PRAY FOR ME

BOOKS BY JAN THOMPSON

Protector Sweethearts (6 Books)
JanThompson.com/protector

Defender Sweethearts (6 Books)
JanThompson.com/defender

Binary Hackers (4 Books)
JanThompson.com/binary

Seaside Chapel (6 Books)
JanThompson.com/seaside

Savannah Sweethearts (11 Books)
JanThompson.com/savannah

Vacation Sweethearts (8 Books)
JanThompson.com/vacation

Keep up with Jan Thompson's book news:
JanThompson.com/newsletter

PRAY FOR ME

VACATION SWEETHEARTS BOOK 5

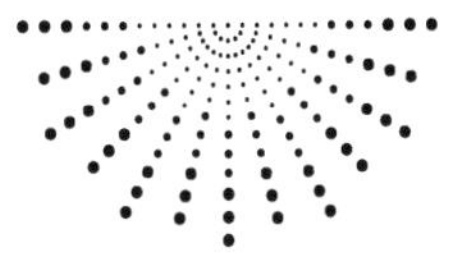

JAN THOMPSON

PRAY FOR ME (VACATION SWEETHEARTS BOOK 5)

Author Website: JanThompson.com
Book News: JanThompson.com/newsletter
Published by Georgia Press LLC

Cover Design: Georgia Press and Deranged Doctor Design

eBook ISBN: 978-1-944188-63-4
Paperback ISBN: 978-1-944188-64-1

To my Lord and Savior, Jesus Christ, who died on the cross to save me from my sins and rose again from the grave to give me eternal life in heaven.

For God so loved the world that He gave His only begotten Son, that whoever believes in Him should not perish but have everlasting life.
—John 3:16

READ A FREE EBOOK!

TIME FOR ME (A VACATION SWEETHEARTS PREQUEL)

When art gallery archivist Sheryl Breckenridge tries to get world-famous sculptor Winton Pace to display his artwork at Simon's Gallery, she doesn't expect him to fall in love with her. Will she reciprocate in this friends-to-more romance?

Read *Time for Me* (A Vacation Sweethearts Prequel) for FREE at the link below. This story starts thirteen months before *Smile for Me* (Vacation Sweethearts Book 1).

Download the FREE prequel here:
JanThompson.com/time-free

Sign up for Jan Thompson's mailing list to keep up with her book news. She writes Christian beach romance, romantic suspense, and suspense thrillers.

Subscribe to Jan's book news:
JanThompson.com/newsletter

ABOUT PRAY FOR ME (VACATION SWEETHEARTS BOOK 5)

A gentleman gardener.
A pastor's daughter.
A friendship blooming into romance.

When his ex-fiancée marries someone else, accountant-turned-landscaper Gus takes a vacation away from his Nassau home, visits his cousin in the

USA, and falls in love with a pastor's daughter. Is it just romance on the rebound? Or is there something serious going on in this friends-to-more travel romance?

Pray for Me is the fifth novel in *USA Today* bestselling author Jan Thompson's Vacation Sweethearts series of standalone Christian travel romances. We first met Gus in *Smile for Me* (Vacation Sweethearts Book 1). At that time, he had left the corporate world and was a landscape gardener in the Bahamas. *Pray for Me* is his story.

UNWANTED TIME OFF...

After losing Veronique to another man, Augustus "Gus" Moss III needs a distraction and a change of scenery. He takes a leave of absence from his landscaping job in Nassau and flies to Atlanta, Georgia, to visit his cousin, Byron Moss. When Byron's whole family is sick, Gus ends up staying at Pastor Fitzpatrick's house, and finds himself drafted into serving in some of Midtown Chapel's summer ministries. He agrees to help because he is a friend of the pastor's eldest daughter, who seems to believe strongly in charity work.

UNEXPECTED MOMENTS...

Women's Ministry Director Tallulah "Tally" Fitzpatrick is busy ministering to women at conferences, and building a village of tiny homes for single mothers. Pulled in multiple directions, she is grateful to have Gus nearby—a steady friend who is around at just the right place and time. Although she has made up her mind to only marry an ordained pastor, she can't help being drawn to Gus, the landscaper with an accounting background and an MBA in finance.

UNAVOIDABLE CROSSROADS...

Are Gus and Tallulah just flirting with each other for the summer, or will the romance last into the winter of their lives? When the man of her dreams arrives in town, Tallulah has to choose between the two. Who will she let go? For sure, both Tallulah and Gus need a lot of prayer.

Pray for Me (Vacation Sweethearts Book 5):
JanThompson.com/pray

Vacation Sweethearts:
JanThompson.com/vacation

Subscribe to Jan's Mailing List for Book News:
JanThompson.com/newsletter

PRAY FOR ME

CHAPTER ONE

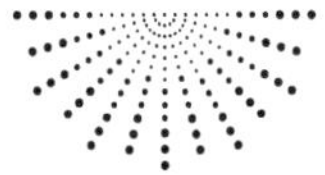

Letting go of Veronique was the hardest thing Gus had ever done in his life.

But let go, I must.

By the time Gus boarded his flight to go on a much-needed vacation, Veronique had been married for six months to another man and was now expecting her first child.

She had told him to forget her when they broke up a year ago, but Gus thought they might reconcile.

A baby with another man meant she had really moved on, didn't it?

So must Gus move on, or his name wasn't Augustus Isaac Moss III. It seemed that every Moss man had to endure heartache of some sort...

All except Gus's cousin Byron Moss.

What was Byron's secret to handling pain? Gus didn't think it had anything to do with Byron being an ordained pastor. He had been strong long before he entered the ministry, back when he was the assistant headmaster at the Chapel by the Sea Christian School in the Bahamas.

In the midst of his grief, Gus called Bryon to share his heart's sorrow.

Multiple phone calls later, Gus was still heartbroken.

When Byron invited Gus to visit him in Atlanta, Georgia, Gus jumped at the opportunity to get Veronique off his mind and out of his system. However, he was able to take only four weeks off due to the various work obligations he'd have to deal with as they approached the next semester.

The Chapel by the Sea Christian School in Nassau was on summer break, and his landscaping crew could easily maintain the grounds without him for a month. They didn't need him. He'd be back in the Bahamas in June and back to work at the school before the teachers returned to campus in July.

Gus napped on the two-hour flight from Nassau's Lynden Pindling International Airport to Hartsfield-Jackson Atlanta International Airport, and woke up wondering what he would do in landlocked Atlanta. No beaches. No ocean. What kind of a place was that?

Exactly.

It would be different from his hometown, although he'd be arriving in late May, when the southern weather warmed up. At least the weather would remind him of home in Nassau.

Gus figured he could handle it. He closed his eyes as the flight attendants collected trash from the passengers on the short flight.

He recalled the Skype conversation he'd had with his cousin just the week before.

"You need a new project," Byron had said.

"A distraction?" Gus asked.

"Well, to reset—or realign—your focus back to God."

"How would a project do that?"

"You move on and you regroup. Recalibrate."

Gus laughed.

"What?" Byron asked.

"You might have left the Bahamas five years ago, but you're still the same Byron I know. Your thesaurus remains. Reset. Realign. Regroup. Recalibrate."

Byron looked amused. "I did that, didn't I?"

"You forgot one word."

"What?"

"Refocus."

"I used it as a noun."

"I supposed you sort of did, Professor Moss."

"Now I'm going to put on my counselor hat and recommend a change of scenery," Byron said. "If you can get away from work for a couple of months, Tina and I would love to have you stay at our house. There's plenty of volunteer work available at church if you want to keep busy and get your mind off you-know-who."

It had been a great idea until this morning, when Byron had texted to say that both his kids, Brielle and Myla, had come down with the flu, and pregnant Tina was catching it too, so would Gus mind staying at Pastor Daniel Fitzpatrick's house for a week until they all got over their sickness?

At first, Gus almost canceled his plans. He could always fly to Atlanta a couple of weeks later when everyone was well. Then his sense of curiosity got the better of him. When he'd visited Byron and Tina a year before, his friend Tally had introduced him to her parents, Pastor Fizz—as they all called him—and Riona, his wife of fifty years. Perhaps they could advise Gus on what constituted a successful marriage, although their three daughters were as yet unmarried, including the oldest one, Tally, who'd become a friend of his, albeit long distance.

Gus spoke to no one as he disembarked from the Boeing 737 and followed the crowd going down the hall and escalator toward the airport train. He could have walked the long way to baggage claim, but he didn't feel like it this afternoon. Besides, he had to get to the MARTA rapid transit for a ride to Midtown Chapel before Byron finished work for the day. They had planned to eat dinner together, just two cousins catching up on life. After that, Byron was supposed to drop Gus off at Pastor Fizz's house in Decatur somewhere.

An hour later, Gus found himself walking out of the MARTA train station at North Avenue, then crossing West Peachtree Street toward Midtown Chapel at the corner of Spring Street and Ponce de Leon Avenue.

With a backpack on his back, he started to whistle "The Happy Wanderer," a campfire song he'd sung as a kid, back in his Boy Scout days. However, the Atlanta heat beat down on him, and his backpack stuck to his sweaty shoulder blades.

Of course, he had to choose the hottest day of the month to visit Atlanta. Eighty-eight degrees on the Fahrenheit scale was no joke.

He wiped sweat off his forehead and trudged on the sidewalk.

The city of Atlanta was huge and sprawling, but this side of town didn't have too many tall buildings. A couple of blocks away was the Fox Theatre, a favorite of Gus's aunt, Nancy. Perhaps the next time she came to town, Gus could take her there again so that she could enjoy the Möller organ, installed in 1929.

Of course, Byron could go too, since Aunt Nancy was his mother.

Since his own parents had passed away when he had been only a teenager, Gus was raised with his cousins by his aunt. These days, Gus was still close to Aunt Nancy. They talked business, even though Gus had left the white-collar field a long time ago. He had a feeling that Nancy had been trying to persuade him to get back into the family business and put his Harvard MBA to good use.

Instead, Gus had chosen to leave the corporate world behind and work as a landscaper and gardener at a small Christian school. He didn't want to return to long working hours and burnouts.

No thank you.

The short walk was easy for Gus. The sidewalk was empty except for a few people here and there.

Everyone else seemed to be driving, and traffic was picking up both ways.

He wondered what all those people were doing out and about. He supposed that some were tourists like him.

Midtown Chapel took up a whole block. Once abandoned, the old nineteenth-century church building had almost been demolished. Pastor Fizz and his historian friends had come together to save the stained glass and pipe organ. They'd raised so much money that they were able to save the entire building and its surrounding grounds also.

Gus walked up to the front door. It was made of old oak wood from St. Simon's Island—from the same grove that had produced wood for the USS *Constitution* tall ship.

The metal knockers looked imposing.

Unfortunately, no one came to the door when Gus knocked.

He texted Byron. Byron texted back some instructions.

"Ah, yes. I knew that. I forgot." Gus pocketed his phone. "The staff door in the back."

He rounded the corner of the building and walked toward the staff parking lot. There were two church buses and several vehicles. A white van pulled up to a side door marked "Staff Only."

The driver's-side door opened, and a woman exited the van. She was wearing a bright tangerine T-shirt, a pair of cargo shorts, and hiking boots.

Gus almost didn't recognize her. She had cut her hair shorter than usual—above her shoulders—and was wearing sunglasses.

"Gus!" she said. "You made it here safely."

Tallulah Fitzpatrick.

Tally.

Gus barely nodded. Maybe he was mistaken. His friend had been as skinny as a twig several years ago, the first and last time he'd seen her in person. Last year, when Gus had visited Atlanta, she was out of town, speaking at a women's conference somewhere.

Today she was filled out in all the right places. Gus didn't know why he noticed that. And she was tanned, like someone who spent a lot of time outdoors.

She smiled that devastating smile that made everything okay, even if his heart still hurt from the recent loss.

"I thought that was you," Tally said.

"How are you doing?" Gus walked toward her and the glass door.

"Busy as ever. You?"

"Same." Actually, no. The first half of the year

had been long and difficult. But he didn't have to tell everyone.

Tally stood by the glass door. "I'm guessing you're going inside."

Gus nodded. "I'm meeting Byron."

Before Tally could pull out her keycard, someone opened the door from the inside. It was Byron. And he was coughing.

"Uh-oh." Tally shook her head. "You too? It's going around."

"The only reason you're not getting it is that you haven't been in the building much this week." Byron coughed again.

"Since you're both able-bodied men, may I ask you to help me carry some boxes from the storage room downstairs to the van?" Tally asked.

"Are you putting him to work right away?" Byron pointed to Gus. "He just flew in for a vacation. And I'm sick."

"Yes, but are your muscles sick too?" Tally looked concerned.

Gus removed the backpack from his back and stretched. "I don't mind. I need a glass of cold water first."

Tally walked back to her van, opened the cargo door, and retrieved a bottle of cold water from a red cooler.

Red, her favorite color. Gus remembered Tally wearing either a red skirt or a red blouse that September she was in Nassau several years ago. She'd spent more time ministering to the women and speaking at their women's retreat hosted at the Chapel by the Sea Christian School, where he worked, than she did walking around campus. He'd only chatted with her at their faculty and church staff dinners, when he wasn't busy with his landscaping work.

Her red outfit and that smile were the two things that Gus hadn't forgotten about Tally.

"Thank you," Gus said.

Tally pointed to Gus's backpack. "That's all you brought?"

Gus nodded, wondering what she was getting at.

"I know you're staying at my parents' house tonight. I'm going there after I drop off the boxes at the warehouse. I could use some help unloading them. If you help me do that, I'll take you to my parents' place afterward."

Byron chuckled. "You're three steps ahead of us, Tally."

"How did you know where I'm staying?" Gus asked. "Other than the fact that Pastor Fizz is your dad?"

"Colette called me. Mom is trying to set her up with you." Tally laughed.

"I'm not interested in anyone." Gus tried not to look stunned that Riona Fitzpatrick was playing matchmaker again. He had heard of her reputation.

"It's too soon, I told her." Tally carried on like it was no big deal talking about a friend this way. "First, you have to get over your grief."

"Grief?" Gus drew a deep breath.

"Yep. Didn't you lose someone you thought you couldn't live without?"

"Ah..." Gus shouldn't have shared that much information with anyone, but who had he told? He certainly hadn't said much in their private group chat.

"My friend, 'grief' is the word." Tally patted his shoulder. "But you're still here. Alive and well. You survived. Don't worry. You'll get over it soon, with God's help."

"Thanks." Gus wanted to walk away and not talk about his private issues, but there was nowhere to go. Besides, he needed a ride to wherever he was staying.

Why couldn't he just stay at a hotel? Away from everyone?

"Everyone knows." Gus stared at Byron. "And here I am trying to get away."

"Not everyone," Tally answered for Byron. "Just his family and my family."

"They didn't hear it from me. I didn't say anything to anyone but Pastor Fizz." Byron lifted his palm in surrender.

"Your counseling pastor, no less." Gus kept his voice down.

"Dad has nothing to do with how we know. He doesn't tell anyone anything, not even Mom," Tally said. "You might have forgotten that Colette and Veronique's sister, Daniella, are best friends."

"They are?" Gus hadn't paid attention to Veronique's sister's friends.

"Yeah. Lots of friendships are made on those ministry trips that Midtown Chapel and Riverside Chapel do together at your church in Nassau." Tally glanced at Byron. "And marriages too."

Byron nodded, and coughed.

"You're sick," Tally said. "Go home, Byron."

She turned to Gus. "Seriously, don't worry. Don't be in a rush to get over it. Grief takes time, and it comes in stages. It took me five years to get over being left at the altar—in Hawaii, no less. But I got over it, with God's help and a lot of counseling from Dad. I'm happily single now, but the downside of that is I can't get help carrying supplies to the warehouse."

"Is that what a boyfriend is to you?" Gus tilted his head. "A porter?"

Tally patted his arm. "See? Humor is part of the healing process. You're on the way."

"On the way to where?" A third male voice said. The man came up behind Tally.

Gus didn't know who the man was, but he could see Tally's face change from cheery to annoyed. She drew a deep breath and turned around.

"You need any help?" the man asked.

"No. Thank you, Silas. I've got all the help I need." Tally's voice was calm, indicating to Gus that she didn't feel threatened.

"I see two beta males." Silas flexed his large arms slightly. "I think you need me."

Gus didn't say a word. Neither did Byron, who was texting on his phone. Gus knew Byron well enough to know that he would defend himself. Perhaps this Silas dude was a known troublemaker and the best way to deal with him was to ignore his taunts.

Gus waited to see how Tally handled Silas. Perhaps he could take his cue from her.

Tally glanced at her watch. "You better hurry, Silas. If you're late again, my dad might not want to meet with you this late in the day anymore. It's past his usual office hours."

"Okay. See you." Silas ignored everyone else and made a beeline for the staff door, which was now locked.

Byron put away his phone and unlocked the door for Silas. "I'll walk you to Pastor Fizz's office."

Only Tally and Gus were left, standing outside in the afternoon sun.

"Is he a member of the church?" Gus asked.

"A visitor. I was hoping to be out of here before he arrived, but I was caught in traffic getting back from the warehouse, so my timing isn't good today."

"Is that the warehouse in Decatur?"

She raised an eyebrow. "You know about it?"

Gus nodded. "Byron told me it was an answer to prayer when someone paid for a year's use of it."

"We have way more donations than we have space."

"What kind of donations?"

"Since we started building those tiny homes as a part of our affordable housing ministry for single mothers, donations have poured in from all over the place."

"Sounds like a good ministry."

"Yep."

"What is it called?"

"Midtown Chapel Village," Tally said. "I had suggested we name it after our theme verse, James 1:27, the one that says, 'Pure and undefiled religion before God and the Father is this: to visit orphans and widows in their trouble, and to keep oneself unspotted from the world.' However, my women's ministry team decided that some of the single moms we're trying to reach might be turned off by something so declarative."

"Isn't being a Christian declarative as it is?"

"I know, right? But I got outvoted, so we settled on the idea of a village, a community, where the kids can feel safe."

"And you put the verse somewhere."

"Everywhere." She turned around to show the words on the back of her tangerine T-shirt.

"You're not wearing a red shirt," Gus blurted.

"Red?"

"You got outvoted again?"

"No, actually. We have T-shirts of many colors. I bought one of each and wear them in rotation." She stepped aside to reveal the side of the van. "Here's the verse again."

"James 1:27" was emblazoned on that side of the van in bold letters.

Tally smiled. "Want to put your backpack in

the van? I'll lock it as we haul stuff out of the church."

"Good idea. Thanks."

Tally handed Gus another bottled water and a hand towel.

"What's this for?" Gus squeezed the hand towel.

"You're sweating bullets." She pointed to his forehead.

Gus didn't realize he was sweating. "It's a hot day."

The hand towel was soft and smelled of lavender. He gulped down the water.

"I apologize for the micro-plastic you're ingesting, but these were on sale, so I had to save ministry money."

Gus nodded. He was trying to get used to Tally's jokes. Then again, maybe she wasn't joking.

Tally locked the van. "Can't be too careful in Atlanta."

"Can't be too careful anywhere in the world these days," Gus said.

"I know, right? However, truth be told, I've forgotten to lock the vehicle door a couple of times, and nothing happened."

Gus nodded. "At the end of the day, only God can truly keep us safe."

He followed Tally into the church building. The air conditioner was still on at full blast even though it was past five o'clock, and most of the staffers had gone home on a slow Friday.

Tally took off her sunglasses, revealing light brown eyes. They were kind eyes, unlike Veronique's more intense ones.

"We're going to need a couple of carts. We can get them near the church kitchen." Tally led Gus down the hallway. "Thank you so much for helping me."

"No problem at all." And he meant it.

CHAPTER TWO

Driving the cargo van with the windows down, Tally heard a train in the distance. She figured that by the time they reached the railroad tracks, the train would have passed.

She glanced over to her unexpected passenger. Gus sat silently, looking out the window. The summer wind played with his wavy black hair, and just like that, Tally wondered what it would feel like to run her fingers through his hair—

Forgive my sinful thought, Lord.

Well, Gus was single again, although that was none of her business.

"I'm sorry," Tally said.

"For what?" Gus turned his head.

"About what I said back there. I mean, regardless of what Colette told me, it's none of my business what happened between you and Veronique."

Gus shook his head. "It's life. Besides, if Veronique told her sister anything, it meant she didn't care if Daniella blasted it to the known world, as she apparently did."

"Well, my sister Colette is not 'the known world.' I wish she'd never told me anything."

Gus smiled. "How's she doing these days, by the way?"

"You know that Colette is a wedding planner. She's been doing a lot of weddings at Lakeside Resort that my grandmother owns at Lakeside." Tally turned onto a side road. "Have you ever been there?"

"Not yet. I've heard of it though. Pastor Dixon mentioned it a few times at church, when we prayed for it. Florida, isn't it?"

"Yep. Lakeside is a small town outside of Orlando, about two and a half hours from Sunset Island on the Gulf of Mexico."

"That's far away from the beach, by island standards, but within driving distance."

"There are beaches closer to Lakeside than Sunset Island. You can still drive to any of those beaches on either side of the Florida peninsula, so in a way, Lakeside has the best of both worlds."

"I've heard of Sunset Island. Aunt Nancy played some golf there in the past. Why did you mention it? Is your church starting a new church there?" Gus asked.

"How did you know?"

"I guessed."

"Midtown Chapel and Lakeside Chapel are starting a small church on Sunset Island, and some people from our two churches are going over to the new Sunrise Chapel to minister for a couple of years."

"Under three hours between the two churches. That means people could drive back and forth."

Tally nodded. "I'm not involved in that church plant, so I have no idea how Pastor Kim is handling it. All I know is that the idea for the church came from Seaside Chapel, who is helping to fund the new church but is not involved in the day-to-day operations. They're leaving it to Lakeside Chapel and Midtown Chapel to make the calls."

"I've heard of Seaside Chapel on St. Simon's Island. Another sister church to Midtown."

"Yep. Seaside on St. Simon's, Riverside in Savannah, Midtown in Atlanta, and Lakeside in Florida are all sister churches. They've come together to fund Sunrise Chapel."

"Just as they funded Chapel by the Sea in

Nassau many years ago when Pastor Dixon started it. Perhaps our church might invest in the mission fund too."

"Donations are always welcome in a ministry supported by the people. In fact, someone who has lived on Sunset Island all her life loaned out the prime lot to build the church for the next hundred years." Tally didn't say who.

Gus chuckled. "Sunrise Chapel on Sunset Island."

"I know, right?"

"Are you going to do some ministry work at Sunrise or Lakeside anytime soon?"

"I don't know. I do speak at women's conferences, so if the churches invite me, I'll go. Or if Dad preaches there, I might tag along."

"Do you use your vacation time?"

"Ministry time if I get to speak or if I'm assisting Mom in some useful way during the conference or workshop or event."

"Sounds like a good thing."

"Truly, I only go because I worry about them driving the RV by themselves. Dad might only be seventy, but has heart problems, and Mom has arthritis."

Her parents had bought the recreational vehicle out of necessity at first, but after a while, they grew to enjoy taking trips here and there, not only for Dad's work but also on the weekends.

"What kind of RV?"

"Winnebago. Thankfully, only a Class C. I can't drive something bigger and longer."

"Does it drive like a regular truck?"

"Pretty much. It's quite roomy too. Sleeps five people, but it's usually just my parents and me, but we make space for Colette and Adalia, just in case they join us," Tally said. "If my sisters go with us, then we take turns driving. It's seven hours to Lakeside."

"Each one drives part of the way. Not bad."

"After that, it's an easy two-plus hours to Sunrise Chapel if Dad preaches there. Once we get there, we have several beaches to choose from on Sunset Island."

"Reminds me of home." Gus chuckled.

"Yeah." She sighed. "Mom and Dad have been hinting they want to move to Lakeside to be near Grandma. Then they could drive their RV to Sunset Island every now and then to help get Sunrise Chapel going."

"You don't seem enthusiastic about it."

"Don't I?" Tally stopped at a red light. "Don't get me wrong. I'm all for church planting. It's bittersweet for me, maybe?"

"How so?"

"It means my entire family would move out of Atlanta, where we've been for decades. My parents married here. My sisters and I were born here. Then again..."

"Then again?"

"Then again, 'this world is not my home,' as the old hymn says."

Gus started humming the hymn.

"You know the song. It's Dad's favorite hymn." Tally started singing along.

Gus stopped humming and simply stared at her.

"What?" Tally asked.

"I love your voice."

Tally's face warmed up. She brushed it off.

"Anyway, Grandma wants Colette to take over her resort business at Lakeside. She's persuading Dad to move too. Dad's considering it because Lakeside Church asked him to take over the pulpit from their retired pastor, who is only five years older than Dad." Tally took a deep breath. "So Dad said he'll only do it for a year, while training up a permanent pastor. That's what they want too, so they're working out some plan. Thing is, if Dad carries out the plan, I'll be alone in Atlanta."

Gus smiled.

"What?"

"You talk a lot when you get nervous," Gus said quietly.

"Do I?"

"Yes, you do. Are you nervous right now? I'm not a stranger."

"No, you're not." Tally lost her train of thought. "Where was I?"

"Your dad is working on a plan to help Lakeside Chapel get a more permanent pastor."

"Dad has his Timothy or Titus in mind." Tally hoped Gus wouldn't ask who it was.

"Who?"

Oh, he had to ask.

"You'll have to ask Dad because I'm not involved. He has a few candidates in mind." Especially Malachi Jacobs.

"You said you'll be alone in Atlanta. What do you mean? Are both of your sisters moving to Florida too?"

"My youngest sister, Adalia, is Dad's ministry assistant. Wherever Dad moves his office, there she will be. However, at the moment, Adalia has taken two weeks off to help Colette at Lakeside Resort. Which makes me wonder why..." Tally paused. "My guess is that she's thinking Dad will most likely accept the position at Lakeside Chapel, even if it's only for a year or two."

"You, on the other hand, prefer to stay in Atlanta."

"I wouldn't say that's what I must do. I am open to God's leading, you know," Tally explained. "Yes, I've spent many years building up Midtown Chapel Village, but that's not my ministry. That belongs to God."

"Paul watered. Apollos planted."

Tally was impressed. "You know your Scripture too. First Corinthians 3:6."

"Which says, 'I planted, Apollos watered, but God gave the increase.' Not that we're Paul or Apollos, but we're team players doing God's work."

"Exactly."

"But the beach though..." His voice trailed off. "Lakeside is two hours away from the beach."

"You move there, then." Tally laughed. "I guess we like what we are used to. You grew up on an island, so you must like the coastal atmosphere a lot."

"I wouldn't want to live anywhere else."

"Not in a landlocked city like Atlanta?" Tally laughed.

"If God moves me, I go where He moves me. Easier said than done."

"I agree. It's a good opportunity to pray and seek God's will," Tally said. "That's how I have to look at it. Our family has been in ministry all our lives. If going to Lakeside means having to do personal sacrifices for the sake of the gospel, so be it."

"Right now your ministry is in Atlanta."

"God has called me to minister to downtrodden single mothers in the metro area, to provide them with food and shelter until they can find their way in the world, to send them to vocational schools for skill training, and to find them jobs so that they can support their kids." Tally felt that she had just recited her mission statement.

"Midtown Chapel Village does just that." Gus looked at her.

"However, my dad always reminds me that we cannot put God in a time capsule. If God calls me to do something else tomorrow, next week, next year, I should drop everything and go with God."

"Yes. I also want to obey the Lord willingly."

"I hold on lightly to the ministry He has given me, you know? I cling to Christ and only Him." Tally stopped the van at another traffic light. "How about you?"

Gus drew a deep breath. "I love my job at the school. I get to be outdoors most of the time. It doesn't pay very much, but enough for me to support myself. I don't know if I'll ever go back to accounting or finance, but I can't burn my bridges. All those years of school must amount to something."

"Can you do both?" Tally asked.

"I am, actually, since I do my own accounting in my landscaping business. However, it's not the corporate setting I worked in for a long time. I burned out on that."

"I don't know how you can burn out on a tropical island, unless you're out on the beach." Tally laughed. "I want to go back to the Bahamas someday. I love the island feel of it, the Caribbean atmosphere. I felt like I was on a real vacation the last time I was there, even though I had a conference to attend."

"Next time I'll be your personal tour guide."

"I'll take you up on that." Tally made another turn toward the front entrance of the warehouse.

Five miles from Midtown Chapel's affordable housing project, the old warehouse sat in an industrial area, isolated from the rest of Decatur. There were no cars in the parking lot, which meant that Levi Theroux had left.

The warehouse manager came to work at the crack of dawn and didn't leave until nightfall—

except tonight. He had started dating someone from church, and Friday nights were their date nights.

Tally drove to the back of the warehouse, where the loading docks—

One of the garage doors was open.

She slammed on the brakes.

"What?" Gus asked.

"That door shouldn't be open." She parked the van and texted Levi. He replied instantly. "Just what I thought. He closed everything."

"Is the place alarmed?" Gus asked.

"Well, we have no money to pay for that service at the moment, but it will be funded in the next quarter's budget." Tally unbuckled her seat belt.

Gus grabbed her arm. "What are you doing?"

"I want to see what's going on."

"No. Call the police right now." Gus's voice sounded urgent.

Tally thought for a quick second. "You're right."

She locked the van doors, rolled up their windows, and called 911.

The operator told her to park on the street, away from the open garage door. As Tally backed out of the parking lot, she prayed for God to handle this. "Thank You, Jesus, that Levi was not in the warehouse when whatever-it-was happened."

Gus's stomach rumbled.

"I'm sorry," Tally said. "I'll call Dad to come pick you up."

"No, no. I haven't eaten since lunch in the airplane, but don't worry about me. Take care of this first." Gus drank the rest of the bottled water that Tally had given him earlier.

Tally parked the van by the side of the road and glanced at her rearview mirror. No police cars had appeared yet.

Frankly, she was afraid to get out of the van. At the back of the van was a cooler with some snacks inside. She could offer that to Gus—if she could get to them from the driver's seat. Unfortunately, there were boxes in between her and the back of the van.

"Let's pray," Gus said.

"Please." Tally closed her eyes. She wanted to cry. This wasn't the first time the warehouse had been broken into. Last time, the alarm had been on —when they could afford it. The burglars hadn't cared.

Tally's hands shook.

She opened her eyes slightly to see Gus preparing to pray. His hands were on his lap. Tally put her hand on his left arm. He didn't push her away. Instead, without even opening his eyes, he reached over and covered her hand with his warm palm.

"Lord Jesus, we come before You now, knowing You are almighty and can do anything," Gus prayed. "We ask for protection for everyone who works at this warehouse. If this is a burglary, I pray that the police would catch the criminals—"

Sirens interrupted him.

"In the name of Jesus, I pray. Amen," Gus said quickly.

"Amen." Tally blinked.

"Are you okay?"

Tally nodded.

"I'm here," Gus said quietly.

"So you are." Tally had no idea what she was saying.

"Maybe God placed me here at this time to help. I was looking for something to do on my vacation besides hanging out with Byron's family."

Tally chuckled. "You're trying to make me feel better, aren't you?"

"What do you mean?"

"You want to do summer ministry projects at Midtown Chapel while you're here?"

"Yes." He felt sure.

"Be careful what you ask for."

Now he didn't feel so sure. "What do you mean?"

"We've known each other for several years, but how well do you know my father?" Tally asked.

"Not too well. I know he's the counseling pastor at Midtown Chapel. He used to be the senior pastor until he stepped aside to let Pastor Eldon Kim lead. Now your father is free to do ministries."

"Bingo. That's the word. Ministries. Dad is never short of ministries. You want work, you got work." Tally got out of the van.

Standing by the van, she waved to the two police vehicles coming down the road. She wasn't sure whether it was okay to wave to them or not, but she was happy they came so quickly.

After the police officers introduced themselves, they asked for Tally's identification and her connection to the warehouse.

"I'm the women's ministry director at Midtown Chapel, and this is our rental warehouse," she explained. "We store donations people give to the church to be used in our affordable housing project in Decatur. We also donate what we can't use to help the poor elsewhere in metro Atlanta."

"And you?" the officer asked Gus.

"Augustus Moss. I'm on vacation from the Bahamas, and here in town to visit my cousin. He's one of the associate pastors at Midtown Chapel." Gus showed them his passport and Bahamian driver's license.

"First day on vacation, huh?" one of the officers said.

Gus nodded.

"Welcome to Atlanta." He grinned.

"Thank you, sir."

The officers told them to remain in the van while they checked out the warehouse.

"Do you want the remote control to open all the garage doors?" Tally asked.

"Won't hurt to have it handy."

Tally handed them her master key as well. After the two police cars drove to the back of the warehouse, she opened the back of the van to find her cooler. It was barely accessible, so Gus helped her lift a box off the top of the hard-case cooler.

"I have some snacks in here." Tally opened the cooler. "Sweet potato chips. Power bars. One apple. More water."

"No plantain chips?" Gus asked.

"Oh, you're so hard to please." She chuckled, knowing he was only kidding. "No peanuts for you."

"Let's share." Gus took whatever Tally gave him.

They went back to their seats. To be on the safe side, she locked the van doors. She handed Gus a container of hand wipes.

"Shall we thank God for these snacks?" Gus asked.

Tally almost hesitated. She didn't recall ever saying a blessing before she ate snacks. She nodded slightly, thinking that Gus was more religious than any of the pastors she had worked with.

After Gus prayed, they dug in.

There was the matter of the apple. Tally didn't have any knife in the car to split it. "You can have this apple, Gus."

"No, you can have it."

"You sure?" She eyed the apple.

"Yep. I'll just take one bite and you can have the rest," he said.

"What? No. I'm not eating an apple that has your saliva on it!"

"I thought we were friends." Gus laughed.

"I don't even eat things with my sisters' saliva on them."

"But friends who eat together, stay together."

"Really?" Before Tally realized he was only kidding, her phone rang. It was Levi.

"Yeah, the police are here." Tally tapped on the Speakerphone icon.

"Are you alone?" Levi asked.

"No. Gus is with me."

"Gus who?"

"Byron Moss's cousin." Tally turned to Gus. "Say something to Levi Theroux, my warehouse manager. He also attends Midtown Chapel."

"Hello." Gus handed Tally the rest of the sweet potato chips.

"I'm twenty minutes away," Levi said. "I'll drop Soline off and then go over."

"I thought you were at dinner," Tally said.

"We were getting seated. It's okay. We can do this another time. I need to help you inventory what's missing, like last time."

Gus's eyebrows rose. "Last time?"

Tally ignored him. "Thanks, Levi. I appreciate it. I hope they didn't take too much this time."

"We should just leave a couple of barrels outside and label them 'Take these instead.' Plus leave some gospel tracts on top of the barrel."

"Do it," Tally said.

"I was joking."

"I'm not. Hey, Levi, what restaurant are you at?"

"Chinese."

Tally turned to Gus. "You like Chinese food?"

"I eat anything."

"Levi, could you do us a favor and order us some takeout dinner? I'll pay you when you get here."

"Sure thing. That's what we're doing now. Tell me what you want."

"Get me shrimp lo mein and stir-fried vegetables." Tally looked at Gus. "You?"

"Ah… Same. Thank you."

Levi took their orders and hung up.

Tally realized that Gus had barely eaten any of the sweet potato chips in the bag. "Don't you want more?"

"Waiting for my shrimp lo mein," Gus said.

As they waited, Tally asked Gus if he was tired.

He shook his head. "It was only a two-hour flight plus airport wait. No big deal. I'll sleep tonight."

"You won't if you stay here with me."

Gus seemed to give it a bit of thought. "I can help with the inventory if you tell me what to do."

"Levi can. He's our warehouse manager, like I said, and he's trained lots of workers." Tally texted her parents to tell them what happened and to let them know they would not make it to dinner tonight and that she'd drop Gus off later in the evening.

Mom called her back almost immediately on video. "Again? Move the warehouse already."

"Don't worry, Mom. The police are here."

Mom made a face on Tally's small screen. "We'll have leftovers for you tomorrow. When do you think you might come home?"

"I'm just dropping him off."

"If you get here late, I want you to stay overnight. I'll put clean sheets on Colette's bed for you."

"All right." No use arguing with Mom.

Tally had moved out ten years ago to her own little townhouse near her parents' old house, but Mom still thought that Tally might come "home," as if Mom's house was the only home the Fitzpatrick girls ever knew.

In many ways, it was. Mom's house was where they gathered for birthdays and celebrations, for Thanksgiving, Christmas, and Easter meals. Grandma had owned the house a long time ago, before she decided to move home to Florida for the weather.

"I don't know, Mom. We're doing an inventory tonight to see what's missing."

"You don't have to do it tonight right away, do you?" Mom asked.

"We have to know."

"You've always been like that. You have to get things done just so. It's no wonder you still haven't married at thirty-five years old."

"Mom!" Tally glanced over at Gus. "Gus is sitting right here."

"What? Oh, I forgot. Turn the phone. Let me see his face."

Tally wondered if it was one of those days or if Mom was losing her memory faster than they had expected. She recalled telling Mom just minutes ago that she would drop off Gus late. Perhaps she had not made it clear that Gus was inside the van with her.

Gus waved to the camera. "Hello, Riona."

"How old are you?"

"Forty-one." Gus looked perplexed, as though he wanted to ask why.

It also hit Tally that he was six years older than her. Did it matter? She wasn't sure.

"You're closer to Tally's age than Colette," Mom said. "Colette's thirty-two. Adalia is twenty-nine."

Tally wanted to end the phone call right now, but Mom was still talking.

"Tally's my firstborn, but she'll probably marry last," Mom added.

Tally counted to ten. "We have to go now. The

police will be back soon."

"Okay, dear. Text me before you get here. I'll leave the porch light on for you."

"Thank you. Love you, Mom." Always.

After she hung up, Tally covered her face with her palms. She could hear Gus chuckling too.

"She doesn't drink, or else I'd tell you she's drunk," Tally finally said. "She's in a hurry all the time, you know? Says she's three years to seventy and still doesn't have grandkids."

"Did they have kids late?"

Tally nodded. "My parents married when Mom was twenty years old, but it would be twelve years before they had their first child. Mom was thirty-two when I was born. She gave birth to three kids one after another, and then they couldn't have any more."

"At least you still have your mom with you," Gus said quietly. "Treasure her."

"We do."

"Good." Gus looked out the window again. "I was an only child. My parents died while I was a teenager. My dad died of cancer, and then my mom died of a heart attack at the funeral."

"I'm sorry," Tally said. "Sometimes homeless teens show up at the Village, and their parents are either dead or have disappeared."

"Teens? Sorry to hear that. What does your church do about that?"

"The kids get into the foster care system, but we provide support in any way we can. Part-time jobs for them at the Village, tutors, clothing, and after-school food whenever needed."

"The Lord's work," Gus said. "I'd like to see the Village."

"I'll take you there whenever you want," Tally said. "Maybe you can find something you can volunteer in—not that I'm trying to put you to work."

"I would be happy to help," Gus said. "I'm a landscaper by trade."

Tally didn't say that she knew he had an MBA. In fact, he had burned out as an accountant to begin with. Then Gus went to graduate school to become a financial analyst. Neither career panned out.

"You get to be outdoors, like you said earlier."

"You heard me say it."

Tally nodded. "I'm a good listener."

However, at this point, she wasn't listening to Gus. Either that, or Gus wasn't talking.

They were both looking at the one police car driving through the warehouse parking lot. Tally heard sirens and glanced behind her to see an EMT vehicle coming up the road toward them.

"What's going on?" Tally asked as she watched the police officer park near the entrance, get out of his vehicle, and wave to the EMT, directing them.

After the EMT drove on, the officer walked toward Tally's van. He came up to the driver's-side window.

"Ma'am, do you know of a young man—maybe a teenager—with blue hair and a tattoo on his right arm?" the police officer asked.

"I'm not sure. Many teenagers come and go at the Village, and I minister to single moms and teenage girls primarily. We also hire people of all ages to work at the warehouse. You might ask our warehouse manager, Levi Theroux, if such a teenager is on the payroll. He's on his way here. Why do you ask?"

"I'll let you know in a minute." He walked back to the car. Then he was on his phone before he returned to Tally's van. "Ma'am, the paramedics have confirmed that the person we found in the warehouse is dead."

"What?" Tally gasped. "Who?"

"That's what we're trying to find out," the officer said. "I'm going to get more information from you in case we have any questions."

"What's happening now?" Tally asked as a couple more vehicles came barreling down the road toward the warehouse.

On the side of one of the vehicles, a decal said "DeKalb County Medical Examiner." The officer let that one through. He stopped the second vehicle, an old Mazda.

"That's Levi." Tally got out of the van.

Levi was instructed to back up and park on the side of the road. Levi got out, carrying a bag of takeout containers.

Tally had lost her appetite.

"What's happening, Tally?" Levi looked concerned, but he clearly had no idea what had just transpired.

"They found a dead body in the warehouse," Tally said.

"What? Who?"

"That's exactly what I asked. Waiting for more information from the police. For now, they said it's a kid with blue hair and tats. You know who?"

"Hmm..." Levi handed the food containers to Tally. "Julian is my newest hire, but he has black hair. Who recently dyed his hair blue and came in today without my knowing?"

Tally took the plastic bags from Levi. "I don't know if I can eat right now."

She handed the food to Gus through his rolled-down passenger's window. When she turned to talk to Levi, he was walking to the police car.

In her entire ten years of ministry work at Midtown Chapel, she'd had to deal with deaths, especially when older church members passed away. If it was an elderly woman, Tally would often deliver the eulogy, especially if the woman had no next of kin.

While Tally was familiar with deaths, she didn't want to get used to it.

Tally watched Levi talk to the police officer. She wasn't sure what she could do besides pray as she walked toward them.

"...notify his family," Levi said to the officer.

Tally wondered if Levi knew who had died in their warehouse.

"I sent everyone home for the weekend." Levi nodded. "I don't know how he got in. I have the keys, and I locked up the entire place before I left."

Keys.

Tally raised her hand.

"Yes, ma'am?" the officer asked.

"I gave you my master key and the remote for the garage door. When will I get them back?"

"They're with another officer," the officer said.

"Could you give them to Levi when you're

done?"

"Yes."

"Thank you."

"Can she go home?" Levi asked the officer. "I'll stay here. Considering I'm the warehouse manager and she is not, I know more about the warehouse than she does."

"Yes." The officer tuned to Tally. "Stay in town in case we need to contact you."

"Will do." Tally turned to Levi. "What about the donations in the van? We were going to drop them off."

"How about you leave the van and take my car?" Levi handed her his car key. "I'll drop the van off at church tomorrow, and Soline can pick me up. You can return my car to me on Sunday."

"Thank you, Levi. You're the man."

"Tell that to Soline. She's not sure." He laughed nervously.

Girlfriend trouble? Tally didn't ask.

The officer turned to Tally. "We'll call you if we need anything more from you."

"Please do. You can call the church office and ask for me, or my cell phone directly." Tally returned to Gus in the van. "We're going take Levi's car, if you don't mind. He'll take care of the van and drive it to church on Sunday."

Gus got out of the van, and between him and Tally, they transferred the cooler, Tally's tote bag and purse, Gus's backpack, and their dinner to Levi's old avocado-colored Mazda.

Tally decided she would tell Mom and Dad about the dead body only after they arrived at their house. She wanted to drop off Gus and go home to her own townhouse to take a warm bath. However, her parents had to know what else had happened. Dad could then tell Pastor Kim and the senior staff at church.

Tally felt rather tired all of a sudden.

"Would you like me to drive?" Gus asked. "I do have an international driver's license, and I've driven in the USA before."

"Yes please." It seemed like a small gesture, but Tally appreciated it very much. "We can use my phone for the GPS if you'd prefer to look at a map than listening to me tell you to turn here or turn there."

"We can do both."

"All right."

As Tally buckled up on the passenger's side, she thanked God that Gus was here on the right day and at the right time.

She was convinced that God had sent Gus.

CHAPTER THREE

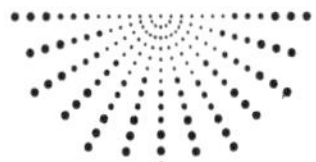

Gus didn't want to eat alone at Pastor Fitzpatrick's kitchen table, so he invited Tally to join him. After all, they both hadn't eaten dinner, and if Tally were to take the Chinese food home to her townhouse, it would be an even later dinner for her.

Well, she declined. Said she had to go with her dad to the Village to see the mother of the deceased.

The takeout containers ended up in the refrigerator. Gus couldn't eat either. He hadn't regained his appetite since he'd heard that a blue-haired teenager had been stabbed to death. He worried about Tally being so close to danger and wondered how he could protect her.

"Prayer is the best thing I can do," Gus said

aloud as he rolled his suitcase into the guest bedroom in Pastor Fitzpatrick's house.

He showered and changed, checked his email, and texted Byron—he didn't reply—before his stomach rumbled again, loud enough to remind him that he had eaten very little food since lunch. If Aunt Nancy had been there, she'd be upset.

Gus left his phone charging on the small desk by the window as he went downstairs. The kitchen was fairly large, but it was closed in on all sides in the old 1920s house. Gus had seen some of those back in the Bahamas, a throwback to the old British colonial days. This house was not built by the British though. It was built by Pastor Fitzpatrick's grandparents and handed down to the pastor's parents and then to him as a wedding gift.

Gus found a dinner plate and reheated his Chinese food. While waiting, he sat down at the kitchen table, fascinated by the alder wood. He knew that alder was a type of birch. The wood was soft and easily scratched, but this table was well maintained.

"Staring at the table?" Tally's voice reached him before he realized she was standing in the kitchen.

Gus looked up. "You're back."

Tally nodded. "Just now having dinner?"

The microwave pinged. Gus got up from his seat. "Yes. Would you join me?"

"Sure. I'm famished." She washed her hands at the sink and retrieved a dinner plate from the cabinet. She took her takeout containers from the refrigerator and dumped the content of both boxes onto her plate, piling it up. She found an unlined paper plate in another cabinet and covered her dinner before reheating it in the microwave.

"How long did you put yours in for?" Tally asked as she leaned against the cabinet near the microwave.

"Two minutes," Gus said.

Tally nodded.

"How did it go?" Gus asked.

"On the drive to the Village, Levi called and filled in more details. He's still at the warehouse as far as I know."

"What details?" Gus offered her some bottled water from the refrigerator.

"Someone broke into his office. Took his laptop."

"Just his?"

"There's only one laptop."

"Ah. Okay."

"He said he should've taken it home, but he was in a hurry to get to his date night." Tally waited for the microwave to beep. When she checked her plate, part of her lo mein was still cold. She put the plate back into the microwave.

"I'm so glad Dad went with me." Tally blinked. "It was gut wrenching to watch Jacinda weep over her youngest son. I can't imagine what it must feel like to lose a child."

"I'll remember to pray."

"Thank you. Sheldon was only seventeen years old. Came out of rehab twice. His mother lives in one of our tiny homes with four other kids. Sheldon came and went."

The microwave pinged again. This time Tally decided the food was warm enough.

"What did the police say happened at the warehouse?"

"I'll tell you more in a minute." Tally sat across the table from Gus. "Would you please ask God to bless our dinner?"

Gus nodded. "Lord Jesus, we come before You now asking for Your mercy and comfort to surround Jacinda, whose son, Sheldon, died today. I pray that You will give Pastor Fizz and Tally the words to say to the family. I pray that You will give Levi wisdom to handle the mess at the warehouse. I thank You for the takeout dinner we have, and may it provide nourishment for our bodies. In Your holy name I pray. Amen."

"Amen." Tally dug in. "About your question earlier, we don't know what the police know. Levi looked at it from his perspective as the warehouse manager."

"So his laptop was missing. I gather that meant it wasn't found with Sheldon's body."

"Exactly."

"Someone else was there, obviously."

Tally nodded. "There were signs of breaking and entering, some ax work, but no weapons were found around Sheldon."

"That would explain why the medical examiner was called to the scene," Gus said.

"Yeah. Levi said that otherwise the EMT would take the dead body to the morgue, and the ME would check it out there." Tally shrugged. "Truth be told, I don't know much about that sort of thing."

"I'm assuming your surveillance videos might be helpful."

"No money for surveillance videos," Tally admitted.

"No alarm. No surveillance." Gus felt bad for the ministry.

"That's pretty much it. We had a massive

budget cut a few months ago, and the first thing to go was warehouse security. The powers that be decided that used clothes and donated cookware weren't much to protect. Monetary donations are dwindling and expenses have gone up." Tally stirred the food on her plate.

"I don't mean to pry, but are you operating in the red?"

"Midtown Chapel has been funding us—since it is part of the church ministries—but we were hoping that the Village would turn a profit. We tried to plant a vegetable garden so we could sell produce, but how much can you plant in such a small space? We primarily get donations from sympathetic people."

Gus wasn't sure how to suggest an audit on Midtown Chapel Village finances. He couldn't do it because he hadn't renewed his Certified Public Accountant license in America. Besides, it had been for Florida, not Georgia.

"I wasn't a finance major, nor am I an accountant," Tally said. "My degree was in English."

"English?" That surprised Gus. "How did you end up as the women's ministry director?"

"After my master's program, I taught English at a local community college," Tally said. "On weekends and in the summer, I volunteered at church, primarily in the women's ministry. I was heavily involved in the literacy program, tutoring inner-city kids. I got to know the moms, and we found that those most in need were single moms. That's how Midtown Chapel Village began. When our women's ministry director retired, I applied for the position and got it."

"How many people are hired in the ministry?" Gus asked.

"Just my assistant and me. Everyone else is a volunteer." She looked at him. "You're in finance."

"I can't look at your finances."

"Why not?"

"Because I'm not a CPA in Georgia. I don't want to get into legal problems."

"A CPA? Are you a CPA in the Bahamas?" Tally's eyebrows rose.

"In a previous career, I was—although my MBA was in finance."

"And your present career is in landscaping." Tally drank some water.

"I still believe none of our old careers would go to waste. God will use them all for our good."

"That's not what I meant." Tally forked a shrimp. It seemed to be the last shrimp on her plate. "I meant that you and I are similar. We both have degrees in majors that we don't use now."

"I still use my accounting background to run my landscaping company," Gus countered. "I'm not trying to be contradictory."

"You're not. I still use my English degree in some ways in the reading program at the Village. And I write my own documents and reports at church—plus my own speeches at women's conferences."

"Useful." Gus wondered whether she meant teaching little kids, or were there adults learning to read too? He decided not to ask. Instead, his thoughts moved back to the events of the day. "Are you safe going to the warehouse?"

"Levi's still there. He's replacing the door so nobody else breaks in."

"Replacing the door himself?" Gus asked.

"Yeah. He's handy that way. He can fix anything." Her voice sounded like she admired Levi.

Gus didn't want to read too much into the relationship between the two, although he wondered if Tally was interested in anyone at the moment.

Tally glanced at Gus's plate. "Do you want a pair of chopsticks?"

"No need. A fork is enough."

"We do keep extra chopsticks in the kitchen because we sometimes get takeout."

"Is this what you usually order?" Gus asked.

"No. Sometimes I get rice instead of lo mein. I do like seafood."

"Someday when you have time to visit Nassau, I'll take you to eat all the seafood you want." Gus meant it.

He and Tally had known each other as friends for a while, but this was the first time he had much to do with her ministry or her family. The last time he was in Atlanta, he had hung out at Byron's house and visited with Tina and the kids.

"Deal," Tally said. "Maybe next week we can check out Atlanta. I'm sorry we're so busy."

"No, no. Byron invited me to town," Gus said. "If his family hadn't caught the flu, I wouldn't be staying with your parents, and I'd be out of the way."

Tally made a face. "I don't mean you're in the way. In fact, I'm glad you were with me at the warehouse. I wouldn't have wanted to sit in the van alone."

"I didn't do much." Gus twirled lo mein noodles around his fork, like they were spaghetti.

They ate quietly for a while.

"Would you like more water?" Tally asked, getting up.

"I'm fine. Thanks." When he saw how tired

Tally looked, Gus was concerned. "Maybe you'll get to sleep in tomorrow."

"Me? Nope. I have to get up super early to meet the architect. We're building more tiny homes."

"How many more?"

"A dozen or so." Tally smiled. "We could use more volunteers, if you're looking for something to do."

"To build houses? I wouldn't know what to do." Even as Gus said it, he knew he wanted to help.

"A willing heart is all we need. Besides, there's more than construction work. We need a landscaper too, and the women would like to plant more vegetables."

"I can help with that."

"Then you're on."

Gus cleared their plates for them and loaded the dishwasher. Tally hung around even though he told her he didn't need her help. As he was wiping down the table, Tally's mom walked in.

Riona Fitzpatrick looked like an older version of Tally, with gray hair but few wrinkles on her face. She was shorter than her daughter, but her mannerisms were similar in some ways, like that smile on her face.

"You don't have to clean my table." Riona tried to take the dishrag from him.

"Already done, ma'am. Thank you for letting me stay here for a few days."

Riona nodded. "Don't mention it. We host missionaries all the time, so we have visitors coming and going. Did you get enough to eat?"

"Yes." Gus wrung the dishcloth and hung it over the sink.

"Have you showered?" Riona asked.

"Yes, ma'am." *Why is she asking me that?*

"Good. I'll start the dishwasher. Otherwise, the dishwasher will use up all the hot water and you might end up taking a cold shower."

"Mom, I still don't believe that," Tally said.

"Think what you want. I'm telling you that we run out of hot water altogether if I run the dishwasher, the washing machine, and the hot tub."

"But a shower?" Tally hugged her mom.

Gus didn't like to see people argue over trivial things. He opened the refrigerator to grab a bottled water to take to his room.

"Riona, thank you again for letting me stay here," he said. "I'm going to turn in. Long day."

"I guess I better go home." Tally yawned.

"You agreed to stay tonight, dear."

"I did?" Tally looked at Gus.

Gus shrugged.

"Yes, on the phone when I called you." Riona held her daughter's hands. "I don't want you falling asleep at the wheel."

"You worry too much, Mom. I'll be fine."

"You still have to come over at seven o'clock in the morning to pick up your dad."

"Right."

"Colette is at Lakeside the next two weekends for several weddings at Lakeside Chapel, so you can have her room," Riona insisted. "You and she are about the same size anyway, and you've worn her clothes."

"All right." Tally hugged her mother. "I can go to bed right away instead of driving home."

Riona smiled. "Besides, they haven't caught the killer yet."

Yikes.

Gus stared at Tally. She didn't seem too worried, as if the killer had nothing to do with her. However, he needn't remind anyone that the murder had happened in her rented warehouse, though.

Gus went upstairs to the guest room and found his phone buzzing on the charger. He had missed Byron's text and phone calls.

Gus called him back on FaceTime.

"I know, right?" he said after Byron finished saying how stunned he was that Gus's first day in Atlanta was met with literal death.

Byron repeated what he knew. "You didn't see the body."

"Tally and I didn't go inside at all. We saw the open garage door, and called the police immediately, thinking it was a break-in."

"I told Levi they really need to install a security system."

Gus nodded. "I wish I could look over the women's ministry finances. They really need to budget for more security."

"You worry about Tally."

"Is it that obvious?"

"Yes. Let me check on that for you. If Pastor Kim says okay, then you can do an informal audit. I know accounting is what you used to do."

"Thanks. It's a good idea to get that approval from the top, considering I'm not a church member."

"Exactly." Byron coughed and sneezed.

"How's the family?" Gus asked.

"Everyone is still sick. If we don't turn a corner by Monday, we're all going to see the doctor," Byron said.

"Get well soon. I'll pray for a quick recovery."

"You'll have to get someone to take you to church on Sunday. Doesn't look like we're going to make it. Wouldn't want to get the whole church sick."

"Don't worry. I'll ask Pastor Fizz."

They chatted for a bit. Gus fell asleep shortly after that, drifting into the strangest dream of becoming Tally's bodyguard and keeping her safe from unknown attackers.

CHAPTER FOUR

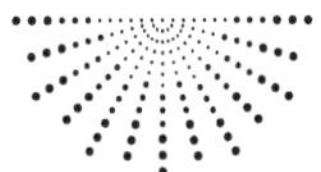

Tally woke up before four in the morning, unable to sleep. Usually, she'd get up at five o'clock, so she could've used another hour of sleep.

Colette's bed wasn't uncomfortable, but it wasn't Tally's own bed in her own townhouse. However, Colette's old T-shirt and shorts were super comfortable cotton, and she wondered if her sister would let her keep them.

Lying in bed, she tried to hear noises in the night. She had left the window open, but all she could hear was...nothing but her own thoughts, not even early summer insects. She glanced at the window. It was dark outside. The screen prevented summer mosquitoes from invading her sister's bedroom.

Tally drew a deep breath and tried to decide what to do. Should she get up and read her Bible now, or should she try to go back to sleep? Mom had said before that sometimes God stirred Christians to pray in the night, but only one person came to Tally's mind.

Jacinda Everett.

The poor mom who had lost her teenage son.

How could Tally explain to Jacinda that God had allowed it? Almighty God who wanted everyone to be saved had somehow allowed Sheldon to die without Christ.

"Lord Jesus," Tally whispered. "Didn't You say in 2 Peter 3:9 that You don't want any to perish? 'The Lord is not slack concerning His promise, as some count slackness, but is longsuffering toward us, not willing that any should perish but that all should come to repentance.' Lord, why did Sheldon die?"

Then again, perhaps Sheldon might have received Jesus Christ on his last breath. If so, he would be in paradise with God.

Tally remembered that passage of Scripture that her father had preached so often about the two thieves crucified on both sides of Jesus at the cross in Luke 23:39–43. One of them scolded Jesus, but the other pleaded for his own soul.

> *Then he said to Jesus, "Lord, remember me when You come into Your kingdom." And Jesus said to him, "Assuredly, I say to you, today you will be with Me in Paradise."*

"Lord Jesus, help me minister to Jacinda." Tears rolled down Tally's cheeks and onto the pillow beneath her head.

Ministering to women at church seemed like a light task. Tally loved talking to them, hugging them, and sharing Bible verses with them at Bible studies, retreats, and conferences. Then everybody went home to their own lives.

Back at the office, Tally organized the ministry, but she had been insulated from directly counseling anyone—simply because she was not a trained counselor. She could be trained, but there were plenty of counselors at Midtown.

Perhaps she needed to get some training so that she could be a better pastor's wife.

Ah, that.

To be a pastor's wife, she would need a pastor for a husband.

"And there is none." Tally said it aloud and laughed.

She had no idea how time passed by her. At thirty-five and unmarried, Tally kept hoping that a single pastor would show up for her to marry...

Malachi Jacobs.

She felt embarrassed as his name popped into her head. Malachi first came on her radar about ten years ago when Riverside Chapel in Savannah had a joint missions conference with Midtown Chapel and Seaside Chapel. The three churches had banded together to fund missionaries all over the world.

Malachi was one of them. He had followed the seminary footsteps of his great-grandfather, the Reverend Hiram Jacobs, who had passed away some eight or nine years ago now. At the missions conference, Malachi had presented himself as a new missionary who needed funding.

Tally sent his missions agency a check, and she received his emails and newsletter updates. Every time Malachi was in town, he would spend time with the Fitzpatricks, and Tally had seen him as often as her mom had.

Tally wanted to take their relationship to the next level, but Malachi kept leaving the States for overseas mission fields.

To this day, Tally still felt something for him, as if she could not let him go. After all, she had the idea that she would marry a pastor.

Tally sighed and rolled out of bed.

After washing her face and brushing her teeth, she swiped her phone to read her Bible. She preferred to read her leather-bound study Bible, but she had left it in her townhouse. She hadn't planned on staying overnight at her parents' house.

She remembered Dad saying that a pastor and his wife had to be prepared at all times for the unexpected. Mom set a good example of taking everything in stride. Sometimes people came crying at odd hours of the night—

Tally heard something.

It sounded like the doorbell.

She had barely read a verse in her Bible.

The doorbell rang again.

Her first thought went to her parents. They were still asleep. *Let them sleep.*

Her phone in her hand, Tally ran downstairs as the doorbell kept ringing. Someone banged on the door.

She looked outside through one of the glass panels on either side of the front door. The small light shone on a woman she recognized as one of the women who had started attending Midtown Chapel recently.

"Karissa?" She unlocked the front door. "Karissa? What's wrong?"

Karissa's hair was askew, and her pajamas were torn. Her face was streaked with something. "Help me."

"Come in, come in." Tally prayed for calm as she locked the door behind Karissa and turned on the foyer light.

In the light, she saw it.

Karissa's face was bruised, and one eye was swollen. "What on earth?"

The woman burst into tears.

Tally swept her into her arms and held her as she shuddered and wailed.

"Everything is going to be okay," Tally found herself saying. "You're safe now. God knows."

Karissa was still crying when all the lights came on. Mom and Dad came out of their master suite down the hallway. Stepping down the stairs, Gus looked like he had just woken up. His legs were muscular—

Busy right now.

Tally patted Karissa's back and held her tightly, like she held Colette and Adalia when they needed an older sister's shoulder to cry on.

"Let's go in the living room," Dad said.

"I'll put on the coffee." Mom walked to the kitchen.

Gus said nothing. He stood at the landing, as if wondering if he should go back to bed or come downstairs and see what was happening.

"You can pray, Gus," Tally said.

Gus seemed surprised. He nodded and went back upstairs.

Tally almost smiled that she had apparently read his mind. She walked with Karissa to the living room, which faced the back of the house. She grabbed a box of tissues on the way to the big couch, where she sat down with Karissa.

Dad sat across the carpet from them, his Bible already in hand. He never went anywhere without that old Bible.

Tally immediately felt so much better. Dad was here and he'd know what to do. God would guide him. And all would be well.

Now she understood why God had allowed her to wake up so early this morning, although she suddenly felt tired, as if this was too much for her to handle.

Poor Karissa. It wasn't the first time she'd had problems at home, but it was the first time she had come all the way here to the counseling pastor's house.

Tally handed Karissa more tissues. Everyone waited for her to calm down a bit.

Sometimes it was best not to say anything but to pray silently and wait for the right time to do everything. If there was anything that Dad had taught Tally, it was patience.

A fruit of the spirit.

Karissa was still crying, and now Tally was crying along with her.

How could life be so hard for this poor woman? Perhaps it was better not to marry at all if marriage was like this.

Then again, Tally only had to look to her parents to see the best marriage ever. They were her examples, not Karissa and her drug-addicted estranged husband.

"Cruz found me," Karissa finally said. "He broke down my door last night and passed out in my bedroom. I thought I had enough time to pack up and leave, but he caught me as I was walking out the door. Dragged me back into the house and beat the tar out of me."

She shifted and made a sharp hissing sound. She reached for her ribs and yelped.

"We need to get you to the doctor." Mom stood by Dad's armchair.

"I'll be all right," Karissa said.

"You don't look all right." Tally lifted a strand of hair from Karissa's face.

"I'm not bleeding."

"Under your skin, you might be."

"I drove here myself." Karissa sounded proud. "I stood up to Cruz. That means something, doesn't it?"

"He's three hundred pounds, and you're barely one ten," Tally said. "By the mercy of God you made it out here."

"How did you get to the car?" Mom sat down next to Karissa.

"I went to the neighbor's house, and they let me drive away while they held Cruz down."

"Did they call the police?" Tally asked.

Karissa nodded. "But it won't do any good. Cruz will get out and find me again."

Tally felt a sting in her eyes.

The smell of coffee wafted through the living room.

"So this is what we're going to do," Dad finally said.

Everyone looked at him.

"We're going to pray right now, then we're all

going to the twenty-four-hour clinic to have your wounds looked at. We're going to file a police report, and then we'll talk."

Tally nodded.

"Thank you, Pastor Fizz." Karissa's eyes were fiery and strong in spite of all that she had suffered.

Tally knew that it was time for Karissa to leave town and go somewhere where Cruz would not be able to find her. The women's ministry had connections with battered women ministries and halfway houses all over the country.

Fortunately, Karissa didn't have any children.

"He's not a bad man," Karissa said.

"Stop defending him," Tally said. "No good man would beat up a woman, especially his own wife."

"It's the drugs. Maybe he needs to go back to rehab."

You think? Tally pursed her lips, just in case she misspoke.

"Let's pray," Dad said. In his baritone voice, he prayed for God's mercy and provision. "Oh Lord, who sees all things and cares for all Your creation, show us what to do, where to go, how to solve this problem. And we give You all the glory and praise. In the name of Jesus, I pray. Amen."

"Coffee's ready," Mom said. "I just need my purse."

"I need my shoes and wallet." Dad followed Mom back to their bedroom.

Tally almost reminded them to brush their teeth, but they were adults.

"Would you like some coffee?" Tally asked Karissa.

"Yes, please. I love coffee."

"Let's get some." It might seem out of place, but Tally knew something had to be *normal* for Karissa. Maybe coffee was a slice of routine that marked the start of a brand-new day.

To Tally, that normalcy would be to get up early in the morning and read the Bible—which she hadn't gotten to yet because the doorbell rang.

However, she had run through two verses from memory before she got out of bed. As soon as she had time this morning, she would read the Bible. Perhaps she could read it to Karissa on the way to or at the doctor's.

When Mom and Dad came out of their bedroom again, Tally approached them. "I'm going to get my purse from Colette's room and tell Gus where we're going."

Dad nodded.

"I think we need to pull Karissa's car into the garage," Tally added.

"Not my car," Karissa corrected. "My neighbor's car."

"Good idea," Dad said. "Cruz knows where we live."

"Do you have the car key?" Tally asked Karissa, who was drinking coffee calmly. If not for her face, no one would know she had just been assaulted.

"I left it in the car."

"Okay." Tally's shoulders felt tense, as though her muscles were tightening up. Silently, she prayed that God would lift her stress. She felt sorry for Karissa, but Dad had reminded her not to internalize other people's grief, or she would lose her objectivity to deal with the situation.

How do I not feel for poor Karissa?

Tally ran up the stairs. As soon as she reached her bedroom, she remembered she hadn't showered. Quickly, she changed into clean clothes—Colette's T-shirt and a pair of matching capris—and grabbed her purse and phone charger.

In no time, she was knocking on Gus's door. She told him what they were going to do. As she spoke, she started to lose it. Tears puddled in her eyes. She held her breath, as if that would stop the flow.

"Shhh..." Gus wrapped his arms around Tally.

His chest was warm, like a blanket. Tally wanted to go back to sleep right there. She rested her head on his shoulder and smelled fresh soap. He had taken a shower.

And she hadn't.

She pulled away and wiped her eyes. "I haven't showered."

"I don't care." He smiled. "I've prayed, and will keep praying. I'll stay here until you get back."

Tally nodded. "Don't let anyone come in. If you see this man, call 911." She swiped her phone to show him a photo of Cruz.

"Will do."

"Call Byron. He knows what to do, including mobilizing the prayer ministry to pray." As she walked away, she reminded herself to call her administrative assistant. Maggie Jacobs would let the women's ministry staff know. Plus, she would call the women's shelter and make arrangements for Karissa.

Tally thanked God for the people He had put together for her at the women's ministry. While Tally was a big-picture director, she had a few able assistants who had eyes for details. In fact, many of her staff and volunteers were closer to the women they ministered to.

Maggie was probably still at the Village. She had volunteered to stay with Jacinda overnight in case she needed prayer. In the morning—it wasn't even dawn yet—lay counselors would get there and take over.

Ultimately, this was God's work. All Tally could do was minister to the women as the Lord would direct her. She knew she had found her calling even though ministry work was never meant to be easy, nor was it always planned.

On the schedule this morning was another Saturday of construction and gardening at the Village. A few more tiny homes would be ready by next week. Yet it wasn't safe for Karissa to stay there. If Cruz found her there, what would happen to her?

The couple had attended several counseling sessions with Dad at Midtown Chapel until Cruz purportedly found a new job out of state somewhere. Karissa continued the counseling alone for months. Now Cruz was back.

At the foot of the stairs, Tally remembered something. She turned around to run up the stairs, but Gus was right there behind her. He had followed her downstairs.

"I was going to give you my spare keys to the

house." She dug into her purse and fished them out. "Here. Lock the doors after we leave."

"Yes, ma'am." He looked calm. "Do you have Levi's car key?"

Tally handed it to him. "I'll call the house phone in a bit to give you Levi's number. He's supposed to be at the Village this morning, if you're looking for something to do."

"I'll go there unless you need me here."

"I don't need you." Tally moved on. "Mom made coffee. Have some breakfast—or if you can get to the Village by seven o'clock, Hiroki is bringing Chick-fil-A for everyone."

"Hiroki?"

"Hiroki Yamada, our chief architect. You might meet him today. Most days he's in Savannah, but today he's in town."

"Okay."

When Tally reached the garage, Mom was getting out of Karissa's neighbor's car. Dad's SUV was idling on the driveway. Tally found her sandals and ran after Mom.

"Lock the doors!" Tally called out to Gus.

CHAPTER FIVE

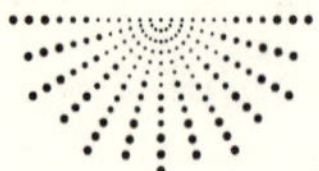

When Gus arrived at the Midtown Chapel Village, he wasn't sure where to go or what to do. The only person he really knew was Tally, and she was at the police station with her parents and the stranger in the night.

However, he had briefly met Levi and remembered what he looked like. If Levi came to the Village today, then Gus would know a friendly face. Someone to talk to. After all, Gus had driven Levi's car.

Thankfully, as soon as Gus parked behind a church van, Levi came up to him.

"Fancy seeing you here." Levi extended his

hand and shook Gus's. "Thanks for bringing my car back."

Gus handed Levi his car key. "From Tally."

"Does it drive okay?"

"I didn't go over the speed limit."

"I mean I've had problems. Did you hear any rattling?"

"A little." Gus had prayed aloud in the car on the drive here, so it hadn't bothered him.

"Thank God you made it here safely." Levi slapped Gus's shoulder.

"Maybe you should take the car to the mechanic."

"I've had problem after problem with that car. I think the transmission is probably going too. I need a new car."

"We'll pray that God will provide." Gus meant it.

"Thank you. Speaking of prayers, the next time you see Tally, be sure to tell her we prayed for Karissa just now."

"Will do."

Gus had expected Levi to know what was going on. After all, Gus had called Byron as soon as he'd locked the house door after Tally left, and Byron was supposed to tell everyone else who needed to know.

"You didn't just drive here to drop off the car, did you?" Levi asked. "I'm sorry you missed breakfast."

"I ate before I came. I have all day if you need another volunteer."

"Good. We need all the help we can get. Lunch is provided, by the way."

"What can I do?" Gus asked.

"I hear you're good at gardening."

Tally must have told him. "Well, I can help with that."

"We'll have to get some potting soil from the warehouse, but why don't I take you to the vegetable garden and show you what we have so far. You can take a look at the area and make some recommendations."

"Sounds good to me." Gus followed Levi down a cement path flanked by colorful and assorted huts. They might not be called huts, but they looked like huts or cabins or one-bedroom studios.

"Aren't these tiny homes something else?" Levi asked. "They're functional and practical."

Ah, tiny homes. Gus forgot what they were called. "Very economical too."

"Right. God has provided."

"He has."

The houses were painted in pastel colors, and

some even had porches and window boxes. The colors were not as bright or intense as the beach houses back home—oh, he missed the beaches—but they were colorful nonetheless.

They looked like bubblegum colors, but Gus didn't want to note that. "How big are each of these?"

"Each is under three hundred square feet. Want a tour?"

"Let me do that," a woman's voice said.

Tally.

Gus recognized her voice even without seeing who it was. Unless, of course, he was mistaken and it was one of her two sisters or her mother.

Both men turned around.

Sure enough, it was Tally.

Levi waved. "I thought you're busy with Karissa."

Tally walked toward them. "Mary Anne from the women's shelter took over. Karissa's in good hands. They're taking her somewhere safe."

"Restraining order in place?" Levi asked.

"Yeah."

"How did you get here so fast?"

"I dropped Mom and Dad off at the house and came here—after I took a shower."

Tally's hair was tied up in a bun at the back of her head, so Gus couldn't tell if it was still wet.

"Fast as lightning." Levi laughed.

"Not really. It's been at least two hours since we went to the police station."

Levi looked stunned.

Gus checked his watch. Sure enough.

Tally spoke with Gus. "Has Levi put you to work yet?"

"I volunteered to do some gardening."

Tally held out her palm toward Levi. "You got the van key? We'll need some gardening equipment from the warehouse. Plus those giant flowerpots."

"Gave the key to Maggie," Levi said. "Let me find her."

"Sure."

Gus wanted to ask about the police investigation at the warehouse, but he figured that could wait. It hadn't even been twenty-four hours yet, and so much had happened at Midtown Chapel.

If this kept going, Gus wondered if he should just go home to Nassau, where life was peaceful and quiet.

Then again, he'd be stuck in his flat, bemoaning and lamenting his losses in life.

He wondered how Veronique was progressing with her pregnancy—

No, don't go there.

Gus cleared his throat.

Tally turned toward him. "I haven't forgotten about you."

"No, no." Gus's face reddened. "I was thinking about something else. I wasn't even listening to you two."

Levi smiled. "Let me text Maggie to get you the van key. She's here somewhere."

"This way." Tally led Gus down a stone path. "I've got some container gardening in mind, but I'm not much of a gardener. You can help me."

The tiny homes were arranged in such a way that there were four squares forming a common area. In the middle of each square was a firepit.

"We do campfires year round," Tally explained. "Several people would play instruments–guitar, harmonica, violin, and even an occasional banjo–and we sing hymns and have Bible studies about once or twice a week."

"Sounds fun. When's the next one?"

"Wednesday night. We did this to mirror Seaside Chapel with their Firepit Service. Have you attended one of those?"

"Seaside Chapel on St. Simon's Island?" Gus asked.

"Yeah."

"Never been to St. Simon's."

"Well, we should take you—or someone should. Best barbecue I've ever had is on that island."

Gus mulled over the idea of taking a mini vacation within his vacation.

"How far away is it?"

"Five hours of driving. Or an hour of flying." Tally stopped at a giant flowerpot that had a variety of flowers growing in it. "You can get a ride with some of the Seaside Chapel volunteers. They'll be here in a couple of weeks to build more houses. Then you can fly back here."

It seemed like a lot of trouble to go to the coast.

"Or I can take you there. Dad is preaching one Sunday morning in June. Mom's not driving much anymore, and my sisters are too busy. So I'm taking a week off to take my parents to St. Simon's. We're staying for a few days so Dad can prepare his sermon. That Sunday morning, he's preaching at Seaside Chapel. After church we'll drive up to Savannah, where Dad will be preaching at the evening service at Riverside Chapel. The next day we'll drive back to Atlanta."

"Are you the only one driving?"

"Yep."

"I can split the driving with you."

Tally leaned toward Gus. "Can you drive an RV?"

A recreational vehicle. "I'm game."

"Okay. You'll need to bring your international driver's license and passport with you on the trip, but you knew that."

Gus nodded.

"It's only five hours each way, but maybe we can let you drive a little bit. Oh." Her fingers touched her forehead. "Seriously, you don't have to drive."

"If I go, I'd be more than happy to drive. It will give me something to do rather than nap all the way in the vehicle."

Tally chuckled. "Is that what you do on road trips?"

Gus shrugged. "I wouldn't know. There are no long road trips in the Bahamas, as you know. A small island surrounded by ocean."

"I'd be lying if I said I don't miss the Bahamas," Tally said. "I'd like to go back if I have the opportunity, but most of the projects that our church sponsors these days have been with the summer camps at your school."

Gus nodded.

Since Chapel by the Sea had been adopted by the trio of sister churches—Riverside, Seaside, and

Midtown—various mission teams had visited its Christian school to run Vacation Bible School every year.

"I know that mostly the teams worked with kids," Gus said.

"If I go over the summer, I'd just be doing support work, like making snacks for the kids. I'd prefer to minister to moms though."

"You know our church hosts women's conferences in the fall. Maybe you can get involved in that."

"Our church also has women's conferences in the fall." Tally looked disappointed that she couldn't do both. "If they're not in the same week—or month—I might be able to do both."

"Don't do too much. You'll need time for self-care as well."

Tally nodded. She said no more, as if the conversation about all the things she had to do this fall had concluded.

They kept walking. Gus saw some empty flowerpots stacked up beside bags of soil.

Gus stepped toward the flowerpots. "What do we have here?"

"Since we don't know how many houses we are going to build, Hiroki and I decided that we would plant flowers in containers instead of in the ground. That way, we can move the flowerpots around if we need more space to pop up another home."

Hiroki and I.

Gus recalled that Tally had mentioned Hiroki before she left her dad's house in the morning.

Before Tally could say more, someone came over to ask her this or that.

Of course, she knew everything about the Midtown Chapel Village.

Gus wondered when they could start work. Perhaps they should cut the tour short.

They rounded a corner, and someone popped out of one of the tiny homes and stopped Tally.

Tally had the brightest smile when she hugged the resident, but Gus could see the tiredness in her eyes. He wondered how much sleep she'd had.

"My friend Davila wants to know if she could get on the waiting list," the resident said to Tally.

"Of course, but I have to tell you, we can only build the houses as fast as we have volunteers," Tally said.

"Davila wants to volunteer. She used to work in construction, back when she was homeless. She's living in a halfway house, but she could help."

"She's pregnant, isn't she?"

The resident nodded. "Seven months along.

That's why she wants to live here, where she can raise her baby safely."

Gus waited to see how Tally would respond, and he saw tears well in her eyes.

"Then I won't have her working in construction at this time. She can volunteer doing other things like gardening and cooking, if she wants. I'm not saying that she can't climb scaffolding while seven months pregnant—or maybe I am saying that."

The resident was so excited that she jumped up and down. "She could stay with me, you know."

"You have one full-size bed."

"I can sleep on a cot, and Davila can sleep in the full-size bed with her baby when the time comes."

"We'll have someone take a look at the layout of your house, but if I remember correctly, you have a corner space for a hammock," Tally suggested.

"I can sleep on a hammock. I can sleep anywhere as long as there's a roof over my head."

Gus wanted to cry, but he held it in. He wondered what he could do to help build more tiny homes or speed up the process. Volunteers, he'd heard Tally say. What if he paid a construction company to do the rest of the work here, thus freeing up volunteers to do more important things, such as ministering to the hearts and souls of these people?

"So here's what we're going to do, Lena." Tally tapped on her phone. "Ask Davila to sign up for a home by tomorrow. We have a committee meeting on Monday to decide on needs, and as you know, we prioritize pregnant women and mothers with small children."

Lena nodded profusely. "Thank you, thank you."

"No guarantee that Davila will get a number next week, unless there's no one else more pregnant than she is, you know?"

"Yes, ma'am."

"Also, she has two months to go, right?"

"She's due end of July."

Tally nodded. She made another note on her phone. "Is she seeing an ob-gyn?"

"No."

"What do you mean no?" Tally looked up. "Go to the Village website and get her a list of doctors. Free of charge to her."

"Oh, I didn't know that. I thought we have to pay a bit, like copay or something."

"She's a single mother, pregnant, and out of work, am I right?"

Lena nodded.

"The church will pay for the balance of her medical expenses and childbirth, whatever the state doesn't cover."

Lena cried. "How can I help?"

"We have baby showers every other month. Can you help with decorations and finger food?"

"Yes, I can. I'll go sign up right now." She ran off, then came back and gave Tally a big hug.

Gus was processing all that he had heard. His heart said to donate some money to Midtown Chapel for their medical ministry, but his head said to give plenty enough to the Village to cover all expenses its residents needed, including medical.

"Tally." He tapped her shoulder.

Her fingers wiped her face.

Gus walked around her and faced her. She was crying. Gus hadn't seen her in this state before. Without a word—and with all his own protocols flying out of the window—Gus gathered her in his arms and let her head rest on his shoulder.

He said nothing.

Just as quickly, Tally pulled back. "Where were we? Ah, the tour. This way, Mr. Moss."

Circling the squares, they ended back at the containers by the sidewalk—and Tally's face returned to normal.

Someone was waiting for Tally.

"Jacinda." Tally's voice was low as she hugged the woman tightly. "We've been praying for you."

"Thank you." The woman's voice broke. She wiped her eyes. The tears wouldn't stop flowing. "Sheldon would be happy to know that so many people care."

What on earth? So many people crying today.

Gus should have brought a box of tissues. Why were there so many broken hearts in this place?

Gus stood there silently, watching Tally console the poor mother. Putting two and two together, he gathered this was the mother of the dead kid in the warehouse.

Gus could not imagine losing a child. He had lost his parents, and that had been devastating, but what did it feel like to lose someone you gave birth to?

He wondered how he could help. Money, he had plenty of. But it looked like they could use manpower also. Human resources.

He glanced around to see if there were other teenagers. School was out for the summer, and perhaps some of the teens had jobs they could go to. Were there teenagers without parents here? Homeless teens perhaps?

Gus decided to ask Tally about them later.

Maybe he could set up a scholarship fund for their high school and college expenses.

Gus had no clue how that idea popped into his head, but his parents had died when he was still a minor. He could sympathize with orphans in some way, even though his rich aunt had taken him in and raised him.

These people here had nobody but the church.

And God.

Gus wasn't aware that Jacinda had left. When he looked up from staring at the ground, Tally was staring at him.

"Something on your mind?" she asked.

"Are there teenagers living here—maybe homeless ones without parents?" Gus asked.

"You mean runaways? We don't take runaways. If their school tells us that they're homeless, we have foster parents who can provide them shelter and food. Teenagers don't live here in the Village on their own."

Gus nodded.

"They can, however, volunteer here. We take all volunteers." Tally pointed to the community building. "We have a day care and after-school program in the community center over there. We do pay people to work there, but there's a limited number of positions. In any case, the programs we have allow single moms to go to work during the day."

Gus decided that if he were to start a scholarship fund, then it would have to be for every child at the Village, not just teenagers. He decided he would pray about asking Aunt Nancy to help him seed the fund.

"Does Midtown Chapel have an academic scholarship fund for the kids?" Gus asked.

"Not yet." Tally waved to someone. "Maggie! Over here."

Maggie and another woman made their way toward Tally and Gus.

"Maggie, Soline, this is Augustus Moss—Gus," Tally said. To Gus, she said, "This is Maggie Jacobs and Soline Ang-Ferrera. You might have heard their names yesterday when Levi and I talked outside the warehouse."

Gus shook their hands. He didn't remember much, but it didn't matter. He did recall, however, that Soline had a date with Levi on Friday night.

"Maggie is my able assistant," Tally said. "I don't know what I'd do without her. She has a keen eye for details and fills in all the potholes I miss along the way, running the women's ministry at church."

"Teamwork," Maggie said.

"If I retire, the ministry goes on," Tally said. "If Maggie leaves us, our ministry is doomed."

"We'll be sure to train people to continue the work." Maggie pointed a finger in the air. "To God be the glory."

"See what I'm saying?" Tally nudged Gus with her elbow. "She has the foresight."

Ultimately, a Christian ministry should depend primarily on God, and Gus was sure that Tally knew that. Gus himself had trained his landscape crew at his school well enough that if he should quit and find a new career or move elsewhere, Chapel by the Sea Christian School would still be well taken care of.

After Tally took the van key from Maggie, Tally invited Gus to go with her to the warehouse. "We can get more flowerpots there and some potting soil. We also need to stop at Pike's to get some seedlings."

"What kind of seedlings?" Gus asked.

"Whatever flowers they have."

"Anything?"

"Whatever you want." Tally laughed. "Unless someone requests specific flowers in the planters, we just leave it to the volunteers, as long as it's within budget."

Gus made up his mind to pay for the flowers,

but he didn't tell Tally at this point. He followed her to the van. It was the same van from Friday, but it was emptied out.

Tally climbed into the driver's side. She was silent for a long time. Her hands were on the steering wheel, but her head was bowed.

Gus thought she was praying. He didn't say a word as he buckled in.

Tally's left hand reached over to massage her right shoulder. When she looked up, her eyes were red. She quickly put on her sunglasses.

"You okay?" Gus asked.

"I'm fine."

"Are you lying?"

"What?" Tally put the van in gear.

They rumbled down the road before Gus spoke again. "I don't mean to pry, but..."

"Don't."

"Okay." Gus decided to pray for Tally instead. He could not imagine the pressure she might be under from the last twenty-four hours.

The rest of the drive would have been in silence except that Tally played some Christian songs from her phone playlist through a Bluetooth speaker. They arrived at the warehouse with Tally humming "10,000 Reasons" by Matt Redman.

They had sung that at Gus's church in Nassau also. He sang along.

Tally put the gear in reverse and backed up the van so that the back door faced the loading dock. "You have a nice voice."

"Thank you." Gus stopped singing.

"Don't stop singing." Tally chuckled. She unbuckled her seat belt and tapped her phone. "Let me text security to let them know we're here."

"I forget the rest of the words." It was true. He blanked out after the compliment.

"Next time I'll remember to let you finish before applauding." Tally unlocked the van door and opened it. One foot was out of the vehicle, when Gus grabbed her arm.

"Is it safe to be here so soon after...?" he asked.

"Life goes on, right?" Tally said. "We have to get the potting soil and the containers."

"What if the killers return?" Gus asked.

"We all die sooner or later."

"I don't want to die today."

"Okay. So stay in the van, and I'll roll out the potting soil for you."

The door to the building opened from the inside. A big man stood at the door. He wore a security-guard uniform.

"Joey," Tally said. "Have you met Gus?"

They shook hands. The man's hand was so big that Gus thought Joey's little finger could break his thumb.

"Joey works at security at Midtown. Pastor Kim sent him here today. This afternoon, the security company is installing a new system," Tally said. "You don't have to worry, Gus."

"Not when I'm here." Joey didn't laugh or smile. He ushered them inside the warehouse and locked the door behind them.

The warehouse was half-filled with boxes and things. Somewhere between stacked chairs and tables was a chalk outline. Joey walked around it, and Tally followed.

Gus's feet were glued to the floor where he'd entered.

"Sheldon was here," Tally said quietly.

Gus made himself move toward Tally, as if he had to stay close to her. To protect her? Or to feel safer himself?

"Anything I can help with?" Joey asked.

"Yeah. We need some potting soil and containers." As Tally spoke, her phone rang. She tapped the Answer button. "Dad?"

Gus waited for Tally to talk to her dad.

"Next week? Wow. Really? I see. When are you leaving?" She waved for Gus to follow Joey.

Gus didn't want to leave Tally standing by the chalk line, but she didn't look afraid. For one thing, she had almighty God with her, but there was also Joey the Muscle Man.

And me, Gus. Just Gus.

"You're volunteering at the Village?" Joey asked. It sounded like an interrogation.

"I'm on vacation from the Bahamas, visiting my cousin Byron Moss."

"Vacation, you say?" Joey laughed. It was a deep laugh. "People go to the Bahamas for vacation, not the other way around. If you haven't noticed, Atlanta is landlocked."

"I know. I needed a change of scenery."

"We all do. Welcome to Hotlanta. Hope the weather is not too muggy for you."

"Not bad so far."

"Just wait until July. How long are you going to be here?"

"June. I'm only here for four weeks."

"In a few days you might wish you were back on the beach. Is it nice out there in the Bahamas? I've never been." Joey found a cart for Gus just as Tally joined them.

"Yes, very nice. Tropical weather year round." In a small way, Gus missed home, but he didn't miss the pain that his former girlfriend had left him.

Why had Veronique decided to leave him? She'd said this and that, but Gus didn't believe those were the real reasons. They had been together for a few years.

It was clear to Gus now that Veronique had considered him boyfriend material but not husband potential.

Maybe God had other plans for him. Clearly, He had other plans for Veronique.

"The potting soil is a few aisles over." Tally's voice echoed in the warehouse. "Joey, maybe you can give us a hand."

"Sure. I got nothing better to do while I wait for the alarm company to show up." Joey walked alongside Gus, who pushed the cart.

As they were loading the potting soil, Joey's phone rang. "Must be the alarm company."

He was off the phone in no time. "They're on their way."

"Good." Tally dragged a giant plastic flowerpot. "This is surprisingly light."

"Or you're a strong woman." Joey laughed. He carried a stack of four flowerpots.

Gus pushed the cart full of soil. It was heavy. He didn't complain.

At the loading dock, they filled the van. Then Tally and Gus drove off.

"I'm glad the warehouse is getting an alarm system." Gus adjusted the AC for the passenger's side.

"It wasn't my decision not to renew the last alarm service," Tally explained. "However, we were paying monthly, and the rate went up. Giving is usually slow in the summer months."

"But you have new funding overnight."

"Yes. God provided."

Gus didn't ask where the money had come from. If he donated to the church for these ministries, the only person who would know was Pastor Kim.

"Usually, someone hears about the needs," Tally said. "That's how God provides for us."

Gus began to get it. "You get only what you need."

"Yes. When we need it."

"Just like manna from heaven."

"You know your Old Testament."

Gus barely nodded. "I'm still learning."

"Byron says you teach Sunday school at your church."

"Yes, but learning about God is a lifelong process." Gus drew a deep breath.

"Tell me what you've learned this week." The question seemed sudden.

Gus was taken aback. Yes, Tally was a friend, but not a friend so close that he could share what he'd really learned this week. He could tell her something in general, but that wouldn't be what he had learned this week.

"Nothing?" Tally asked.

She was getting personal. Perhaps her directness was a result of her being a counseling pastor's daughter. Or maybe that was how she was.

Do I really know this lady, after all?

"I'm sorry," Tally said as she drove the van.

That was all it took for Gus to begin to understand where she was coming from. "Why do you ask me about my personal lessons?"

"Maybe I just need to see what others are learning so that I can better handle my own present situation," Tally said. "One of the things I enjoy about our Sunday school class is that we share with one another what God has taught us."

Gus agreed. "Sometimes, by learning vicariously through other people, we won't repeat the same mistakes ourselves."

"That too." Tally slowed down as she turned onto a road.

"Truth be told, I've been in a mess for months," Gus said.

"I don't need the details."

"You asked, and I am going to tell you."

"Do I want to hear it?"

"There's a happy ending."

Tally smiled. "God wins."

"Yes, but I'm not out of the woods yet."

"Huh. So where's the happy ending?"

"In the future."

"And now?"

"Now I'm recovering. Since you already knew about Veronique, I will tell you my side of the story," Gus said. "I sort of got over the fact that she married someone else instead of me. It's been half a year, so I should move on, right? However, the memories of her keep coming back to haunt me, so to speak."

"Dad would say that you have to make a decision to let her go, and then your feelings will follow."

"I should have talked to your dad a while back then. It took me months to grasp that." He wanted his emotions to follow.

"Better months than years." Tally parked the van as close as she could to the walkway next to the community center at the Village. "If you need distractions, you've come to the right place."

"Byron says there's never a downtime at Midtown Chapel."

"He's right. You'll be so busy you won't have time to think about Veronique." Tally laughed as she texted on her phone before she got out of the van.

Gus followed her to the back of the van. Maggie and Soline appeared, along with Levi.

Gus noticed that Soline and Levi didn't talk to each other. As they carried the plastic flowerpots, Levi leaned toward Soline and said, "Sorry."

She didn't reply.

Gus grinned. Soline reminded him of how Veronique was when they'd fought. He had to be the first one to say he was sorry. Or the rest of the week was ruined.

Tally nudged him. "Hush."

"What?" Gus couldn't stop smiling.

"Two days." Tally lifted two fingers. "I give them two days. They'll be all over each other again."

"I don't know them."

"Watch." Tally tried to lift a bag of potting soil. It was too heavy for her. "Whoa."

"Let me do it." Gus stepped in.

"It looked easy when you and Joey carried them to the van."

"They're fifty pounds each."

"Glad you're here, is all I can say." Before Tally

could thank him, she slapped her forehead. "We forgot something."

Gus laughed. "Oh yeah. The seedlings!"

"So let's just drop everything off, and then we'll go to Pike's." Tally started to push the cart, when Levi and Maggie returned.

"Where's Soline?" Tally asked.

"She's doing something else." Levi sighed.

"Tell her we're having an organizational meeting with dinner tonight," Tally said.

"A meeting tonight?" Levi swiped his phone. "It's not on the calendar."

"Well, I'm adding it now. Since we have Gus here, we need to talk about our plans for the next few weeks."

Gus nodded. "I'm available to help in any way I can."

"Okay." Levi didn't sound too sure. "But Soline and I had a fight, so we're not talking anymore."

"Oh dear. Does that mean you can't be in the same space with her?" Tally asked.

Gus watched the interaction and felt for Tally. This was why he discouraged workplace romance among the staffers at his landscaping company. If the couple had a fallout, it could affect their daily operations.

Case in point: Veronique and him.

Although Veronique didn't work in his landscaping company, she did work at the school where his company provided lawn-care services every week.

Then again, love was love. If it happened, who could stop it but God?

"I'm sorry," Levi said. "I could apologize to her, although it's her fault."

Tally lifted a palm. "If you need counseling, make an appointment with Dad. As to your personal matter, I don't want to get in the middle of it. Soline's a friend of mine too."

Levi nodded.

All this time, Maggie had stood there silently next to Tally. She was on her iPad.

Gus wondered what she was doing.

"Maggie," Tally said. "Ask Soline if she can make it tonight. If not, it will just be you, Levi, and me."

Since no one protested, Gus guessed that Maggie and Levi had both agreed to the last-minute meeting.

"Meet at my house as usual. Dinner's on me. Spaghetti okay?" Tally handed the cart to Levi.

"Free food is always okay," Levi said.

Gus waited to be invited to the meeting. Had Tally forgotten him?

Tally turned and bumped into Gus. He held her arms. She stepped back. "Sorry."

Maggie seemed to pretend like she didn't see the interaction.

Tally cleared her throat. "Gus and I are going to Pike's to get some flowers. You need anything?"

"No." Maggie's eyes went back to her iPad.

"Nope. Thanks." Levi left with the cart.

Back in the van, Tally was texting again, mumbling to herself as she did so. She stopped and looked over at Gus. "You're invited to dinner at six o'clock, followed by a meeting about the Village. Is that okay for you?"

"Sure. I have nothing else to do," Gus said.

"For real?"

"Yes, ma'am. I'm fine." Gus meant it. He wondered whether she had misunderstood him. He really had nothing else to do tonight.

"I can ask Levi to pick you up."

"That's great. Thanks. When does the meeting end? I'd like to get to bed by ten o'clock."

"Good for you. I'm having a hard time these days. I don't get enough sleep, and I'm feeling stressed over what happened yesterday."

Gus liked her honesty. "I will pray for you."

"Thank you."

"In fact, let's pray right now."

Tally closed her eyes and bowed her head as Gus prayed for her and the ministry, for the decisions she had to make on the fly. Gus was impressed with her people skills, but he could see an undercurrent of stress as Tally juggled all these ministries.

CHAPTER SIX

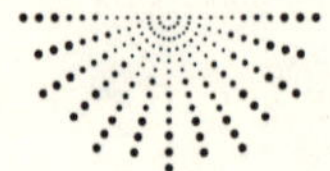

After Gus prayed in the van, Tally felt embarrassed that she had started crying before Gus finished his prayer. The pressure valves burst, and she realized that the burden of the women's ministry was simply too much for her to bear.

How did Mom juggle her ministry work and life after work hours before she retired? Had it been ministry all the time for her?

I need a break from people problems.

Gus patted her shoulder and suggested that she take a break the rest of the day. The work in the Village would still be there on Monday.

Tally took his advice. After they bought the

seedlings and flowers from the nursery, Tally dropped off Gus at the Village and went home to her townhouse.

There, at the front door, was a box. It was addressed to her, but it seemed to have been hand delivered. After entering her townhouse, she checked the security cameras.

Silas.

On the recorded video, he was wearing a baseball cap, but he looked like Silas.

"How does he know where I live?" Even as she asked the question aloud, she remembered an old church directory that the previous pastor's office had published. It was only shortly after she had moved out of her parents' house. That might be where Silas obtained her house address.

"What is this?" She opened the box. There was a cake inside. It said *Happy Anniversary*.

"What anniversary?"

Tally did not take the cake out of the box.

She had no idea what sort of anniversary Silas was celebrating.

She did not want Silas to come back, whether she was at home or otherwise. What to do?

She drew the curtains on all her windows. It was a bummer, because she liked natural summer sunlight. However, he could be watching her through the windows.

She sat down on her couch in the living room and called Dad on Skype. "What's going on with Silas?"

"Honey, you know I can't tell you that," Dad said. "The counseling sessions are confidential."

"Well, what I'm experiencing right now is not confidential. He dropped off an anniversary cake at my front door."

"What anniversary?" Dad asked.

"Exactly."

"And why would he do that?"

"You tell me, Dad." Tally crossed her legs. "I feel like I need security, but who has the money to hire someone to stay with me at all times, right?"

"When was the last time you talked to Silas?" Dad's voice was measured.

"Friday afternoon just before he went for his counseling session with you. I was outside the staff entrance, chatting with Byron and Gus, when Silas walked up to us."

"What did he say to you?"

"Not much. I was loading up the van, and he offered to help. That was all, as far as I can remember."

"He's been doing that a lot, hasn't he?"

"I don't know if I'm reading too much into it. After all, I work at the church. Anyone who comes and goes is bound to run into any church staff."

Dad was silent. He simply stared at the camera.

"Dad?"

"I'm thinking."

"Okay." Tally knew that meant Dad was also praying for wisdom. Thinking and praying went hand in hand for Dad.

"Considering that Sheldon was murdered at the warehouse yesterday, and then the cake arrived today, why don't you move home for a few weeks until we figure out what's going on?" Dad finally said.

"You have a guest," Tally reminded him. "Gus will probably stay there until flu season is over at the Moss house."

"Your mom has decided that if you take Colette's room again tonight, she'd rather have them sleep downstairs in the basement."

"Them? Are you expecting more guests?" Tally knew that Gus was there, but who else was Dad inviting to the house?

"Malachi Jacobs is coming to town," Dad said. "He and Gus can share the basement. There's my man cave, which I hardly use. Plus the spare bedroom. One of them has to sleep on the pullout sofa, but they can toss a coin to see who gets the privilege."

Wait a minute.

"Did you say Malachi?" Tally's dream man, her potential future husband—if only he knew that he could be.

Then again, Malachi was rumored to be engaged, although Tally couldn't get intel on whether it was with Bethany Baker, his former girlfriend. Perhaps they had reconnected while away from Atlanta.

"Is he coming alone?" Tally had to ask.

"Yes, dear. Why wouldn't he be alone?" Mom's face was stoic.

"Is there something I don't know?"

"About?"

"Malachi. Is he engaged, like they said he is?"

Mom smiled that knowing smile. "No, he's not engaged."

Now she understood why Mom didn't want the men to sleep upstairs on both sides of her bedroom. Mom knew about her longtime crush on Malachi.

"When is he coming?" Tally asked.

"Tomorrow, he says." Dad's voice echoed in the kitchen.

"Maggie hasn't said anything." Maggie would have told Tally.

"She doesn't know. He wants to surprise his little sister, so don't tell her yet. He'll just show up at church tomorrow."

"Little sister? Maggie is twenty-nine, Dad." Tally laughed.

"Once a little sister, always a little sister."

"Well, knowing Malachi, he's unpredictable when he springs surprises," Tally said.

Mom and Dad both turned their heads. "Meaning what?"

"Remember the last time he said he'd surprise Maggie on Sunday night?"

"No," her parents said in unison.

"He showed up Saturday night. He preferred to keep Sunday sacred," Tally explained. "Dad, did you tell him about the dinner tonight?"

Dad nodded.

"Maggie will be at dinner tonight," Tally said. "If Malachi shows up at the same time, then the surprise will have to be tonight."

"Regardless, I've already invited Malachi to stay at our house."

"How long is he staying?"

"Did you mean in town or at our house?" Dad asked.

"Both."

"Two weeks in Georgia, but not necessarily in Atlanta all the time. He's going to visit his sponsor churches in various cities. I think he mentioned Valdosta, Columbus, and Macon." Dad looked like he tried to remember more, but his memory failed him. "He'll sleep here tonight. Then he'll leave his things with his sister as he travels across the state."

Either way, it meant that Malachi might pop into their office at church every now and then for the next two weeks. Or not.

"I told you that I'm going to fill in for Diego at Riverside two Sundays from now," Dad said.

"Yeah. You called me at the warehouse," Tally said.

"I didn't tell you that I'm sending Malachi to preach in my place at Seaside Chapel the following Sunday."

"Now I know." Tally wondered if Dad was slowing down before her very eyes. One moment he had scheduled himself to preach at both Seaside Chapel on St. Simon's Island and Riverside Chapel in Savannah on the same Sunday. The next moment he had given his Seaside preaching duties to Malachi while he filled in for another guest speaker at Riverside one week earlier than planned.

It also meant that Tally would not be spending any time with Malachi on St. Simon's Island. In fact, they weren't going to that island at all this time.

"You know how it goes with ministry," Dad added. "Sometimes things change on a dime. We have to be flexible. I wasn't Diego's first choice, but it doesn't matter. The pastor who was going to preach in Diego's place has a crisis in his family with one of his kids in rehab, so Diego asked me and I said yes."

"You told me."

"I did?"

"Uh-huh." Was Dad simply forgetful, or was this a symptom of a greater underlying medical issue? "Two weeks from tomorrow."

Tally checked her calendar again to see how much time off she had left for the entire year. And it was only May. It meant that she had to change her vacation time to one week earlier so that she could drive Dad and Mom in their RV to Savannah.

However, if she could also speak to the women at Riverside, then she could count it as official ministry work and she could leave town without using her vacation time.

"I invited Malachi to go a day early with us to Jacobs Landing," Dad said.

Tally's heart skipped a beat. She could not imagine camping out that close to Malachi.

"He said no."

Tally's shoulders sagged.

"Said he's going to spend some time with his sister that last weekend he'll be in town, and then he's going back to the field after preaching at St. Simon's."

"Where is he going next?" Tally had tried to keep up with Malachi, but he traveled a lot.

"He's helping with a church plant in Kentucky."

"Minnesota last month and Kentucky this month. Sounds like he's staying stateside for a bit."

"Doesn't it?"

"I thought he preferred overseas assignments?"

"If you ask me, I think he's preparing to look for a pastoral position."

"That so?" Tally waited. Dad wouldn't say things for no reason.

"I'm going to ask him to assist me at Lakeside Chapel."

It was all news to Tally. "I thought you were only visiting Lakeside. You preach there in a few services and then come home to Atlanta. Same with Sunrise Church."

"You remember what I said, Tally?" Dad asked.

"You said so many things, Dad."

"Something that applies to this situation."

"The instability of it?"

"You're close."

Tally felt that her brain was too tired for pop quizzes. However, Dad always taught. Day and night. Night and day. If she didn't answer his question now, she could be sure that he'd do a makeup test soon.

"Something you said recently?" Tally fished for clues. She gazed at her phone, stared at Dad on the other side of the video call, hoping to see something in his face.

"Let me give you a hint. It's in Proverbs."

Tally rolled her eyes. "Dad, you've preached on every verse in the book of Proverbs. It could be anything."

"I'll give you a hint. I did not plan to go to Savannah next week, but when Diego called, I felt led to go."

"Ah. Got it. Proverbs 16:9."

Dad clapped. "Go on."

"It says, 'A man's heart plans his way, but the

Lord directs his steps.' God changed your plans next week. He might change your plans for Lakeside Chapel as well. Is that what you're saying?"

Dad nodded. "Even though I don't plan on staying at Lakeside Chapel, that church is so close to Orlando that it has many visitors. It's growing."

"What does that have to do with Malachi?"

"If he wants to take up a permanent position, I can recommend him to be an assistant pastor at Lakeside Chapel."

"Lakeside doesn't even have a senior pastor since Pastor Gottlieb passed away last year."

"Right. They've been rotating through a list of invited guest pastors because the deacons are not sure who God wants them to hire," Dad explained. "However, they are sure they want me to preach for one year while they pray about it. That way the church is stabilized and the members won't wonder whether to find another church."

"You're taking the opportunity to train up a Timothy or Titus."

"Exactly. Why not kill two birds with one stone?"

"And Malachi is your Timothy."

"For one year he could be my assistant pastor. When I'm preaching in Atlanta or Savannah or St. Simon's, he could fill in."

"Sunrise Chapel needs a pastor too."

"That has an interesting development that I'll tell you about later."

Tally wanted to know now. "Hint please."

"You know that Byron Moss is out of seminary. Midtown ordained him a few months ago."

Byron.

Gus's cousin.

Tally could guess where Dad was going with it, but she didn't want to say.

"That island boy in him has been homesick for the coast," Dad said.

Tally recalled that earlier in the warehouse, Joey had reminded Gus that Atlanta was landlocked. Gus had said something about a change of scenery.

"Byron has been here for some years now," Tally said. "However, he takes his family to the Bahamas every Christmas."

"He vacations in Florida the rest of the time. Why doesn't he go up to the mountains?" Dad asked.

"You tell me. You're the counselor."

"He misses the ocean."

"So you're going to talk to him about applying for the senior pastor position at Sunrise Chapel on Sunset Island." Tally leaned toward her phone. "How many times have you prayed about this?"

"Every time I see Byron at church and every time I pray for Sunrise Chapel."

Tally drew a deep breath. "It seems like God has prepared these men for such a time as this. Missionary Malachi, with his vast experience in many countries, would do well at Lakeside Chapel, which gets many international visitors coming to the Orlando and Winter Park area."

"And Byron Moss is now ordained and ready to take over the helm of a church of his own. Maybe it's Sunrise Chapel."

"Which isn't just any church, but a church on an island in Florida that has weather closer to the Bahamas than Georgia does."

"It seems that God has ushered these young pastors that way." Dad looked pensive, as if his years had waned and that it was time to hand the torch over to the next generation of pastors.

"Dad!" Tally suddenly said.

Dad wasn't startled. He was used to three daughters and their decibels at home. "What?"

"You're only seventy years old and Mom's only sixty-seven. Stop sounding like you're ninety. Even at ninety, you'd still be younger than Hiram Jacobs, who passed away at a hundred and four, preaching his last sermon from his deathbed."

Dad nodded. "Maybe Malachi will be blessed with longevity genes like his great-grandfather had."

"Speaking of Malachi, will he stay at his sister's house Sunday night then, once he's surprised her?" Tally asked.

"You'll have to ask him." Dad moved on. "Colette's with your grandma at least until Christmas, if she doesn't decide to stay at Lakeside permanently."

"Dad, this is so unlike you."

"What is?"

"Your house guests are two single men, and you want me to also stay there, albeit on different floors. That doesn't sound like something you'd put up with."

"I've known the guys for years. I trust them. Besides, didn't you stay here last night? Gus was next door to you."

"It was late at night, and Mom insisted. Besides, I barely had four hours of sleep, with Karissa's crisis so early in the morning." Tally shrugged. "How long do you want me to stay there?"

"Until the murderer is arrested."

"That could take years."

"I don't want you to stay here for years, although your mom would love it if all three of her daughters lived at home forever with her." Dad laughed. "We'll pray that they will find the murderer soon."

"It might not have anything to do with Silas."

Dad didn't react. He simply said, "The police are interviewing everyone."

Tally wondered if Dad knew more than he was saying. After all, the counseling sessions would reveal Silas's motives. If he was a bad guy, then her staying at Dad's house would put both her parents in danger too.

Regardless, it couldn't happen today. "I'll go over tomorrow after church. I have a dinner meeting tonight at my house. I was going to cook for everyone."

"Have the meeting here," Dad said. "What were you planning on cooking at your house tonight for your dinner meeting?"

"The only thing I can cook without burning."

"Spaghetti. How about you do it here and just cook extra for your mom and me? She'll even make a salad if you ask her."

"Well..." Tally didn't want to impose on her parents.

"Let me cook," Mom offered. "I'm never tired

of spaghetti, but I want to eat something else tonight. I know you're very busy today. Dinner's on us."

"Mom..."

"We insist." Dad's voice sounded grave. He looked concerned on the video screen. "We're twenty minutes from your house."

"Which begs the question of whether it's safe at either location, right?"

"I know, honey. If we're together, then your mom won't worry too much about you."

"I'm thirty-five, Dad. Not a teenager anymore."

"You're still my daughter."

"And I'll always be your daughter."

"You got that right. Pack up and come over." Dad had spoken.

Tally could still say no. However, the death on Friday shook her up a little, and she would be lying to say she wasn't afraid. She knew she should not fear. And yet Psalm 23:4 came to her mind.

> *Yea, though I walk through the valley of the shadow of death,*
> *I will fear no evil;*
> *For You are with me;*
> *Your rod and Your staff, they comfort me.*

Then again, she had a feeling she might not sleep at all tonight. She might leave all her lights on.

Silas knew where she lived.

It felt creepy.

"Okay, Dad. You win," Tally said. "I'll text everyone to tell them about the change of venue."

"It's not a matter of winning an argument, honey. You knew that."

Tally nodded. "I know. It's about safety first."

"Right. Do you want your mom to make some salad and bake a pie?" Dad asked.

"What kind of pie?"

"Apple. Your favorite. I bet she has all the ingredients."

"Are you a betting man now, Pastor Fizz?" Tally laughed.

"No, but I always win with apple pies."

"Because it's your favorite too."

"Sure is. If you come over soon enough, I'll make you a sandwich for lunch."

"Dad." Tally shook her head.

"What? Ham and melted mozzarella. Another favorite of yours." Dad lifted his eyebrows and grinned.

"Why did I ever leave home?" Tally asked.

"Exactly. Free rent, free food. What's not to love about your childhood home?"

After Dad hung up, Tally felt a hundred times better as she called Maggie to move the venue for tonight's dinner meeting. She also texted Gus herself since he was still at the Village.

Then Tally packed for one week away from her house. She knew that she had to take time off on Thursday to drive Mom and Dad to Savannah. Over the weekend at Jacobs Landing, she'd do laundry at their coin laundromat, and she'd have enough clothes for another week. Same clothes, but they'd be clean.

Tally made it to her parents' home around noon, in time for the comfort food she needed today. She planned to go back to the office at church after she'd eaten—

Wait. It's Saturday.

The church office was closed. She had been so busy working every day that the days had all collided with one another.

Bothering her was the thought that Silas also knew where Dad lived. Would they be safe anywhere?

After a quick lunch, Mom and Dad went to the grocery store because Mom decided she would do the cooking tonight instead of Tally. They didn't want Tally to go with them. Instead, they insisted she take a nap.

They knew she hadn't had enough sleep since they'd begun the Village mission.

While her parents were out shopping, Tally carried her suitcase upstairs and rolled it into Colette's room. She would sleep here at least for the weekend.

She took out her Bible and fell asleep before she could read a verse.

She woke up to the smell of cooking wafting up the stairs from the kitchen. It was five thirty! She took a quick shower and went downstairs to help Mom.

Something was off. She did not smell spaghetti sauce.

When she reached the kitchen, Gus was making salad per Mom's instructions. His hair was still damp—probably from a shower—and he had changed into a T-shirt and shorts. His legs were muscular and so were his arms.

"Hello," Gus said to Tally.

"Had a good nap?" Mom asked.

Standing at the sink, doing dishes already, was Tally's ministry assistant Maggie Jacobs. She lifted her gloved hand, greeting Tally.

"You're here early," Tally said to Maggie.

"I came straight from the Village," Maggie said. "It's closer to just drive here than to go home, wait fifteen minutes, and drive out again."

Tally nodded. She didn't want to talk about money, but it cost more to rent apartments or buy homes nearer to Midtown Chapel. Otherwise, Maggie wouldn't have to drive an hour every weekday through rush-hour traffic to get to work at the church.

"Sorry I overslept." Tally stepped toward Mom, eyeing the dutch oven on the stove. "What are you making?"

"Roast, dear. It should be ready soon." Mom lifted the lid of the dutch oven and showed her the beef surrounded by potatoes, carrots, and onions.

"What happened to my spaghetti?"

"You can cook that another time. Beef was on sale at Whole Foods, so I had to get it." Mom handed Gus a cucumber. "Peel that and cube it for the salad."

"I love cucumbers," Gus said.

"How can I help?" Tally asked.

"Please set the table." Mom checked her two apple pies in the oven.

"Maggie and Levi should be here soon."

"Soline?"

"She's no longer doing anything that Levi is involved in."

"I'm sorry to hear that. Okay, so we have Maggie, Levi, Gus, you. Adding your dad and me, we'll have six. Plus an extra plate, just in case." Mom winked at Tally. "Enough room at the dining table."

Plus an extra plate for Malachi.

Tally almost forgot he was showing up tonight. She glanced at Maggie, still at the kitchen sink, seemingly unaware that Mom had been referring to her brother.

Tally walked past Gus in the kitchen on her way to the dining hall. He was washing and peeling the cucumber. The salad he was making looked colorful.

"Do you want the salad on the table or in the fridge until everyone comes?" Gus asked Mom.

"In the fridge please. I think we won't eat for another half hour."

Tally felt bad that she had woken up just in time for dinner, not in time to help in the kitchen.

Just then, the doorbell rang.

"Get the door, Tally," Mom said.

Tally put down the dinner plates on the dining table. She hesitated for a minute because she wondered who was at the door. Heaven forbid it was Silas.

"I'll get it." Dad's booming voice echoed in the dining room.

Before Tally could tell him to be careful of strangers at the door, she heard the door chime.

"Malachi!" Dad said. "You're here!"

Tally's thirty-five-year-old knees went weak. Nearby, Maggie screamed her way to the front door to greet her older brother.

CHAPTER SEVEN

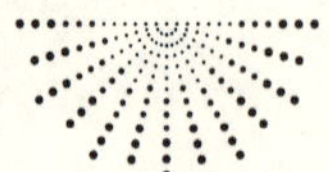

Gus could clearly see the change in Tally, sitting next to Malachi Jacobs at the dining table. She hardly talked to anyone else—not to Maggie, Levi, Gus, or even to her own parents. Every now and then Maggie got a word in with her brother, but otherwise Malachi seemed lost in Tally's words—uh, world.

Tally confirmed yet again what Gus had learned about her. She seemed to talk more—and chatter—whenever she was nervous.

Amused, Gus took his mind off Tally by chatting with Pastor Fitzpatrick and Riona. "Delicious, ma'am. You did a great job."

"I had a good helper." Riona smiled. "Want more?"

"No thanks. I'm about full."

"You know you'll eat roast beef sandwiches after church tomorrow if we don't finish this tonight." Pastor Fitzpatrick gave him a look.

"Are you saying if we finish the roast tonight, we get to eat out after church?" Riona looked terribly excited.

Her husband nodded.

"Seconds for everyone," Riona joked.

Gus glanced at Tally, still talking with Malachi. The chandelier above the dining table cast a warm glow on her face. Her brown eyes looked darker and so did her brown hair.

Gus wondered if brown was her original hair color. Riona's hair was dyed black. Gus hadn't seen Colette or Adalia on this trip thus far and wouldn't know what their hair color was.

What am I doing thinking about Tally's hair?

He cleared his throat.

Tally looked his way.

Gus smiled. "Anyone want more water? I can refill your glasses."

No one wanted more water.

Gus got up anyway and started to take the plates to the kitchen. In the kitchen, he loaded the dishwasher. The open floor plan of the house meant that he could hear the dinner table conversations from where he was standing, and they could all see the dishwasher being loaded.

"Now that's the kind of son-in-law I'd want," Riona said aloud to her husband. "If only Colette were in town. That girl hightailed it out of here when I mentioned Gus to her."

Gus's face reddened. "I'm not in the market at the moment."

Not so soon after his breakup.

"It's been nearly a year since you broke up with Veronique," Riona reminded him.

Has it been?

"I had no idea you kept up with my personal life," Gus said, more to himself, but apparently it was loud enough for everyone to hear.

"You forget that your aunt and I are friends." Riona put silverware in the sink.

Gus turned the faucet on. "Well, still..."

"I'm sorry. Nancy and Byron are like family to us, and we extended that to you."

Gus was touched. "Thank you, Riona. Does that mean I'll always have a place to stay in town?"

"Of course. Even if your cousin has room, you can always still stay here. We don't have little kids running around."

"Peace and quiet?" Gus rinsed off the plates before putting them in the dishwasher.

"What peace and quiet?" someone asked. Gus glanced over his shoulder. It was Tally. With the water running, he hadn't heard her coming into the kitchen, carrying two plates.

"Here, in our house," Riona said to her daughter.

"Wait until you have grandkids." Tally placed the plates on the counter next to the sink. "Mom made you work?"

"I volunteered."

"I'll help."

"No, no. Go have conversation with...uh..." Gus couldn't finish his words.

"With Malachi?" She said it with ease.

Gus nodded.

"He's talking to Dad about his mission work."

"What about your meeting?"

"We're digesting. We're having our meeting with dessert." Tally tied an apron around her waist. "Let me help. Then you can come to the meeting too."

"I don't need to be at the meeting," Gus said. "Just tell me what to do later."

"Are you always this stubborn? Move over a bit." Tally bumped Gus to the side with her hip. "I'm helping and it's final."

Gus was taken aback by her assertiveness. "Are you always this pushy?"

"She can be." Riona laughed. "That's how you get things done in the women's ministry. If you're not decisive, if you don't set the schedule, you're going to have a bunch of women chatting endlessly for hours and getting nothing done."

"Mom." Tally threw her a glance. "I'm just helping with the dishes. Could you check the dining room to make sure the table is cleared?"

Mom left without a word.

"I don't want to tell her what to do, but we have to get the dishwasher loaded in ten minutes," Tally said.

"We do?" Gus tried to speed up. "Doing dishes is therapeutic, and I was going to take my time."

"You can still do dishes every day while you're here if you ask Mom. She'll let you do your daily therapy undisturbed."

Gus wasn't sure how to respond. He sensed that Tally was anxious about something. Should he ask her?

"What?" Tally stared at him.

"What *what*?" Gus rinsed off a serving bowl. It had a pretty blue-and-white design on it. It looked like a form of Blue Willow, but not quite.

"You looked like you almost wanted to ask me a question," Tally said.

"You could tell?"

Tally nodded. "What's the question?"

"Nothing, really. I was just wondering if you're tense about something."

"Tense?" Tally shrugged. "I'm not worried about anything at the moment."

"Malachi?"

"Ah." Tally smiled a little. "I saw you greet him when he came in the door before dinner. I was surprised that everyone knew him."

"Our church in Nassau supports him after Riverside introduced him to us. Ten years ago—or so—he came over to tell us about his mission field."

"You met him then?"

"Yeah. I showed him around Nassau, and he stayed at my house. We've been friends ever since—albeit long distance."

Tally scraped off food from one of the serving bowls into a container. "What's he like?"

"Overall nice guy. A gentleman. Doesn't smoke or drink. No tattoos. And he can sing and play the guitar at the same time." There, he said it. Malachi was definitely the perfect boyfriend—if there was such a thing as perfect.

Gus used to think that Veronique was the perfect girlfriend.

"No tattoos?" Tally laughed. "Why did you say that?"

"You asked me what he's like, and I supposed you were asking if he's boyfriend material that your dad might approve."

"Wow. How did Dad get into the picture?" Tally put away the leftovers in the fridge. Then she put more silverware into the dishwasher.

There were only a few plates left for Gus to wash. "We're about done. Go to your meeting. I'll join you after I wash these."

"Thank you." Tally took off her apron. "We'll be on the back porch."

"Okay. See you then."

Before Tally left, she gently and briefly squeezed Gus's shoulder. "You're a good judge of character. I'll ask you more questions later."

Gus didn't say a word as he watched Tally go.

That was the fourth time they had touched each other today. Before the crack of dawn, she had cried in his arms. Then she cried again on his shoulder at the Village. Minutes ago, she bumped him by the kitchen sink to tell him to move over so she could help do the dishes. And now she just squeezed his shoulder.

Why was he keeping track? Did he think the next step for them was to hold hands?

Why wasn't Tally nervous around him? Well, to begin with, they had been friends for a while.

That was probably it.

After he started the dishwasher, Gus stood by the kitchen island to slowly drink a glass of water. He spotted Mr. and Mrs. Fitzpatrick chatting in the living room by themselves. They must not be attending Tally's meeting.

Gus went to them to ask if they'd like some pie.

"Not at the moment," Pastor Fizz said. "Maybe in five minutes."

Riona laughed. "I'll get it for him. You get it for yourself. The ice cream is in the freezer."

The sliding glass door to the porch opened, and Maggie entered alone. She smiled at Gus and then Tally's parents.

"I hear that your apple pie is the best, Riona." Maggie walked slowly past the trio.

"Thank you. Eat as much as you want." Riona turned to Gus. "Please can you show her where the dessert plates and forks are?"

"No problem." Gus felt at home.

He guessed that Maggie must not have come here often. They would have seen one another more at church than in any of the pastors' homes.

Gus ended up carrying dessert plates, forks, and napkins, while Maggie carried the pie and knife out to the porch.

It was a warm May night in good old Georgia. The ceiling fan spun above them.

Malachi was sitting in a rattan armchair. Levi was near him on a freestanding hammock. There was a binder on another armchair, which Gus guessed belonged to Maggie.

"If anyone wants ice cream on top of your pie, you'll have to go get it yourself from the freezer." Maggie put the pie and knife on the coffee table between Malachi's armchair and Tally's love seat. "The tub will melt out here."

Tally was sitting on a rattan love seat. She patted the cushion next to her. "Seat is yours. Nobody else wants to sit next to me."

"Why not?" Gus put down the plates and forks.

He sat down next to Tally, wondering why nobody sat next to her. "Maybe because the seat is uncomfortable."

"Maybe so," Tally said.

"I meant physically uncomfortable." Gus pointed to the thin cushion beneath him. "But I'm never uncomfortable with *you*."

"I agree," Maggie said. "I saw both of you at the Village yesterday and today. You looked like good friends. Seems to me that you two have known each other for a while."

"Four years," Tally said. "But we haven't seen each other in person since then. Last year Gus was in town, but I was away at a conference."

"Interesting." Malachi put down his empty plate. "Did you come all the way here to see Tally?"

"No," Gus said. "I'm supposed to be visiting my cousin Byron, but his whole family came down with the flu. I ended up staying at Pastor Fizz's house, and here I am, volunteering at the Village and attending this top-level meeting."

"Speaking of the Village, let's get back on topic," Tally said. "Do you know everyone here, Gus?"

"Yes." He had pretty much met everyone prior to tonight. He was surprised that Malachi sat in on the meeting, considering he wasn't involved at the Village.

Excluding Malachi and himself, the leadership core of the Midtown Chapel Village comprised of Tally, her assistant Maggie, and the warehouse manager and Village supervisor, Levi.

Gus was surprised that Tally was not only the women's ministry director but also the Midtown Chapel Village director. How many positions could this lady hold?

No wonder she was still single.

Was that by choice? Or perhaps she hadn't found anyone special yet.

Throughout the meeting, Gus didn't say much. He was there to observe and eat his slice of apple pie. Malachi was the only one who wanted ice cream on top of his apple pie. Everyone else did without.

Malachi left for the kitchen in his *quest à la mode.*

Without Malachi sitting there, looking at her, Tally seemed to relax a bit. She had a checklist of things to discuss with her small committee.

Gus felt tired for her. There were so many things that she had to get done.

"You're speaking to the women's conference in Valdosta the same weekend that Malachi will be there," Maggie reminded Tally.

Gus noticed the sudden brightness in Tally's eyes.

Was there something going on between Tally and Malachi? Gus wondered.

"Which week is that?" Tally checked her phone.

"First week of June."

"Whew. Okay. I haven't updated my calendar,

but I'm driving Dad to Savannah the week after next." Tally told Maggie the date.

"When you get back, you'll have to turn around and drive to Valdosta," Maggie said. "Maybe you can carpool with Malachi."

Tally went silent for a bit.

Gus waited.

Malachi returned from the refrigerator, a pile of ice cream on top of his apple pie. "Who's carpooling with me?"

He sat down as Maggie pointed to Tally. "She has a conference in Valdosta on the same Saturday you're meeting with donors for the school project."

"We'll take my car," Malachi said. "I can drive you there in under four hours."

"N-no," Tally finally said. "I think I'll drive on my own. I'm coming home Saturday afternoon. I'm guessing you'll be in Valdosta until after Sunday church."

"Yes, I'm preaching Sunday morning," Malachi said. "You don't want to hear me preach?"

"I've heard you preach many times. I just need to get home because I have a lot of work to do. If I take an extra day off every time I go to a conference, I won't have time left to do anything else but speak at events."

"I hear you." Malachi continued eating, devouring his dessert like a little boy.

Gus noticed that Tally hadn't eaten her slice of pie.

"Would you like me to heat up your piece of pie?" Gus asked Tally.

She seemed surprised by the gesture.

"Well..."

"Yes or no?" Gus asked quietly. "No trouble at all."

"Yes please." Tally almost smiled. "Fifteen seconds."

Gus went indoors and saw that the Fitzpatricks were no longer sitting in the living room. All was quiet in the house, except for the low noise coming from the dishwasher. Every now and then he heard water pipes behind the dishwasher.

Gus warmed up Tally's apple pie the way she asked for it: fifteen seconds in the microwave.

He didn't think the pie was warm at all.

He texted Tally.

Your pie is still cold.

Now he felt bad that he was interrupting her.

She didn't reply to her text. He heard the sliding door open and close. Tally came to the kitchen. She added another fifteen seconds on the microwave.

"Sorry I took you out of the meeting," Gus said.

"No worries. I don't eat cold pie, so it'd just sit there until I warm it up. How did you know that I would've wanted it microwaved?"

"I didn't. It was a guess."

"Thank you." Tally gently tapped his upper arm with a fist.

What was that for?

Gus had no idea.

He followed Tally out to the back porch and spent the next hour listening to her conduct the meeting. They talked about securing the warehouse, funding the Village, adding counselors, and finding jobs for the single mothers living at the Village.

"This one's for you, Gus—housing homeless teens," Tally said.

Gus nodded.

"We don't have funds right now, and we have to find families to foster the homeless kids, but we could look into independent living for teens. Some local fast-food chains will hire teenagers as young as fourteen years old, so that can be a way for them to earn some income to support themselves."

Gus didn't want Tally to deal with homeless teens on top of her already full schedule, but he wasn't officially in the committee.

"Chaplain Ben over at Seaside Chapel on St. Simon's Island works with teenagers, so maybe I'll call him and ask what he's doing," Tally said. "If we can do a joint project somehow, it could save time, labor, and money."

"Thank you." Gus was impressed that Tally had connections and practical ideas.

"Our problem right now is all three," Tally said. "We're stretched thin at the Village, we don't have enough volunteers, and we need funding."

Gus didn't want to say anything right now without getting more information, and he had to pray about starting up something he couldn't finish. After all, he was going home to the Bahamas in June.

"Looks like something to pray about," Gus said.

"Certainly. None of our projects could ever happen without God's blessings."

"We need God's blessings in life as well."

"In all aspects of life," Malachi chimed in. "Including love."

Gus didn't know what he was getting at.

"We go where God calls us. We do what He leads us. Such is the life of a person in ministry," Malachi said.

"I know that my calling is to minister to women," Tally said. "It's not easy, because these women at the Village have way more experience than I do in life. They've seen it all—broken homes, marriages, motherhood, homelessness, poverty. Compared to them, I live a sheltered life. However, God calls me to this task of ministering to them. Sometimes I feel that I don't have what it takes."

"But you do," Gus said before Malachi could say a word. "You have Christ in you, you have the Holy Spirit of God in you, you have the Word of God. As a Christian, you have everything those women need. Salvation in Christ the Son. Sanctification of the Holy Spirit. Sweet relationship with God the Father."

"For a moment there, I thought you'd find a word that starts with 's' to complete your alliteration." Levi sounded serious.

"Sweet starts with 's' though," Malachi said.

"Sweet is an adjective in 'sweet relationship.'"

"He could say 'serenity of God' and it would start with 's,' although that would change the meaning of it." Malachi looked at Gus.

"Yes, it would change the meaning," Gus said quietly.

"Are we missing the point?" Tally looked at Levi and Malachi.

"I was replying to Tally's statement that sometimes she feels inferior and inadequate," Gus said.

"Colossians 2:10 says that we are complete in Christ. John 15:5 says that we achieve nothing apart from Christ. Colossians 1:27 says Christ in us is the 'hope of glory.' In other words, yes, on our own, we are inferior and inadequate. However, in Christ, we are 'more than conquerors,' as it says in Romans 8:37."

Maggie clapped. "Wow. You should be a preacher."

"But that's not my calling." Gus shut it down.

Then he worried that he had offended them, especially Tally. He did not want to offend Tally. In fact, he wanted her to think well of him.

Why? He wasn't sure exactly.

CHAPTER EIGHT

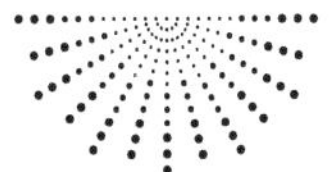

"Would you like some coffee?" Tally asked Gus as they sat down in the front row in her Sunday school classroom.

She felt antsy because Malachi Jacobs was giving a mission report this morning—out of the blue—and she wondered how long she could stand staring at him from the front row. She needed a distraction.

"I can get it myself." Gus got up.

"No, no. Let me do it. You want cream and sugar?" Tally was on her feet. She put the bulletin on her seat, as if to save the seat.

"Just cream," Gus said. "Thank you."

When she got back to her seat, Malachi was sitting on the other side of it.

"Is that coffee for me?" Malachi teased.

"Black?" Tally handed him her own cup of coffee.

"Any coffee. Thanks."

She decided not to go back for another cup. The class was about to start. She handed the other cup to Gus.

Gus thanked her and then went to the back of the class to get her a cup of black coffee. It surprised Tally that he had paid attention. She had given Malachi her black coffee, which meant she drank it black.

Gus sat down again just as Joseph went up to the podium. The class director handled all announcements, and then someone else taught Sunday school. Tally knew that Byron was sick at home, so she wondered who was teaching this morning.

"I'm filling in for Byron, who's at home with the flu," Joseph said. "After the announcements, we're going to hear from a missionary whom our church supports. He has traveled the world over, so let's see where he is these days. Some of you already know him from years past or might have met him today."

Sitting next to Malachi in Sunday school sent shivers up her spine, but Tally knew that a lot could change after all this time. In her twenties she had been sure that Malachi was her ideal husband. Six years later she wanted to explore her feelings today to see if it was still the case.

Needless to say, she could hardly concentrate when Malachi took the podium. She busied herself writing in her church notebook on her lap, trying to stay calm even as her heart beat wildly.

Calm down. You're thirty-five.

"Some of you know that I've been traveling in North America this year," Malachi said. "I just got back from Minnesota after spending three weeks there. I'm meeting up with my team in Kentucky on Monday, and we're going to visit some of our supporting churches."

His team? Tally scrawled something. Might that include where Bethany Baker attended church?

"We'll be gone for a few weeks, and then I'll be back again in Georgia," Malachi continued.

"Your team?" Joseph asked. "We'd like to meet them and hear from them too."

"You will." Malachi glanced at Tally just as she looked up. There was a hint of apology on his face. Then it was gone.

Tally didn't want to think too much about it, but they had almost dated six years ago. Almost. He had taken the initiative to hint that he was interested in her.

And then Bethany Baker had shown up at Midtown Chapel. Malachi dated her instead, albeit briefly. Bethany was transient, coming and going as she pleased. When she was in town, Mom took Bethany under her wings for reasons unknown to Tally. It wasn't as though Mom needed a fourth daughter.

After Malachi got over Bethany, he stayed in town for two more years, but nothing happened between him and Tally, for reasons that he hadn't explained to this day. Not a single time did he show Tally any interest after Bethany.

After Malachi left the country to oversee the construction of a school in North Africa, Tally had regretted their nonstarter relationship, but it was too late.

This Sunday morning, Tally felt uneasy with Malachi sitting next to her. If he had gone through with the rumored engagement with Bethany, no one had told Tally. Sometimes she wished that men wore engagement rings as well. At least in Asia somewhere, couples wore couple rings. Not here in the Western Hemisphere.

After Sunday school, Tally tried to avoid walking near Malachi. Since she couldn't hide in the busy ladies' rooms, she went to her office downstairs in the basement to take a quick break. Staff workers were here and there, doing their own things, and Tally said hello to all of them.

How could Malachi still affect her after all these years? It seemed that she hadn't let him go.

If Malachi decided to go with Dad to Lakeside Chapel, then what was she going to do? Every time she'd visit her parents, he'd be there.

Perhaps it would be best to avoid Lakeside at all cost—until Malachi got married, or until she did.

Me? Marry? Banish the thought.

Tally didn't bother to freshen up in the restroom, and regretted it as soon as she walked up the stairs to the Midtown Chapel sanctuary. What if her makeup had run? What if she had smudges around her eyes? What if...

She made a dash for the restroom as the sanctuary orchestra began their opening piece. She checked the mirror. Her face looked fine. Her hair was messy, though. She patted it down with her fingers.

Her phone in her purse buzzed. She checked the text message. It was from Gus.

Gus: Sitting next to your parents. Saved you a seat.

Tally: Thank you. On my way.

Tally knew where her parents usually sat. She did not always sit with them, but this morning she was running late, and if Gus had saved her a seat, she'd take it.

When she entered the sanctuary, she made a beeline to the section where her parents usually sat. To her surprise, Malachi and Maggie were sitting next to Mom at the edge of the pew. That meant Tally had to walk past them in the narrow space between them and the seats in front of them, and past Dad and Gus, before she could get to her saved seat right in the middle of the pew.

You'd think they'd save me a seat at the end of the pew, but no.

"Let's all stand to sing," the music pastor said through the microphone.

Perfect timing. Everyone stood up, and Tally made her way down the pew to her seat on the other side of Gus.

When she put her Bible down, she saw that she was one seat away from Seth Moreno, known on television as Chef Stephanos. Tally made a mental note to keep in touch with him in case she needed a celebrity chef for future fundraising dinners to benefit the Village. Or if she wanted a judge for a bake-off or cook-off. Media personalities like him might be interested in charity work.

Tally didn't feel like singing today, but she sang anyway. Dad had told her that when she walked by faith, she had to watch out for her feelings. Whether she felt like it or not, she had to do what would be required of her faith—if she wanted to walk with God. Dad often cited Hebrews 11:6 when it came to faith versus feelings.

> *But without faith it is impossible to please Him, for he who comes to God must believe that He is, and that He is a rewarder of those who diligently seek Him.*

Right now her feelings were confused, so walking by her feelings would be foolish indeed.

Should she continue her dreamy pursuit of Malachi or let him go? If nothing happened six years ago, would anything happen between them now?

Truth be told, it wouldn't work out with Malachi because he traveled across the world to help local churches and mission projects. It was as though he was on a permanent short-term mission status. He'd go to one place, stay for three to twelve months, then move on.

Such a life would make him perpetually single,

unless he found another Christian missionary who loved to live out of a suitcase.

Me, I prefer stability.

However, Dad had hinted on Saturday that Malachi might be considering winding down his world travel and staying put in one spot. Tally remembered what Dad said.

If you ask me, I think he's preparing to look for a pastoral position.

Could that be another reason he was traveling in the United States this summer instead of overseas?

Tally had never told Mom and Dad about her feelings for Malachi. Knowing them, they might have guessed, but since nothing happened between her and Malachi, there was nothing to talk about or speculate.

Pastor Kim preached another part of his sermon series on sacrifices, but it was more than Tally could handle today.

Lord, I have sacrificed so much for Your work these past ten years.

Tally tried to focus on the sermon but felt that she was pulling away from God. After all these things she had done at church, she was still a lonely single woman at the end of the day.

"Let's read in Luke 18:10. 'Two men went up

to the temple to pray, one a Pharisee and the other a tax collector.' Do you remember the story?" Pastor Kim asked from the lectern.

Tally remembered the story. Her dad had preached it before—a countless number of times.

"The high-and-mighty Pharisee prayed, 'God, I thank You that I am not like other men—extortioners, unjust, adulterers, or even as this tax collector. I fast twice a week; I give tithes of all that I possess.' Luke 18:11–12." Pastor Kim paused. "Does that describe you?"

Tally wondered in her heart whether it did. Then again, as a pastor's daughter, her life was commendable. She had kept her reputation clean in her entire thirty-five years of life. She had never gotten into trouble, never cussed, smoked, drank, gotten a tattoo, whatever. Nope. She hadn't been one of those pastor's kids who rebelled against their parents—

"Luke 18:13 tells us about the other worshipper that day. 'And the tax collector, standing afar off, would not so much as raise his eyes to heaven, but beat his breast.' Read with me what he said. 'God, be merciful to me a sinner!' Do you get it now?" Pastor Kim's voice spoke volumes into Tally's ears.

She lowered her head.

Guilty as charged.

"What did the Lord say about the tax collector?" Pastor Kim asked the congregation. "We find that in the next verse. 'I tell you, this man went down to his house justified rather than the other; for everyone who exalts himself will be humbled, and he who humbles himself will be exalted.' Luke 18:14."

Tally felt that all her sacrifices for God burned like a heap of ashes. Had she been behaving more like the proud Pharisee than the humble tax collector? Both were sinners, but one received God's mercy.

Growing up in Pastor Fitzpatrick's house meant that her life had been sanitized since birth. Mom and Dad would never allow the sordid world to taint any of their three Christian daughters. Sheltered they were not, but protected from the world, yes.

And now the girls were grown up, but their social circles were very small. The number of eligible men worthy of marrying a Fitzpatrick lady was laughably small as well.

Perhaps God had not wanted her to marry. If He had, why hadn't He brought a nice Christian gentleman–single and unattached–to her doorstep? After all, she had lived a clean Christian life. Surely there was a reward for that?

"What do you have that you have not received from God?" Pastor Kim stood next to his lectern. "This week I challenge you to be aware of your own self. Examine your heart. Don't be conceited. Humble yourself before the living God. Do away with pride. Stop looking down on others. You're no better than they are—save for the grace of your Lord and Savior, Jesus Christ."

Tally's eyes watered as Pastor Kim prayed.

Lord, be merciful to me, a sinner. Help me to be humble.

After the closing hymn, Tally made a mental note to check herself this week. It would be hard to do so, especially since she was going a mile a minute. She had meetings the whole week long, plus that fundraising hike up Stone Mountain on Saturday, one week before she would drive her parents to Savannah.

If she could bail out of the hike, she would, but she had promised Jacinda and several other women at the Village that she would hike with them so they could pray together on top of Stone Mountain.

That hike would be enough exercise to last her a month.

She packed up her Bible and purse, but Dad was still talking to people on the row in front of them. She looked to her left to see if she could get out that way.

She turned to Gus. "I'll wait for you all outside in the rotunda."

"I'll go with you," he said.

She led the way, swiping her phone to see if she had anything else going on today that she needed to take care of. Sunday was a workday for her since she was at church for two services—and sometimes meetings in between.

Saturday was supposed to be her day of rest, but she could not recall a single Saturday off in recent months.

The Bible was clear about working six days and taking the seventh day off. And yet Tally had worked seven days a week for months.

At some point in time, she was going to burn out.

"But not today." She shook her head.

In the hallway, Tally introduced Gus to a number of church members who stopped to chat with Tally. Some made small talk, some asked about the warehouse tragedy—which Pastor Kim didn't announce to the world this morning—and some offered to volunteer at the Village.

Most of the time, Gus didn't say much. Tally

couldn't read his face, and she decided to assume nothing.

"Friendly church," Gus finally said.

Tally nodded. "Been this way as long as I've been here."

Which was to say, since she was born.

Mom and Dad waved from the meet-and-greet rotunda, where the dome above them echoed voices everywhere. Tally wondered who had designed it.

Before Tally could reach her parents, Pastor Kim walked by, shaking Dad's hand. He was accompanied by his wife of forty years, Lydia, and their daughter, Iseul, who was chatting with some friends.

Iseul attended Midtown Chapel with her parents, but her Navy SEAL older brother rarely showed up at church. Oliver Kim was deployed somewhere in the world, and the family didn't talk about him except to pray for his safety. Only God knew the details.

Tally waved to Iseul as she reached the rotunda.

"Hey, Tally." Iseul hugged her.

Iseul had helped a couple of times at the Village, back in the early days after the land had been donated. Iseul and the entire singles ministry had come out to help clear the bushes and land behind the community center.

"You remember Gus?" When Iseul shook her head, Tally introduced the two of them.

Then Dad grabbed Gus to talk with Pastor Kim, leaving Iseul and Tally alone.

"You going to the hike this Saturday?" Tally asked.

Iseul nodded. Pointed to her friend standing next to her. "I'm trying to persuade Leland to go too."

"I'll go if my cousin Cayson goes." Leland Yang-Joule wore no makeup behind her pair of glasses. Her hair was tied up in a bun on top of her head. She looked like she had just walked out of her office to have a cup of coffee before she went back to work again. "We're meeting a late deadline, but if he thinks we can take Saturday off, you'll see us there."

"Exercise is a great way to de-stress," Tally reminded her. "Besides, it's for a good cause. We're raising funds for the pregnancy center and the Village."

"That too. I'll remind him."

Leland didn't take out her phone to add the event to her calendar. Perhaps she had already done so, but Tally wondered if she wasn't going to show up.

As far as Tally knew, Leland and Cayson ran a computer business and worked at odd hours around the clock and around the world.

"Fair enough. Don't work too hard." Tally felt like a hypocrite. She was working too hard herself.

I need a day off.

Mom, Dad, and Gus were still talking to Pastor and Mrs. Kim. Tally's stomach rumbled as she approached them. Her ears perked up when she heard Malachi's name mentioned.

"Might be good to see if he wants to help me when I go to preach at Lakeside Chapel." Dad's voice didn't show stress.

But Tally could always tell when Dad sounded stressed out. This time, something was afoot. Tally could feel it in the air. It meant that Dad had prayed over a plan that was now in motion. He had gone past the "prayer battle" part.

Dad had mentioned Malachi and Lakeside in the same sentence. It meant that was almost a sure thing.

Then again, Malachi was always the wildcard, unpredictable in his decisions.

"What I was thinking too," Pastor Kim said. "As

an associate pastor, he could still go on his mission trips. He has the credentials."

"He grew up in Lakeside, so it's homecoming for him."

"Does he want to go home to Florida though? His grandparents are living in Savannah now, right?" Mom asked.

Dad nodded. "At SSLR."

Tally wondered how often Malachi had visited the Savannah Senior Living Resort to check on his grandparents, who had raised him after his single mother passed away. He had left home to go to seminary in Atlanta.

It was a good thing that Malachi came to Atlanta, or they'd never have met. Tally smiled at the memory.

"Whatcha smiling about?" A familiar voice whispered in her ear.

Malachi.

Startled, Tally dropped her Bible.

And someone caught it before it hit the floor.

Gus.

He handed the Bible to Tally. His eyes met hers, and she was sure hers looked stunned. Her church Bible wasn't light. It was a special heavy-duty Bible with waterproof pages—you know, just in case she got caught in the rain or left it outdoors at the Village.

"Good catch." Malachi gave Gus two thumbs-up.

Gus grinned.

"Are we going out to lunch?" Iseul asked Tally's mom, who nodded.

"Well, how about we go together?" Dad asked, starting the head count. "How many do you have?"

"Leland has to go back to work, so it'll be just the three of us today." Iseul waved goodbye to Leland.

"We have five—including Malachi and Gus." Dad lifted five fingers.

Tally's heart skipped a beat. She knew it might be too late to start any relationship with Malachi, but perhaps seeing him again could help her let him go emotionally. Maybe?

"Name the place," Gus said. "I'm paying."

Dad looked surprised. "That's nice of you."

As Mom and Dad discussed with Pastor Kim and Lydia where to eat lunch, Tally took the opportunity to use the ladies' room. There was a long line outside the one by the rotunda, so Tally walked down another hallway to a lesser-known ladies' room. Sure enough, two people walked out, and there were plenty of empty stalls.

In one of the stalls, someone was crying.

"Are you okay?" Tally asked gently, wondering who it was.

The crying stopped, but Tally could hear soft sobs.

"I just want to make sure you're all right."

No response.

Tally used the facilities and then washed her hands. The stall in question was still closed.

She still heard sobs.

"Hello, I'm Tally, with the women's ministry." She directed the ministry, but this was not the time for titles. She identified the ministry she worked with so that the crying woman would know she wasn't a stranger.

"Tally? That you?" the woman replied. She unlocked the stall door.

It was Jacinda.

"I didn't know it was you," Jacinda said. Her eyes were swollen.

Tally decided not to ask Jacinda to wash her hands first. Instead, she wrapped Jacinda in her arms and let the poor woman weep into her shoulder.

"My poor baby. My poor Sheldon. He could've come to church with me this morning." Then she wailed.

Tally tried not to cry and lose her emotional bearings altogether. "Levi told me that Sheldon accepted Christ a month ago. As such, he is in heaven with Jesus now, walking on the streets of gold."

"I know, but I'm still sad."

"We weep, but not without hope." Tally reminded Jacinda about 1 Thessalonians 4:13–14.

> *But I do not want you to be ignorant, brethren, concerning those who have fallen asleep, lest you sorrow as others who have no hope. For if we believe that Jesus died and rose again, even so God will bring with Him those who sleep in Jesus.*

"My baby." Jacinda moaned.

Tally wanted to say, "...is with Jesus."

But she felt that she was conveying a head knowledge. She had never carried or given birth to a child, so how would she fully comprehend what it meant to lose a child?

She said nothing and let Jacinda cry a bit more as Tally looked around the ladies' room for a box of tissues. She spotted it, but it was too far away from her.

"Let's get you some tissues, okay?" Tally said.

Jacinda nodded. She washed her face at the

sink. She tore off several paper towels, and was in the process of patting her face dry when Tally returned with a box of tissues from a counter near the entrance to the ladies' room.

Jacinda dropped the entire box into her oversized tote.

Tally didn't say a word. This was not the time to talk about church property and community restrooms.

"How about we go for lunch and we can talk?" Tally asked. "Did you come with anyone?"

"No. I came alone. I took the bus."

"You didn't carpool?"

"No, I made a decision too late and the van had left," Jacinda said.

Tally silently prayed that Jacinda's two older children would come with her to church someday. They didn't live with her at the Village.

"Then it's just you and me," Tally said. "What would you like to eat?"

"Anything. I'm okay with Waffle House too."

"Waffle House it is. I want some buttermilk pancakes with bacon on the side. How about you?"

"I like their ham and eggs." Jacinda adjusted her blouse. "Could you wait for me for a minute? I need to put on some makeup."

Minutes later, as Tally washed her hands, she

noticed that Jacinda's face looked better. "Wow. You're really good with makeup. Have you considered going into the beauty business?"

"I've worked retail at one of the stores, but they won't let me put makeup on anyone."

"Maybe google to see what sort of business or franchise you can start?" Tally thought that perhaps a new business venture might be a good distraction from Jacinda's grief.

"You know, you're not the first person who has mentioned that to me. I can do hair too. I used to work as a stylist in Chattanooga, before I moved to Atlanta."

Tally nodded. "Let me text Mom and Dad to tell them I won't be joining them for lunch."

More than informing them, Tally also needed to borrow a vehicle from someone. She had carpooled with Mom, Dad, and Gus this morning.

As they walked toward the rotunda, Tally spotted Malachi coming toward them. She told him that she and Jacinda were going out to lunch on their own.

"Take my car." He dropped his vehicle key into Tally's palm. "I just need it back at the evening service tonight."

"Is it a rental?" Tally asked. If it was a rental, then she wasn't on the list of drivers.

"No. It's the same car I've had all this time. I parked it in Maggie's garage, and she drives it from time to time to keep the battery running. I drove it to Minnesota and back."

"Thank you. Where are you parked?" Tally asked.

"Right next to the church vans in the back, if the vans haven't moved." Malachi paused. "You know what it looks like."

Tally nodded. It was a deep maroon, if she remembered correctly.

So many memories to erase.

CHAPTER NINE

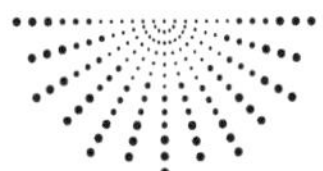

All week long Tally prayed for Jacinda as the latter grieved for her lost son. By Friday Tally wasn't sure what else to pray for her, except repeatedly asking God to comfort Jacinda and give her something useful to do that could take her mind off the grief—not that anything could erase it.

While the poor mother continued her counseling sessions at Midtown Chapel, Tally and Maggie provided her with as much support as possible. Tally spent every day at the Village, even working from the community center to be nearby.

Malachi had gone to Kentucky, and Tally needed something to take her mind off him. Ministering to Jacinda and preparing for their Stone Mountain hike seemed to do the trick.

Gus was at the Village, planting flowers, weeding the yard, and mowing the lawn. He really did a lot of work and never complained a single time. In fact, Tally couldn't go from the community center to the tiny homes without seeing Gus here and there.

"How are you doing?" Tally stopped at the water fountain where Gus was filling up his water bottle.

"Hot." Gus wiped sweat off his forehead. "I wish I had brought my brimmed hat."

"You didn't think this would turn out to be a working vacation, did you?"

"Not labor-intensive like this." Gus laughed. "How's Jacinda?"

"Grief takes time."

"I know. When I lost my parents, it took me years to get through the grieving process."

Tally nodded. She hadn't lost anyone close to her yet. When Grandpa passed away, she had been a toddler and fully unaware.

She knew that someday her grandmother and her parents would die, and she would have to grieve. Until then, she didn't want to think about death.

"I had my aunt supporting me in many ways," Gus added. "Glad Jacinda has her church family."

Rivulets of sweat washed down Gus's face.

"You look hot. Maybe you'd like to sit inside the community center for a while to cool down?" Tally suggested.

"I should have brought a change of clothes. I didn't think I was going to work past noon."

Before Tally could say anything, Levi showed up. "Good news, Tally. Someone's donating two tiny homes. They'll arrive tomorrow."

"That's great. What time?" Tally swiped her phone to add the event.

"Ten o'clock."

"One hour before our meeting. Do we need to reschedule the meeting?"

"Maybe not," Levi said. "It's a drop-off. We can start construction next week."

"Sounds good." Tally clicked Save. "Speaking of drop-off, Maggie said the sponsored T-shirts are still at the warehouse. We need those for the hike tomorrow."

"Yeah, we left there this morning and forgot to pick them up."

"I'll go get them." Tally had brought her car today. She turned to Gus. "You want to come with me? We have donated clothes. You might be able to find a T-shirt and shorts your size since we're not going home anytime soon."

Gus glanced at his watch. "How long are you going to be here?"

"Probably past dinnertime. So much to do."

"I'll take a break. The weather should start to cool off soon, right?" Gus asked.

"Yeah. Like way over there in October." Tally laughed.

"I don't want to get your car seat wet with my sweat," Gus said.

That was considerate of him.

"I have some old towels I carry around in my trunk. You can sit on them." Tally found her keys in her cross-body purse.

The twenty-minute drive with air conditioning at full blast cooled both of them down.

"Doesn't it get hotter come July and August?" Gus asked.

Tally nodded. "Because we're landlocked."

"Poor you. No ocean."

"Ocean says 'vacation' to me," Tally said. "I haven't taken a vacation in years."

"Well, when you can take a vacation, come see us in the Bahamas," Gus said.

Us? Not "come see me"?

"Thank you. Byron and Tina invited me—and

my parents, of course—but I haven't gone."

"I know. Your parents visited our church last year for their anniversary."

"Paid for by the church. They took up a special offering." Tally coasted into the parking lot behind the warehouse.

"Uh...Tally." Gus's voice was grave. "They haven't found the murderer yet, have they?"

"No. It's been a week. No news from the police." Tally parked the car. "I'm not afraid to go inside. We have new security, plus a new system. A bit late, but I'm not the finance department."

"Safety first."

"Yes, but giving is down, and I get it when they have to ration tithes and offerings."

Gus got out of the car. "Why is giving down?"

"For a number of reasons. It could be anything, including people being out of work, moving out of town, refusing to tithe. Statistically, most people tithe less than ten percent. That's in a regular year." Tally locked the car and walked with Gus toward the loading dock. "It gets worse in the summer. Even fewer people tithe over the summer. They might be on vacation."

Tally texted the security guard to tell him they were at the door. He didn't reply right away.

"Shall we wait a bit? He hasn't replied," Tally said.

Gus looked worried.

"Don't worry—"

Click.

Joey's face appeared. He pushed the door open. "Hey, you two. Get out of the heat."

"You remember Joey?" Tally asked Gus. "You met him last week—or was it Saturday?"

"Saturday, yes." Gus followed Tally into the building.

"Picking up more potting soil?" Joey asked.

"No. T-shirts for the hike tomorrow. We were supposed to get them on Wednesday, but they had missed a new sponsor on the back because they used an outdated design file. They had to redo the screen-printing," Tally explained. "But then, instead of dropping them off at the community center, they brought them here."

Joey chuckled. "Sounds like a company you'd never want to do business with again."

Tally didn't say anything. She'd ask her leadership team for their opinions on the matter soon enough.

"I'll be happy if the hike goes well tomorrow," she said. "We're praying for cloud cover."

"You're going to need it. Or bring umbrellas."

"That will be a sight to see. A hundred umbrellas hiking up Stone Mountain."

Joey laughed and waved as he went down a hallway to return to whatever he'd been doing.

Tally turned to Gus. "Let's get you some dry clothes first. Then I'll go get the T-shirts from the office, and we'll meet back at the loading dock door."

"Sounds good."

~

The good news was that Gus had clean, dry clothes on. The donated T-shirt was comfortable, albeit crumpled, and the shorts had an elastic waistband. He rolled up his wet clothes to take back with him to Tally's car.

The bad news was that after he exited the men's restroom, he got lost in some hallway he had never seen before. He texted Tally to ask her where to go, but she didn't reply.

That was not a good sign.

Gus tried to backtrack to the restroom. He kept going in the wrong direction because he couldn't find the restroom. He was so exhausted from all that yard work under the sun today that his brain was barely functioning, and he couldn't remember which way he had come from.

In fact, all the hallways looked the same once he left the main warehouse area.

Anyway, he wandered around for a while, hoping to run into Joey.

He was almost sure he was in the right hallway now, until he nearly slipped on some paint on the floor. Under the lights, the paint looked dark red. Why hadn't anyone cleaned it up?

Gus looked around for some of those orange cones to put near the paint so that nobody else slipped on it, but he didn't see any.

He kept walking, and there was more paint on the concrete floor, as if someone had dragged a mophead on the floor.

See? They didn't even mop up the spill properly.

Gus shook his head. "Hard to find good help these days."

He turned a corner and froze. The ceiling lights were brighter in this hallway, shining down on the streaks on the floor.

That's not red paint.

The trail ended at a door.

Gus's eyes widened as he wondered what to do. If he had more information about what he was seeing, he could assess the situation better and perhaps take a more decisive action.

Like call 911.

In seconds he was tapping on the phone.

He stepped back into the shadows and prayed for wisdom from God.

Obviously, he shouldn't open the door to see where the trail led to.

The best thing to do right now was to run for his life—

But where's Tally?

"Hello?" he whispered into the phone when an operator answered. "I'm at..."

Then he realized he didn't have an address. "I don't know where this place is, but it's in Decatur. Can you ping my location using my cell phone?"

"Sir... Wh...?"

Gus couldn't hear anything else. No reception. He moved to another position in the shadowed hallway. "Hello? Hel—"

A blow to his chin caught him off guard as the phone flew out of his hand. He heard it crash against the floor or wall or something hard.

Someone kicked his head and neck, sending shots of pain through his skull.

He felt another kick to his chest, and it took the air out of his lungs. He collapsed on the floor.

Something strong clasped around his ankle, followed by a tug. His legs lifted off the cement, and his body was dragged across the floor.

Someone very strong—or a machine—was doing this.

Gus tried to open his eyes, but he was seeing stars in the dark.

Then he heard a woman scream.

CHAPTER TEN

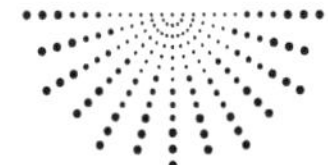

As soon as the light came on, Tally saw Joey sprawled on the floor just inside the door, a pool of red liquid under his head. His hair was matted, and his eyes were closed.

She screamed.

Her wrists were still tied behind her back, and her ankles were tied together in front of her. She leaned forward, away from the wall where she'd been sitting, next to a stack of boxes containing donated housewares and knickknacks they hadn't sorted yet. Most of the windowless storage room was empty because they had distributed many boxes to the needy out there.

"Joey? Joey, wake up! Wake up!" Tally tried to scoot toward Joey.

Just then she saw Silas Graham come in through the door, dragging something heavy on the floor behind him.

Silas had no emotion on his face. His hair was askew. His security-guard shirt looked soaked through with something. Sweat?

Silas was a big man, and Tally couldn't see what he was pulling into the room. Her eyes were still on Joey, unmoving on the floor.

Silas trudged past Joey and then stopped. He reached into his pockets and pulled out a switchblade and some rope. Then he walked around what he had been dragging.

Tally's eyes widened.

It was Gus. He had bruises on his forehead and arms. He was passed out.

"Oh no! Gus!" Tally turned to Silas. "What are you doing? Let him go!"

Silas ignored her.

Tally prayed for the right words to throw at Silas. "How are you going to explain this to my father?"

Maybe if she made it personal, using "my father" instead of "Counseling Pastor Fitzpatrick," she might be able to make a connection with any sensibility in his brain.

Silas stopped unraveling the rope. He turned to

Tally and smiled. "At this point, Miss Tally, I don't care what your father has to say."

"Please, Silas. Please." Tally lowered her voice, hoping it would help.

Silas ignored her. He tied up Gus's ankles and wrists, just like he'd done to Tally earlier when he knocked her out outside the security office.

"Gus, wake up!" Tally yelled.

Silas glared at her. He walked to another part of the big room, where he found a roll of duct tape on some stacked boxes. He waved the duct tape in the air. "Shut up or I'll tape your mouth."

"I'm allergic to duct tape, I told you. My lips will break out in a rash." *Forgive me, Lord, for lying.*

"Why I didn't do it. Hate to ruin our engagement kiss." Silas pulled Gus by his ankles to another corner of the room, away from Tally.

"Silas, please," Tally begged. "Joey needs a doctor."

"No, dear. Joey needs a mortician." He laughed as he dragged Joey's body out of the room.

"Where are you taking him?" Tally didn't know why she asked.

Silas didn't answer. He slammed the door shut. Tally heard the lock click, so she suspected that Silas had locked the door.

The door was solid and didn't have any windows for Tally to look through.

She thanked God that Silas had forgotten to turn off the light.

Tally turned her attention to Gus. "Gus!"

At first she tried to scoot over to him, but the distance was too far away. Instead, she lay down on the floor and rolled lengthwise all the way to him. She came to a stop when she slammed up against his legs.

"Gus! Gus!" Tally sat up, facing him.

Gus moaned.

Tally tried to kick his legs, but she couldn't get her tied-up feet to cooperate. She scooted on her bottom toward the wall and sat alongside it in the same direction as Gus, whose mouth was duct taped.

Tally saw a bump forming on his forehead. There were scratch marks on his right cheek, as though his face had scraped the concrete floor. Maybe in the hallway?

Gus had bruises on his upper arms and neck. Other than that, he seemed all right. No blood anywhere.

She whispered in his ear. "Gus, wake up."

His eyes slowly opened. He looked in Tally's direction.

He winced. A muffled sound came out of his mouth behind the duct tape.

"Gus, if we can lie down on the floor somehow, and you can get your face near my hands behind my back, I can peel off your duct tape from your mouth."

Gus nodded.

"It could be painful." Tally hadn't paid attention to whether Gus had shaved this morning. Even if he had, his facial hair would've started to grow again by the afternoon.

Gus shook his head, as though it was the only way.

At least, it was the only way that Tally thought of. "All right, let's do this."

They rolled onto the floor, side by side. Then Tally rolled over to her side. Gus also did so, and then scooted down to her hands.

She could feel his face. "I am not responsible for any accidental whatever that might result from this action."

Gus chuckled.

"Are you ready?" Tally asked.

Gus nodded again.

"Take one." Tally's fingers gripped one end of the duct tape. Slowly, she peeled it—

"Oww!" Gus's grunted.

"Sorry. Sorry." Tally expelled a breath. "I think we need to do this fast. It's like waxing your legs. I'm going to pull the strip off fast. It'll sting, but it'll be off, and you can speak again."

She couldn't tell if Gus nodded or not.

Tally's fingers gripped one end of the duct tape and peeled it off at one quick go.

Gus yelled out in pain.

Tally threw away the duct tape and turned back to face Gus. "You okay?"

"I won't need to shave for a while." Gus sat up. Held his head.

"Are you all right?"

"Just a bit of a headache. No worries." Gus wiped some blood from his forehead. He rubbed his shoulders. "No broken bones. Thank God."

"I'm glad you're tough like that."

Gus winced. His jaw dropped as he looked in the direction of the door. "What's that smear on the floor?"

"Joey's blood," Tally said quietly.

"Joey the security guard?"

Tally nodded.

"Is he dead?"

"Silas says he is." Tally sat up and scooted over to Gus.

They were shoulder to shoulder. That way they could keep their voices down.

"What else did Silas say?" Gus asked.

Tally shrugged. "Very little."

"Where did Silas pick you up?"

"I was looking for Joey and you. Half the lights in the hallway weren't working, and I got lost. Then I saw Silas. I was a bit surprised to see him wandering around with a flashlight, and I thought of Sheldon immediately."

"Interesting. I wonder if the two situations are connected."

"Yeah. One week ago to the day, Sheldon was murdered in this very warehouse. Today, Joey died."

"You're not scared of dead bodies." Gus looked from Joey's blood trails to Tally.

"I work at church, remember? Lots of funerals over the years. Sometimes open casket. I don't want to say I'm numb to it, but it's easier to grieve when a Christian dies."

"Joey?"

"I don't know what his spiritual condition is, but if he's a Christian, he'd be in heaven right now."

Gus agreed. "We're in shock."

"You mean it's all going to sink in soon."

Gus didn't answer her. Instead, he talked about his own encounter with Silas.

"I tried to call 911 out there in the hallway, but he found me." Gus tried to adjust his sitting position.

Tally couldn't help him. Her hands were tied.

"Speaking of which, I guess either Silas took my phone, or it's still out there in the hallway."

"He took my phone," Tally said. "Levi is expecting us to go back to the Village this afternoon. If we don't show up and Levi can't contact us, he will call 911—if Mom doesn't call first, which is probably what she'd do the moment Levi calls her. We just need to wait."

"This Silas guy..."

"You met him a week ago. The first day you arrived in town."

"Just before his counseling session with your dad. I was uncomfortable when he came up to you."

"I was too, but I'm sort of used to it. He was harmless, you know."

"Maybe he snapped. Does your dad know about it?"

"I've talked to him about Silas," Tally said. "If Dad thinks I'm in any kind of danger, you can be sure he'd call the police and talk to security at our church. Our security department has a lot of off-duty and retired police officers working in it. They'd give him advice on what to do."

"Am I supposed to be comforted by that?" Gus asked.

"I don't know." Tally swallowed what little saliva she had. She felt thirsty and wondered if Silas would feed them.

"What time is it, I wonder?" Gus asked.

"Probably still late afternoon and not quite dinnertime."

"Dinner?" Gus's voice told Tally that perhaps she should be more worried about getting out of there alive than about dinnertime.

"Dad said that when you are in a stressful situation, you need to be practical and stay in the here and now, doing simple things that need to be done at the moment, instead of worrying about a future that hasn't come yet."

"A future like our impending deaths, you mean?" Gus asked.

"Focus on the here and now."

"Shouldn't we be focusing on God?"

"Yes, of course. Focus on God while being all here."

"I don't want to be here." Gus grinned.

"With me?"

"I'm fine being with you," Gus said. "I meant that I don't want to be a hostage on my vacation."

"I know what you mean. I was only joking to make myself feel better." Her voice cracked. "Uh, how about let's pray? Dad said that the first thing we'd always want to do in a crisis is to pray. Tell God everything, even though He already knows."

Gus nodded. "How do you want to pray?"

"Do you remember choral readings in Bible class? We'd go around the room, and each person reads only one verse, right? So we can pray that way too. I'll pray about one thing, and you pray about one more thing, and then it's my turn again."

"Sounds good to me. You start."

"No, you start."

"Why?" Gus looked at her, like he really wanted to know.

Tally had no reasons. "Because you're older?"

"That's not a good reason to be the first to pray."

"We can argue until Silas comes back," Tally said.

"Argue? Have we ever argued with each other?"

"There's always a first time." Tally didn't look at him. "All right, I'll start."

Gus closed his eyes.

Tally couldn't believe he'd be that petty. If Dad were here, he'd take the lead and pray first.

Was Gus shy?

She'd never peg him as shy.

"Are you praying or not?" Gus asked, his eyes still closed.

Tally's lips quivered. No words came out. She closed her eyes.

"Father God, thank You that You're with us," Gus prayed. "When I got up this morning, I had no idea what would happen to us, but You knew it all. Yet You allowed this, so there must be a reason. I know that we can trust You to deliver us out of this situation in whatever way You deem best. I don't want to guess what that might be, nor do I want to tell You what to do with us."

As soon as he paused, Tally prayed.

"Lord, I want to go home to my mom and dad and sisters," Tally whispered. "They must be worried about me. Dad has heart problems, Lord, and You know that, so I pray that You will keep his heart stable. Don't let him stress over this. Please let Gus and me be rescued soon."

"I also pray for my family. Give Byron wisdom about speaking with his mom about this, and don't let Aunt Nancy freak out. She'd want to hop on the plane and fly to Atlanta to take me home, but she knows I'm not her little boy anymore."

Tally chuckled.

"Lord Jesus, I pray that You will deal with Silas. If he needs help, please provide for him the right kind of help. I have no idea all that is going through in his mind, but since it has come to this, I don't know whether I should feel fear."

Or maybe Tally was still in shock. Never in her life could she have imagined being imprisoned.

"Father God, we are not even close to being like Paul and Silas—the good Silas—in jail, singing at midnight, but I pray that You will guide Tally and me to handle this calmly," Gus prayed.

"And please send help ASAP. Thank You, Jesus," Tally said.

Gus waited.

Tally had nothing more to pray at this time, but she might pray more later.

"In the holy, matchless, peerless name of Jesus, we pray. Amen." Gus closed the prayer.

"Amen." Tally opened her eyes.

Now she could feel her shoulder shiver a little.

"Is the room cold for you?" Gus asked. He leaned closer to Tally so that they were shoulder to shoulder. "Warming up a bit?"

Tally shook her head.

"Do you think we should try to untie our hands and then we could untie our ankles and get out of here?" Gus asked.

"I think he locked the door."

"Let's find out." With great effort, Gus rose to his feet. His ankles were tied, just like Tally's. He bunny-hopped to the strong door. Then he turned around to let his hand grip the doorknob.

He jiggled.

The door did not open.

"Okay." Gus kept his voice down as he made his way back to where Tally was sitting. "We could ambush him when he comes back."

"Throw pots and pans at him, you mean?"

"Pots and pans?" Gus hopped back to his seat near the wall.

Tally pointed to the boxes near them. "Donations."

"I see."

"Would it be better for him to chase us out there in the hallway, or would you rather have him come back here and finish us off?" Tally wondered aloud.

Gus jiggled his wrists.

"He tied the knots well," Tally said. "Silas used to be a sailor."

"I used to be a Boy Scout," Gus said. "I know a thing or two about knots. Let's try."

Tally nodded. "If we look at each other's wrists, maybe we can study the knots and see if we can unravel them without looking, like if we were blindfolded."

"Good idea. Turn to your right so I can see how he tied them."

Tally did what Gus told her to do. He made some small remarks.

"Now let's sit back to back so that I can reach your wrists," Gus said.

It was worth a try, so Tally scooted around until they were both sitting back to back.

Before Gus could figure it out, the door opened again.

"Getting cozy, aren't we?" Silas smiled. He closed the door behind him. In his right hand was a handgun.

Tally gasped.

Silas swaggered toward them. "Sitting together, are we?"

Tally and Gus did not answer him.

Silas squatted down in front of Tally. He smelled of sweat—like he hadn't showered in days—plus cheap cologne, beer, and...gasoline?

"Miss Tally." He casually pointed the handgun

at her face. "Marry me."

What?

Tally knew that she should be afraid of the muzzle, but for some reason, she wasn't. It felt like she was in a play and that Silas wouldn't shoot her for real.

Because he wanted her to be alive. That was the only way he found satisfaction: when Tally answered him, talked with him, like they were best buddies.

Tally prayed about her response. Slowly, she met Silas's gaze. "No."

"No?" His jaw dropped. "Why?"

"Is this how you propose?" Gus said. "She's all tied up."

Silas turned the muzzle toward Gus. "Did I ask you a question?"

"No, but I can see you want a positive response from Tally."

Silas cocked his head.

Tally could see that his pupils were dilated. Was he on drugs? If so, it might explain his unusual behavior today. What happened to harmless Silas?

"If you're going to propose to Tally, you might consider a candlelight dinner," Gus continued.

"Go on."

"Maybe you can find a folding table somewhere. Bring it here with two chairs. Get some takeout dinner that you both like. I'll be your humble server."

"Server?"

Gus nodded. "I'll pour water and light the candles and all."

Tally couldn't believe what Gus was saying, but she went along.

Silas turned to Tally. "Where can I find a folding table?"

"I don't know. Joey would, but then look what you did to him."

"I didn't think he'd be useful."

Useful?

Tally prayed for Gus. If Silas didn't think Gus could be useful, the former might kill the latter.

"It would be best not to end a life prematurely because you have no idea what God has in store for the person. For all we know, Joey could be the father of a future president, but now we won't ever know because he died before he could see his little kids grow up."

Silas rolled his eyes. "If there's one thing I dislike about you, Miss Tally, is that you make no sense half the time. But I put up with it."

Likewise.

"Where can I find plates and a candlestand?"

Silas asked.

Tally pointed with her chin to the boxes near them. "Those boxes are donated stuff from the community. There are pots and pans in there, so I think we might be able to find some plates and potentially forks and spoons."

"Donated stuff?" Silas asked.

"They're in good condition."

"But we'd have to wash them."

"There's a break room somewhere near the security office."

Silas thought about it for a few seconds. "Nah. Too much work, too much trouble. We'll just eat off paper plates and use plastic forks."

That meant Silas had bought Gus's idea.

Tally wondered why Gus suggested it. To buy time? A delay tactic?

Silas's free hand touched Tally's face. She flinched.

"Good. I want you to be afraid of me," Silas said.

Tally wasn't sure whether she should look fearful or whether she should try to be friendly with Silas to bring his guard down.

"Did you wash your hands before you touched my face?" Tally asked.

Silas smiled and stood. "I know you care for me.

What kind of food do you like?" He put his handgun away in his waistband.

"I eat all kinds of food, but I'm thinking of fajitas right now," Tally said.

"Chicken or beef?"

"Chicken."

Silas was about to leave the room, when Tally called his name.

"Are you getting some for Gus too?" She asked. "He's serving. Luke 10:7 says that 'the laborer is worthy of his wages.' My dad always insists that you pay workers."

Silas smiled at Tally. "Of course I want to please my future father-in-law. What do you think we should get for Gus?"

"Are chicken fajitas okay with you?" Tally asked Gus.

He barely nodded.

"Two orders of chicken fajitas then," Tally told Silas.

"Three." Silas left the room and slammed the door.

Tally heard the lock.

"The gamer is coming back soon. We might not have a lot of time." Gus jiggled his own wrists and then tried to see if he could somehow move his tied arms from the back to the front.

Tally also tried, but her arms were not flexible enough. "Maybe if I'd exercise more..."

"I have long arms, so let me try. Only one of us needs to be successful." Gus contorted until his arms actually went under his thighs, then knees, then feet, and then his arms were in front of him.

"Quick! Untie me, Boy Scout." Tally spun around on the floor.

The door opened.

"Figured." Silas shook his head as he walked into the room, leaving the door wide open.

Outside the door, Tally spotted a folding table and two folded chairs.

Silas pulled his handgun out of his waistband and pointed it at Gus. "First you remove the duct tape from your mouth. You think I didn't notice?"

Neither Gus nor Tally replied.

"I was playing along with you. Now you've changed the position of your hands. Maybe I should just shoot you."

"No," Tally blurted. "Then who will serve dinner?"

"I ordered Taco Bell. No server needed."

"But what about my chicken fajitas?" Tally asked.

"Next time, baby."

"Did you get a ring?" Gus asked.

There was nervousness in his voice since the gun was still pointed at him.

"No ring." Silas reached for Tally. She scooted back. "She says yes, and I'll go get her a ring. She says no, and I'll start shooting."

Tally realized that they were dealing with someone who needed psychological help. If only Dad were here. He was a trained professional.

Still, Tally had to survive this, and she'd do whatever it took for her and Gus to get out of this warehouse alive.

Lord, please.

Then again, if she died tonight, she would go to heaven. She would see Grandpa again and the elderly ladies in her women's ministry who had passed away.

Her parents and sisters would grieve, but they would know where she was.

If Silas died tonight, he would be lost forever. Was there hope for him? Could she and Gus talk to Silas about Jesus? Or was he too far gone?

What could Silas understand at this point, with a loaded gun in his hand?

Assuming it's loaded.

She prayed that Gus would not do something as stupid as to wrestle the gun out of Silas's hand. She wasn't sure how much exposure Gus had in the

Bahamas with weapons, but it might not be as much as Americans did.

Even so, Tally had never held a weapon.

What to do with Silas? How far could they play along before he snapped?

When are the police coming?

"There is a reason I tied your wrists behind your back," Silas explained to Gus, like a schoolteacher did to a rebellious student. He was about to correct it when his phone beeped.

He checked his messages. "Tacos are here. Delivery at the front door. You stay put."

Silas left them the same way he had every time: locked door.

"Let's do this," Gus said.

Tally turned around again, her wrists in front of Gus. He unraveled the rope around her wrists. Then she untied his wrists before they both worked on the ropes around their own ankles.

Tally leapt up, and they both ran to the door.

It was locked from the outside.

"As expected." Tally ran to the boxes. "Let's look for something we can use as weapons. Like bats or something."

No baseball bats. Only pots and pans, spatulas, labels, dinnerware.

"A stainless-steel pot with a handle might work, if you can swing," Gus said.

"Good idea. Did you play baseball as a kid?" Tally asked.

"Football—or soccer, as you call it here."

"I played baseball." Tally picked up a large non-stick frying pan with a long handle. "This is heavy."

"I'll use it." Gus took it from her.

Tally found a three-quart stainless sauce pan with a lid. She removed the glass lid and held the saucepan in her hand.

Gus was at the door. "Let's turn off the lights."

Tally rushed to his side, then nodded for him to turn off the lights.

They waited by the wall. Gus was nearest the door. "I'll swing this and hopefully knock the handgun away when he steps in."

"Okay."

They were quiet for a while. Tally tried to hear noises from outside the room, but she couldn't hear anything. She tried to pray, but no rational phrases formed in her head.

I can't pray, Lord. Please just send the police.

She drew a deep breath. She held the saucepan in both hands.

"Don't be scared. I'm here," Gus whispered.

"I should be scared, but I'm not. I'm just in a daze."

They were standing in the dark, and Tally couldn't see Gus, but she felt his hand squeezing her arm. "It's going to be okay. God is keeping us safe."

Tally nodded but didn't think Gus could see her. "Yes, the safety of my life is in God's hand. Psalm 91:1 says, 'He who dwells in the secret place of the Most High shall abide under the shadow of the Almighty.' Dad had my sisters and me memorize this verse when we were kids, and now I'm glad we did."

"That's a good verse," Gus said. "Let's pray it back to God. Would you like to pray?"

"Sure." She took a deep breath. "Father God, thank You that You are always with us. Thank You that we can dwell safely in Your shadow. You are the Lord God Almighty."

"Amen," Gus said.

"Father God, I am reminded of Psalm 4:8, which says, 'I will both lie down in peace, and sleep; for You alone, O Lord, make me dwell in safety.' Even though I don't plan to sleep right now, I know that if You can 'make me dwell in safety' as I sleep, You can also keep us safe when we're awake."

She waited for Gus to pray also.

"Dear Heavenly Father, You said in Proverbs 18:10 that 'the name of the Lord is a strong tower; the righteous run to it and are safe.' Thank You that we can run into Your strong tower and You will keep us safe," Gus prayed.

"Thank You, Jesus."

"Psalm 46:1–3 also comes to mind," Gus said.

Tally knew that one. Somehow they recited the first three verses together.

God is our refuge and strength,
A very present help in trouble.
Therefore we will not fear,
Even though the earth be removed,
And though the mountains be carried into the midst of the sea;
Though its waters roar and be troubled,
Though the mountains shake with its swelling.
Selah

They finished their prayer in the name of Jesus. Tally felt better, but she also knew something that Gus might not know.

"I still don't believe that Silas is going to kill me," Tally whispered. "You, maybe. But not me."

"Why not?" Gus asked.

"Because he can't marry a dead body."

CHAPTER ELEVEN

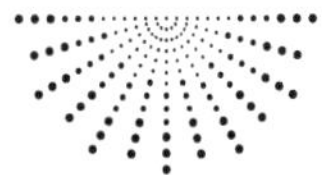

They waited for a while in the dark room with the lights off, but Silas didn't return. The door had no window, and Gus couldn't see outside. They'd have to rely on their ears.

Right now they heard nothing.

"Wonder what's happening?" Gus asked in a whisper. The frying pan was getting heavy in his hand. His head throbbed. "How long does it take to get from this room to the front door?"

"I don't know," Tally said. "If the lights were on, we'd look silly holding pots and pans against Silas's handgun."

She was standing so close to him that he could feel her right arm against his left arm. They still stood by the wall, waiting for the door to open so that they could take a swing at Silas. The bruises on his arm hurt when Tally pressed on them, but he didn't want Tally to move away, so he bore the pain quietly.

"I thought I heard something." Gus pinned his ear to the wall.

There was some sort of roaring sound. He wasn't sure what it was.

Then an explosion rocked the building. He heard things fall, glass shatter.

He extended his hand to touch the door. It was warm.

"Uh-oh."

"What?" Tally asked.

"The door is warm. Is this a fire-rated door?"

"I don't know."

"I think we better move away from the door. I'm afraid there's a fire on the other side." Gus flicked on the light.

He looked down to see Tally still holding on to his arm. He winced.

"Oh." Tally released her grip. "Sorry. Sorry."

"It's all right."

"I think we can find some blankets." Tally put down her saucepan and went to work digging through the boxes. "I know they're not wet blankets, but maybe we can hide underneath them if we need to."

"I was thinking that we need to roll up cloths and put them at the bottom of the door, like draft stoppers, you know?" Gus pointed to the door.

"Good idea. If it's a fire door, then as long as the smoke doesn't come through around it, we can wait until the firefighters come to get us out."

Tally nodded. She found some blankets and comforters. Gus rolled them up and put them at the base of the door.

Then they went to a far corner of the room and sat down.

"We shouldn't hide behind the boxes because the firefighters might not be able to find us," Tally said.

They sat side by side against a wall.

Fearless Tally who wasn't afraid of Silas or of dying was now visibly shaking.

Gus wanted to say, "It's just a fire," but the timing wasn't right for jokes.

"I want to be raptured," Tally said. "I don't want to die in a fire."

"Like you said, Levi has probably called the police. If they knew this was a hostage situation, they would have surrounded the building, right? Then if a fire breaks out, they can see it right away."

"I know. And yet..." Tally folded her arms across her chest.

"Are you okay?"

Tally didn't reply.

Gus tried to think of something to say to take Tally's mind off the idea that they could potentially die, being trapped inside this locked room with fire all around them.

Tally tried to get up.

Gus grabbed her arm. "What are you doing?"

"Try to open the door."

"It's locked from the outside."

"We can break the lock."

Gus got up. Started looking into the boxes near him. "We can try to find something that can break the lock. Or maybe a screwdriver to dismantle it."

Tally was at the door, pounding it with her bare hands. "Help! Help!"

Gus reached her before she scalded her palm on the warm door. "We need to stay away from the door until we find a tool."

Tally didn't scream or anything—it wasn't her style—but the look of panic in her eyes made Gus want to wrap his arms around her...

And die together?

He brushed off the thought. He pointed to the boxes. "You start on this side, and I start on that side. We're looking for tools to help us break the lock."

"Like a hammer?" Tally asked.

Good. She's switching mode.

As they worked, Gus tried to think of something to say. "How long have we been friends?"

"Four years. Why?" Her voice was nervous. "Is this the time to make small talk?"

"Pep talk. Do you trust God?"

"Always. You don't even have to ask, Gus."

"Do you trust me?"

"I don't know."

Gus could hear the hesitation in her voice. "Well, we better trust each other. I might be the last person you see on earth."

"I'll see Jesus next if I don't make it out of here, so what's your point, Gus?"

Gus grinned. "I forget what I wanted to say."

"You were trying to cheer me up."

"Failing at it."

"No, you're sweet."

When it got quiet again, Gus could hear the fire outside the room. Eventually they'd be cooked alive. "Look for some sort of fire-retardant blankets."

"There's so much artificial fiber in these boxes that we'd probably die just breathing in the fumes when they go up in flames." Tally's voice faltered.

They huddled together, listening.

"I'm thinking of all the things I regret not having done," Gus said.

"Like what?"

"Kinda embarrassing to say it."

"Suppose I'm the last person you'll see on earth. Will you tell me?" Tally asked.

Gus was quiet for a bit. "Uh..."

"Didn't peg you as shy." Tally pushed away a box and looked into another. "Why don't I start?"

"Go on."

"I wish I'd gotten married and had kids," Tally said. "Then they could get my house and savings, and my parents could have the kids to remind them of me."

"Huh."

"Is that all you can say, Gus?"

"I don't know how to respond to that. When you talk about marriage, that hasn't worked out for me. The woman I thought I'd marry left me, married someone else, and is now pregnant with his child."

"So you came all the way to Atlanta for a change of scenery, and look where you end up."

"With you, Tally."

"How ironic."

"Why did you say that?" Gus waited.

"When I first saw you at the school in Nassau, I thought you were such a good-looking Bible-toting guy. I asked around about you, did you know?"

"I didn't know. I'm flattered."

"Don't be. They all told me you were taken."

"Taken?"

"You had just started dating Veronique. I came late."

"Ah."

"You were such a gentleman to us visitors to your church and school. You always said 'ladies first' to me, and you found chairs for us latecomers at some of the outdoor meetings."

"I was trying to be nice to everyone who was in the Bahamas for the first time," Gus said.

"It was the year after Tina went there for the first time and met Byron. They fought a lot."

Gus smiled. "Yes, they did. However, the next time she returned to Nassau, they fell in love and eventually got married."

"And lived happily ever after." Tally couldn't help smiling.

"No, actually. The Christian marriage ends at death."

"Figure of speech, Gus."

"I know. Unlike them, you and I have been friends since you went to the Bahamas. We have never fought."

"We didn't interact much with each other to do any of that. Veronique made it clear to all the women that you were off the market. Friendship was all we had."

Friendship?

Was that all he wanted too? Gus was a free man now. He could date whomever he chose. Would he want to date Tally? He hadn't thought about it.

Until now.

"Yes, I'm a one-woman man. I had just started to know Veronique when you visited my church, and my focus was all on her," Gus explained. "Long story short, she and I weren't meant for each other."

"Why not? I mean back then. Clearly you aren't now."

"I lost my individuality dating her. She liked us to wear matching clothes, she wanted more than I could give her, and the world revolved around her, even though she's a Christian. If I didn't do what she said, she accused me of not loving her enough."

Gus felt like a big burden had just unloaded from his chest. He had to tell someone besides his cousin Byron. Not to elicit sympathy, but as his last confession.

"Is that TMI?" Gus had surprised himself today. He rarely disclosed too much information with friends.

He hadn't considered Tally special until he came to Atlanta—and spent time with her.

"You're free now," Tally said. "Free to date someone new."

"Not that I'm looking to."

"I hear you." Tally nodded. "You know, another regret of mine is being too busy to say yes when someone I liked asked me out. He never asked me again."

"Oh? He's not for you then."

"That so?"

"I have no idea." He laughed. "I said it randomly."

"You wanted to make me feel better." Tally lightly punched him in the arm.

"Owww." Gus pretended like it hurt more than it did. Actually, his head and shoulders hurt more than Tally touching him.

"You're not a wimp, Mr. Moss."

"No, I'm not." Gus drew a deep breath. "If I ask you out, will you say yes?"

"We may not survive this." Tally sighed. "I

haven't found a thing in all these boxes. Lots of household items. I think we've picked through them in the last few months."

"Suppose we do survive this, by the grace and mercy of God. If we do, how about let's go out for dinner somewhere?" Gus asked. "Why should we let past memories prevent us from finding out what we're missing in life? Let's create new memories."

He warmed up to the idea of more conversations with Tally. They got along well, and Gus wanted to see where it would lead.

Where God would lead them?

"All right," Tally said. "Let's go out to dinner. Like a survivors' club meeting or something."

"Survivors' club?" Gus was thinking that it was more like the start of something new.

"Why not? Two survivors having dinner together," Tally said. "It's not like it's a date night."

Gus felt deflated. He so wanted it to be a date night.

However, he'd asked Tally out just like that, and so he couldn't expect much. If she were surprised that he had asked her out, and then thought that it wasn't anything unusual because Gus was a friend, then he wasn't going to make her wish she hadn't said yes.

"You promise not to bail out?" Gus asked, just in case.

"I gave you my word." Tally looked at him kinda funny.

"You can't change your mind."

"I won't. After all, we nearly died together." Tally laughed.

"We're not out of the woods yet—"

Then he heard it. A loud crack. Something cutting wood and steel.

"Anyone in there?" someone shouted.

"Yes! Help! Help!" Gus rushed to the door and pounded it with his fists.

Tally showed up next to him with her saucepan in hand, which she proceeded to pound on the door with. The deafening noise attracted attention.

"Stand back!" someone shouted from the other side.

Gus pulled Tally back and away from the door. His hand was on her arm. Tally's other hand reached across her chest to cover his hand.

The door handle fell off, and the door flung open.

Two firefighters appeared, fire and smoke behind them. "Tally and Gus?"

"Present!" Tally and Gus said in unison.

~

Once Tally was outside the warehouse, her knees buckled, but before she went down, Gus and a firefighter pulled her back to her feet as they led her to safety a far distance away from the building, where the paramedics waited to examine them.

The night was dark, but all the parking lot lights were on. Together with the lights from the fire truck and emergency vehicles, the place looked like it was ready for an outdoor concert. Fire hoses and firefighters were everywhere, along with fire trucks, emergency vehicles, and police cruisers.

The scene was surreal in the night, like it couldn't possibly be real.

Tally was able to walk on her own, so they let her. Thank God they didn't try to carry her because Tally had gained twenty pounds since Christmas, and it was the reason she wore loose-fitting T-shirts and blouses these days.

She kept telling herself she had to walk off all those Christmas cookies that the ladies at church so expertly made, but she had no idea today might have been the day her weight was put to the test.

At least Gus hadn't tried to carry her.

His arm was around her waist though—where all the flab was.

As soon as Tally and Gus were with the paramedics at a safe distance away, the firefighters from the search-and-rescue team of the fire department asked Tally again about Joey.

Tally had told them that she saw Silas drag Joey's body out of the storeroom.

"I don't know if Joey was dead," Tally repeated herself. "He looked dead, but I kept thinking it was his body, though at the back of my mind, I wanted to think that he was only injured."

"I asked you before, but you didn't answer. Was there anybody else in there besides the four of you?" the firefighter asked.

"I don't know. Is Levi here? He's the warehouse manager. He's in charge of shifts. He'll know if someone else was there with Joey. Gus and I were on our own. We did not see anyone else in there besides Joey and Silas, when we were there this afternoon."

The firefighter spoke into his two-way portable radio just as a small explosion shook the ground they were standing on.

Tally ducked, and Gus covered her head with his arms.

"Stay back, everyone!" the firefighters yelled as they ran toward the explosion.

Tally saw Mom and Dad trying to stay out of the way of the paramedics, who were examining her and Gus. Tally didn't have a single scratch on her except for the abrasion around her wrists from having been tied up.

A police officer came over to ask Tally and Gus questions. That was when Tally realized that she didn't have her purse or phone with her.

"I dropped my phone just before Silas attacked me," Gus said.

"I'm taking your statement next," the officer said to Gus. "But first, the whole building is a crime scene—again. If we see your purse and Mr. Moss's phone, we will notify you."

Tally and Gus gave the officer their phone numbers.

As soon as the paramedics released Tally, Mom and Dad descended on her and hugged her as though they had lost her and found her again.

"Mom, Dad! I'm all right." Tally stroked Mom's hair as they cried together. Dad wrapped them in a big bear hug.

All right. That's enough.

Tally wasn't one for mushy hugs, but her

parents were. She was more worried about a particular someone.

Gus.

He had been beaten up more than Tally. He seemed to be fine inside the warehouse, but now he looked exhausted.

He said he felt dizzy, but he didn't want to go to the hospital.

Gently, Tally leaned toward his face. "Gus?"

"Yes?"

She kissed his unscratched left cheek.

Gus stared at her.

"I'll go with you." In her heart, Tally was divided on this. She felt that she had to go with Gus, but she also wanted to drive with her parents.

"You need to get checked too, Tally, just in case," Dad said. "We'll follow."

"Okay then." Tally climbed into the ambulance, and held Gus's hand.

He stared at his hand in hers. And then at her.

She said nothing.

He didn't pull away. His hand warmed up in hers.

"Where are we going?" Tally asked the paramedic sitting next to her in the ambulance.

"Decatur Memorial."

Tally called out to her parents. "Did you hear that? Decatur Memorial."

"Got it." Dad and Mom waved as the ambulance door closed.

~

Tally received the all-clear from a doctor at Decatur Memorial Hospital. A nurse gave her some antibacterial ointment for her wrists. She had minimal smoke inhalation.

They adjourned to the waiting room to wait for Gus, who had to undergo a bunch of tests on his head and shoulders. Dad bought some sandwiches from the cafeteria and distributed them to his wife and daughter.

"Tell Tally what we know so far, dear." Mom patted Dad's arm.

"A taco man went to the warehouse door and met Silas," Dad said. "Silas thought something was fishy, ran off, and for some unknown reason, set himself on fire surrounded by a bunch of boxes. That set off a ring of fire all around the first floor of the warehouse."

"How did you know all that?" Tally asked.

"I heard the officers talk to one another when I was on standby to talk with Silas. I'm still his counselor, you know. Don't go telling everybody about what I just said. I'm sure the police will let the public know what went on soon enough."

Tally tried to put the timeline together. "I can add to that. When Silas came back to see us, he smelled of gasoline."

"You need to give that information to the police," Dad said.

"I will. They know we're going to the hospital."

"Silas has severe burns all over his body," Mom said. "The first ambulance left before you came out of the warehouse."

"Did Levi call you?" Tally asked. "How did you know that Gus and I were held inside?"

"Levi and Silas both called me," Dad said. "I called the police, and they asked me to go to the warehouse to advise them on Silas's psychology. Don't worry. I was at a safe distance away."

Of course, Mom always tagged along. Dad didn't go anywhere without Mom.

"Wait." Tally's eyes widened. "Why did Silas call you?"

"To ask for your hand in marriage," Dad answered.

"Is that private information?" Mom asked Dad. "Counselor-patient confidentiality?"

"No, dear, we weren't doing a counseling

session. I was the father of his future un-bride when he called me. I didn't put on the counselor hat at that time. So I called the police, and then I called Levi back."

I'm the un-bride now.

"I figured Levi also called the police." Tally checked her phone. No messages from Levi.

"Yes, Levi and I both called," Dad said. "In fact, thank God for Levi. He was on the alert since last Friday. He thought you and Gus had forgotten to return to the Village. He tried calling your phone, and it wasn't like you not to answer."

"Right. I knew he'd be suspicious. He'd figure it out and call the police. I'm glad he called you too, Dad." Tally closed her eyes and said another prayer.

She was thankful to be free.

Levi Theroux arrived at the waiting room, and rushed over to give Tally a big hug. "Thank God you're alive. God is good!"

"Yes, He is," Mom and Dad said in unison.

Levi pressed a palm to his chest. "I don't know if this thirty-something heart can take this sort of thing two Fridays in a row."

"You can't quit." Tally pointed a finger at him. "What are we going to do without you?"

"How did you know to call the police?" Mom asked.

"I know Tally very well," Levi said. "She was going to the Warehouse and then back to the Village. If there was a change of plans, she would have texted me. Tally's like that. When she didn't, I wasn't concerned at first. People forget, you know?"

"I rarely forget to text you or Maggie," Tally said.

"Exactly. However, since last week I've been extra vigilant about that warehouse. I know we have security now, and I know it's Joey's shift. I called the security desk, but no one answered. Then I called his personal phone to see if both of you were still here."

"Did you talk to Joey?" Tally asked.

"Unfortunately, no. By the time I called, someone else had his personal phone."

"Silas."

"He used the same phone to call Pastor Fizz, it turned out." Levi looked at Dad. "He and I put two and two together."

"Your mom and I drove there as fast as we could," Dad added.

"I'm sure you meant that you kept the speed limit." Tally waited for Dad to reply.

He didn't.

"When I reached the warehouse, the police were already there." Levi pointed to Tally. "Your car was parked outside. So now three people needed to be rescued from the warehouse—you, Gus, and Joey."

"Joey." Tally blinked away the image of the dead security guard lying on the floor of the storage room. "Did they find Joey?"

Levi said yes.

Tally started to cry softly.

Mom hugged Tally. "But it's over now. As soon as we see Gus, we'll go home, okay?"

"Let's pray before we forget." Dad bowed his head and closed his eyes.

There was no either-or with Dad. If he wanted to pray, Mom would be right there next to him, praying. The rest of the people could stay or leave.

Levi bowed his head immediately.

Tally closed her eyes just in time to hear Dad start his prayer.

"Dear Father God, You are the creator of this universe in which we live, and all the natural things therein, including fire that burned inside the warehouse, and natural wood and fabric that are in the warehouse."

Tally took a deep breath as she remembered her

time with Gus in the warehouse. By a miracle, Silas hadn't hurt them more.

Someone touched her arm. She figured it was Mom, but the hand felt larger.

She opened one eye to look.

It was Gus.

He had a couple of Band-Aids on his forehead. The gashes on his arms were still there, but they were not bleeding anymore.

Gus reached down to hold her hand.

Tally closed her eyes again to listen to Dad. One thing about Dad that was most calming to Tally was his prayers in that baritone voice of his. By the time he finished thanking God for all the details she hadn't considered putting into a prayer, her heart would have calmed down.

And so she listened to Dad's prayers, not out of obligation but because Dad always prayed heartfelt prayers.

"You made her in her mother's womb, those tiny fingers and toes we first saw some thirty-five years ago." Yes, Dad was still praying. "Patiently, we raised our first-born child, our lovely daughter, whom we cherished and adored all those years and made sure she never skinned her knees on the little pink trikes she loved to ride."

"Knee pads," Mom whispered.

"Little did we know that thirty-five years after she was born, she'd be caught in a warehouse fire that could have taken her life—and that of her good friend Gus—if the firefighters had not gotten there in time. Baking them a cake or bringing them food is not nearly enough to show our gratitude."

Her good friend Gus?

Tally was smiling now. The tension had left her shoulders.

"Yet the biggest thank-you of all goes to You, Lord, for rescuing Tally and Gus from Silas and from the fire. You shielded them and protected them from serious harm, and they have come out of the warehouse alive. Thank You, Father God, for Your tender mercies even as we will now deal with the psychological damages that might have come out of such an experience."

He wasn't done.

No one said a word or made any noise as Dad continued.

"And now we pray that Your hand will be upon the police and detectives and arson investigators as they figure out what really happened inside the warehouse." Dad paused. He expelled a deep breath. "As much as I'm upset about it, I still pray for Silas, that he will get the help he needs. Up until this point, he hasn't shown any sign of being harmful to himself or others, but he snapped, and here we are. Lord, You knew him before we did. I pray that You will heal his mind and also his burned body. Let him no longer refuse Jesus Christ, the Great Physician."

Dad finally closed his prayer, and there was a collective sigh of relief—except from Tally. She wanted Dad to keep praying.

"Gus!" Levi nearly slapped his shoulder.

Gus evaded Levi's hand. In the process, he let go of Tally's hand.

"Oh sorry. Forgot. Are you all stitched up?"

"No stitches needed. These bruises will heal." Gus turned to Tally. "No brain injury. Only bumps on my head, and scrapes on my face. I might have some small scars."

"No concussion?" Tally asked.

"No. Thank God."

"Wow. God must've given you a hard head." Tally blinked. "Did the police talk to you?"

"Yes." Gus stood close enough to touch Tally again, but he didn't. "I gave my statement while waiting for my test results."

"Can we go home now?" Mom's eyes were teary, and she hugged Tally again.

"Let's go home," Dad declared as he walked out of the waiting room with Levi and Gus.

Mom held Tally's hand tightly, as though she were still a little girl trying to cross a busy street. "I think you need to rest at home tomorrow instead of going on the Stone Mountain hike. Maggie can handle it."

"I forgot all about the hike tomorrow." Tally turned to Levi. "That's why we were at the warehouse, to pick up the T-shirts for the hike."

"I'll look for them, but I tell you, there'll be a lot of damage from the fire," Levi said. "I think we should postpone the hike."

"I agree," Tally said. "Joey is dead, and we need to contact his family right away, even if the police already have. He drew his paycheck from Midtown Chapel, after all."

"Let me handle that," Dad said.

"As for the hike, the sponsors would want people to wear shirts advertising their companies, and looks like we won't have access to the warehouse until the police are done with the crime scene investigation." Tally turned to Dad. "Your counsel, Pastor Fizz?"

"Postpone it," Dad said.

"Good advice. Let me text Maggie... Oops. No phone. Borrow yours, Levi?"

Levi handed Tally his phone. Maggie was still awake, and called back. Tally rescheduled the hike to another Saturday. She didn't have her calendar with her, but she figured it had to be the Saturday after she drove her parents back from Savannah.

"What's the probability of the same warehouse being attacked twice two Fridays in a row?" Gus asked.

"They have to be connected," Dad said.

"I've given all the information to the police." Levi sighed. "Let them figure it out. It's their job."

Tally and Mom walked arm in arm out of the hospital to the parking lot. After letting Levi go, they went to the family vehicle, an SUV that seated eight people. Dad preferred to drive his pickup truck, but it only seated two. Gus sat in front with Dad because Mom refused to leave Tally's side.

"What time is it?" Tally asked, peeking at the dashboard in between Dad and Gus. "What? It's only midnight? How did I think that it's almost morning?"

"Feels like it, doesn't it?" Gus glanced back at Tally.

Tally nodded. "I'm glad you were in the warehouse with me, Gus. You were calm and collected, like Dad. Dad's always calm, no matter what happens."

"Like me?" Dad looked in the rearview mirror.

Tally looked away. "Figure of speech, Dad."

No, it was literal, and Tally knew it.

She had just complimented Gus in front of her parents. She hoped they didn't think too much of it.

Otherwise, if it didn't work out, she'd never hear the end of it.

Wait a minute.

What might not work out?

Sometimes Tally had no idea where her heart would take her. Perhaps she was simply exhausted, and her mind was going places.

Yeah, that's got to be it.

CHAPTER TWELVE

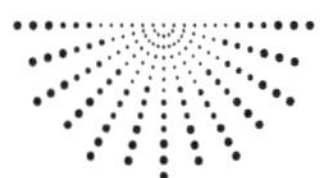

When the news reached Midtown Chapel on Monday morning that Silas Graham had passed away from fourth-degree burns in his self-immolation on Friday afternoon, there was mourning at the Fitzpatrick household.

Dad spoke with the police about counseling Silas. Thing was, Silas had shown no sign of violence all those months he'd been getting free counseling from Dad. He sometimes attended church and Sunday school, was friendly with everyone, and liked to follow Tally around. She thought he was harmless because Dad hadn't said otherwise.

Now Silas was dead.

Dad shared Tally's sentiments that it was a shame that Silas hadn't made peace with God before his death. The words that Dad left her with before he went to meet with Pastor Kim at church resonated in Tally's mind.

Believing in Jesus is an individual decision. Each person has a choice to believe in Christ or not. No one can force anyone to believe what they don't want to believe.

Mom insisted that Tally stay with them for some days until she was ready to go back to work. The church allowed Tally to use up her sick days to recover from the trauma of having been imprisoned against her will, even though it had been for only several hours and Gus had been with her.

"I don't know if I can be absent for that long," Tally said.

"You've aways been healthy and rarely used up your two weeks of sick leave each year," Mom said. "Now is the time."

"If I take two weeks now, there's only one week left between June and December. What if I get sick?"

"That could happen. Then you just need to take your vacation days or unpaid time off."

"Isn't that taking advantage of the church's generous sick days and vacation time?"

"Is it? Getting two weeks of sick leave and two weeks of vacation days is your reward for being a faithful worker all these years."

"I'd rather get my reward in heaven."

"Tally, if you don't rest and recover from your trauma, you will get to heaven sooner than you think. Stress can kill you. Just ask Uncle Ian."

"Uncle Ian is dead, Mom."

"Precisely. Dropped dead at the pulpit because he never took a sick day in his life."

"I don't think that makes sense. If he took sick days, that meant he was sick. Uncle Ian was rarely sick. He died because it was time for God to take him home. He was ninety-nine years old, Mom."

"Could've lived to be a hundred if he'd gotten enough rest."

"Mom, that's not a good argument, and you know that. Every hair on our head is numbered. Obviously, it's not my time to go, because I'm still here."

Mom sighed. "Why are you like your dad? Always using logic and Scripture against me."

"I do not."

"We were talking about sick leave. All I want is

for you to rest. I don't want you stressed out over what happened on Friday." Mom sniffed.

Tally wrapped her arms around Mom and hushed her as she cried softly. "There's a reason I was in the warehouse that day and not you. You'd have fallen apart."

"Yes, I would've. You're more like Dad. You can survive anything."

"See, Mom?" Tally handed Mom a tissue. "You agree that I'll be all right. God protected Gus and me."

Mom nodded.

"How does Dad handle a crisis?" Tally asked softly.

Mom looked up. She nodded. "You're your father's daughter all the way."

"So I need to go back to work. It will keep me distracted."

"Going to Savannah this Thursday will help too."

Tally nodded. "Until then, the Village needs me."

"The warehouse is badly damaged, so a lot of the people working on the Village landscape and construction are at the warehouse, helping Levi to clean it up," Mom said. "Few people are at the Village today. I asked Levi."

"I can still help." *No, I can't go back to the warehouse.*

"I don't want you to go to the warehouse. I'm concerned that you might get nightmares about what happened."

"Shouldn't I have felt scared when Silas pointed a handgun in my face?" Tally asked. "Why wasn't I?"

"Because you've dealt with Silas so many times at church, that you knew him well enough. You knew that he wouldn't pull the trigger. You told Dad this morning that Silas wouldn't marry a dead person because he liked to converse with you. Dad told you that it's because Silas had always been mistreated, and when someone talked to him like he was a normal person, he appreciated it."

"It's so sad that only Dad and I talked to him normally."

"Most people at church avoided him. I did too. I didn't have the energy to deal with him, even though I felt sorry for him." Mom stroked Tally's hair. "God has gifted you with a special way to deal with people. Most of the women at the Village would come up to you and tell you everything. You can always get the truth out of them. You should've been in counseling. You're so much like your dad."

"It's too much responsibility."

"I hear you. You're doing well as the women's ministry director, so I'm happy for you with your career choice. You speak at conferences and do workshops for women."

"I don't have any the rest of this year, Mom. Once the entire Village is completed, and we have housing for as many needy women as possible, I will go back on the speaking circuit."

"Which do you prefer? Do you like to work at the Village more than speaking at conferences?"

"Each has its own pluses. As long as I can minister to women, I'll do the work. However, I do lean toward conferences. I feel that I can reach more people that way in a shorter period of time."

"The Village is harder. More challenges of all sorts."

Tally blinked. "Right. We encounter individual problems more in the Village. In workshops and conferences, I deal more with groups. There are individuals with problems, but I don't have to handle one-on-one situations, like Jacinda's."

"Oh, that poor mom." Mom wiped a tear from her eye. "I cannot imagine losing any of my daughters, although if any of you died, I've had you all for at least twenty-nine years. Sheldon was only seventeen. Too young to die."

"I hope the police find the murderer so that Jacinda can have closure. However, she is broken emotionally, and that closure can only come from God. Until then, I can pray with her. I think I should go to the Village."

"No," Mom said. "Trust me. You need to just chill and stay here with me. You're probably still in shock."

"It's been three days."

"Sometimes people get PTSD and still have problems months or years later."

Did Mom think she had post-traumatic stress disorder? "You and Dad are watching me closely, and you're letting me talk and cry about it."

"It helps that Gus is very strong spiritually and emotionally. I suspect that you would be worse off now had he not been in that storeroom with you."

Tally agreed. "God has brought him here for such a time as this."

"You told me that you were scared to death until Gus showed up. Then, even with Joey dead, you and Gus managed to survive. You bounced strengths off each other, and you prayed and relied on the Lord to deliver you through the furnace."

"The fiery furnace. It was hot when they pulled us out of there. Smoky and hot." Tally grabbed her waist and hip. "I need to lose some weight. Thankfully, neither Gus nor the firefighters carried me out."

"You're not that overweight. You're only twenty pounds above your ideal weight."

"Do you know how much time it'll take me to lose twenty pounds?"

"Then you better start walking more. Exercising is also a good way to relieve stress. When we get to Savannah and Tybee, you'll have plenty of time to exercise while your dad is preaching here and there. I'll ask Gus to accompany you so that you won't have to go out alone."

"I'm fine by myself, Mom."

"You two survivors need to help each other during this time of recovery. Talk to each other. Pray together. If you think you're feeling too sad, you tell me, all right?"

Tally nodded.

"I can't thank the Lord enough that you survived." Mom hugged her. "God must have a special plan for you and Gus."

Speaking of Gus, he had been quiet all day long. He came downstairs for breakfast and lunch, helped load the dishwasher, and then disappeared back into his bedroom.

Tally knew that Gus had an appointment with

Dad on Tuesday about whatever he wanted to talk about. They'd meet at Dad's counseling office at church so that Gus wouldn't feel the pressure of being cautious about what he said.

Tally wanted to ask Gus how he was doing today, but she didn't know how to do it. She figured that if she'd grown up with brothers, she might know how to handle a guy. Dad wouldn't be a good example of a typical male because Dad was extraordinary, in Tally's eyes. Few men could measure up to Dad and his fortitude.

By late afternoon Tally felt the weight of her experience, and burst into tears in Mom's arms. Mom let her cry for a while, listened to her ramble on about her concerns.

One thing that surfaced over and over again didn't concern Silas at all. Tally hadn't been surprised that Silas wanted to marry her, because suddenly all his behavior in the past made sense.

However, Tally was more bothered by the other thing—what she had told Gus when she thought Friday was her last day on earth.

"What exactly did you tell Gus?" Mom asked over green tea and oatmeal cookies.

They were sitting in her favorite room in the house, a small sunroom that caught the afternoon sun. Normally, it would be hot this time of day in

May, but the curtains kept out a little bit of the sun. Tally sat in an armchair away from the sun, but Mom sat on the sofa, which was basking in the afternoon sunshine.

Mom had grown up in Key West and enjoyed the sunshine she missed so much. Tally believed that she wouldn't hesitate to say yes if Dad asked her to move home to Florida.

Tally sipped hot tea as she mulled over how to explain her embarrassment to Mom.

Hot tea was served year round in the Fitzpatrick house. It was a comfort drink for everyone. All problems could be solved with a cup of tea, almost.

Except this one.

This one had taken wings and flown out.

"Go on," Mom said. "You can tell me."

Meaning she'd tell Dad and no one else.

"That I was somewhat interested in him four years ago before I found out he belonged to someone else at that time," Tally said.

"You didn't act on it, and neither did you pursue it after you found out he was taken."

"Right."

"When you told him that, how did Gus respond?"

"He didn't freak out."

"Good."

"I don't remember everything he said, to tell you the truth. In fact, that Friday was a big blur to me. I'm not sure what else I said to him. Somehow after all that, he asked me to dinner."

"He did?" Mom's eyebrows rose.

"We're both single now, so it should be all right."

"Of course."

"Just felt that maybe I shouldn't have told him that I had noticed him. I backed off after I found out he already had a girlfriend."

"In the past." Mom nodded. "When's your dinner date?"

"I don't think it's a date. We're calling our own survivors' club meeting." Or was that what she had suggested? What had Gus thought about it? She couldn't remember.

Mom ate another cookie. "Our ladies at church make the best cookies. Isn't it nice of them to bring us meals?"

"Yes, indeed. These look like Marsha's cookies." Tally chewed slowly. "I'm sure it's hers. She puts bits of walnut in her oatmeal cookies. I'll be carrying memories of these delicious bites around my waistline, to be sure."

Mom laughed. "Me too."

They ate some more.

"I'll have to get the recipe from her." Mom sipped tea. "What else did you tell Gus on Friday night?"

"You know me, Mom. I'm a private person, even though I do share some personal things at conferences and workshops. However, this is about what I felt way back then about a particular person. I would never even talk about such things to anyone outside our family. There I was, spilling my heart to Gus—only the person in question."

"He could've been the very last person you talked to on earth."

"That's why."

"Some things you just talk to God about, not to people."

"It's Gus's fault that I find him easy to talk to. He's not judgmental like a lot of other guys. Or maybe he judged me quietly."

"If you don't know him well enough, it's better to hold back your opinion and not speculate about his personality."

"You're right, Mom."

"Do you want Dad to speak with Gus about confidentiality?"

"I can talk to him myself." Tally picked up her

phone, which she had placed on the coffee table next to the plate of cookies.

She didn't remember putting down the phone, but there it was.

The phone had scratches all over it. The waterproof casing had survived the firefighters' hoses that Friday night. Tally might get a new phone later, but since it still worked, she wasn't worried about it.

She was glad that Gus also had his phone back. They had been texting each other all weekend whenever they were in their own bedrooms.

"I'm going to text him now to meet me on the porch," Tally said.

"It's hot out there. Meet here." Mom patted the cushion on the sofa she was sitting on. "I'll leave you two alone. While you do that, I'm going to call Marsha and ask about her cookie recipe. Then we'll do dinner. How does that sound?"

"Good."

Mom was about to stand up, when she seemed to realize something. "If your dad was home, he'd say we need to go to the Lord in prayer. We just talked about it and forgot to pray to God about it, you know?"

"We did. Sorry I forgot."

"I did too. So let's pray." Mom motioned for Tally to come over and sit next to her on the sofa.

Tally did, and they held hands as they prayed for God's wisdom to handle the aftermath of what could have potentially been a tragedy for two families. As it was, Silas had no family, which had been why the church had taken him in.

After Mom prayed, she said, "Wait here."

She returned from the kitchen counter with a small stack of cards and a pen in her hands. "I have four thank-you notes that you and Gus need to sign. One is to the police, two to the firefighters, and one last one to the women at church who cooked us meals for this entire week."

"Two for the firefighters?"

Mom nodded. "Yes. They sent a search-and-rescue team into the building while it was on fire to find you, while another team put out the blaze that Silas started."

"Oh." Tally took the pen and cards from Mom. She placed them on the coffee table before texting Gus upstairs. Upstairs, because after Malachi had left that Sunday, Dad told Gus he didn't have to stay in the basement all by himself.

Tally: Are you in your room?

Gus: No. I'm in your dad's library.

Tally: We need to talk.

Gus: Name the time and place.

Tally: Back porch. Any time.

Gus: How about now?

Tally: Okay. Give me five minutes.

Five minutes should be enough for her to wash the dried tears from her face. She did not feel like putting on makeup today. She was at home anyway, and her parents didn't care if she had makeup on.

Gus was on the porch reading a book when Tally opened the sliding glass door. A gush of hot air assaulted her body, and she realized she hadn't put on any lotion or sunscreen on her face.

Oh well.

He stared at her.

"I have four cards that Mom wants us to sign to thank everyone for helping us." Tally handed the cards to Gus. "Here's a pen. I haven't signed them yet."

Gus put down the book on the side table that separated his rattan chair from where Tally chose to sit down. He put the cards on top of the book.

"Are you all right?" Tally asked.

"Just carrying on with my life."

"Same."

"Does the counseling with your dad help you?"

"Yes, tremendously. Dad's good with grief counseling also, and I'm still not over Sheldon's death last week, and now Joey is dead. Thing is, I didn't know these two people very well, so the impact is not as severe, although I am sorry for their mothers."

Gus nodded.

"Anyway, Dad said we'll do a few more sessions. He had to run to a meeting with Pastor Kim. However, Mom's at home, so I talked to her."

"It's a strange feeling," Gus said. "I've never been imprisoned or held hostage in my life."

"Neither have I. If you need someone to talk to..."

Gus looked at her.

"You can talk to me, if Byron doesn't have time." Tally felt bold enough to say it.

"Thank you. I've already chatted with Byron this morning, and we'll talk again soon. I might see Byron after my meeting with Pastor Fizz tomorrow since they're both at church."

"Is he back at work? How's the flu they all had?"

"They got over it. I think in a few days I might move over to their house, since they were supposed to host me on this trip anyway."

"You're leaving us?" Tally asked.

"Not leaving you. Just staying over at Byron's house instead of here. Then Byron and I can talk more. I'll still help you at the Village, so we'll see each other."

Tally nodded. She felt a strange feeling of being abandoned. Perhaps it was because they were both survivors.

Then again, she had God.

"I'm doing this so that you can have some privacy," Gus explained.

"Oh?"

"I was coming downstairs earlier and heard you cry. Are you okay?"

"You heard me talk?"

"No, I didn't hear you say anything. You were already crying. I turned around and went back upstairs. Your dad had told me I could read in his library, so I went there instead."

Tally decided to believe him.

"My parents are leaving for Savannah on Thursday, so we'll be gone all weekend until Monday," Tally said. "If you decide to stay here, you'll have the whole house to yourself for four days."

"You're going with them." Gus seemed to be thinking about something. "I'm assuming you're driving the RV."

"Yep, I always do, ninety-nine percent of the time. If I can't do it—like I'm out of town at a conference–I'll pay Levi to drive them. This time I have two weeks off, although my sick leave will turn into a ministry leave in Savannah. Both are paid leaves, so those are just labels."

"Don't you think you should rest after having gone through a traumatic experience?" Gus asked.

"Mom said the same thing, but I think I need the distraction."

"I need a distraction too."

"Savannah will be a change of scenery on the coast." Tally wasn't sure why she invited him without asking her parents. They might not want him to be there with them.

"I want to go," Gus said. "How far is Savannah?"

"About five hours of driving."

"I can drive."

"I want to drive this time."

"Let's take turns. We can keep each other company. Survivors, remember?"

"I suppose we can. I need to check with my parents to see if it's okay for you to come with us. I forgot to ask, you know?"

"He's welcome to go with us!" Mom shouted through the walls, it seemed.

"I thought I closed the screen door," Tally said.

"The window is open!" came the reply from inside the house.

Tally chuckled, and so did Gus.

"Do you like my mom? She's a hoot." Tally laughed.

"She cooks very well."

"That too." Tally smiled. "So now you've been invited to Savannah. Thank you for offering to drive. I rarely turn down volunteers."

"It might be fun to get out of town. I've had enough drama in Atlanta."

Tally turned pensive. "How much do you remember about Friday? Or are you blocking it out of your mind?"

"Distractions are welcome, but I remember a lot of things about Friday."

Uh-oh.

"About what I said..." Tally swallowed.

"Which part of our conversation in prison? You said many things."

"I thought that was my last day, but God sent rescuers," Tally said. "If I'd known we would get out, I wouldn't have said all that I did to you."

"Like what?"

"About being interested—somewhat—in you four years ago."

"I like honesty."

"That was a piece of confidential information between us."

"Okay."

"So I need you to sign a nondisclosure agreement," Tally said.

Gus laughed. "You're serious?"

"That will keep my reputation intact."

"You mean the next time you see Malachi, you don't want him to think that you were actually thinking of someone else—a single man who stayed in the same house with you for a few days."

Tally's jaw dropped. "No, you got it wrong. Why did you mention Malachi?"

"Because I saw you in Sunday school and at church last weekend. Was he your childhood crush?"

"No, no." Tally didn't want to talk about Malachi. "Look, I want you to promise me you won't tell anybody else all the things we talked about on Friday at the warehouse."

"All right." Gus lifted up Tally's palm and wrote on it with his finger. "There. I signed your NDC."

He signed my nondisclosure clause with his finger?

"What's that? Invisible ink?" Tally laughed.

"Feel better now? It's good to laugh." Gus grinned.

"Why do you make me feel at ease, Mr. Moss? Like I could tell you everything. Next time we'd better not be in trouble together."

"Or you'll reveal to me your deepest secrets?"

"Keep dreaming, hunk."

CHAPTER THIRTEEN

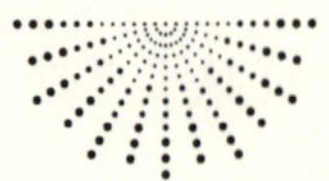

Gus offered to fly the Fitzpatricks to Savannah to save Tally from having to drive at all, but Pastor Fizz said they'd have to rent a place to stay for a week, and it would cost too much. Gus offered to pay for lodging as well but was told to give that money to the church instead.

Gus didn't want to argue that he could do both. He just checked his accounts via a secure channel on his laptop in the guest bedroom to confirm it.

Sometimes he felt that he had lived too frugally and saved too much. What would he do with all the money and investment income he'd earned above and beyond his landscaping business profits?

The Lord's counsel to the rich ruler in Luke 18:18–23 came to his mind, and he wondered whether he'd been a good steward of all that God had blessed him with. He had heard Pastor Dixon at his church preach Luke 18:22 at least once.

> *You still lack one thing. Sell all that you have and distribute to the poor, and you will have treasure in heaven; and come, follow Me.*

Gus was sure that the Bible wasn't saying he should live in abject poverty but that he should consider being significantly more charitable with the stock windfall. There was plenty where that came from because God had continually blessed him in his investments.

Gus knew that he had an aptitude for finance and accounting and anything related to investments and money management. He wasn't sure how he acquired the knack, but it was a gift from God, for sure.

Then what am I doing in landscaping?

He knew the answer, and it always came to him whenever he dealt with introspection. He wasn't in finance anymore because he was running away from the fire, so to speak. The work was too hard, and the people were impossible to deal with. He was tired.

Gus shut down his laptop and unplugged the power cord. He put them away in the laptop compartment of his backpack.

Then he folded his clothes from the closet and packed them into the largest compartment in his backpack. He'd brought enough clothes for five days, so every fifth day he had to do laundry.

He hadn't expected to be doing laundry at Pastor Fitzpatrick's house. He'd feel more comfortable if he was staying at Byron's house. Byron said his entire family had recovered from their flu, but since Gus was leaving town anyway, he decided to wait until after he returned to Atlanta before he moved to Byron's house. It would save a lot of packing and unpacking.

The trip to Savannah would take four days, and he hoped they had decent washers and dryers at the campground on Tybee Island some twenty minutes away from Savannah. He checked the amount of laundry detergent he'd brought with him and made a shopping list to get some more when they reached Savannah.

Tally had told him that they'd buy some groceries but would probably eat out at some twenty-four-hour diner he'd never been to before down by the river in the oldest town in Georgia. He looked forward to seeing something historical.

He put his toothbrush, toothpaste, razor, and soap into a ziplock bag and put the bag into one of the side pockets of his backpack. His sandals and hiking boots went into the bottom compartment.

There. All done.

He checked the bedroom one more time to make sure he hadn't left anything behind, before he went downstairs to help the Fitzpatricks load up the RV, which they stored at a nearby storage facility whenever the RV was not in use.

This old house didn't have a garage big enough to keep the RV out of sight, and the homeowners' association forbade any RV parking within the property line except for loading and unloading.

Tally and her dad had gone to pick up the RV that morning, and they should've been back. Earlier, at breakfast, Gus had made his airplane proposal. After the Fitzpatricks rejected it, they'd made sure he didn't feel bad. Riona had made him extra pancakes, and Tally had given him a hug.

Yes, that's right.

Tally had given him a hug. Her hair smelled like clean shampoo, and her face was smooth and clear. No makeup again.

Gus wasn't sure when their relationship had

turned—or if it had at all—and he'd hate to factor Silas into the equation. However, if Gus and Tally hadn't been locked in the storage room together, they wouldn't have shared their thoughts, thus breaking the ice and moving their relationship from platonic friends to...

To what?

At the foot of the stairs, a train of luggage and shopping bags lined up all the way to the front door. Riona was dishing out instructions to her husband. Tally was probably outside, loading up the Winnebago.

Tally came in just as Gus offered to help Riona carry stuff out. Tally was pushing an orange cart with four wheels. Her dad was chatting with her about something.

She smiled at Gus.

Gus tried not to read too much into it.

Well, did he expect her not to smile?

"How can I help?" Gus asked.

"We're loading everything as fast as possible," Tally said. "Dad wanted to leave by ten, and it's almost eleven o'clock."

"We never leave on time," Riona said. "It's too bad that we couldn't pick up the RV last night."

For various reasons unknown to Gus, they

hadn't done that. He didn't pry and figured it was a small matter. Even if they left at noon, they'd still be in Savannah by six o'clock at the latest. The sun would still be up in the sky.

Gus took over the cart from Tally and loaded up the suitcases. He hadn't seen the RV parked outside, so he had no idea whether all these things would fit. His job was to cart them all out to the RV and let the Fitzpatricks figure out what to do.

Tally walked with him down the makeshift ramp outside the front door and to the long driveway surrounded by well-manicured yard. From listening to mealtime conversations, Gus knew that they paid the HOA money to handle the landscaping for them. He liked the way the box hedges were pruned, but he'd have preferred to see more flowers. As it was, green was everywhere.

The Winnebago, painted red and black, wasn't very big. It was about the size of a small school bus. Somehow, four or five people would be able to sleep in that thing.

However, it wasn't a concern for Gus, as he'd called ahead to Jacobs Landing to book a place to stay for the night. They were all rented out, and Gus thought he'd have to camp outside in a tent for four nights. However, the management called back half an hour later—divine providence!—and said that someone canceled a weeklong booking for a vintage caboose. Gus snapped it up, even though he had to pay for an extra three nights he wouldn't be using.

Pastor Fizz appeared at the RV door. "Thank you for your help, Gus."

Riona came up behind Gus and patted his arm. "Yes, thank you."

She turned to Tally. "This is what you get if you marr—"

"Stop, Mom." Tally raised a palm in the air. "Don't say anything that's going to make all of us feel uncomfortable. We have to drive together for five hours."

"But you're both survivors. Live a little."

"Mom, I don't even want to ask what you mean by that." Tally rolled her eyes.

Riona chuckled as she handed a tote bag to her husband. "Fruits for the journey. We don't have to refrigerate them."

"All right." Pastor Fizz looked so serious.

Gus lifted a suitcase off the cart. It was pretty heavy.

"That's mine," Riona said. "It goes in the back."

Gus carried it into the RV.

Tally greeted him. "I'll take it. Thank you."

She rolled it down the narrow aisle, past the small kitchenette and the shower to the bedroom at the end of the RV. Beyond the folding door was a double bed, which was probably where Pastor Fizz and Riona would rest at night.

Gus felt that he was taking a peek into their RV life. It seemed personal in this small space with no permanent walls separating the bedroom from the kitchen and the living room. What living room? The dinette containing a square table and a bench seat seemed to be where the family would gather.

When he returned to the RV with the next suitcase, he saw that there was a bunk bed above the driver and passenger seats. However, the roof was right above it, so whoever slept there had to crawl into it.

"You're wondering how five people could fit in here," Tally said as she put some perishables into the small refrigerator.

Gus nodded.

She pointed to the dinette. "The bench contains a pullout bed. That's where I'll sleep because I don't want to climb a ladder."

She pointed to the bed above the driver's seat. "If you can't find a place to stay at Jacobs Landing, you'll have to climb up there."

"Or pitch a tent outside."

"You can do that too, but mosquitoes could eat you alive."

"Mosquitoes don't usually bite me," Gus said.

"They don't like me either. We must not be sweet enough." She chuckled.

"I'm forty-one. No time to be sweet."

"Thirty-five. Same." And Tally high-fived Gus.

The last rolling suitcase belonged to Tally. Gus guessed it was hers without even looking at the tag. It was Christmas red.

"This is yours." Gus checked the luggage tag attached to one of the handles. "Tallulah Fitzpatrick."

"You guessed right." Tally picked up two tote bags, one in each hand.

"What other colors do you like besides red?" Gus asked.

"All shades of red."

"Still red."

"How did you guess though?"

"You wore a lot of red when you were in Nassau four years ago," Gus said. "I remember one of those break-the-ice meetings in which we had to talk about something personal. You and a few others talked about Christmas memories, and you mentioned that it was why red is your favorite color."

"How do you remember such details?"

"Only because a contrasting color to red is green, and that's my favorite color. Outdoor green and grass green and, yes, Christmas green."

"I'm trying to recall," Tally said. "Were we the only ones who preferred Christmas colors?"

"Yes, of all the people in the room." The only reason Gus remembered this was that he'd been trained as an accountant to notice patterns. In their case, one liked Christmas red and the other liked Christmas green.

"I barely remember."

"That's because I wasn't important to you. You'd remember if I was."

"You were taken, Gus. I'm only interested in single men." Tally put the bags on the floor in front of the kitchen counter.

Then she took her suitcase from Gus. They were facing each other, with Gus about three inches taller than Tally—in her platform sandals that looked like a pair of Dr. Martens.

"And now?" Gus asked softly.

As soon as the words left his lips, he regretted asking because he shouldn't have put her in an awkward position. Five hours of driving were coming up, and this question would hang over their heads all the way to the coast.

Tally smiled, but she didn't answer his question. "How tall are you?"

"Why are you suddenly asking me that question?" Gus felt confused.

"Are you six feet tall?"

"Your guess is pretty good," Gus said. "A hundred and eighty-three centimeters back on the island."

"I'm five seven. You're five inches taller than I am." Tally lifted a foot to show him her shoes. "My sandals have an almost two-inch heel."

Gus wasn't sure what she was getting at—except perhaps to chase a rabbit trail because she didn't want to answer his question. Or maybe it mattered to her.

"Is my height a problem to you?" Gus asked.

"No, no. I was just curious."

Before he could say anything else, Gus heard someone call Tally's name.

Tally left her suitcase and walked past Gus out of the RV. "Mom, what do you need?"

"Come help your dad carry his monitor."

Gus came out of the RV and watched Tally talk with her mom.

"Why a monitor? Isn't he bringing a laptop?" Tally asked.

"He wants a big screen. Just go help him, will you, before he brings his entire home office?" Riona laughed.

Tally laughed with her, and her laughter sounded like her mother's.

She turned toward the RV. "This is why we haven't left town. By the time we get rolling, it's time for lunch."

Gus chuckled.

He wasn't sure where to put his own backpack. He wondered if things would shift while the Winnebago was on the road. He'd never driven one before. However, his driver's license allowed him to drive big trucks and school buses all over New Providence, so he was certain he could drive this RV.

After they loaded everything, Tally rolled the cart around the back of the Winnebago to an external storage area. Gus followed Pastor Fizz to see if he needed anything.

"We're only going to be gone for four days," Pastor Fizz said. "However, I want the comforts of home, you know. I'm too old to wing it or to camp out."

"Glamping!" Riona shouted in an excited voice from inside the RV.

The windows must have been open for her to have heard her husband.

"We have a full tank of gas, so now it's up to you and Tally to get us there," Pastor Fizz said. "Tally knows the directions. We've been there many times."

"I'm still going to use the GPS," Tally said from an open window. "It tells us how bad the traffic is and how much time we have to get from town to town along the way. Plus we might want to stop for lunch."

"We can eat lunch on the go to save time," Riona said.

Gus took out his phone and snapped a photo of Riona and Tally at the window. Tally made the victory sign, and Riona grinned broadly.

This family must love going on road trips. Gus supposed there were more opportunities for driving in America because of the size of this country. He wondered how many months it would take for him to visit all fifty states in an RV.

When they all climbed aboard the RV, Pastor Fizz went through his checklist.

Most of it was Tally this and Tally that.

"Did you lock the doors, Tally?"

"Set the thermostat and lights?"

"Did you set the alarm, Dad?" Tally turned the

tables on her parents. "Bring your toothbrush? Extra socks? Flip-flops? Bathing suits?"

After they went through everything, it was closer to noon than to eleven o'clock.

"Now it's time for lunch," Pastor Fizz declared. "Where shall we go eat?"

CHAPTER FOURTEEN

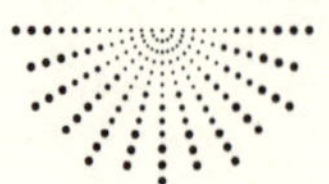

After lunch Tally drove the Winnebago to Macon. They encountered the usual traffic going out of Atlanta on Interstate 85 where it merged with Interstate 75. Thankfully, they were driving between the morning and afternoon rush hours.

However, there were many vehicles and trucks going south this afternoon—as there were on the other side of the highway going north.

"You get used to this traffic, don't you?" Gus asked from the passenger seat.

Behind them, all was quiet, as Mom and Dad had decided to take a nap. Tally couldn't stop them from turning the Winnebago into some sort of sleeper bus. She would rather they sit on the bench and put on their safety belts, but they had eaten big lunches, both of them, and must now take a nap.

"I-75 is coming up. The split will help with traffic." Tally adjusted the air conditioner.

Then she pulled down the driver's-side sun visor. It wasn't able to move much since it was attached to the ceiling.

"Where are your sunglasses?" Gus asked.

"I have no idea. I might have left them in my car."

Gus handed her his. "Wear mine."

Tally took a glance at the pair of sunglasses. "Cartier" was engraved on the gold temple.

Cartier?

"Looks fancy," Tally said. "I'd better not wear them."

"Don't worry about it."

Tally shook her head. "No, thanks. I don't want to break them."

"Aunt Nancy bought them for me, if you must know," Gus said. "I didn't buy them myself."

"That's even worse. I don't want to owe your aunt anything." Tally sighed. "I get my sunglasses at Target or the thrift shop, you know."

A small cloud cover floated in, helping her see better through the windshield. She glanced at the

GPS on the dashboard. "Looks like we'll be in Macon in an hour and a half."

After they drove past Interstate 285, traffic was better until they reached Stockbridge, where there was a wreck ahead of them on the highway outside the city. The GPS told Tally the delay would add twenty-five minutes to their drive.

"Sit back, relax, and enjoy the ride," Tally said.

"Does anyone sit here with you when you drive your parents around?" Gus asked.

"Sometimes my parents take turns. Most of the time I'm here by myself. I don't mind the quiet, really. I talk to God and think about things." Tally glanced at Gus. Oh, he looked good in those sunglasses. "I didn't mean that I don't want to talk with you. I'm just saying that I'm okay with driving quietly, but I'm also fine with talking."

"I didn't misunderstand you," Gus said. "When I drive the school bus for Chapel by the Sea summer camps, I don't always want to talk to people. Kids in buses can be noisy, but I rarely play music. What about you? Do you listen to music when you drive?"

"I do every now and then. Maybe light pop or classical or hymns. I rarely listen to talk radio because it can be distracting to me. Music is in the background, pretty much, so I can focus on the road."

"Makes sense."

They were quiet for a while. Tally wasn't sure what to say to Gus. Driving the RV on road trips was always stressful for her, so the road was all she could focus on, and she didn't have it in her at this time to come up with topics of conversation. All she wanted was to get her passengers safely to Jacobs Landing on Tybee Island, and then that was the end of her job for the weekend.

Once they got there, Riverside Chapel would provide them with a car to drive around town. Dad said that it was Pastor Diego Flores's car, free for them to use while the pastor traveled out of the country with his family on a two-week vacation in Italy. Someone else was supposed to fill in for Pastor Flores, but his mother had passed away, and he had to leave for Tennessee to make the funeral arrangements.

So they called in the backup pastor: Dad.

Tally needn't have worried about driving long distance with her parents—although she did, every single time—because they always prayed before they left on a road trip, and today was no exception.

"Why did your parents name you Tallulah?" Gus asked.

"You really want to know?"

"Yes."

"My parents have Irish roots, as you can tell from our last name," Tally said. "They'll tell you that they named me after Mom's grandmother, Tallula Kelly—no 'h' at the end of her first name—whom I've never met. She lived in Ireland somewhere."

"However..."

"You knew that was coming." Tally laughed. "Truth is, when my parents were engaged, they went on an October hiking trip to Tallulah Falls in North Georgia and decided that if they ever had a daughter..."

"So they named you after a waterfall."

"Doesn't it look that way?" Tally laughed. "They had a June wedding the following summer. They've been married for forty-seven years."

"Wow. How old were they when they married?"

"Mom was twenty and Dad was twenty-three."

"So young."

"Yeah. They like to tell people that they had a twelve-year honeymoon because it took them that long to have a child. Fortunately or unfortunately, they didn't forget to name their first child Tallulah."

"Twelve years, huh? Nice long time for them to get to know each other after the wedding."

"When Mom had me, she was three years younger than I am now, and by the time she was my age, she already had three kids. I don't even have a boyfriend." Tally hoped that Gus wouldn't ask about her past history.

Yes, she had dated in college. A seminary student.

No, he wasn't the one.

Yes, she'd had a boyfriend when she first started working at Midtown Chapel. He was an intern who'd left to take a position in a church on the other side of the country. And she hadn't seen him since.

No, she wasn't about to tell Gus all that.

And neither was she going to tell him about her next crush that never was.

Or about her ill-fated wedding in Hawaii that had almost happened.

She had already told him enough on Friday when they'd been stuck together in a crisis.

She could see them now, all tied up. She could see Joey's body on the floor. Silas's gun in her face. The warehouse on fire.

She blinked.

Why was she feeling scared now?

"Tally," Gus called her name.

She didn't answer.

"Tally?" he asked again.

"What?"

"Are you all right?"

"I suddenly thought of what happened on Friday." Tally kept her eyes on the road.

Gus sat up. "At the next exit, pull over."

"We just left Atlanta. We're not even in Macon yet."

"Trust me. Stop at the next gas station. It will be fine."

"Why?"

"I need to go to the restroom." He sounded genuine.

"Didn't you just go at lunch back there at the barbecue place?" Tally asked.

"I have to go again."

"For real?"

Gus nodded. "Yes, for real."

He wasn't lying. He had to go, but then Tally felt that he had used that as an excuse, because after she returned from the convenience store with four of bottles of cold Gatorade, she found Gus at the wheel.

"Gus, I'm driving to Macon." Tally glared at him.

Dad walked up to them. He'd been walking

around the RV, it seemed. "If he wants to drive, let him. You'll have plenty of driving to do once we get to Savannah."

Tally shrugged.

She had a feeling that Dad and Gus had conspired somehow.

"Where's Mom?" Tally asked.

"Still sleeping."

"Is she breathing?" Tally didn't know why she asked.

Gus had no reaction to her question. He simply looked at her with the kindest eyes she had ever seen in a man.

"Yes, she is. Don't worry about her." Dad's voice was calm. He took the shopping bag from Tally. "I'll keep her Gatorade in the fridge until she wakes up. Let's get back on the road."

Or we'll never get there.

Dad didn't say his usual whole sentence. Normally, if they dillydallied on the road, Dad would say, "Let's get back on the road or we'll never get there."

This time he left off the second half of the statement. Why?

Tally climbed into the passenger side and fastened her seat belt. She didn't say anything to Gus. She felt that she had been tricked somehow.

"I don't like to be tricked," she said as Gus pulled the RV out of the parking lot of the gas station.

"Let me explain."

"No."

"If you want to know the truth, let me explain."

"The complete, honest, real truth?" Tally asked. "I hate it when people dissimulate the truth beneath a story they make up."

"I hear you."

"Do you know why there are very few people I consider to be my real friends?"

"Because they think they can lie to you and it wouldn't matter." Gus's voice was soft.

"Right."

"They don't respect you and the importance you place on truth."

"Exactly."

"And a lot of these people are Christians."

"Precisely."

"I want to always be honest with you," Gus said. "In matters big or small. I don't want to have secrets between us."

"Are we close enough to not keep secrets from each other?" Tally asked. "We're only friends, so if you have secrets you can't tell me, that's one thing, but don't lie about it to me, especially to my face."

"I've made you angry."

"No. I'm being honest with you. Now tell me what you wanted to say."

Gus cleared his throat.

They were back on the highway now, and Tally wondered if this was a bad time to start an argument. However, she had just been yanked out of her driving duty, and she wanted to know if it was an honest action on Gus's part or if he had conspired with Dad because they thought she had PTSD and shouldn't be behind the wheel.

Dad was a counselor and had seen everything under the sun.

What was it that Dad saw that she wasn't seeing about herself? Even if she lost a bit of her trust for Gus, she still could trust Dad, based on her lifetime of seeing his good track record.

"When you told me that you were having flashbacks of Friday, I was worried that it would affect your driving and we'd get into a traffic accident."

"And kill us all?" Tally asked.

"No, no, not like that." Gus eased into traffic going southbound on Interstate 75. "Just so happened that I had drunk too much tea at the barbecue place, so I had to go to the restroom anyway. Your dad and I were talking, and I said that my instinct told me I should drive. It's only a few hours to Savannah. Let you rest. If you feel emotional about Friday, you can sit in the passenger seat and mull over it, and you won't be stressed out at the wheel."

"I was stressed driving through downtown traffic, but that was over."

"Maybe that stress lingered and triggered your flashbacks."

"Don't know."

"I don't know either," Gus said. "However, on the road, our number one concern is always safety."

"Right.'

"Having driven many passengers—including schoolchildren—in Nassau, I think I can handle stressful situations at the wheel, so I wanted to drive to free you up to relax and take it easy."

Tally wasn't sure how to respond.

"I want to be clear that I'm doing this because I care. If your dad was at the wheel and I felt like he was under stress, I would offer to drive in his place. So it's not just you."

Tally thought he was trying to say that it had nothing to do with gender.

"I wish someone would do that for me too," Gus continued. "If I should take a break from driving due to the conditions at hand, then I hope that someone would say, 'Hey, let me drive, since it's a long road.' And I'll gladly let them drive."

"What conditions at hand?"

"Tomorrow marks a week since our adventure in the wonderland."

"Don't you think about it?" Tally asked.

"Not all the time. I am not thinking about it right now, especially with my emotions. I'm thinking about it from an objective point of view. Maybe I can do that because I'm not local. I come from another country and am only visiting. I am not emotionally attached to anyone in Atlanta—except maybe... Never mind. The point is that I'm not from here, and I don't know people."

He wouldn't say their names. Tally decided to do it for him. "Silas and Joey."

"Et al. I met Levi recently. I met your parents last year. I hope never to see the police or firefighters again for the rest of my vacation. Midtown is not my home church. The Village is not my project. You can say that I'm basically a passerby."

"All that to say that Friday's events did not affect you as much as they affected me."

"I'm not saying that I'm shielded, but I'm saying that God is invincible." Gus stayed in the same lane and let the other vehicles speed past the RV. "Romans 8:37 comes to mind. 'Yet in all these things we are more than conquerors through Him who loved us.' I don't have Romans 8:38–39 memorized, so if you have, could you recite it? I find it encouraging to read God's Word aloud."

"I know the verse, but I can't recite it word for word. Let me read it." Tally swiped her phone and searched for the verse in her Bible app. She'd already had it bookmarked. She read it aloud.

> *For I am persuaded that neither death nor life, nor angels nor principalities nor powers, nor things present nor things to come, nor height nor depth, nor any other created thing, shall be able to separate us from the love of God which is in Christ Jesus our Lord.*

"What does that say to you, Gus?"

"It says that no matter what happens to me, I won't ever be separated from the love of God," Gus replied. "That is to say, the events of Friday night cannot affect my relationship with God."

"I agree. Maybe I'll get emotional, but it doesn't change God's love for me. God is still God."

"If I keep my eyes on Jesus in heaven, then I can better handle the mess on earth."

"That's a good way to put it." Tally highlighted the three verses in her Bible app. "Romans 8 is also where the other famous verse came from. Romans 8:28, remember?"

Gus nodded. "God does work out everything for our good."

"Including Friday." Tally looked up to see signs saying that they were almost near Macon.

"Yes, including the tragedies on both Fridays." Gus kept in the same lane he'd been in for a while.

Tally thought that Gus was a good driver because he drove the RV steadily. He made no sudden moves, didn't change lanes here and there.

In a way, the way he drove was like his personality, she had come to understand.

"You're a very steady man," Tally said.

"What do you mean?"

"*Unshakable* is the word that comes to mind. It's like the world around you can explode, and yet there you are, depending on God wholeheartedly."

"You get that by watching me drive?" Gus chuckled.

"Not only now, but on Friday you were calm in the storeroom and you talked Silas out of messing with me. I was slightly afraid when he brandished the handgun at me, but I knew that he wouldn't hurt me."

"You assumed he wouldn't hurt you. Anything could have gone wrong. Since you perceived you were not in a huge danger, you didn't see Silas as a threat."

"I don't know if he saw you as a threat to him because we went to the warehouse together."

"We will never know."

"It's also likely we might never know who killed Sheldon," Tally said.

"If Silas was the one who killed Sheldon. If the two cases are not connected, then you have a major security problem at the warehouse."

"The police are still investigating, so we'll wait for the results."

"We can pray while we wait. Romans 8:28, after all, also applies to that situation."

Tally scrolled up to Romans 8:28 in her Bible app. "Romans 8:26–27 are also good verses, as well as Romans 8:29–30."

"I forget what the first set of verses are."

"I'll read it to you." Tally read it aloud as clearly as she could, with the air conditioner on and the RV engine whirring.

> *Likewise the Spirit also helps in our weaknesses. For we do not know what we should pray for as we ought, but the Spirit Himself makes intercession for us with groanings which cannot be uttered. Now He who searches the hearts knows what the*

mind of the Spirit is, because He makes intercession for the saints according to the will of God.

"I'm always thankful to God that when I cannot pray, when I have no words, the Holy Spirit of God prays on my behalf," Tally said.

"When my parents died, I was in that state," Gus said. "I was already a teenager, but it was a double funeral. A lot of grief. My faith grew tremendously that year."

"I bet. I like the fact that the Holy Spirit prays for us 'according to the will of God.' His prayers are perfect."

"He prays for us when we are weak," Gus said. "I know the next set of verses. Do you want me to recite it?"

"Go ahead, and I'll follow along in my Bible."

"The translation I memorized it in might be different than what you're reading."

"That's all right. Go ahead."

Gus did, and Tally followed along in her Bible app.

And we know that all things work together for good to those who love God, to those who are the called according to His purpose. For whom He foreknew, He also predestined to be conformed to the image of His Son, that He might be the first-born among many brethren. Moreover whom He predestined, these He also called; whom He called, these He also justified; and whom He justified, these He also glorified.

"I should memorize that too," Tally said. "I used to memorize a lot of Scripture verses, but these days I feel that I could look them up on my phone."

"Pastor Dixon said that we should remember God's Word, like it says in Psalm 119:11. 'Your word I have hidden in my heart, that I might not sin against You.' Also, memorizing verses helps our overall memory."

"I enjoy our discussions about God's Word," Tally said. "Whenever Mom and Dad are free, we read the Bible together. We used to have a weekly family Bible study when my sisters and I lived at home. Now Adalia and I have our own houses, and Colette has moved to Lakeside. We rarely get together for Bible studies these days."

"I want to say that's too bad, but I understand. It's not easy to have Bible studies with my friends either, so I attend the ones at church." Gus had one hand on the steering wheel and the other elbow on the door.

"Sorry you're missing your Bible studies at church. Byron teaches one at Midtown, so you might consider joining him for the summer."

Gus nodded. "I plan to, as soon as we get back to town."

"This has been some vacation for you, hasn't it?"

"I'm here for the adventure."

"Plenty of it, no doubt. You might never want to return to Atlanta again." Tally laughed. "I hope this doesn't give you a poor impression of the city. If you read about violence in the news, for example."

"I understand. Sometimes the statistics are clumped together. If the results were more granular, then you can get a better study of each city's state of violence."

"In the case of Friday afternoon, we can see that it had an explanation. A supposedly deranged man held a woman captive because he wanted to propose to her."

"At gunpoint."

Tally didn't want to dwell on that. "Her colleague unwittingly got caught in the net and ended up being imprisoned together with the woman."

"God freed us, and we live happily ever after."

Did Gus... What was he saying?

CHAPTER FIFTEEN

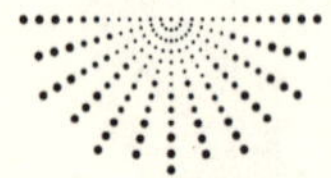

Gus opened his eyes at five o'clock and listened in the dark while he remained under the comforter in the vintage caboose tiny home. The blanket came up to his neck, and he felt a cool breeze even though the air conditioner had shut off.

He reached over the mattress to the small side table and groped for his phone. The screen light was bright enough for him to find the switch on the table lamp. He turned it on.

The room filled with a soft glow.

Then he realized how small the space was. Really tiny. Surrounded by wood panels, he felt like he was inside a coffin. Well, a gigantic coffin—

with a queen bed, dinette, kitchenette, and a shower. No room for a bathtub.

He pushed back his blanket and sat up on the bed as he checked his phone. His weather app would show him the current temperature of the location he was in, something he always checked as a landscaper, just in case.

"Almost seventeen degrees in Celsius." Gus converted it to Fahrenheit, just in case he had to talk about the weather with Tally later. "Sixty-two degrees."

He had no idea why America still used the old units of measurement, when most of the world used the metric system. And he had no idea why that thought popped into his head at this early hour.

"Looks like it's going to be cloudy this morning," he said aloud to no one.

He had lived alone for so long that he'd been talking to himself awhile now. He supposed that if he had a pet, he could chat with the pet.

He felt groggy, like maybe he hadn't gotten enough sleep.

Maybe he should go back to bed. However, he couldn't because he didn't want to oversleep. He'd promised Tally that he'd go walk on the beach with her at sunrise. She had told him that sunrise would be at six thirty, and it wasn't supposed to rain until the afternoon.

He could sleep another half an hour and wake up at five thirty, but he wanted to read his Bible and shower before he met Tally outside for their morning walk to the beach. Tally had mentioned that if Dad would let her use Pastor Flores's car, they could get to the beach in five minutes.

After Gus read the next chapter in Leviticus, he wondered how long it would take for him to reread the Bible through from Genesis to Revelation. He had started this round back in January, but for some reason he hadn't read a full chapter at each sitting.

He underlined Leviticus 20:7, and prayed about committing the verse to memory.

Consecrate yourselves therefore, and be holy, for I am the Lord your God.

Back at home, Pastor Dixon preferred to preach out of the old King James Bible, and in his Bible the first word would have been "sanctify," as in "sanctify yourselves." Whether "consecrate" or "sanctify," the results had to be the same: holiness.

Gus prayed about how he could sanctify

himself, when he realized God had answered his question in the next verse, Leviticus 20:8.

> *And you shall keep My statutes, and perform them: I am the Lord who sanctifies you.*

Only God could sanctify him.

"Lord, You're so amazing!" Gus nearly clapped. He closed his eyes and prayed for a deeper understanding of God's Word. "Father God, help me to obey You all the way. Thank You for sanctifying me and making me holy, as You are holy."

Gus understood that he still had a long way to grow spiritually as a Christian.

He made a note on his phone to teach Leviticus 20:7–8 the next time he had to fill in for a Sunday school teacher at church.

"How do I apply these two verses to my life today, Lord?" Gus asked aloud before he headed to the shower.

He heard it just as he turned off the showerhead and stepped out of the shower.

A distant rumble. Then a nearby crackle overhead.

Rain pelted the roof of the caboose as Gus changed into a T-shirt and a pair of jeans. It was too cold for him to wear shorts this morning.

With a towel over his head, he ambled to his phone near the bed and checked the weather forecast again. "Five percent chance of rain just happened."

He texted Tally to cancel the beach walk.

No reply.

Gus resumed drying his hair with a towel while he waited for Tally to reply. If she had no other plans, he'd go back to bed.

The knock on the door was faint at first, and Gus didn't quite hear it in the rain until it got louder.

There was no peephole on the door. Gus looked out one of the two small windows on either side of the door.

Tally.

He opened the door. There was Tally under a red umbrella and carrying an insulated lunch bag. The rain came down all around her.

There was no awning or roof in front of the door.

"Come in," Gus said, like it was no big deal. "Don't get wet."

He stepped aside, the towel still over his head. When he realized it, he tossed the towel on the coffee table in front of the sleeper sofa.

Tally handed him the lunch bag. She stepped

inside the caboose, shook the umbrella outside the door, closed it, and leaned it against the door.

She took the lunch bag from him and retrieved a stainless-steel mug out of the bag. "Oh good, I didn't spill it."

She handed it to Gus. "Hot coffee for you, with a shot of cream."

"Thank you." Gus was impressed that Tally remembered how he liked his coffee. It had been two weeks since Tally had brought him coffee in her Sunday school class at church.

Gus sipped the coffee. "Very good."

"And muffins." Tally lifted out a paper plate with four muffins on it. "Mom baked them last night."

"Last night? After dinner?"

They had arrived in Savannah at seven o'clock and had dinner at Piper's Place. There, Pastor Fizz picked up the car key from Isaac Untermeyer, the chef de cuisine, who had kept the key for Pastor Flores. His small car was parked in the back lot of the restaurant for convenience.

Dinner went on and on because Pastor Fizz liked to tell stories. Gus followed Tally's cue. She simply listened to her dad, as though it were the last time she'd hear him speak.

By the time they picked up some milk and eggs

at the grocery store and drove Pastor Flores's car and the RV to Jacobs Landing, it was almost eleven o'clock in the evening. Everyone was tired.

"While we were all sleeping, Mom baked these banana-and-walnut muffins."

"How much sleep did she get?"

"Not much. That's Mom. She gets excited on trips and can't sleep." Tally looked around. "This caboose must be no more than ten feet wide. It's bigger than some of our tiny homes at the Village."

"I read up on it," Gus said. "It's an original from 1931. It weighs twenty-five tons."

"Wow."

"They put a lot of wood paneling on the walls, but behind those are probably metal."

"That might've been rusted out?"

"I don't know."

"Otherwise why would they cover it up?"

"Good point." Gus followed Tally's gaze upward. The cupola added height to the caboose.

"Bet you get some sunlight in the day—if it isn't raining like now." Tally walked under the cupola toward the tiny kitchenette. To get there, she had to walk past Gus.

Normally, he'd feel uncomfortable being in such a small space alone with a woman, but he did not. He really didn't. Tally didn't seem concerned either.

Why?

Perhaps it was because they had been trapped together in a room a week ago. Had they become better friends as a result of that shared experience?

Gus wasn't sure if he wanted to be "better friends." He'd be lying if he didn't admit feeling a bit of attraction for Tally.

Then again, wasn't this too soon after breaking up with Veronique?

Okay, it's been one year.

"Do you want me to heat up the muffins now?" Tally placed the plate of muffins on the counter.

"Have you had any?"

"No. I rushed here to bring you hot coffee."

"Thank you. That's very thoughtful of you."

"You can always heat up cold coffee in the microwave, but it doesn't taste the same."

Gus nodded, enjoying his hot coffee. "Have you had any coffee?"

"I drank one cup in the RV, and that's all I wanted this morning."

Tally looked past him and surveyed the rest of the room. Her eyes settled on the bed.

Gus hadn't made the bed. Normally it wouldn't have mattered, but...

He put down the coffee mug on the coffee table near the towel. He then pulled the comforter to cover the entire bed, ran his hands on it to smooth it out.

Tally sighed.

"What?" Gus asked.

"The bedsheet underneath the comforter?" She pointed.

"What about it?"

"Step aside," she ordered.

Gus did as he was told.

Tally lifted up the comforter. "See, your bedsheets are all crumpled up underneath."

"You don't have to make my bed," Gus said.

"Just this one time."

Gus kept silent as he watched Tally correct his shoddy work.

"You can heat up the muffin if you want," Tally said. "Thirty seconds should do it."

"Sure." Gus washed his hands in the small kitchen sink. Then he removed the plastic wrap from the plate. "Shall I heat all four muffins?"

Tally nodded. "Two for you and two for me."

More thunder and rain.

"I texted you earlier," Gus said.

"Sorry. I forgot to charge my phone last night.

It's all out of juice." Tally straightened the comforter. "There you go."

"Thank you. Please sit before you decide to clean my kitchen and scrub the bathroom." Gus almost pointed to the sofa, but then realized maybe it wasn't a good idea for them to sit together on the sofa.

Instead, he sat down at the small dining table. It was no bigger than the size of a square folding card table, with chairs on opposite sides. That way, they didn't sit on the same side. Why would it matter? Gus didn't know.

"I was going to use Dad's phone to tell you that we have to cancel our beach walk this morning, but he doesn't have your number." The microwave bell dinged, and Tally went to get the muffins. "Dad could call Byron to get your number, but it was too early to call people, you know?"

Gus nodded.

"I was going to bring you coffee anyway, so here I am."

"Did you walk here? I didn't pay attention outside." Gus drank more coffee.

"I walked. You're five yurts away from the Winnebago." Tally put the muffin on the dining table, along with folded paper towel she found near the sink.

When Tally sat down, her knees bumped against Gus's. "Sorry."

"No worries."

Both of them dragged their chairs back.

Outside, the rain continued.

"What time is it?" Tally asked, looking around. "There's not a single clock in this place."

Gus got up to find his phone. "Six thirty."

"We have an hour before Dad cooks eggs and bacon for breakfast. What they bought at the grocery store last night." Tally placed a muffin on her folded paper towel.

"Oh? I thought *this* was breakfast." Gus sat down with his phone.

"Just a little muffin, Gus." Tally grinned. "All carbs and no protein."

"What about the walnuts you said your mom put in?" Gus waited to see if Tally would say grace before she ate the muffin.

"Too little to count." Tally held the muffin in her hand. "Would you like to say a blessing before we eat this muffin?"

Gus chuckled and prayed for them. He tasted the muffin. "Wow."

"Too sweet?" Tally asked. "Mom put raw honey in it."

"No, it's perfect."

"I know, right? Mom is the best baker I know." Tally savored the muffin. "She dreams of opening a bakery someday. I told her she'd better do it sooner than later. She's going to hit the big seven-oh in three years."

"Isn't seventy the new sixty?" Gus asked.

"Tell my mom that and she will adopt you." Tally laughed. "And what are we, the new twenties?"

Gus shrugged. "Sometimes I feel older than in my forties. Landscaping under the Caribbean sun is no joke. You get used to it, but it does a number on your skin."

"I hear you. When I go to the Village without sunscreen, I can feel the effects of the UV rays."

"Wear a hat?"

"I should. I keep losing my hats."

"And sunglasses?" Gus asked. "Have you found yours?"

Tally shook her head. "I'll look when we get home to Atlanta."

"Another five hours of driving on Monday."

"Right. I think at some point in time, my parents won't want to do this anymore."

"You mean go on road trips?"

"Yeah. I've been trying to talk them into taking it easy and not working as hard as they used to. They need to retire and enjoy life, you know?"

"Doesn't your dad get paid when he travels to each church?"

Tally nodded. "Yet his income mainly comes from Midtown Chapel. He's been the counseling pastor there for the last twenty years."

"How will he support himself after he retires?"

"My sisters and I will continue working, and we will pay for their retirement fund."

Her filial piety came as a surprise to Gus. He didn't know what to say.

"We career people have no idea what it means to have time on our hands," Tally said.

"Do you like your job?" Gus asked.

"I love my job. I'm tired all the time, but that's because I lack exercise and I've gained... uh...weight."

"I always gain weight on vacation."

"What do you do for exercise?"

"I work in the yard at the school and church, so that's the bulk of it, but I also jog and run sometimes. I lift weights in the gym."

"I was hoping to get back to walking more," Tally said. "It's May, and I'm still working off the cookies I ate at Christmas. If you've never had Mom's cookies..."

"Better than these muffins?"

Tally nodded. "And the calories stick to you forever."

They laughed.

"What about after work?" Gus asked. "Any hobbies?"

"I'm always short on time, but I'd love to travel more. When I speak at conferences, I go a day early to check out the town. They're mostly in Georgia, but there are so many little towns I haven't visited in this lovely state."

"You could go farther if you flew," Gus said.

"Yes, but I have to balance the two things I want to do. I don't want to spend all my time at conferences and no time at the Village. My ministry is to women, and the Village offers a more direct and personal interaction."

"Makes sense. What about vacation time for travel?"

"I'm using it all up to drive my parents around."

Gus reached for the second muffin. "If my parents were alive, I'd spend time with them every day if I could."

"You have Aunt Nancy, yes?"

"Have I mentioned Aunt Nancy to you?" Gus asked.

"In passing, yes. However, I know that she's

Byron's mom and that she raised you, and I've actually met her at the women's conference four years ago."

"Interesting. I have lunch with her two or three times a week, although lately I've avoided her because she wants me to work in her company."

"Oh?"

Gus sighed. "Byron has a family in Atlanta now and won't ever go back to Nassau except to visit. His brother, Donovan, is busy with Moss Resorts in the Caribbean. At first he was also in charge of Moss Cruises, but handed that back to Aunt Nancy because he had other things he wants to do, like partying."

Gus wondered if he had spoken too much.

"So the only person she can turn to now is you." Tally wadded up the paper towel. She did not eat her second muffin. "You can have that."

"Don't you want it?"

"I'm waiting for bacon and eggs at seven thirty." Tally looked at Gus. "Tell me more about your dilemma."

"Confidentially, okay?"

"Yes. I'll pray for you and with you."

"Aunt Nancy wants to semiretire. She's in her seventies."

"What I said about my parents. They've worked hard. It's time to take it easy."

"Unfortunately, she has no one to trust."

"Her VPs?"

"She only trusts her family."

"Ah. She trusts you, but you'd rather be gardening."

"I've been into gardening for a very long time, ever since I was a teenager helping out in the garden at Moss Cay." He wasn't sure he wanted to get into all that.

"Cay? Isn't that a little island of some sort?"

"It doesn't have to be little, but this one is. Byron's grandfather left it to him, but he shares it with everyone."

"How pretty is the garden?" Tally asked.

Gus swiped his phone and showed her a few pictures of Moss Cay. "The garden surrounds the main house."

"Looks pretty. The flowers are very bright."

"If you go to the Bahamas, let me know, and I'll show you around the garden."

"Deal. So you'd rather be outdoors than inside a corporate office."

"I burned out in a corporate job." There, he'd said it. Gus hadn't talked about this to many people.

In fact, only Aunt Nancy and Byron really knew how he'd crashed and burned as an accountant.

"Doesn't mean you can't do office work," Tally said. "How did you burn out? Why did you burn out? It could be many reasons. You didn't get an MBA in finance for nothing."

Gus didn't know how to respond to that.

"Are you happy doing landscaping?" Tally asked.

"Yes, but I also miss... I shouldn't."

"Miss what? Miss working in finance?"

Gus nodded. He drank the last of the coffee in the travel mug. "I suppose I went to university because I wanted to get a good job, but when I graduated, I didn't want to work for Aunt Nancy."

"You don't like her?"

"I don't want to mess with our relationship."

"I hear you. Where did you work after college?"

"At an accounting firm in Miami."

"Miami?" Tally's eyes widened. "No wonder."

"No wonder what?"

"I don't know how to explain it, but Byron had a British accent when he moved to Atlanta. Five years later his accent is wearing off and he's sounding more and more American every day. Maybe Tina's southern accent is rubbing off on him."

Gus wasn't sure where Tally was going with that. "Anyway, I burned out in Miami, and I went home. I didn't do anything for months. Aunt Nancy stopped pressuring me then. About nine months later I started working in landscaping at the church and school. And then they hired me, so I started a company to handle the administrative work."

"And finances."

"I've been happy ever since. I guess it's because I liked gardening to begin with. It's my hobby."

"Not all hobbies become careers, but you knew that."

Gus didn't reply.

"If I have a hobby that I cherish, I'd protect it as a hobby so that it doesn't become a full-blown job that eventually might tire me out. If it loses the 'happy hobby' label, it's no fun anymore."

I get her. "Like traveling?"

Tally nodded. "I prefer to travel for pleasure rather than work."

"Some people would love to combine both."

"If it works out for them, great. Each of us is different."

"Of course." Gus finished the last muffin. "If you could travel anywhere in the world with the idea that you might move there—or at least stay there for an extended period of time—where might you go?"

"I have to think about that for a bit." Tally went quiet. "All my work trips have been for ministry or mission. I told you I take extra days for my own mini vacation."

Gus waited.

"I suppose that the most memorable trip I've been on was the women's conference at your church in Nassau."

"When we walked by each other in the hallway. This time you're welcome to sit with me in church."

"I don't know if I can afford to take a vacation at this time."

"I'm inviting you to Nassau, all expenses paid. I'll show you around the islands to see things you might have missed."

"Don't get me wrong. I don't mean money," Tally said. "I'm talking about the cost of time. I have so much work to do at the church that I can't afford to be away from the office other than with my parents."

"Oh, I see." Gus wondered if he should ask the next question, but then he decided to go ahead. "Hypothetically, would you live in the Bahamas?"

"I can live anywhere God sends me. So yes, I

suppose I could live in the Bahamas—if I have a reason to."

For some reason, Gus liked the answer.

"Could you live in Atlanta?" Tally asked.

"If I have a reason too. A good reason."

"I was just asking in kind because you did. However, truth be told, the flight between Nassau and Atlanta is so short that you can visit your cousin whenever you want."

And you as well.

It might be a short flight between the two places, but it seemed like the longest distance between two hearts. He wondered if there was a chance that Tally might look at him differently.

She seemed at ease with him because she considered him to be a friend.

What if he wanted to be more than a friend? Would that kill their friendship?

"What time is it?" Tally reached over the table and tapped Gus's phone. The time popped up. "Almost seven fifteen. We better run, or we'll be late for breakfast with my parents."

"It's still raining, and I don't have an umbrella," Gus said.

"We'll share mine." She got up. Cleared the table. "That's Dad's travel mug, actually, so he'll want it back."

"Should I wash it?"

"No need if you want more coffee. I'll wash it later." She grabbed the lunch tote. "Ready to go?"

Gus might never get a chance if he didn't ask her now.

"Since it's just the two of us here, may I ask you a question?" Gus said.

Tally's eyes widened. "Go ahead."

"About what you said in the warehouse..." He didn't come near her.

Her answer could determine whether he stayed in this caboose all weekend by himself.

"I said so many things last Friday because I thought we were going to die," Tally said.

"You said that Silas wasn't going to kill you."

"I know, but it was fifty-fifty, right? I know one thing. I wasn't afraid. I knew God was with me, but He also sent you. With you around, I wasn't afraid."

"God is good."

"Now that we both survived, I hope you don't tell anyone about our conversation—not even Dad."

"I haven't."

"So what is it that you want to ask me about?" Tally was standing at the door, the wet umbrella in her hand.

"You said that when you were in Nassau four years ago, you considered me..."

"Arrgghh." Tally's face turned red. "I should never have told you that."

"I'm glad you did. Sorry it didn't work out then. But now..."

"Now what?"

"Well, the other day in Sunday school, I saw that you were nervous around Malachi."

"Don't bring him up, please." Her shoulders slacked.

I have to know if there's a chance for me.

"If I tell you, it will be difficult for me to face you," Tally said. "I'm embarrassed already thinking about it."

"Are you saying that what's happening between you and Malachi is a one-way street?" Gus asked.

Tally sighed. "To put it plainly, he family-zoned me the moment Dad took him under his wings as his Timothy. Dad knows that Malachi wants to settle down and raise a family. He's traveled all over the world."

Gus wondered if Tally's love for traveling started because of Malachi.

"Because I also love to travel, I thought that maybe we could be a pair... Why am I telling you all this?"

"Because I asked?"

"Look, Malachi doesn't look at me the same

way he does his ex-girlfriend who left him. If you ask me, they're meant to be together and I have no chance."

"Unrequited love?"

"I had this idea that I should marry a pastor and not take anybody else."

Gus remembered what Pastor Fizz had told him.

"It has ruined my love life because I wouldn't date in my twenties due to that ill-conceived idea."

Gus barely nodded.

"If I had sought the Lord more, I might have realized that maybe what I was looking for was not a pastor like my dad—who can replace him?—but a Christian man with a pastor's heart instead of at the word 'Reverend' in front of his name, you know?"

"I know many godly men who have a pastor's heart," Gus said.

Tally raised her free hand. "Do not introduce them to me."

"Don't worry. I won't. Why would I introduce..."

Rivals?

"Don't make it worse for me." She shook her head. "Let's just go for breakfast, shall we?"

The umbrella turned out to be too small for the both of them. They stood inside the doorframe, umbrella between them, and unable to go out in the rain.

"We need a golf umbrella." Tally laughed. "How are we going do this? One of us—or both—will get wet."

"I'll get wet. It's okay."

Tally seemed to ignore what he said, or maybe she didn't hear him. "I have an idea, but we can only do this because we're friends."

Please don't friend-zone me.

"Have you ever been in a three-legged race?" Tally asked.

"Yes."

"So if we put our arms around each other's waist, we can walk tightly under the umbrella and stay out of the rain."

Tightly?

"Is that a good idea?" Gus asked. "Won't your dad see us walking like that and wonder what we did in the caboose to cause us to be that close to each other?"

"Will he? I'll explain why to him and he'll understand. He's a logical man."

I'm logical too.

Yet right now his own logic went out the window as his feelings confused him. Was he falling in love with Tally? Why? Just because they got along every day without fighting each other, it might not spell love.

Logically, the reason they got along was due to their individual maturity, right? Both of them were older now—if forty-one was "older" and thirty-five was not far behind—with no time to waste on trivial things. Both of them would rather get to the point.

So why don't I just come right out and tell her I'm interested in her?

"Ready?" Tally asked.

"Let's go for it."

As they held each other's waist, Gus tried to keep the umbrella centered above their heads.

Her arm was warm around his waist. It gave him a feeling of belonging, something he hadn't found with Veronique.

Perhaps Veronique was never the right one for him.

Then who was?

Gus liked holding Tally's waist. She wasn't on the chubby side around her waist, and Gus liked his girlfriend to be more filled out.

What did I say?

Well, maybe he wasn't thinking straight.

In any case, Tally had a big heart. She was kind to everyone, regardless of their condition in life. She tried to help everyone, as evidenced at the Village.

That mattered to him more than all the Christmas cookies she believed she had put into her waist and hips.

"Our challenge is to go five yurts without getting rained on," Tally said.

"A new unit of measurement I've never heard of in my life." Gus laughed. He turned his face to find Tally's lips only inches away from his.

Her eyes were big and round and bold and warm. Was she as surprised as he was?

She turned away.

But she didn't let go of his waist.

And neither did he let go of hers.

CHAPTER SIXTEEN

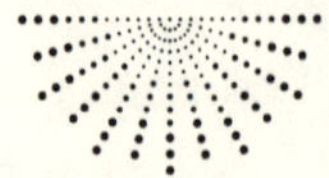

The Super Saints of Riverside Chapel banished the two "young'uns" to their own table to order from the "kid's menu." The fact that they had reserved a rare table by the window for Tally and Gus at this busy Friday lunch hour made Tally feel better about being prevented from listening to Dad tell jokes about his three daughters when they were little kids.

As she and Gus followed the server across the room to their window seats, Tally glanced back a few times to the party of twelve sitting at a long table by the wall.

"They'll be fine," Gus said. "We're only across the room."

"Why can't we sit with them?"

"Because we're underaged." Gus chuckled. "You heard Jerome and Rhonda."

"Rhoda," Tally corrected him. "Rhoda Untermeyer-Pendegrast."

"Sorry." Gus waited for Tally to pick the side of the table she wanted.

"What a nice gentleman you are," Tally said after Gus helped her with her chair.

"I don't do it for just anybody."

"That so?"

The server left them after taking two orders of mineral water—with lemon for Tally and no lemon for Gus.

Tally looked outside the window. Some tourists didn't have umbrellas, and they were soaking wet.

"When is the rain going to stop?" Her fingers flew to her mouth. "I'm sorry."

"For what?"

"I'm such a complainer today."

"You're comfortable with me. That's why you speak your mind. Am I right?" Gus picked up the menu from the table.

Tally had to think about it. She felt safe with him. Perhaps it had something to do with their Friday drama, even though that had been...

"It's only been a week," Tally suddenly said.

"A week?"

Tally nodded. "Sometimes it feels like it just happened, and sometimes my mind blocks it. Do you feel the same way?"

"I keep busy." He pointed to her menu. "I'm not trying to rush you, but you might want to order. We should eat at the same time as the Super Saints so that we'll finish at the same time as well."

"Good idea." Tally stared at the menu. She almost always ordered the same things when she was here. "What are you having?"

"Fish, I think."

"Fish? I thought you were a beef guy."

"We're grilling hamburgers and hot dogs tonight, so I don't want to be *hamburgered* out."

"Is that even a word? *Hamburger* is a noun."

"I think you can turn any noun into a verb these days."

"Oh? Give me another example."

Gus was quiet for a few seconds. "I can't think of any right now. When it pops up, I'll let you know."

Thunder crackled in the distance.

"I don't know if we'll ever make it to our beach walk this weekend." Tally felt disappointed. "It'll be a shame for us to come all the way to Savannah, and stay on Tybee Island, but not make it to the beach."

"Rain is rain."

"Yeah. Can't be helped, but I still feel like we're missing something, you know?" Tally lifted her menu up as she was reading.

Fingers appeared on top of her menu. Gus gently pressed down the menu toward the table. "The next time you go to the Bahamas, we'll walk on the beach."

Tally couldn't help smiling. "Does that mean you want to see me again?"

Gus retracted his hand, but his eyes were on hers. "Yes."

"I appreciate honesty and transparency." Tally went back to the menu and figured out what she wanted.

As if on cue, the server returned with their mineral water. "Are you ready to order?"

Tally looked at Gus. He nodded.

"I'll have your Very Berry Salad topped with grilled chicken," Tally said. "Please put the dressing on the side."

"Very good, ma'am. For you, sir?" the server asked Gus.

Tally watched Gus as he ordered salmon on couscous and wilted spinach. It sounded better than her salad.

After the server left, she regretted what she had

ordered. But she didn't say a word. Actually, there was nothing at Piper's Place that she didn't like. Her salad would come with blueberries and sliced strawberries, as well as a fruity berry dressing. Perfect for lunch. She looked forward to it.

Outside, the rain kept pouring.

Her red umbrella was in the umbrella stand by the restaurant entrance, among a bazillion other umbrellas. She'd buy a new one if it went missing—but it was the same umbrella that she and Gus had shared this morning.

Something had changed in their relationship before breakfast with her parents today. Tally wasn't sure what precisely.

Gus looked around. "This must be a popular place. The restaurant is full, and every table is occupied."

Tally pointed outside the window. "People are waiting in the rain to be seated."

"How many floors are there in this restaurant?"

"Three. They open around the clock, but they're closed on Sundays now. They used to be open on Sundays, until Piper met Jesus."

"Piper. Ah, the namesake of this establishment."

"Her grandmother named it after her."

"Knowing she'd take over?"

"I don't know the details. All I know is that it's the go-to hangout for Riverside Chapel members," Tally said. "It's a miracle we got this table. Unless you reserve days in advance, the main floor is always booked."

"Some connections then?"

Tally shrugged. looked in the direction of the Super Saints. "Rhoda over there is Chef Isaac's mom, but I know that Chef Piper is always fair, so I think there was a cancelation."

"Otherwise?"

"Otherwise we'd be sitting with the Super Saints, which is what I wanted in the first place."

"I'm sorry that you have to sit with me." Gus's voice was one of regret.

Tally's jaw dropped. She reached over the table and touched Gus's hand, then pulled away almost immediately. "Don't get me wrong. I enjoy talking with you. It's just that I'm bummed I can't be a fly on the wall over there. Dad sometimes says the ugliest jokes about my sisters and me—especially me. Everybody always laughs, but at my expense, you know?"

"In that case, it's a good thing that you're not sitting over there getting stressed out and not enjoying your lunch," Gus said.

"Oh. I hadn't thought about it that way."

"Let's have some pleasant conversation to offset whatever it is they're joking about."

Just then, peals of laughter came from the Super Saints table. Tally stared at them as people were wiping tears from their eyes. Dad was, as per usual, in the center of it all. Mom had her hand on his arm, as though telling him to stop already. He went on and on.

Tally sighed.

She looked outside the window. She couldn't see too far in the rain but could point in a certain general direction. "Over there, docked on the river, is Riverside Chapel."

Gus peered. "I can't see a thing in this rain, but I look forward to visiting the church tomorrow morning."

"Then you can tell your friends when you get home that you attended a church on a riverboat."

"It would be interesting, although I've attended church services on a cruise ship. Same thing, right?"

"I don't know, Gus. I've never been on a cruise."

"You haven't?" Gus swiped his phone. "Let me add that to the list of things to invite Tally to."

"Invite me? Like we have time?" Tally laughed.

"If you had time, would you go on a cruise?"

"If I had time, I could do a lot of things." Tally

wondered why he asked her that sort of question. "Right now ministry work will probably keep me busy for years to come."

"When was the last time you took a real vacation—not one where the church considers it a ministry?"

"Everything I do is ministry."

"Is that right?"

"Uh-huh. I told you. I tag on a day or two here and there to an event, and that's all the time I have." Tally sipped her mineral water. "If my parents move to Lakeside, and I go with them, then I'll feel like I'm living in a place where people vacation, you know? Then I think I can go on day trips here and there, and those would be real vacations."

"Day trips?"

"Right."

"Back home, we do have day cruises. You can have dinner cruises up and down the coast."

Tally nodded. "Same with the riverboats here. You can have dinner on board as they sail down the Savannah River."

"Have you been on a riverboat cruise?" Gus asked.

"No time." She smiled. "You know, the airplane is a marvelous invention for busy people like me. Fly in, fly out, get on with life."

"Have you ever relaxed?" Gus finished his mineral water and asked for more.

"Like what you're doing in town for the summer?"

Gus was about to answer her when Tally received a text from Maggie Jacobs. Tally's administrative assistant was still in Atlanta, managing the women's ministry while Tally was gone.

"Oh no." Tally drew a deep breath.

"What?" Gus looked concerned.

"Remember Jacinda Everett? Her son Sheldon was murdered in the warehouse?"

Gus nodded.

"The police have no more leads. Jacinda had a mental breakdown this morning. She's in the hospital now." And Tally couldn't be with her. "The Village needs me."

"No, Tally. The Village needs God." His voice was firm. "Paul and Apollos, remember?"

Tally sighed. "That's right."

"It's only been two weeks," Gus added. "Sometimes investigations go for a long time."

"Two weeks too long. With the warehouse burned, they couldn't find more clues there if they wanted to. If Silas was a suspect, then the suspect died with the lost evidence. What to do?" Tally mumbled. But she knew what the answer was. "We have to pray for God to handle it."

"I'm not trying to conjure up conspiracy theories, but was Silas the kind of person who would burn down a warehouse?"

"I don't know him well enough to have an opinion about that," Tally said. "However, the delivery man said that he saw Silas set himself on fire."

"He'd wanted to marry you minutes before that."

"I smelled gasoline on his clothes."

"What if someone else manipulated him into burning down the building?"

"For insurance purposes, you mean?"

"That piece of land is so close to the city of Atlanta that it must be valuable, for example."

"Wait a minute. You're suggesting that the owner of the warehouse might have something to do with the fire?"

Gus shrugged. "I'm just running scenarios in my mind. I'm sure that the detectives are on it."

Tally tilted her head. "Are you sure you're just a landscaper?"

Their lunch came, interrupting their foray into the world of conspiracy theories. After Tally said a blessing for their meal, they made small talk and didn't speak about the warehouse at all, until five hours later when the rain finally stopped—at least on Tybee Island—and the Fitzpatricks and their guest walked across the campground to the pergola, where Jacobs Landing held its Friday night community cookout.

Tally didn't want to bring up the warehouse matter again, but she ran into Sabine Wei, whose husband, Ming Wei, was a private investigator in Savannah. He usually worked with Sabine's sister, Helen Hu, the private investigator who had done some work six years ago for Byron Moss—only Gus's favorite cousin.

"I heard you were falsely imprisoned against your will," Sabine said after giving Tally a hug.

A longtime member of Riverside Chapel, Sabine had befriended Tally when Dad started to fill in for Pastor Flores at the pulpit whenever the latter went out of town.

"Yeah, last Friday. It was only for a few hours, but it felt like forever." Tally pointed to Gus standing nearby. "If not for Gus, I'd be freaked out."

"You screamed a lot before I got there." Gus grinned.

"That was because when Silas turned on the

light, I saw Joey's body on the floor." Tally turned to Sabine. "Joey was the security guard."

"Oh? Why did Joey let the suspect into the building?" Sabine asked.

"Good question."

"I saw in the news that the suspect didn't work at the warehouse. He just showed up and the security guard let him in. Why?"

Gus gave Tally a look, as if saying, "Told ya something's fishy."

Sabine's husband came walking toward them with two drinks. He gave one to his wife. He said nothing at first, but then Tally had to open her mouth.

Tally pointed to Gus. "He thinks there's something else happening beneath the surface."

Ming waved to Gus. "Hi, you must be Augustus Moss. I'm Ming Wei, Sabine's husband, and father to all her kids."

"Gus."

"Gus. Nice to meet you."

Gus shook hands with him. "You saw the police report?"

Ming didn't answer, but he asked something else instead. "What theories do you have?"

"I was only guessing," Gus said.

"But they were very good guesses." Tally felt she had to defend him, for some reason.

Tally didn't want to pry, but why would Ming look into the matter? "Did Pastor Kim ask you to see what's going on?"

"Word is going around, so one way to quell rumors is to find the truth," Ming said. "The two deaths occurred almost back to back in the same warehouse rented to the church."

"Right."

"So maybe we can talk about this during dinner," Ming suggested.

Tally nudged Gus's arm. "Looks like you're not the only one who has questions."

She turned back to Ming. "Who's paying you for the investigation, Ming?"

"I'm doing this as a favor to my sister-in-law," Ming said. "The church called her, but she's busy, and I happen to be available."

"Are you going to Atlanta to ask questions?"

Ming nodded. "I might see you at the Village."

"Jacinda Everett—Sheldon's mom—is heart-broken right now. She thinks they'll never catch her son's murderer and that he won't get justice."

"Our God is just," Ming said.

"And there will always be justice," Sabine added.

They high-fived each other.

Tally smiled, watching the husband and wife interact with each other. They had been married for a while now. Tally couldn't remember how many years, but Ming's work was sometimes dangerous, and yet Sabine hung in there.

Could I be that strong?

"Would you like some hamburgers?" Gus asked.

"Like we didn't just have lunch five hours ago," Tally said.

"Then again, it's been five hours. And we had a light lunch."

Tally nodded.

As they walked toward the grill and folding tables with condiments, Sabine nudged Tally.

"Is he..." Sabine didn't say it, but Tally knew what she was asking.

Tally didn't know what to tell her. She really didn't.

Why wasn't Tally surprised that Dad was at the grill with Thomas and Hunter?

Thomas was getting up there in age, with the deep lines on his face. His senior dog had just died, and he had been grieving. His wife, Delilah, was out of town, visiting relatives in the extended Jacobs family.

Delilah had been the owner of Jacobs Landing until she married Thomas and decided to sell the campground to her nephew, Hunter Jacobs, whose day job was as a novelist.

Tally waved to Dad.

Dad waved back with the stainless-steel spatula in his hand. At the next grill, Hunter waved to Tally as well.

Tally went up to him. Hunter had met Gus when they'd checked in late on Friday night, and no introduction was needed.

"Is Priyanka here?" Tally asked Hunter.

"She's home with the baby," Hunter said.

"How are both of them doing?"

"Great health, thankfully. Pri's dad is going to be here next week. He might stay awhile."

"Oh good. He can visit with his new grandchild." Tally didn't say more. Priyanka's father had lost his wife to cancer and now lived alone in India, retired to their beach house, surrounded by servants.

Tally had a lot in common with Priyanka because their families had three daughters each.

The last time Tally was in Savannah, she'd had lunch with Priyanka, who'd said that she hoped her father would move to the Savannah Senior Living

Resort, where Priyanka worked, so that she could keep an eye on the retiree.

"He needs a new hobby," Priyanka had said. "But he's bad at golf."

That made Tally wonder what would happen to Dad if Mom passed away. Or vice versa.

Then it dawned on her.

She glanced at Dad at the other grill. Maybe that was why Dad and Mom might move to Lakeside. If something happened to him, Colette and Adalia could take care of Mom.

What about me in Atlanta?

Everyone knew that Tally was too busy. Her schedule filled to the brim. If not for the warehouse tragedy the week before, she would have been at work all week. If not for this short trip to Savannah, she'd be working long hours every day.

"You all right?" Gus asked quietly. He handed her a plate with two buns and two hamburgers. "Can you eat both?"

"I'm famished. I think salad is ninety-nine percent water." She chuckled.

"My new friend, Ming, wants to talk to me, so we're going to chat a bit. I'll come find you later."

Tally nodded. She wasn't sure why Gus would want to find her later, but as soon as he left, she felt bereft, like she had to be with him.

No way.

I'm not falling in love, am I?

Tally took her plate of hamburgers and went to the side table to slather them with ketchup and sweet pickles.

Mom was squirting mustard on hers when Tally arrived.

"I know you don't like onions, so I'm getting yours." Mom smiled.

"I love you, Mom." Tally gave her a one-arm hug.

"What? Am I dying?" Mom asked.

She knew how to defuse the situation.

"I was just thinking."

"I can guess, but this evening I want you to focus on putting together the best hamburger you can," Mom said. "Then let's go sit in a swing and watch people."

"The swing is one of the favorite spots. It might be taken by the time we get there."

"Then we'll sit at the pergola. Watch the world go by."

"Okay. Let's do that."

Tally picked up extra napkins, and mother and daughter made their way through the crowd to the swing.

Of course it was taken.

An elderly couple sat there, saying nothing to each other.

Tally and her mom were about to head for the pergola, when their camping neighbors got off the swing. "All yours. We have somewhere to go early tomorrow morning, so we're turning in."

"That's nice of you," Tally said. "Thank you."

"Did you get enough dinner?" Mom asked the neighbors as she staked out her side of the swing.

"Yes, ma'am. And we're getting some hot dogs to go," the man said.

"Good night," his wife, or companion, said.

Mom said a blessing before they ate the hamburgers.

"I didn't eat much at lunch today," Mom said.

"I had salad."

"I was trying to keep Dad from his TMI rabbit trails, that I barely ate. The food got cold, and I didn't want to take it to go. So I wasted food today, and I'm very sorry for it."

Tally didn't say anything. Her eyes were on the campground, looking for...

Gus.

The lanterns lining the community area were not very bright. There were strings of lights on tree branches, and shadows appeared everywhere.

"Who are you looking for?" Mom asked.

"No one."

Mom smiled. "Do you remember how your dad and I met?"

Tally nodded. "At church."

"He was a visiting evangelist, traveling with his dad, when they came to our church to preach in our revival." A grinned crept up Mom's face. "I fell on top of him."

"I've heard that many times before, Mom. It was an accident."

"No, it wasn't exactly."

Tally stopped chewing. She looked at Mom. "Truth telling, Mrs. Fitzpatrick, is fundamental to the Christian life."

"I know." She expelled a breath. "It feels good to finally get it off my chest. I didn't want to say it when Astrid was alive."

"Who's Astrid?"

"The woman your dad would've married had I not fallen on him."

"And fallen for him at the same time." Tally shook her head. "For thirty years you said it was an accident."

"There was an accident though, but I didn't create it. A real one. When your dad walked into the dining hall, he said he 'accidentally' turned my way and stopped in his tracks. I was at least five or six tables away from him, but his eyes were on me."

"Are you sure he wasn't looking at other people?"

"Nope. He told me later that he saw me for the first time and he was in love."

"Mom, I don't know if I necessarily believe in love at first sight. Don't you need to get to know the person a little?"

"There's time for that, dear, but single young men were scarce at the church in my little town because all the men left for work in the big cities."

"Then don't get married."

Mom made a smacking sound with her lips. "Let me tell the story."

"Go on, while I eat." Tally started on the second hamburger.

"I tell you, your dad was so tall and good looking, that all the eligible girls in my church were going for him. They surrounded him and offered him food. He could've started a harem that evening at church suppertime."

"Mom!"

"Just kidding, of course." Mom wiped the corner of her lips with a paper napkin. "In any case, it became a contest of which girls' dishes your dad would love to taste. All I had was a tray of my banana-and-walnut muffins."

She sighed.

"What happened next? I'm still looking for the accident."

"Before I could take it to your dad, Astrid picked up *my* muffins, walked over to him, and said she made them and would he like to try some?"

"How dare she!"

"I know. Then again, the recipe wasn't mine. It was Grandma's."

"Still, in the same family. Could Astrid have made the muffins herself if she had the recipe?" Tally asked.

"That's what she told me later. She was going to learn it and somehow retroactively fix the old lie with the new truth."

"In a church, no less."

"Exactly. As though God wasn't watching. Your dad ate it and loved it. He said he'd never tasted muffins that good." Mom stared right ahead. "So I snapped."

"You snapped?"

"I stormed up to Astrid in my bell-bottom tartan-plaid jeans and my favorite frilly blouse—I was trendy in my own mind in the late seventies —and I told Astrid to her face that she was lying in the house of God about who made the muffins."

Tally could imagine Mom doing that.

"She pushed me hard, so hard that I fell backward, my tartan pants going up in the air, and I nearly landed on the green linoleum floor on my head. If that had happened, my neck could've snapped, and I would've been in bad shape."

"However..."

Mom put up her index finger in the air. "However, your dad, my hero, caught me. Only thing was, he needed more exercise because he wasn't strong enough to catch me. So I fell on top of him. In a way, he cushioned my fall. But it was in front of everybody at church."

"Why didn't you tell us this story instead of some silly 'I fell on top of your dad but it was an accident and I won't tell you why' nonsense?"

"I told you why. Astrid was still alive. She passed away three weeks ago."

"Oh. I'm sorry."

"If I had known she was sick, I would've gone to see her. Madison is only an hour's drive away from our house."

"I would've gone with you."

"It's too late now. She's dead and buried."

"Did she know the Lord?"

Mom shrugged. "We all think that if we grew up in a church, that we must know the Lord, more likely than not. That's not always true, you know? We won't know if Astrid was saved until we get to heaven. If we don't see her there, she didn't make it."

"So you keep this story for forty-seven years because you didn't want to tell a funny story at her expense."

"Right."

"Dad said he wasn't hurt. Is that true?" Tally asked.

"Are you questioning our very existence?" Mom laughed.

"Just checking the facts."

"He wasn't hurt at all. We got off the floor. He ate the rest of my muffins and asked me to marry him."

"What?" Tally choked on her hamburger.

Mom slapped her back.

"For forty-seven years, you said that Dad proposed to you at church, but you didn't say it was on the first day you met."

"Now you know." Mom looked away. "We don't want to make jokes at the expense of others."

"Dad always made people laugh at the expense of his own daughters."

"Pastors' kids have privileges."

"I don't like this kind of privilege."

Gus's laughter came to Tally in the wind. She had started to pick out his light accent from among the crowd. Now she could recognize his laugh.

What is happening to me?

She turned toward the sound of the laughter. Dad was chatting with Gus like they were old friends.

"Dad seems to get along with Gus," Tally said quietly.

"Is that a good thing, in your estimation?" Mom asked.

Tally shrugged.

"I like him too." Mom nibbled on a pickle.

"You do?"

"Uh-huh." Mom turned to Tally. "Did something happen between you and Gus?"

"Like what?"

"Like maybe love at first sight?"

"It can't possibly be that, Mom. We've known each other for four years." Unlike Mom and Dad, who fell in love at first sight some forty-seven years ago, Tally had never experienced such a thing. Even her interest in Malachi had been a slow burn. Then it had fizzled out.

"So it's way past time then?" Just like Mom to pry. "Is that what you're saying?"

Tally had no response. "I don't know what I'm saying."

"Then pray, Tally. Pray for God to show you His will."

Tally nodded. "I have, I am, and I will."

CHAPTER SEVENTEEN

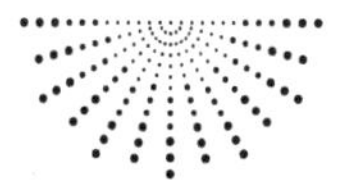

"Pray for me, Byron." Gus went straight to the point. He adjusted the phone in his hand so that the video showed his entire face. "I might have fallen in love with a friend, and I'm afraid it will affect our beautiful friendship."

"In what way?" his cousin asked on the other end of FaceTime.

Byron's tone made Gus curious. However, Gus knew that he could be frank with Byron and share the deepest concerns of his heart. Over the years, Gus and Byron had given counsel and advice to each other.

"Well..." Gus leaned back on the small sofa in the caboose. "For four years, we've been platonic

Christian friends. Now I don't want to be just friends anymore."

"Does she know this?"

Gus shrugged. "We almost went for a walk on the beach—just the two of us, alone—yesterday and this morning, but it was rained out. The fact that Tally was all right with not inviting her parents or any of her local friends on the beach walk with me tells me that she might be feeling the same thing as I do."

"Are you two about the same age?"

"I'm six years older than she is." Gus didn't think age mattered. "She looks younger than thirty-five, and I look older than forty-one."

"I don't care about how you look," Byron said. "I was wondering if you two grew up in the same era and have common interests, you know? Might explain why you get along so well."

"We do get along on the basis of our thinking perspectives and worldview. We're both mature Christians, to begin with. Now we've both survived a dangerous situation together."

"It seems that way. Also, you've spent a lot of time with her since you arrived in Atlanta two weeks ago—more time than you've spent with me."

Gus nodded. "I've been helping at the Village with their landscaping and container gardens."

"Thank you for that. Did Tally ask you to help?" Byron asked.

"She gave me a tour, and I volunteered. I needed something to do while I'm in town."

"Have you disagreed on anything while at the Village?"

"That's the problem," Gus said. "We discuss things, share our opinions, and end up agreeing. She and I haven't had any friction in our relationship, not even on the Friday we were held hostage together. The lack of friction scares me."

"A crisis is probably not a case study for everyday life."

"That too. However, I love talking with Tally about things. She's intelligent, articulate, knows her Bible, and doesn't mess around. She's mature both spiritually and emotionally. Maybe that's why we don't quarrel as much. If we cultivate our friendship, we're going to be best friends. If we start dating each other, it could very well ruin our friendship. What if we start quarreling with each other?"

"Are you trying to reconcile how to have a best friend and a girlfriend?"

"Maybe that's it." Gus got up and went to the fridge. His phone was still in his hand. "I'm getting some cold water. The AC isn't all that great in this caboose."

Gus returned to the sofa with two bottles of cold water.

"Isn't your significant other supposed to be your best friend?" Byron asked. "If not, then you have two people you go to when you have problems in life. Do you go to your best friend for one thing and then your girlfriend or wife for another? What if they both give you opposing advice?"

"I hadn't thought of that." Gus drank some water.

"Ideally, your wife is also your best friend."

"I'm only at the 'should I get a girlfriend' stage, Byron." Gus laughed.

"Tina and I are both best friends and spouses. This way I tell Tina everything, and she does the same. We have no secrets. If we need to ask someone else for advice about a matter, then we both decide who we should go to. Usually we'll agree to ask someone who is older and wiser than us, like Pastor Kim or Pastor Fizz."

"Must be nice to be able to talk freely with Tina about everything."

"In confidence too. I'm married to my best friend, and she talks with me, prays with me, cares for me, loves me. I love living life with her."

"I'm glad it worked out. I know she wasn't always your best friend," Gus said.

"You know our history. We were enemies when we first met." Byron laughed. "When she taught art camp eight years ago at the school, she hated me and cried all the time because of me. After summer was over, I missed her for the next two years. When she returned to teach again, our relationship changed from enemies to friends, and then we fell in love and I married her. Five years and three kids—including one in the womb—later, here we are."

"I'm happy for you."

"Compared to me, you skipped a step, Gus. You didn't have to fight a duel with Tally."

"Hard times could be coming."

"How so?"

"Tally has a good job and ministry in Atlanta. I want to go home to Nassau. We will be two hours of flying apart."

"We had that problem too. However, you have to seek the Lord's wise counsel on that." Byron reminded him not to get too far ahead of himself. "After all, you're just now getting to know each other."

"Feels like we have a foundation in our four-year friendship."

And yet would that be enough?

"As your favorite cousin, I want to remind you

not to be in too much of a hurry," Byron said. "Remember when you were dating Veronique?"

"I'm trying to forget a lot of memories with her. What situation are you referring to?"

"You started dating Veronique after Tina went to Nassau for the second time," Byron reminded him. "If I remember correctly, you were tired of being single, and Veronique happened to be interested. She's a Christian, and you thought God had sent you a girlfriend."

"I still believe God did, but only as a girlfriend. I was so lonely I'd take any girlfriend. I don't want to say Veronique was simply available, but she pursued me, and she passed my checklist test."

Byron nodded. "We can say that on the one hand, God must not mean for you to marry her because she's now married to someone else."

"That's how I have to look at it," Gus said. "We broke up a year ago, and six months later she married someone else. When we broke up, I was somewhat relieved. But when I saw the wedding invitation—she invited me, can you believe it—I felt a sense of loss."

"Did you think that perhaps Veronique was supposed to marry you, but on her own accord, she married someone else instead? The Veronique we knew was headstrong sometimes."

"Did you mean that God allowed her to marry someone else, but it wasn't His perfect will for her?"

"I'm not saying that's it, but it has happened to other people."

"There's another possible thing though," Gus said. "It could also be that Veronique and I weren't supposed to be dating, but that we did on our own will, not in God's will. That might explain why our relationship didn't last."

"And why you and Veronique fought all the time in your tumultuous dating years."

"We had very little in common except food, church, and workplace."

"I have a lot more in common with you."

"So dating Veronique might not have been in God's perfect will."

"Which brings me back to the point that God saved you from a bad marriage," Byron said. "To be sure, don't get me wrong. It doesn't mean that just because my wife and I get along that it's the end of it. We're best friends on earth, but you know who should be your best Friend of all."

Gus nodded. "Jesus Christ."

"Precisely. John 15:15 says, 'No longer do I call you servants, for a servant does not know what his master is doing; but I have called you friends, for all things that I heard from My Father I have made known to you.' But you knew that, Gus."

"I do." It became clear to Gus at that point where Tally would stand if she were to become an integral part of his life.

Yes, a part of his life.

She could never be his life. That position was reserved for his Lord and Savior, Jesus Christ, and Him alone.

"Jesus is my best Friend ever," Gus added.

He wasn't supposed to put Tally on a pedestal. He appreciated Tally as a good friend, and they could become best friends after their shared experience together, but it still remained that Tally was a human being.

As much as he appreciated—and loved her—she was still human.

Never would he want to make the same mistake he'd done with Veronique: revolve his life around her.

No, his life should be focused on God instead.

Gus cleared his throat. "Before I talked to you this morning, I was divided. In my mind, if Tally becomes my best friend, I will lose the chance of dating her."

"I don't want to bring our age into the picture, but we're not spring chickens anymore, you and I."

Byron's voice sounded cautious. "We're at the age when life might speed up soon. My kids will suddenly be in school and then college. When people said 'time flies,' I used to laugh. But you and I know that if we don't speak our minds now, we might have to forever hold our peace."

"What do you mean?"

"If you like Tally, you need to let her know and let the chips fall where they may. I know about Malachi."

"What about Malachi?" Gus felt somewhat threatened, but then again, this was the elusive man who didn't look at Tally the way she wanted him to look at her. Gus recalled that Sunday school morning when Tally brought Malachi coffee—just the way he liked it—but he only looked at her like someone would his...sister.

"Malachi is coming back to town next week. He might be going with Pastor Fizz to minister at Lakeside for the rest of the year."

"Isn't that a good thing?" Lakeside was about seven hours south of Atlanta. If Malachi went to Florida, then he wouldn't be near Tally in Georgia. Gus would still be in town for another two weeks of summer. Enough time to spend with Tally and see where they could go from this point.

"He's your rival, and you might not be able to

beat him because he is most like Pastor Fizz. Tina told me that Malachi was Tally's crush back when she was in her twenties. She waited for him for so long that she didn't date anyone, with the exception of the man she almost married in Hawaii—which her dad had thought was on a whim, although the man who left Tally at the altar was a pastor's son."

Tally would have been thirty years old at that time. Gus didn't know why that mattered, but when he had turned thirty himself, he took stock of his life and changed his career. Maybe, just maybe, Tally thought time was running out or something, and that she had to marry.

Nah. Tally's not like that.

She was thoughtful and brave. Why would she marry someone "on a whim," like her dad had thought?

"Was he a Malachi look-alike?" Gus asked.

Byron shrugged. "I'm only telling you what I know in confidence so that you can make better decisions, and so that you don't get your heart broken again."

"I didn't know about the would-be groom's background. But Tally might have mentioned the wedding briefly when I first arrived in town."

"Why would she tell you that on the first day you got here?"

"Because she was trying to comfort me about Veronique. Told me that I was grieving the loss of her and that grief takes time. She did say it took her five years to get over her relationship."

"It's the Fitzpatrick genes," Byron said. "Has Pastor Fizz told you about how he met Riona?"

"No.'

"Not yet, you mean. Just wait. He's going to tell you. It was love at first sight, and they've been married for almost fifty years—forty-seven, if I remember correctly."

"Love at first sight? That's the stuff for fairy tales." Was there such a thing? Gus began to doubt his own skepticism.

Four years ago... Had Tally fallen in love with Gus at first sight?

Ah, probably not if her heart was for Malachi, whom she'd known longer than she had known Gus.

"They fall in love easily, and they remain fiercely loyal to the ones they fall in love with—assuming they don't get dumped." Byron sighed. "You got your work cut out for you, cousin. You're in the hit-or-miss zone. If she has already fallen in love with Malachi, then you have no chance unless she lets him go. Otherwise, in her heart, there will always be a Malachi, and you don't want to share room with him, you know what I mean?"

One thing he loved about his cousin was his frankness. When Byron was falling in love with Tina years ago in the Bahamas, he had sought out Gus's counsel. Gus had spoken his mind and given him an honest opinion. Now Byron was doing the same for him.

"How many Fitzpatricks do you know?" Gus asked.

"Pastor Fizz has two younger brothers. Both are pastors too. They told their stories when they came to town. All three pastors are happily and faithfully married to the wives of their youth."

"Good."

"The question remains with the Fitzpatrick daughters. All three sisters are not dating anyone at the moment. If you ask them—and Tina did—they'd tell you that they're looking for someone who is like their dad. That's a tall order. Pastor Fizz is the gold standard no man can reach."

But Tally shared an umbrella with Gus in the rain on Friday morning. She had initiated the three-legged imitation walk across the campground.

Oh, come on, Gus. Like that counted.

What about that afternoon in the warehouse

one week before the umbrella event? Tally had held his arm a lot.

Gus could say that she had been under stress and fear, plus they could have lost their lives that evening. That had been why she'd shared her heart.

And told him that she had been interested in him when she'd visited his church four years ago.

One year after she had almost married that unnamed pastor's son in Hawaii.

Oh.

Gus didn't know what to think now.

Perhaps...

"Everyone says that Veronique broke my heart one year ago, but now I realize that she isn't the one for me. It was a blessing that we broke up when we did. I've had one year to get over her, and I truly feel nothing for her now."

"As of when?"

"A week ago." There, he admitted it.

"Oh, when you and Tally were held prisoners in the warehouse."

Gus nodded. "Bad news is that I'm going home in two weeks."

"Time is in God's hands."

"Sometimes God brings people together in strange circumstances," Gus said.

"So you feel ready for a new relationship."

"With Tally."

"But you don't know how she feels about you."

Well...

Gus wondered if he should tell Bryon what Tally had told him about when they'd first crossed paths at Chapel by the Sea in Nassau four years ago. Had that been love at first sight, the Fitzpatrick way?

Gus wondered if her feelings for him were still there. It might explain why she felt comfortable with him, chatting with him, showing him around at the Village, entering his caboose alone...

And most of all, inviting him to watch the sunrise with her on the beach—which had yet to happen.

"I pray that you're not falling in love on the rebound," Byron said. "Please don't hurt Tally, or I will never hear the end of it from my wife."

"I'll be careful. We're both adults. Don't worry."

Even as Gus said it, he began to worry about it himself.

CHAPTER EIGHTEEN

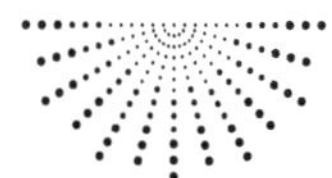

"What are your plans after you go home to Nassau?" Dad asked Gus point blank as he pressed two graham crackers together to sandwich a big piece of chocolate and a giant roasted marshmallow. He handed it to Mom.

Tally wondered what Dad was getting at, but she dared not ask, in case Dad got the wrong idea. Or worse yet, in case Gus got the wrong idea about her.

She rotated the marshmallow at the end of her steel roasting stick over the firepit. Gus was sitting next to her, so she couldn't see his face.

"This is the first time in years that I'm taking more than a week off from work," Gus said.

"A long vacation, or a sabbatical?" Dad asked.

"I hardly know which one. Fortunately, I have enough workers at both the school and church that they don't need me."

Tally handed the marshmallow to Gus, who sandwiched it between crackers.

"You can have this," Gus said to Tally.

"Thank you." Tally took it from him.

As she ate it, Gus took her stick and skewered two marshmallows at the end of it.

Tally and Gus were sitting in camp chairs that Dad and Mom had hauled all the way over here from their RV. If not for the rental golf cart, it would be hard for them to walk that far, carrying two ancient—heavy!—camp chairs to Gus's red caboose.

Across the firepit, Dad and Mom shared a log. Mom was leaning on Dad's shoulder. Dad roasted marshmallows directly across from where Gus was sitting. Their steel sicks were pointing at each other, and every now and then their marshmallows looked like they were going to duke it out right there in the fire.

Behind them were low-wattage Christmas lights strung out across the caboose roof. Nearby, the golf cart was also strung out in Christmas lights.

And it was only May.

Tally supposed that Jacobs Landing simply

hadn't bothered to change out the lights after Christmas five months ago.

"Are you going back to landscaping after you get home?" Dad asked. "I'm just curious, is all."

"You're always curious, Dad." Tally laughed. She turned to Gus. "Say no if he offers you a job."

Gus chuckled. "Seriously, though, I keep my life flexible enough so that when I hear from God, I am prepared to move in the direction He leads me."

Dad's eyes brightened. "So you're on a personal retreat, waiting to hear from God."

"That's a good way to put it." Gus's marshmallow caught on fire.

"Throw it on the ground here to let it cool down." Tally pointed to the sandy clay around the firepit. No grass grew there.

She handed Gus the bag of marshmallows, half-full. "We have plenty left. I think we're going to run out of chocolate soon."

"How did you end up doing landscaping?" Mom asked Gus. "Byron tells me that you have an MBA from Harvard, no less."

"Isn't life always full of ironies?" Tally asked.

"No, it isn't." Dad didn't mince his words.

"I've always loved the outdoors, even as a teenager," Gus said before Tally could open her mouth. "When I became an adult, I got busy and had to make time to spend outdoors. I started with container gardens on my balcony, and that grew into something that filled my free time. While other people golf or do sports, I go to my little garden. It's peaceful when I'm with my plants."

"No wonder you're such a help to us at the Village," Tally said.

"Glad to help."

"Balcony?" Mom asked. "You live in a condo?"

Like there were no condominiums in the Bahamas. Tally didn't want to correct her mom, so she bit into a s'more.

"I would think you'd have a house with a garden, the way you said you liked gardening," Mom explained.

"I'm in a flat—a condo—because it's across the street from the school." The way Gus looked at Mom told Tally that he wasn't offended. "I can walk to work every day and not have to drive."

"Wouldn't that be nice if we lived that close to the church..." Dad sighed. "Atlanta traffic is no trivial thing."

Tally laughed.

"We'll be within walking distance to the church in Lakeside," Mom said.

"For only three months. And then we'll be back in Atlanta."

"We can stay longer if God calls us."

Dad squeezed Mom's arm. Unspoken words between them, but Tally thought that had been the premise of their entire ministry and marriage: answering the call of God.

Mom turned her attention back to Gus. "I heard that you take care of the gardens on Moss Cay. You must be very good with it."

"You know about Moss Cay." Gus smiled.

"Full disclosure," Mom said. "Your aunt Nancy and I are friends. And Tina showed me her wedding photos on the island."

Gus didn't show an expression one way or another, but Tally began to wonder. Was that a good thing that Mom knew Nancy Moss? Everyone who had ever been to Chapel by the Sea had met the matriarch of the Moss family empire.

"Both Nancy and Byron have invited us to Moss Cay, but we haven't been able to find the time." Mom turned to Dad. "We need a vacation, dear."

"Are you asking me to semiretire?" Dad's finger gently rubbed Mom's chin.

Tally thought they were almost going to kiss again. They didn't know that she'd been catching them cuddling and teasing each other in the

Winnebago. Maybe the small space pulled them together, or maybe their long marriage did.

"No, honey. I'm asking you to find time for a vacation. Even Pastor Dixon has invited us to the Bahamas several times."

Gus stacked together another s'more and quietly handed it to Tally. She was surprised, and thanked him.

"I'm inviting you too." Gus looked at Tally's parents and then at Tally. "Let me know when you're free, and I'll see if Moss Cay is available."

Why is he looking at me?

Tally supposed that anyone with the last name of Moss could invite people to the island cottage. She brushed it off. She wasn't sure if she wanted to go to Moss Cay, wherever it was. The last time she was in Nassau, the women's conference took all week, and she didn't have time to explore the little islands. She'd spent most of her free time on New Providence Island, and hadn't taken any boat trips.

Tally waited to see where the conversation would go. Clearly Mom and Dad had asked Gus poignant questions about his career by way of asking him about the detour he was on.

"Gus, are you at a crossroad in your career?" Dad asked suddenly.

"He's relentless," Tally said to Gus quietly.

Gus didn't answer her. He looked across the firepit. "I'm at a standstill, sir."

"Honesty." Dad turned to Mom, and they nodded in unison.

I knew it.

Tally knew that her parents were assessing Gus. For what though?

"When you're at a standstill, it's sometimes a good idea to look back to where you've come from, the long journey you have traveled to get to where you are," Dad suggested.

"Good idea."

"So how about you give your salvation testimony at church tomorrow?"

"Me?" Gus looked surprised.

"Five minutes," Dad added. "All I can give you."

"Dad!" Tally exclaimed. "You only gave me two minutes last year. Why is he getting five?"

Dad smiled. "You know it depends on the church and what they're asking me to do."

"I didn't know about the testimony time," Mom said.

"Neither did I." Tally nibbled on a cracker.

"I'm going to preach five minutes less tomorrow," Dad explained.

"Please don't do that on account of me." Gus

stopped rotating the marshmallow stick over the fire.

"I want to hear your testimony," Dad said. "You do okay in front of an audience?"

"I've given my testimony at my church."

"Then it's not a problem." Dad reached for two pieces of chocolate to stick into his s'more.

"No problem at all."

"Even at the last minute?" Dad raised an eyebrow.

"I've been saved awhile, so it's the same story," Gus said. "I could add in how it affects my life today."

Dad nodded approvingly.

Tally was curious about what Gus was going to say, but she didn't pry. She'd find out in just over twelve hours.

In the meantime, they made small talk until they finished the entire box of graham crackers and all the chocolate. The only leftovers were giant marshmallows—because Mom had bought an extra bag.

Dad looked up in the sky. "Nice and clear."

Mom pointed out a few constellations.

"We should take a walk." Dad looked into Mom's eyes.

"Let's do."

In the light of the firepit, they looked like they were still in love with each other after all these years.

Quietly, Tally thanked God for her parents' marriage and prayed that she too might have such a privilege to have a godly marriage built on Christ, as her parents had.

Dad stood up from the log and stretched. "How about we let you two clean up? Your mom and I are going to take a walk and look at the sky."

"Sure. Go. I'll drive the golf cart back to the Winnebago in a little bit." Tally waved them off. "Don't stay up too late."

"You too." Mom waved to Gus. "Come get us at eight o'clock for church. Don't let us leave without you."

"Will do, Riona."

Tally watched them go, two people holding hands and looking at each other so lovingly. She turned to Gus. "Do you think we'd leave you behind?"

"In between the lines, your ,om was telling me to be early. I'll be knocking on your Winnebago door at 7:45 a.m."

"That works. You'll enjoy Sunday school in the hour before the church service," Tally said. "I'll introduce you to all my friends who weren't here at Friday night's cookout."

"I'm almost jealous of your parents' relationship," Gus said. "Is there such a thing? Can there be such a thing?"

"What? Your jealousy?" Tally laughed as she picked up the marshmallow sticks and used a paper towel to clean off remaining marshmallow bits stuck to the end of the sticks.

"No, I meant a loving married life after so long together." Gus used a pair of long tongs to check the logs in the firepit. "Your parents get along so well with each other."

"Believe me, they argue too."

"I suppose that's normal."

"However, my parents argue less nowadays. They've achieved a level of relationship maturity."

"That so?" Gus picked up some pieces of trash and threw them into a nearby trash can. There wasn't a lot of trash, so he was done in one round. Some of the trash was old and looked like it came from previous caboose renters.

"After forty-seven years together, my parents have learned to respect and honor each other. Whether they agree or not about a situation, they still love each other." Tally's heart warmed as she thought about her parents. "They're my role models for a godly relationship. They put Christ first in their marriage, and they exhibit the fruit of the spirit."

"Galatians 5:22–23."

"Right. 'But the fruit of the Spirit is love, joy, peace, longsuffering, kindness, goodness, faithfulness, gentleness, self-control. Against such there is no law.' I'm particularly drawn to 'longsuffering' because patience is key."

Gus nodded. "Two verses later, it says, 'If we live in the Spirit, let us also walk in the Spirit.' I can tell that your parents are dedicated to God, not only in their ministry but also their marriage and personal walk with the Lord."

"You're right." Tally tied up the trash bag in the small trash can.

"I'll ask the manager's office for a liner in the morning," Gus said.

"They're closed on Sundays."

"Oh."

"There might be a liner in the caboose. Check the kitchen cabinets."

"Be right back." Gus took a step and then turned to Tally. "I don't want to leave you out here. Will you be safe?"

"Sure. I think we're safe here. This is not like downtown Atlanta."

"Still, stay where I can see you."

Tally was taken aback by what Gus told her. "Do you want me to go look for a trash can liner?"

"I'll douse the firepit with water. I don't trust that the fire is totally out."

"Let's sit around for a little bit before we do that. It's a nice night, like my parents said." Tally didn't know why she had said that.

"What time is it?" Gus asked.

"Oh, I forgot you have to prepare for your testimony tomorrow morning."

"No, not that. I just want to know the time."

"Are you being honest with me?"

"Yes, Tally. I am. My phone is in the caboose, so I'm asking you what time it is."

Tally didn't want to belabor it. She checked her phone. "Nine o'clock. Oh."

"Oh what?"

"We forgot to take a group photo earlier when we were grilling s'mores. What a wasted opportunity." Tally looked at the firepit. "Fire's almost out now."

"We didn't make a big fire. Maybe we'll have to do this again and remember to take photos."

Tally almost wanted to suggest that she and Gus could take some photographs, but then she did not want to overstep her boundaries.

"Okay." She walked up the steps to the red caboose. In the night, the caboose looked darker than its Christmas-red paint. "Do you want some water?"

"There are some cold waters in the fridge," Gus said.

Tally entered the caboose. Inside, it looked nice and clean, and Gus had made his bed the way she had shown him the day before.

Tally walked to the small kitchen cabinet and started looking for a trash can liner big enough for the outdoor trash can. She cringed as she remembered how she had overreacted to Gus asking for the time when Tally suggested they sit around until the fire went out on its own.

Was that too direct?

Truly, she didn't mean it.

She found a single trash can liner and left the caboose.

Gus was stoking the partially burnt logs in the firepit to keep what little was left of the fire going. It seemed to be mostly embers now.

When he saw her going down the steps, he went to get the trash bag from her.

As Tally handed it to him, she missed a step and tripped. Gus reached for her, but she spread her arms and landed on her feet on the gravel.

"That was close," Tally said.

"I was about to catch you." Gus looked at her shoes. "Are you all right?"

"Yes, I'm fine. Didn't sprain my ankles."

Gus put the liner into the trash can. "For your information, I could have caught you. If it ever happens again, I'm going to make sure you don't fall."

"I didn't fall. I made a perfect landing on two feet."

"Do you want me to give you a perfect ten score?"

Tally laughed. "You're funny."

"Am I? Do I want to be funny?" Gus walked back to the firepit with Tally.

They moved their camp chairs a bit so that they could watch the fire and still see each other. They drank water and watched the remaining logs turn to ashes.

"Truth be told, my parents don't have a fairy-tale marriage," Tally said. "Don't put them on a pedestal."

"They seem to have a biblical marriage."

Tally pointed at him. "Precisely. That's more important."

"I agree."

"Why did you ask me about their relationship,

though?" Tally wondered if she should be curious, but she found it easy to be honest with Gus. He was unassuming and nonjudgmental toward her.

"After...uh..."

"After what?"

Gus hesitated. "All right, since we're friends, I'll say it. After Veronique, I wondered whether there was such a thing as a happy marriage and whether I might as well stop looking."

"Wouldn't you look to God and let Him handle it?" Tally asked. "I'm sorry to be blunt, but that's what I told myself after...after Hawaii."

"We've both had our hearts broken badly."

Tally didn't want to burst his bubble by saying that she had been quite relieved she didn't marry that man on a whim in Hawaii. She had been reacting to Malachi's non-interest and had found a man who'd wanted to give her the world, until he decided not to on their wedding day.

"At least Veronique left you before your wedding day. It's bad when you're waiting for the processional and they can't find the groom, you know."

"That sounds like a tragic comedy."

"My dad came into the bridal room and told me that the jerk had cold feet, asked his own father to leave my dad a text message—while Dad was standing at the altar, and not a moment too soon." Tally looked into the distance, beyond Gus, the golf cart, and the lamp-lined stone path. "He didn't have the decency to tell me to my face that it wasn't going to work out. He had to ask his own pastor dad to fix it for him."

"You sound a bit disappointed."

"Should I be? It's been five years."

"Maybe it was so baffling to you that it still plays in your mind," Gus suggested.

"Well, it is baffling. Looking back, we should've broken up a long time before he proposed." Tally sipped some water. "He made me doubt my own desire to marry a pastor."

"Where is he now?" Gus asked. "Maybe I shouldn't ask. Don't answer that."

"He's still in the pastoral ministry somewhere. Last I heard, he'd married the church organist's daughter, who can sing soprano."

"Does it matter? Why did you specifically say that?" Gus asked.

"How observant you are, Mr. Moss." Tally laughed. "Now I'm going to reveal a big secret to you."

"I'm all ears." He finished his bottled water. "I will not tell anyone—although you do realize that we're outside in the open and there are yurts and RVs around us. Anyone could be listening."

"The biggest problem L—uh, my ex—had with me was that we couldn't sing a duet at church together. Because..."

"Because?"

Tally didn't want to say more, but Gus seemed like he couldn't guess. "Let's just say that I've always wanted to take voice lessons but have no time."

"Oh, so he had a problem with your singing?"

"I'm not tone deaf. I just don't know most of the songs he wanted me to sing, and I can't read music, so I have to go by ear. By the time we got to the next stanza, I'd forgotten what the tune was, so I tried to go along but sometimes ended up off key."

"You have poor retentive memory."

Tally glared at Gus. "Is that your diagnosis, Dr. Gus?"

"I have no idea. I was trying to figure out why your being able to sing mattered so much to your ex."

"For the wedding, he wanted us to sing our vows. Can you believe it? We fought for weeks over it. No way was I going to embarrass myself singing outside my usual vocal range."

"He could have picked something you can sing, a tune you know, and put the lyrics on top of it."

"Genius. What I suggested."

"Or he could do away with singing vows. Sing later. The marriage vows are sacred."

Tally stared at Gus. "Where were you when I needed a wedding planner?"

He stretched his long legs. "At least you went as far as the wedding chapel. I didn't even get that far."

"Be thankful. The wedding cost me a lot of my life savings. The venue, the reception food, flowers, my wedding gown, my sisters' bridesmaid dresses, and so forth. I paid for everything, including the plane tickets for my parents and sisters and their hotel rooms."

"I hope you got a family vacation out of Hawaii."

"Yes, we did. We had a grand time for a week, when my honeymoon was supposed to be." Tally smiled. "It's been over for a while now."

"You're telling me what happened because you want me to feel better about my own breakup."

Tally was impressed that Gus came right out and said it. "You saw through it."

Gus didn't reply.

"I merely answered your question about a

'happy marriage,' Gus. I'd rather not bring up my own poor experience at my own wedding, but Dad said that it's better not to start a marriage if the person is wrong for you. Guess who rejoiced when my wedding didn't happen?"

"Your dad."

"Exactly. He reminded me that happiness is temporary, after all. He said I should want a biblical marriage that can endure the tragedies of life, not just the happy days."

They stared at the fire for a while.

"Earlier, your mom asked me why I live in a condo," Gus said.

"Don't get her wrong. Please, condos are houses too."

"No, I didn't get her wrong. She didn't say a whole lot, but since she knows Aunt Nancy, she might also know that I bought the one-bedroom condo because it wasn't just close to my work, but also because I was waiting for Veronique."

"Oh?" Tally thought that she should feel something as Gus talked about his ex, but she didn't feel anything. All of it was in the past, and Gus was single now.

Single? Did it matter to her?

Four years ago, when she'd seen him for the first time in the Chapel by the Sea hallway, something happened in her heart. Unlike her parents, she didn't believe in love at first sight, but Gus had made an impression on her.

All that had fallen apart when she found out that he was taken.

"I wanted us to go house hunting and find a nice house we liked, where we could raise our children."

Raise our children?

Oh. He meant Veronique.

"We started to argue more and more at that time, and there was no way we were going to reconcile." Gus seemed oblivious to Tally's thoughts.

"Differences in opinion?"

"Maybe? I don't know. Money was a problem. My landscaping salary was enough to pay the monthly expenses for a small house, but she had grand ideas above my budget." Gus slowed down a bit, as if saying more would be badmouthing a former girlfriend.

Tally waited. Gus seemed to want to tell her, as though it was important that she knew.

Tally's sister Adalia had told her that Veronique had expensive tastes and had expected Gus to take care of her with his Moss name. Unlike Donovan and Byron, Gus was the country-mouse part of the Moss family, but Veronique didn't seem to believe it.

I wouldn't understand. I'm low maintenance.

"If we combined our salaries and bought a huge house, we'd still be stuck with mortgage payments." Gus waited.

Was it time for me to say something?

"When people say they 'bought' a house on a mortgage, they actually owe the bank or lender money. That can go on for fifteen or thirty years here in the States." Tally glanced at Gus. "For that many years, who owns the house?"

"Exactly."

"Several years ago, I bought a townhouse that was being foreclosed on. Paid in cash," Tally said.

"You did?"

"Yeah. It's an older house and only has two bedrooms. But no mortgage."

"Good for you."

"Hiroki said I could've bought a detached house instead of a townhouse, but I wanted a place near church. Intown houses are more expensive. I paid less for the townhouse than I would've a smaller condo in Buckhead or Lenox or Brookhaven."

"Are those districts?"

"Yeah. Within the Atlanta city limits."

"Makes sense. In any case, you have no debt on your house."

"Precisely. I can sell the townhouse later if I want more bedrooms." Two verses came to her mind. "Romans 13:8 says, 'Owe no one anything except to love one another, for he who loves another has fulfilled the law.' And then there's the verse in Proverbs about being a slave to the lender."

"Proverbs 22:7, you mean? 'The rich rules over the poor, and the borrower is servant to the lender.' That's why I want to remain debt-free, especially in a marriage."

"Yes, that verse."

"So you do understand what I'm talking about."

"My parents taught me to live within my means, to save more than I spend, but that's common knowledge."

"Is it anymore?" Gus asked. "I drive a smaller car so that I don't have a car payment. I live frugally for one person."

"Same. This way if I never marry, I'm debt-free and I can support myself."

"Never marry?" There was surprise in Gus's voice, but Tally could hardly see his face in the dim light. "What do you mean?"

"It's up to God," Tally said. "Just as my career is in God's hands, so is my love life. I guess I've been single for so long—with the exception of my little detour, which I won't repeat—that I'm getting used to it."

"Oh."

"Sometimes I dream of a guy I cannot have. I'm coming to a point in my life when I need to be practical, you know?"

Gus turned to look at Tally. "What if God brings someone into your life?"

"Then I would know."

"Would you?"

"I think so."

"How would you know?"

"Wouldn't God tell me?"

"Like how?" Gus pressed. "Sometimes things are right in front of me and I don't see them."

"Same."

"I hate to miss God's will for my life because I'm not paying attention."

"That can happen in any part of life, not just love."

"With regard to that, speaking for myself, I don't want to miss the love of my life if God has brought her to me."

"How sweet, Gus. Be sure to invite me to your wedding."

"You better show up," Gus said.

Tally chuckled. "Unless I'm at a conference elsewhere or not available."

Gus barely nodded.

"You mentioned paying attention to God," Tally said. "I think that praying more and reading the Bible are a part of the process."

Gus didn't say anything. Tally had no idea what he was thinking.

She continued. "To know God's will, Dad said that it requires a surrendered life. If I surrender my life to God, then He fills every moment with His perfect will."

"You're referring to our Christian life after salvation." Gus was back in the conversation.

Tally nodded. "The process of sanctification requires a daily dying to self and living unto God."

"I know that verse."

"Pop quiz, Gus. What is it?" Tally waited in anticipation, even though that was a verse commonly known to believers who were actively studying God's Word and growing in their faith.

"Are you thinking of that verse in Luke somewhere? Something about taking up my cross daily."

Tally swiped her phone, tapped in her pin, then opened the Bible app. She handed her phone to Gus. "Open book."

"Do I get a prize for guessing?"

"We get to end this firepit chat and go back to our trailers." Tally smiled.

Gus searched for the verse. "I already know it's in Luke. Give me a second."

And he was back. "Here it is. Luke 9:23, in the words of the Lord, 'If anyone desires to come after Me, let him deny himself, and take up his cross daily, and follow Me.' That one?"

Tally nodded. She started humming "I Surrender All."

They sang the chorus together.

"What's wrong with your ex?" Gus asked. "You can sing."

"I'm not a soprano, and I have an untrained voice. I am not a professional singer. I talk better than I can sing."

"He wanted to marry a soprano." Gus laughed. "I've never heard of such a precondition for marriage."

"He found his wife, and I found my freedom. It's a win-win."

"Maybe it's a win-win for me too," Gus said. "Veronique found the husband she wanted, and I'm here."

Tally slapped his upper arm gently. "Glad we had this conversation."

"We do get along," Gus said. "I fought with

Veronique every day."

"Are you comparing me to her?"

"Oh no, no. I wasn't trying to." Gus sat up in his camp chair. "I was thinking about your parents, how they manage problems well."

"They have a process. Both are very stubborn people."

"They are? Here I am thinking that one of them yields to the other."

"They both yield to each other. It's never one person doing all the thinking," Tally said. "My parents have perfected the art of calmly debating all the pros and cons before reaching a joyful conclusion. Otherwise, they won't move forward with any decision."

Gus got up to check the firepit. It looked like the fire was almost out. "How long is the process?"

"Depends on the situation. They pick their battles. Some things are easily resolved. Minutes or hours. However, other matters could take a very long time to deal with. Days, months, before they come to a conclusion. For example, whether they should move to Lakeside permanently."

"Couldn't they move there for one year and then make a decision?"

"Yes, they could, but my parents don't want to do that. In the one year they're gone, Midtown will fill the counseling pastor position. If Dad returns to Atlanta, he'd be at least seventy-two years old."

"I see."

"You're not going to see my parents move forward with a decision until they both are in agreement with each other. It won't be the case of Dad dragging Mom to Lakeside and then listening to her complain about it."

Gus picked up their empty water bottles and put them on the steps of the caboose. "I'll take them to the recycle bin outside the office tomorrow."

"Thank you."

He returned to his camp chair. "If your parents don't know all the facts and what's coming, how can they debate the pros and cons?"

"They discuss the situation based on the information they know. As they get more information, they'll discuss again. For example, if they made a decision last year that no longer works this year, they're flexible and objective enough to go back to the table and hash it out."

"Like the Lakeside decision they have to make."

"Right. My parents can keep their lines of communication open because they're always together, always talking with each other. They won't surprise each other with unilateral decisions."

"Model couple."

"Mom is a keen researcher. She'll gather all the facts as they know them, and they will have an open, honest discussion about the good, the bad, the ugly. They don't insult each other. They don't try to one-up each other. They simply go, 'Here's the problem. Here's what I know. What say you?' And they go back and forth until they've exhausted every point. Sometimes Mom even takes notes because they might forget later."

"Sounds like a business meeting."

"People have said that, but if you were in on these meetings, it's eye opening. It solves a lot of problems when a married couple is not hiding secrets from each other." Tally sighed. "Transparency is so important in a marriage, Dad told me."

"I see now. If you were to marry, you'd want to marry someone like your dad," Gus said.

Like your dad.

Tally recalled what she'd said to Gus after their imprisonment and the fire.

I'm glad you were in the warehouse with me, Gus. You were calm and collected, like Dad. Dad's always calm, no matter what happens.

Among the men she knew, even Malachi, Gus was most like Dad.

What did that mean?

"I guess we better call it a night," Gus said. "But I don't want you to go. I enjoyed our conversation. We get along well, don't we?"

"Because you're on vacation," Tally guessed.

"Do you think that's why we don't argue about anything? We even thought of the same Bible verses." Gus grinned. "Should we find something to disagree about?"

"Don't borrow trouble, Gus." Tally thought for a minute. "The reason you and I get along is that we put God first, so everything comes into its proper perspective. My parents taught me that."

"I wish my parents were alive and did not leave me when I was only a teenager."

"Learn from mine then. They're always willing to teach by their example," Tally said. "Also learn from your Pastor Dixon and his wife, our Pastor Kim and his wife, and other older Christians who have been married for a long time."

"Married?" Gus asked.

The word seemed to come easily for him.

Tally wasn't sure how to respond to that. She cleared her throat. "You asked about our friendship. Why we get along like best buddies."

"Best buddies? Is that all we'll ever be?" Gus's voice was soft.

"What do you have in mind?" Tally didn't know how else to phrase the question.

"A lot of things."

"Name one."

"Just one?"

"All I can handle right now." Tally was being honest. She got out of her camp chair and folded it. She bagged it and then carried it to the golf cart.

Gus came behind her with his folded camp chair. He took the chair from Tally and put both of them on the backseat floor of the golf cart.

"Good night, Gus," Tally said, but she didn't move from where she was standing.

Gus's gaze lowered to her chin.

Wait. Is he looking at my chin? Or maybe my lips?

He stepped closer.

Tally wondered if she should step back.

They looked at each other for a while.

"My mind is going blank," Gus said.

"So is mine."

"What does that mean?"

"It's past our bedtime?"

"I mean philosophically."

Tally thought for a moment. "That maybe our next step is an empty slate?"

"As long as we don't fall into the firepit."

"Ooh, a metaphor." Tally laughed at Gus's answer. And just like that, their would-be moment, whatever it was, ended.

She climbed into the golf cart, turned on the headlights, backed out over the cement driveway—which ran in another direction on the other side of the stone walking path—and drove off, waving one last time as she rounded the corner.

CHAPTER NINETEEN

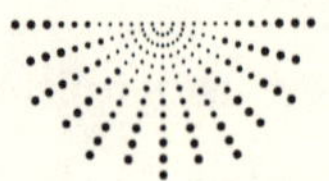

Little did Gus know that his five-minute salvation testimony at Riverside Chapel's Sunday morning service would lead to a twenty-minute sermon in the evening service at the Savannah Senior Living Resort.

After church at Riverside and a hefty lunch in downtown Savannah, Pastor Fizz experienced chest pains and had to see the cardiologist who was on call at the SSLR. It was a good thing for Pastor Fizz that the SSLR director, Roger Patel, had recently opened an on-site clinic for its residents and guests.

It was a bad thing for one Augustus Moss III because, for some reason, Pastor Fizz pointed to him in the clinic waiting room and said, "Gus, could you do a twenty-minute sermon on any topic you want?"

If he had said "Bible study" instead of "sermon," it might not have freaked out Gus as much.

Sitting on both sides of Pastor Fizz, his wife and daughter stared at Gus.

"Me?" Gus asked, as if he hadn't heard it properly. "I must've misheard."

"You grew up with Byron in the same church. You sometimes tag-teamed each other teaching Sunday school. When he was out of town, you filled in for him. You're in various ministry committees at your church."

"How did you know all that?"

"Research," Mom said.

Pastor Fizz put his hand on his chest. "Can you talk about God for twenty minutes?"

Gus didn't know how to reply. Of course he could talk about God, even for an hour or longer. Case in point: he had chatted with Tally for a while the night before around the firepit.

Gus almost said yes because he didn't want to be the reason Pastor Fizz's heart gives out.

"Dad," Tally started to say.

"I would have asked you to teach a Bible study tonight," Pastor Fizz said to Tally. "You could pull up any of your sessions at the women's conferences, and you'd have no problem."

Gus could feel the word "however" floating in the air.

"Gus is on vacation," Tally said.

"Is he on vacation from God?" Dad asked.

"Never from God," Gus said. "Pastor Fizz, I was just stunned a little bit that you think I can do it."

"Would I have asked you if you couldn't?"

No one answered Pastor Fizz.

"Any topic?" Gus said.

"Yes." Before Pastor Fizz could expound on it, the nurse called his name.

Riona went with Pastor Fizz to see the doctor, and they told Tally to wait with Gus.

Tally scooted over two seats until she was next to Gus. Looked at him with her brown eyes. "I'm sorry about Dad putting you on the spot twice in the same day."

"I can talk about God all day long, but I was surprised, is all."

"If you want to go sit in the car and pray alone about this, I have the key to our borrowed car." Tally reached into her cross-body bag.

"What am I praying about?" Gus knew he was

going to pray, but he was curious about what Tally thought.

"Whether to take up the assignment, and if so, what to preach about."

"It's very obvious I should do it."

"Pressure from my dad?"

"Not really. I should thank God for the opportunity to encourage believers in the Lord."

Tally nodded.

"That said, I have to pray about what to talk about tonight," Gus said. "I don't want to give my salvation testimony twice in a day."

"Maybe you could share about how God delivered us through the fire two Fridays ago."

"That thought came to my mind. How did you guess?"

Tally shrugged. "Natural aftermath of an event."

"Would it be all right if I mention you?" Gus asked. "We both went through it, and if you don't want me to say your name, I'll just say 'my friend.' I'm okay either way."

"I know a lot of the people at SSLR, so I think it's all right for you to mention me. However, the whole situation is still raw in my mind."

Gus nodded. "However, by the grace of God, our captivity was short—only a few hours—and I think we were not there long enough to be overly traumatized, although it's still there."

"Right."

"If our experience can draw people to Christ, then by all means mention my name."

"I'm sharing how God rescued us. It can encourage someone."

"I agree."

Gus put his palm up. "Key, please."

Tally gave him the keys. "Do you want notebook paper to jot down some notes, or are you going to use the notebook in your phone?"

"I'll take a piece of paper if you have it." Gus was impressed that Tally came prepared. Then again, she was a speaker at events. She knew to write down ideas when they came to her.

Tally tore off a couple of pieces of paper from her notebook and gave him a pen.

"I'll wait here for my parents, and I'll be praying," she said.

"Thank you."

Outside, sunshine beat down on Gus, and he wore his sunglasses so that he didn't have to squint as he walked to the visitors' parking area at SSLR. May in Tybee Island didn't feel as hot as in the Bahamas, even though both places had ocean breezes cooling down the temperature.

After he climbed into the front passenger's seat of Pastor Flores's car, he checked the weather. He converted the Celsius temperature to Fahrenheit so that he could use the same measurement system as Tally, although it wouldn't matter once he returned home to the Bahamas.

At seventy-seven degrees, Tybee was ten degrees cooler than Nassau.

Gus rolled down the window just a little bit to let the breeze in. Then he began praying. Before he could finish, Hebrews 4:12 came to his mind, along with a couple of sermon points that started with the letter 'p.' They simply popped into his head, as Bible notes usually did when he taught Bible study or filled in for a Sunday school teacher at Chapel by the Sea.

He opened his eyes, jotted down the words before he forgot them, and then continued praying. Somewhere in his prayer, he suspected the worst.

"This is yet another test, isn't it, Lord? What is Pastor Fizz up to?" he wondered. "Does he want to test how much Bible knowledge I have? Is he afraid that Tally and I might start dating, and that I might have less biblical knowledge—or less spiritual maturity—than Tally?"

His jaw dropped when Tally came to his mind. Trying not to get distracted by the memories of his alone time with Tally last night, he prayed again for focus.

"Lord, I want to believe that You have shown me what to talk about tonight in the service, but please clarify it. I want to speak only what You want me to and not speak what You don't want me to."

He finished praying and started jotting down what he was thinking. On top of the paper, he wrote down Tally's words: "How God Delivered Us Through the Fire."

Gus didn't call Byron to ask for pointers. He texted him to ask for prayer instead. Byron texted back and thanked him for helping Pastor Fizz.

The clock in the car said that he had exactly two hours before the evening service started at SSLR. They were already in the parking lot, but Gus knew that they would need to drive Pastor Fizz and Riona back to Jacobs Landing, about ten minutes south of SSLR, and make sure they were resting well in their Winnebago.

Then Gus would borrow the car and drive back to SSLR. Fortunately, both locations were on Tybee Island. He hoped that Tally would accompany him to SSLR this evening because he didn't know anyone there. All he knew was that Hunter's wife, Priyanka, worked there, and the director, Roger, was her cousin.

As Gus looked over his notes, he received a text from Tally saying that they were coming out to the car. Gus smiled at the thought that Tally was thoughtful.

Quickly, he thanked God for answering his prayer about the sermon tonight. He folded his notes and put them into his pocket, praying that he would not lose them. For good measure, he took his notes out again, took a photograph of them using his phone, and then put away the notes again.

"Good backup plan," he mumbled.

Gus spotted the trio coming toward him, and he got out of the car, taking the key with him, just in case. Some cars locked on their own—by design or thanks to faulty wiring—and he wasn't taking any chances.

"How's everything, Pastor?" Gus asked.

"Heartburn." Pastor Fizz chuckled. "I forgot to take a tablet before I went to lunch with y'all. Nearly killed myself on fried food, as you can see."

Riona grinned from ear to ear as she held on to Pastor Fizz's arm. "You write your own eulogy, Daniel Fitzpatrick."

Tally rolled her eyes. To Gus, she said, "I can drive. Car key please."

Gus didn't want to counter her offer to drive. He could drive too. Instead, he gave her the key.

Pastor Fizz and Riona climbed into the backseat. Gus rode shotgun with Tally. During the ten-minute drive, Pastor Fizz wanted to pray and thank God for delivering them.

Gus knew that Tally had learned to pray from him—and her mom too. Father and daughter had nearly the same way of praying.

"I think I can preach remotely," Pastor Fizz said. "You don't need to fill in for me, Gus."

"I've already outlined my sermon." Gus reached into his pocket, took out the folded paper, and waved it for all to see.

"Really?" Pastor Fizz sounded surprised.

Gus would like to see the pastor's face, but he couldn't twist his torso enough while sitting in the front passenger's seat.

"If you'd like to look over my outline, I would be honored to get any tips and advice." Gus unfolded the pieces of papers and lifted them in the air.

"If it's just an outline, I don't need to see it," Pastor Fizz said. "I want to take a nap. Maybe I can introduce you remotely at the start of the service."

"That's a great idea, Dad," Tally said from the driver's seat. "SSLR knows you. They consider you almost a resident there. The familiarity helps. Also, you can update them on your heart condition."

"It's not any worse than it was. We just got a scare today with heartburn."

"I know, Dad, but people will wonder why you don't show up tonight. Many of the residents are always praying for us."

"Right," Riona chimed in.

When they reached the Winnebago, Gus realized that they hadn't stopped at any pharmacy. He asked Tally about it.

"SSLR has a small pharmacy on site," she said. "Dad got some samples and refills for his other meds as well."

"Good to know." Gus watched Pastor Fizz and Riona walk slowly from the car to the Winnebago.

He wondered what Aunt Nancy would be like if her health took a turn for the worse. So far she was pretty healthy. Thank God.

"They didn't used to have a doctor or pharmacy at SSLR," Tally said. "They made an agreement with Savannah Memorial Hospital to send doctors on call over. In exchange, SMH can invite SSLR residents to participate in their geriatric research. After Priyanka started working as the assistant director, she lobbied for a small clinic and pharmacy to be on site. She used to be an ER doctor, you know, so she felt that medical care should be closer to the patient. It would take twenty minutes for a doctor to drive from SMH to SSLR. Now it takes two minutes to walk to the patient."

"Very convenient." It must cost plenty of money to make that happen.

"The residents' families made a sizable donation to make the clinic happen," Tally added, as if anticipating Gus's question.

Tally picked up her parents' Bibles from the backseat. She left her own Bible in the car.

Gus needed his Bible, and he now only had an hour and a half to flesh out a draft of his sermon.

"Does your dad want to see my sermon notes when I have them?" Gus wasn't sure what Pastor Fizz wanted.

"He said he didn't want to see the outline. By the time you finish your draft or key points, it will be time for us to go back to SSLR," Tally said. "So the answer is no. He doesn't need to see your sermon notes. If he invited you to preach, that meant he trusts you."

Gus felt humbled that Pastor Fizz trusted him.

"He heard your testimony this morning, and he approved." Tally locked the car door after making sure she was still holding the key in her hand.

"However, a salvation testimony is not the same

as a sermon. I could make mistakes in a sermon, misquote a verse or something."

"You're too hard on yourself, Gus. If you mess up deliberately, wouldn't you have to answer to God? His discipline of you would be harder than what my dad would say to you."

"Makes sense." Gus sighed. "I'm going to walk back to my caboose and work on the sermon. What time shall I return here for the carpool?"

"The service there starts at five o'clock because they want to have dinner at six. If you get here at four forty-five, we'll have enough time to get to their community center."

"Sounds good to me." Gus was about to walk away when he felt a hand on his arm.

"Thank you for filling in for my dad, Gus." Tally had tears in her eyes. "It might have turned out to be heartburn only, but this is today. Dad has two leaky valves, and the doctor said we have to watch him. His heart won't get better, but it could get worse. He's pushing hard, trying to do as much ministry as possible before the Lord calls him home."

"Seems like he might be better off staying put at one church instead of going all over the place. Driving and traveling take a toll on the human body."

"I agree. So pray for him. Pray for us. Pray for me."

"I will, Tally."

"And I will pray for you too, for God's perfect will to reign in your life."

"Thank you very much."

Tally had promised him some serious prayer. And Gus appreciated it.

CHAPTER TWENTY

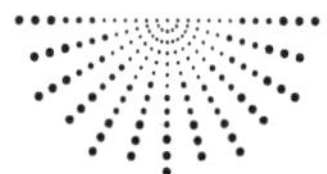

They called Dad a circuit-riding preacher, so he showed up on live video dressed in a plaid shirt and a cowboy hat.

What a showman.

Tally sat in the audience, watching Dad speak on the big-screen television in the SSLR community center. On screen, Dad moved the camera so that it showed Mom.

Mom waved, grinning from ear to ear, knowing that Dad was in his element: preaching to the congregation.

And yet he wasn't here in person, and he had decided not to preach tonight.

SSLR Director Roger Patel walked up to the

podium, and took the wireless microphone from its stand.

"Ladies and gentlemen, Pastor Daniel Fitzpatrick needs no introduction," Roger said into the microphone. "However, due to a health scare after the morning church service today, he won't be with us in person tonight. He has invited a visiting Sunday school teacher, Augustus Moss, to speak in his place. We'll let Pastor Fizz introduce his guest speaker."

Everyone clapped.

Tally smiled as her eyes surveyed the community center, where residents came in all shapes and forms. Some walked, some wheeled in, some looked more fit than their centenarian age, and some looked older than their real age.

Tally and Gus were not the only ones younger than middle age in the crowd. SSLR hired shift workers to work all week long, and they looked younger than Tally.

"Good evening, y'all," Dad's voice boomed across the room. His fingers touched his ten-gallon hat that a friend had sent from Wyoming a few Christmases ago. "How are your bones and titanium knees doing today?"

The crowd began to speak at the same time, and Tally couldn't hear most of what the people said. She heard short phrases like "could be better" and "none the worse for wear," but otherwise she didn't bother to find out what the crowd said in response to Dad's greeting.

She was more concerned about Gus, whether this last-minute thing was something he was used to. He had gotten a taste of what Dad was like.

She glanced over at Gus, sitting to her left side. He was staring ahead. She wondered if his mind was going over the sermon notes he had made this afternoon. She hadn't asked him about it because she didn't want to add to his nervousness.

She reached over and gently squeezed his arm. When he looked her way, she smiled at him.

He smiled back and placed his left hand over hers, which was still on his right arm. His palm didn't feel sweaty at all. In fact, it was warm and cozy, like a small blanket.

Tally felt nervous. She didn't know why.

"I'm sorry I can't be with you in person tonight, but Roger has promised to invite me back soon," Dad said.

"You'd better!" someone shouted.

"What a crowd we have there tonight. Makes me feel bad I can't be there," Dad said. "In any case, do you remember Byron Moss, who preached with me several months ago?"

The crowd answered in the affirmative.

"His cousin Augustus Moss is visiting him in Atlanta, and he helped Tally drive our Winnebago to Savannah this weekend. Back home in the Bahamas, he teaches Sunday school and serves in various ministry committees at his church, Chapel by the Sea. Let's give it up for Gus, and I look forward to hearing his sermon this evening."

Tally let go of Gus's arm, and he walked up to the podium with his Bible and his folded piece of handwritten sermon notes.

Everyone clapped.

"Hello, I'm Gus," he said in his Bahamian accent.

"Hello, Gus!" came the reply.

"So young!" a female voice said.

Tally chuckled.

Every time Gus looked her way, she made it a point to smile at him. She hoped that it put him at ease and he wouldn't be nervous. She wasn't sure if it worked or not, but he didn't seem to mind looking her way and smiling back at her.

"Let's pray," Gus said from the podium, where he had placed his Bible on a small lectern. "Dear Heavenly Father, we come before You now to hear Your Word. Speak to us. We are listening. Tell us great and mighty things that we don't know."

His voice was smooth over the microphone. He did have a speaker's voice. Tally was sure of it. She could listen to him for hours.

Then and there, he had two Scripture verses. Tally jotted the references down in her notebook even before Gus said them. She knew the two verses by heart.

"First Samuel 3:9 says, 'Speak, Lord, for Your servant hears.' When our hearts are ready to hear the Lord, then we can absorb what He says to us," Gus said. "Recently, a friend reminded me to read Jeremiah 33:3 again."

Tally opened the Bible to Jeremiah 33:3 and followed along as Gus read it aloud.

> *Call to Me, and I will answer you, and show you great and mighty things, which you do not know.*

"Two Fridays ago, my friend and I had an unexpected opportunity to see God at work in a harrowing experience in which two people died."

The crowd gasped.

"She's given me permission to mention her name." Gus pointed to Tally. "I'm sure you've met Tally, Pastor Fizz's daughter, who travels with him and Mrs. Fizz."

"Yes, yes" came the collective replies.

Tally smiled and waved.

"Tell your dad we're praying for him," someone shouted.

"I will. Thank you." Tally went with the flow, but she turned her attention back to Gus, as if to say, "An interactive crowd. What to do?"

"Tell you a story. As Pastor Fizz mentioned, I'm on holiday—vacation—in town. I happened to be helping Tally at the Midtown Chapel Village, planting container gardens with the residents and doing whatever is needed in the ministry." Gus walked around the lectern. "Tally and I had to pick up some T-shirts for a charity event we were doing. We went to the warehouse, and the guard let us in. We didn't know that a deranged man was inside, waiting for us."

The crowd was all ears.

"Long story short, we were held captive for several hours." Gus held up his Bible. "The fact that we're here with you testifies that God delivered us."

A chorus of "amen" went up.

"This evening I want to share with you the four ways God delivered us that Friday." Gus flipped through his Bible. "The first word is Protection. If you have your Bible with you, please turn with me to 1 Corinthians 15:55–57, and follow along as I read it."

Tally found the passage quickly because back in her school days, Mom would conduct Bible drills in which all three of her daughters would compete to see who could find the verses first.

> *"O Death, where is your sting? O Hades, where is your victory?" The sting of death is sin, and the strength of sin is the law. But thanks be to God, who gives us the victory through our Lord Jesus Christ.*

"God protected Tally and me that afternoon from all dangers. We knew that even if we had died, we would go to heaven and be with Jesus," Gus said. "Yet God spared our lives. I was beaten up that Friday, but I didn't die. Tally was not beaten, but she was tied up. I thought I had to be strong for my friend, but the truth is that only God can be our strength because our protection comes from Him. Exodus 15:2 reminds us of that fact."

Flip, flip. Tally was there quickly. She read the verse on her own before Gus did.

> *The Lord is my strength and song,*
> *And He has become my salvation;*

He is my God, and I will praise Him;
My father's God, and I will exalt Him.

"I can't say He is 'my God' unless He really is, right?" Gus asked. "Since I have accepted Jesus as my Lord and Savior, I can say that the Lord is truly 'my strength and song' and 'my salvation.' Acts 4:12 says that 'there is no other name under heaven given among men by which we must be saved' except the name of Jesus. Once saved, I can now declare that Exodus 15:2 is true for me. The Lord is my strength, my song, my salvation, and my God."

Gus smiled at Tally.

"So the first word is Protection. God protects us around the clock. The second word is Power. Do you believe that God is all powerful?"

The crowd nodded and agreed.

"Luke 1:37 says, 'For with God nothing shall be impossible.' Yes, God is so powerful that He can do all things, carry us through all fiery furnaces, and comfort us through the difficulties. Do you agree?"

"Yes!"

"I would be kidding if I said I wasn't afraid that Friday. I tried not to show it because I didn't want Tally to say I was a wimp, you know?" Gus did not look in Tally's direction at this point. "However, the only person who can do impossible things—like get us away from the madman—is God, and Him alone."

Gus returned to the lectern, the same way a lot of preachers did. They walked about the podium to break up the screenshot view of a pastor standing behind his Bible all the time. Growing up as a pastor's kid, Tally had seen all mannerisms.

Gus had the style of a pastor, but he wasn't one. In her conversations with him, he hadn't mentioned a call to preach. All he ever said was either landscaping or finance.

Was it possible for someone to have a pastor's heart who didn't take the pulpit full time?

"Of course, nothing is impossible for God. He has the power to keep us safe, and He has the power to send firefighters to rescue us. Why firefighters? Well, while Tally and I were locked up in a storage room, the warehouse caught on fire."

The crowd gasped again. At this point Tally had lost count of how many times the crowd exclaimed as they listened attentively to Gus. If Dad were here, he'd eat it all up. He loved this sort of response.

"You might say, 'Oh, someone called 911.' God is sovereign. By the grace of God the firefighters arrived as quickly as they did. The search-and-rescue team went inside the warehouse and found us. Yes, the door was fireproof, but it was locked from the outside, so they had to hack it down to get us out."

Tally blinked. In her mind she saw herself being led out by the firefighters, away from danger. That was the key—God delivered her away from danger.

She felt better, but only slightly.

Maybe it hadn't been such a great idea to let Gus mention her name. She wanted to run back to the Winnebago and hide under a blanket.

"The third point is Prayer," Gus continued. He looked at Tally, who forgot to smile. His voice lowered. "Look with me at Hebrews 4:12."

Tally was too slow finding the verse. Gus got there first. He read it aloud.

> *For the word of God is living and powerful, and sharper than any two-edged sword, piercing even to the division of soul and spirit, and of joints and marrow, and is a discerner of the thoughts and intents of the heart.*

"Prayer carried us through the hours we were locked up in the storeroom." Gus stepped away from the lectern again. "Tally is a prayer warrior, I tell you. She knows her Bible verses so well that she was able to pray them back to God. I attribute that to the good foundation she has learned from her parents. We spent quite a bit of time talking about God and praying to Him."

Tally's eyes watered, but she held back her tears.

Thank You, Lord, that I am still here today and that You didn't let me die before my parents. Mom would be so heartbroken if I went first.

"We prayed for our captors. We prayed for our families. We prayed for ourselves," Gus continued. "We didn't stop praying or talking about God in our time of need."

Gus looked around the room. "Protection: God protected us. Power: God delivered us. Prayer: God answered our prayers. Finally, the fourth word: Patience. We knew that God would send help one way or another, but we had to wait for it."

Tally wiped tears from her eyes.

"Let's look at the final verse today." Gus's voice was even and clear. "Philippians 4:13 says, 'I can do all things through Christ who strengthens me.' Many of us have committed this to memory. That Friday, Tally and I had to exercise patience as we waited for help to come. Christ strengthened us as we interacted with our abductor and tried to stay alive."

"God is good all the time," Tally whispered to herself.

When she looked up, she was startled to find Gus staring right at her. She managed a smile so that he would turn away.

He didn't.

So she looked away, hoping that he hadn't seen her red eyes. She prayed that she hadn't interfered with Gus's train of thought as he preached. She didn't mean to cry, but having to sit in the room and listen to Gus rehash that Friday's event was perhaps too much for her.

Then again, she had to face it sooner or later. Besides, Dad had counseled her, and his intense counseling the entire week after the event had helped her tremendously, as had Mom's comfort.

Thankfully, their captivity was short lived, and she was not separated from Gus. They'd worked as a team, and they'd survived it, by God's mercy and grace.

I'm a survivor, not a victim.

"Thank God for protecting us, showing His power over our circumstances, giving us the words to pray in a time of crisis, and enabling us to exercise patience as we waited for deliverance. We're victorious in Christ." Gus closed his Bible. "Thank you for letting me share God's Word this evening. Let's pray."

After he prayed, the SSLR crowd clapped their hands. Gus returned to his seat, and without asking for permission, he held Tally's hand.

And Tally let him.

CHAPTER TWENTY-ONE

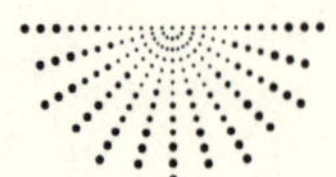

Sunday rolled into Monday quicker than Gus expected, and by late morning they were on the road again. Gus insisted on driving all the way to Atlanta, and Tally chatted with him most of the way to Macon.

Boy, that woman can talk.

Gus didn't stop her, of course, because he wanted to get to know her more, even though their conversations were interrupted by phone calls and potty breaks even before they arrived in Macon.

Somewhere outside of Macon, Byron called.

Gus immediately lifted the phone to his ear.

"Georgia has a hands-free law," Tally told him. "Put him on speakerphone."

Before Gus could do it himself, Tally took the phone from him.

"Keep your eyes on the road." Tally tapped the Speakerphone icon on Gus's phone, but Gus could barely hear Byron with the air conditioner on full blast.

Tally held the phone near Gus's chin so that he could hear better.

"I can talk to you when you get home," Byron said over the phone.

"No problem. Tally's holding the phone for me."

"Nice of her."

"She's nice, yes." Gus heard Tally chuckle.

"I'm charging by the minute," she joked.

"Are you in the Winnebago?" Byron asked.

"Yes. It drives nicely."

"Cruise control?"

"This one has it."

"Very nice. I should borrow it from Pastor Fizz someday. He said I could, but I never do."

"You've flown to your last three vacations in the Bahamas," Gus reminded his cousin.

"Yes, we did. The kids wanted to see their grandmother."

Which reminded Gus to call Aunt Nancy this

week. He hadn't since the warehouse situation because he didn't want her to worry.

"I should call her," Gus said.

"I already told her about what happened to you," Byron replied.

"You did?"

"Yep. She asks about you whenever we talk."

Which is daily? "I should call her, but I don't know what to say to her."

"I figured. She understands. Said she misses lunches with you, but she's happy you're able to get out of town for a change of scenery."

"Does she think I'm sitting around doing nothing?" Gus laughed.

"Told her you're helping out at Midtown Chapel."

Gus waited for Byron to tell him Aunt Nancy's response. When Byron didn't say anything, he had to ask. "What did she say about that?"

"She thinks it's good, but she hopes you don't forget to go home."

Home. Where is home anymore?

Gus used to think that home was wherever Veronique was. Now he wanted to think that he could make a home with Tally.

"Hey, I'll see you when I get to your house tonight," Gus said. "I have to let you go now because Tally's been holding the phone to my chin this entire time."

"Sorry, Tally," Byron said.

"It's no problem at all." Tally's voice sounded like she meant what she said.

Still, Gus hung up. He thanked Tally as he took the phone from her and put it back in his pocket.

After lunch in Macon at a barbecue joint, where Gus filled up on beef brisket and sweet potato fries and a tall glass of iced tea that was entirely too sweet for his palate, the three of them waddled to the Winnebago.

Pastor Fizz and Riona declared that they wanted to take a nap, but Tally insisted that they sit upright with their safety belts on.

"Just in case," she said.

They relented.

Tally also insisted that she drive from Macon to Atlanta, but Gus flipped a coin, and she lost.

So Gus drove again.

They listened to a Christian radio station until the commercials came, and then Tally switched it off.

"I don't care for commercials," she said.

"I don't either, but when I'm driving long distance, it's hard to work the radio knobs while keeping my eyes on the road," Gus admitted. "I mostly line up a bunch of podcasts or my own playlist and then listen to those. Unless I'm driving the school bus, in which case I listen to nothing but the kids. I don't want to be distracted."

Tally was silent for a bit, but then she asked, "Tell me, Gus. What is a man with a Harvard MBA doing driving a school bus and mowing lawns?"

"I told you I burned out."

"Yes, you did. I wondered if there was more to it."

"That's all." That was all he wanted to say. Then again, why did Tally bring it up? He felt cornered, sitting in the driver's seat, unable to run away.

"I didn't want to put you on the spot," Tally said.

"But you did."

"Because I think there's something unresolved."

Gus chuckled. "Are you trying to psychoanalyze me? I'm driving a two-ton RV and must concentrate."

"Keep your eyes on the road." Tally smiled.

She stopped talking. Maybe she felt sorry she had bought up his failures. Yet Gus didn't like having to listen to the air conditioner.

Tally turned on the radio again.

Gus reached for the knob and turned it off.

"Let's talk about my stalled career," Gus said point blank.

Her face brightened up. She looked impressed.

Gus knew for sure that she liked transparency in him.

At the same time, he was fully aware that Pastor Fizz and Riona were in the back. If they weren't napping, they could hear what he was about to say. He trusted Pastor Fizz as a counseling pastor, having been to a couple of helpful sessions with him the week after the warehouse situation. He also trusted Tally, or believed that he did. As for Riona, she would eventually find out anyway, being married to one and a mother to the other.

"I burned out in a corporate setting because I found the environment too stifling," Gus explained. "Even if I went to work without a tie, I could still feel a mental noose around my neck. The demands of the job, having to meet expectations, the daily routine of sitting in an office all year long...make me break out in cold sweat."

"Why don't you start your own financial consulting company?" Tally asked.

"What?" That thought never crossed his mind.

"You saw things as this or that. Either you work in a corporation for an employer, or you quit. You leave behind your knowledge and training in accounting and finance. You run outdoors." Tally put a hand on his arm. "What if you started your own financial consulting company? Or work as an independent consultant? Take only the jobs you want. You work just enough to make ends meet or support a family, and then the rest of the time, you can do whatever else."

Did she just mention a family? What is she asking?

"I already started a company—albeit a landscaping company and not financial consulting." Gus kept his hands on the steering wheel. "I think I can support a family as a landscaper."

"Of course you can. Whom God calls, He provides, as the Bible says." Tally retracted her hand. "I might be wrong about this, but last night, when I was praying for you, I wondered whether God has a plan for your accounting and finance degrees, or whether you've left the field for good."

"You prayed for me?" It was almost all that Gus heard.

Tally nodded. "Is that okay?"

"More than okay. Please pray for me whenever you want. I need all the prayers I can get." For what, he wasn't sure. But he wanted Tally to think about him.

A lot.

Tally's phone rang, and Gus listened to her conversation. How could he not? They were in the same space, after all.

"Levi broke up with Soline again? What's new? How does that affect us? Oh, I see." Tally shook her head. "No, Maggie. You can't take half a day off today. It's her prerogative to call in sick from work, but I need you to run over to T-Shirts 'R' We to pick up the new T-shirts for the Stone Mountain hike this Saturday. Yes, all four hundred T-shirts. Levi can go with you and drive the church van. Whatever you do, don't put the shirts in the warehouse."

She paused for a moment.

Glanced at Gus, who said nothing.

"No, you take them back to church. Find space in our office," Tally said. "We'll sit around the T-shirts if we have to, honey. Ask the other ministry assistants if you can stuff T-shirts into their office spaces. Or find an empty Sunday school classroom that isn't used on Wednesday night. We'll make it work."

Gus didn't say a word, but he felt that in spite of their keeping busy and all, they were still recovering from the warehouse situation. He wondered when Tally would be able to go to any warehouse again.

After Tally hung up, she closed her eyes. Gus wondered if she was praying.

Then she said, "In the name of Jesus. Amen."

So yes, she had prayed.

"Anything I can help with?" Gus asked.

"Will you be there at the hike on Saturday?"

"Yes, I plan to—unless we get rained out."

"Yeah. We'll postpone it again if that happens," Tally said. "Just like our beach walk."

"Two rain checks so far."

"Beach walk and what?"

"We said we'd have dinner together," Gus reminded her.

"We've had dinners together."

"With your parents though."

"Dinner is dinner."

"Do you remember what we agreed to do?" Gus knew she remembered.

"What do you remember?"

"That I owe you dinner—just the two of us—if we survived the warehouse. We did."

Tally brushed it off. "No need to worry about it."

"In that case, we should have dinner."

"All right. We will at some point in time. What's dinner with friends, right?"

Friends? They had held hands on Sunday, and Tally only called him a friend?

What if I want to be more than friends?

Gus recalled what Byron had said to him the week before.

Ideally, your wife is also your best friend.

"You're saying we're missing a beach walk and dinner out," Tally said.

Gus nodded. "When the time comes, will you go for a walk with me on the beach and have dinner somewhere?"

"Doesn't have to be on the same day."

"Great. Will call."

Once they reached Atlanta, traffic picked up.

"Here we go again. Rush hour," Tally said. "Stop and go. Stop and go. Atlanta traffic for you, Mr. Moss."

"I'm getting used to it."

"On Friday you said that you could live here. For real?"

"You mean move and work in Atlanta?" Gus wanted clarification.

"I guess. I don't know what your visa situation

is, but if you could get a job here in town, would you move here?"

"I'll go wherever God calls me."

"My dad would say that's a good answer," Tally said. "Of course, Dad is almost always right. I rarely disagree with him."

They chitchatted about ministry work all the way to Pastor Fizz's house, where Gus parked the Winnebago slightly on the left side of the driveway so that when the RV door opened, they had a bit of cement to step on and not all grass.

The pastor and his wife looked like they had just woken up from a long nap. What was left of Pastor Fizz's hair was frizzled and wiry. Fiona's hair was smashed on one side.

"Would you like to stay for dinner?" Pastor Fizz asked Gus as they unloaded their suitcases from the Winnebago.

Gus felt like they had just eaten, but that had been four hours ago back in Macon—it would've been three if traffic hadn't been so bad on Interstate 285.

"We're ordering out and eating on paper plates, so no dishes," Riona said.

"Oh, I can help with dishes. I'm just wondering whether Byron is waiting for me to have dinner with him." Gus pulled out his phone. "Let me check."

Gus texted Byron.

The answer came back instantly. "Byron's not worried about it. I'll be staying with him until I fly home to Nassau, and there will be time for other dinners. So yes, I'll stay for dinner with you. I don't mind splitting the cost."

"No, no, it's on us," Tally said. "What would you like to eat? Chinese? Italian? Mexican?"

"Whatever you want. I'm not picky." Gus climbed back into the RV to get more suitcases.

"Your call, Mom and Dad." Tally followed Gus into the RV.

They made quick work of hauling things out of there and onto Pastor Fizz's trolley. Tally stayed behind to wipe down the countertops and small refrigerator.

Gus offered to help, but she said no.

She wore gloves and cleaned the bathroom and toilet—or commode, as they called it—and then bagged the trash.

Gus took the trash out to the big trash containers in the garage.

When he came back to see what else could be done, Tally was wiping down the seats and dining table.

"Almost done," she said. "Go sit down somewhere and rest. Dinner will be here shortly. They usually only take twenty minutes, tops. We live very close to restaurants."

"It must be nice to live in town."

"Unfortunately, you hear the city traffic all around the clock. Sometimes sirens, but usually big trucks." Tally rinsed and wrung out her rag cloth, then hung it on the handlebar that went across the small dishwasher. "I almost miss Tybee Island, with its quietness."

"Then you'll love the New Providence Island," Gus said.

"I remember."

"Four years ago. It hasn't changed, by the way. Life is slower and more laid back."

"I know." She sighed. "Every time I travel with my parents to Tybee or Savannah or St. Simon's Island or even Lakeside, I feel as though life slows down a bit in those places. I come home and I feel this. Every. Single. Time."

Gus sat down on the bench chair that Tally had cleaned.

Tally slid in onto the other bench chair across the small dining table. "Don't get me wrong. I love Atlanta. I was born here, grew up here, and love everything about the big city. I can't imagine living in a small town, but I would be kidding if I said that the thought hadn't crossed my mind that after all these years, I need a change of pace."

Gus nodded.

"I don't know why I've been thinking about my work lately, but it might explain why I asked you about your career, why you're doing this or that." Tally smiled to Gus. "It's because I'm evaluating my work in ministry."

"It's not just a career to you."

"Right. Ministry has always been a part of my life ever since I was a little kid. Growing up in a pastor's home makes serving God natural to me. My sisters and I are fortunate in that we didn't rebel against our parents while they served the Lord."

"Because your parents raised you right."

"Well, it's truly by God's grace that we didn't stray. My parents know pastor friends who did everything right and still weep over their kids who hated them, left home, and never returned, or whose kids have gone prodigal, or have been in and out of rehab. The stories are heartbreaking."

"I'm sorry."

"In any case, I feel that if I leave my work at the church..." She sighed. "I don't know what I'm thinking at this point."

"Earlier, you were asking me why I don't just create a consulting company to pick and choose projects so that I don't burn out in a corporate setting," Gus reminded her. "Did you have something similar in mind? Perhaps you were thinking that you could start a non-profit ministry of your own, since you do speaking engagements. With that, you might branch out into podcasts or books."

"I don't want to travel all over the place."

"You're saying?"

"I'm in my midthirties now," Tally said. "I could work in women's ministry for the rest of my life, but I've been so focused on my career that I have no time to think about a family of my own."

You're telling me all this because...

Gus didn't say it aloud.

"I don't want you to get the wrong idea about when I let you hold my hand at SSLR last night," Tally said.

"What wrong idea might I be getting?" Gus couldn't begin to guess.

"I don't know." She sounded genuine.

"Maybe we're both tired after our long drive. Let's take another rain check and revisit this later." Gus smiled to put her at ease.

Tally nodded. She walked toward the door of

the RV, which had been open this entire time. "We'll talk later about it."

Gus stood beside her. "Don't get me wrong. I wanted to hold your hand."

"Same." Tally lowered her face, suddenly looking shy.

"Do platonic friends hold hands?" Gus asked.

"Sometimes, but not usually with the opposite gender—not in my social circle, anyway. Family members, yes, perhaps?"

"Do platonic friends do this?" Gus lifted Tally's chin gently and waited for Tally to respond. She didn't pull away. He planted a light kiss on her forehead. So light it might not have been there at all had either one not noticed.

Tally smiled and put her hands on his waist.

Was that an invitation? Gus didn't move. His thumb and finger were still on her chin. He really didn't know what to do at this point.

Tally stepped toward him and placed her head on his shoulder.

Gus held her in his arms. She was warm and cuddly. Her shoulders relaxed. He could stay there at the RV door and hug her all night, but no, he had to leave soon since he was no longer staying at the Fitzpatricks' home—which was a good thing, considering they had gone beyond being friends at this point.

He thought about his cousin Byron and how he had handled his long-distance relationship with Tina after their summer together in the Bahamas. Byron had wanted to go to seminary long before he met Tina. So instead of finding a Bible college in Nassau, he opted for one in Atlanta, where Tina's pottery studio had moved from Savannah.

It had worked out for them because after he became a reverend, Byron worked as one of the assistant pastors at Midtown Chapel, where he and Tina both attended church. Byron also taught in the Bible college he graduated from. Byron had applied for his American citizenship.

As for Gus and Tally, their story was a bit more complicated. Tally had an established ministry in Atlanta. Gus was sure he'd continue working at his own landscaping company in Nassau. In order for them to be together, one of them had to move. At forty-one years old, Gus didn't know if he wanted to move to America and continue working in landscaping in a foreign country.

If he moved to Atlanta, he'd probably return to accounting and finance—and back into the corporate furnace he had fled from. Would God pull him back that far? He wasn't sure.

He couldn't see how his future with Tally could work out, unless he could do what Tally had suggested—start a financial consulting firm.

I don't know.

He felt tired thinking about having to start something from the ground up. Would he want to do that at all?

Yet he knew he was in love.

And Tally indicated she felt the same about him.

"You go home in two weeks though," Tally said.

Gus prolonged his hug.

"Let's figure out the main thing first and then sort out our careers later," Gus whispered in her ears.

"Sounds like a plan," Tally asked. "What's our main thing?"

Our main thing. She said our.

"For one; we both want to do the will of God," Gus said.

"Yes. So where do we go from here?"

"That is the question."

CHAPTER TWENTY-TWO

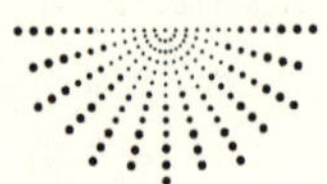

"Oooh. A gentleman." On the video call, Colette clapped. She was sitting on a sofa in her log cabin in Lakeside, dressed in floral pajamas, a Christmas present from Tally some years ago. Her phone camera was on a stand on the coffee table, she'd said.

"I know, right." Tally smiled into her own phone, held in her hand. As she watched her sister drink coffee, she missed her—and their youngest sister, Adalia, too—but Tally had no time to drive down to Florida to see them, with the Village projects still ongoing and incomplete.

"Are you sure all he did was hug you and kiss you—lightly—on your forehead?" Colette's sly smile betrayed her thoughts. She wanted more drama.

"No drama, sis. That was all we did until Mom called us to come inside for dinner." Tally sat back on the sofa in Mom's sunroom.

Outside the bay window, it was still dark. However, Tally had gotten up at five o'clock to shower and get ready for the big day today. Tally and her sister Colette had shared a room back in high school and college, and they'd ended up waking up at the same time every day. It became a habit for them to this day, even though they didn't live together anymore.

Yes, they were early risers, getting up at five o'clock on most days. "Sleeping in" meant that Tally didn't open her eyes until six. "Goofing off" meant she was still in bed at seven in the morning.

"You weren't even aware that the food delivery guy came and went," Colette said.

"Well, we were in the RV."

"You said the door was open. The RV is usually parked outside Mom and Dad's house, near the front door where the food delivery person would've rung the doorbell."

Tally nodded. "I guess we weren't paying attention."

"Are you in love, Tally?" Colette leaned toward

the camera. She had no makeup on, and her freckles spread from cheek to nose to cheek.

Tally simply smiled.

"What about Malachi?" Colette asked. "You've had a crush on him for at least ten years."

"As you can see, if something should have happened between Malachi and me, it would've happened years ago."

"True."

"I was in my twenties. Just got out of college and working and still a kid at heart, I think."

Colette put down her mug on the coffee table in front of her. "Are we late bloomers?"

"What do you mean?"

"We're in our thirties, and yet we haven't found our true loves."

"What are you in, Colette? A fairy tale?" Tally laughed. "Please don't tell me you tried a dating app."

"My friends are."

"Find new friends."

"What do you have against dating apps?" Colette raised her eyebrows.

"Colette. Don't let Henry—or Mom and Dad—hear you."

"See what I mean? We're still doing things—or

not doing things—as though Mom and Dad saw us. Are we not still kids? Not late bloomers?"

"It can happen, I suppose. But I've been focusing on my work and ministry. There's just so much to be done."

Colette nodded. "I'm busy here too. The resort is booming. Our waiting list is one-year long. I don't have time for love."

"We'll grow old together and be roommates again."

"Somehow, I think you'll get married before I do."

"Henry is waiting for you," Tally said. "He's always had a thing for you since college. Followed you all the way back to Atlanta and then all the way to Lakeside."

"I don't know about that. He's a freelance photographer, so he goes wherever there's work. Grandma hired him for the promos, not me."

"Why did Grandma hire him?" Tally asked. "We all know she's a matchmaker."

"I don't need a matchmaker. I can find a boyfriend on my own."

"Says the woman who hasn't dated anyone in the last how many years?" Tally joked. "No, seriously, don't rush. If I'd asked Malachi out, he probably would've gone to dinner with me—since we're friends, right? However, if I had pushed for him, I would've made a big mistake."

"You're giving up on Malachi."

"He was never mine in the first place. He travels a lot and is gone a lot. Even though I travel also because my speaking engagements take me to women's conferences in the region, I don't travel in the same geographic space as Malachi."

"Speaking of geographic space, isn't that a problem for you and Gus though? He's going home to the Bahamas soon, right?" Colette sipped more coffee. "Maybe you should talk with Tina about how she and Byron worked it out. They seemed to be in a similar situation back when they were dating."

"I think we're different," Tally said. "Byron was going to seminary anyway, so he found a Bible college in Atlanta, where Tina owns a pottery studio. On the other hand, Gus has a permanent job he loves in Nassau, and I have a ministry I can't leave in Atlanta."

"Does that mean your relationship is doomed before it begins?"

Tally nodded slightly, but she wanted to cry. "We both have established careers. In our case, I can travel to the Bahamas to speak in women's conference if I'm invited, but most my conferences are in the States."

"You could live in Nassau and fly to those conferences."

"I suppose I could."

"Then you'd be with Gus. And I'd get free room and board when I go visit you. Just make sure it's a beach house or else it's not worth it."

"Putting the cart before the horse, Colette." Tally laughed. "Let's talk about something else. How are Grandma's knees?"

"She's recovering nicely. The PT helped."

"Good." Grandma hated physical therapy, which was another reason Colette and Adalia had gone to see her. They had taken turns to get Grandma to PT every week.

"How's Dad?" Colette's voice was solemn.

"Once he found out it was heartburn, he was ready to bounce back," Tally said. "We had to remind him that he does have two leaky valves and they aren't going to get better for him."

"What's he going to do about it?"

"The cardiologist told him he has to lose weight. That will help with his cholesterol problems and high blood pressure."

"Dad equates losing weight to starving himself."

"I want him with us a little longer," Tally said.

"We all do. Maybe that's why he looks at his three daughters as little girls. He doesn't listen to kids like us when we tell him to exercise."

"You're the one who tells him to exercise. I haven't said a thing—which is a problem, honestly. I don't have the guts to tell him to get in shape because... I mean, look at me. I need to lose about twenty pounds myself."

"Then the key is to get Mom on an exercise regimen," Colette said. "If only they'd move here. We could all walk together around the lake in the early morning when it's cooler."

"You know they're praying about moving to Lakeside to take care of Grandma."

"We'll keep praying."

"For God to show Mom and Dad His perfect will, not ours," Tally said.

"Amen. Is Dad's schedule busy for the rest of the year?"

Tally nodded. "I'm hoping he'll slow down a bit, because I really need to focus on the Village project the rest of summer, and I might not have enough time to drive the Winnebago for them when they travel to speak at churches."

"Tell him."

Tally didn't reply.

"You haven't told him, have you? You try to fit it all in, and then you won't have time for Gus."

"What are you talking about?"

"I'm your sister, and I can tell you as it is."

"That's the Fitzpatrick way." Tally switched hands holding the phone. She sat back on the sofa, waiting to see if Colette would say something she hadn't already realized.

"You've been busy all year at the Village because you depend on volunteers—some of whom don't show up, so you have to wait for other volunteers to come. All that takes time. I don't know how to help you be more efficient, but you're spending a lot of time waiting for people and money."

"That about sums it up, but that's not all I do though."

"Exactly. You also have your women's ministry duties at church, conferences to organize, and speaking engagements to go to. Since you're spread so thin, you rely heavily on your ministry assistant, Maggie, to sort out all the details for you. That's a lot to manage for someone in her position and salary. In essence, she's doing a lot of the organizing for you, fielding calls, fitting all your meetings in."

"Hold on." Tally sat up. "I do a lot of work too. I make all the decisions. I was at the Village all week this week. I spent a lot of time with the single mothers this week, ministering to them. That's my job, Colette."

"I know. I'm not diminishing your role at all. I'm just saying that because you wear several hats, your entire day is spent dealing with ministry." Colette's voice was caring, filled with concern. "After work you barely have time for your parents and yourself, let alone a boyfriend."

"You're saying?"

"I'm not smarter than you are, and I can't cast the first stone—I don't have a boyfriend either—but I know that I have to give up something to make room for something else."

Tally wanted to listen to Colette, but it was painful to hear.

"Sis, it's between you and God what needs to go and what needs to stay on your calendar," Colette said. "I suggest you make a list of the major things you do all week, and pray over them to see if you can fit in life somewhere."

"Life?"

Colette nodded. "You might be in ministry, but truly, your life is embroiled in working around the clock."

"Ministry is work, Colette. A whole lot of work."

"I know. We grew up in ministry. What I'm

trying to say is this. Dad is a pastor, so he's always one. Whether he is awake or asleep, he's a pastor. Whether he's in the office or at home, he's a pastor. He never takes the hat off. On vacations, he's always a pastor. You can tell by how he speaks and what he does when he's on vacation."

"True. His pastor mode never turns off." Tally began to understand what her sister was saying to her. "You're trying to tell me that I've got ministry mode on all the time."

"No, sis. You have *work* mode turned on. Your work mode is disguising itself as ministry."

"I'm not doing busywork."

"I don't mean that. I didn't realize it until I moved to Lakeside, and I'm far enough away from you to look at your circumstances objectively. As much as I love how you're so committed to ministry, you're taking on a lot of sub-ministries under the umbrella of your director position, and when things get busy, you're going through the checklists and completing each task. At the end of the week, it's all work to you. Ministry becomes secondary."

"Ministry is why I work."

"Weren't you exhausted last night?"

Bingo.

"I was very exhausted. We worked very hard at the Village. Someone at church paid a company to help us put up twenty tiny homes this week, and we spent the rest of the time painting and furnishing them. I was bushed at the end of the week."

"Not because of the painting. Because in between the construction work, you also minister to the single moms at the Village. How many people did you pray with this week about their life problems?"

"I can't remember. Many."

"You're only one person. You have to choose your battles. What do you like to do most? Ministering to the moms, speaking at workshops, constructing the Village, providing for the people's needs, driving Dad on his speaking tours, paperwork at the office, fundraising with donors? Which ones would you keep and which ones would you delegate?"

Tally opened her mouth to say something, but her phone alarm went off, startling her. She shut it off. "I have to go. Time to drive to Stone Mountain for our morning hike today."

No, she wasn't picking up anyone. Gus was carpooling with Byron. Mom and Dad had decided to stay home all day. Soline had bailed out also, after her breakup with Levi.

Sometimes Tally would pick up her assistant,

but this morning Maggie was driving her own car because she was skipping the picnic lunch to spend time consoling Soline.

"I'll let you go. Think about what I said." Colette raised her mug in the air. "I'm praying for God's best for you."

"Thank you." Tally hung up the phone and then picked up her Bible from the coffee table.

She had read the Bible before calling her sister but totally forgot to share the verse she'd read this morning. How could she forget the Word of God?

Then again, the passage was long and required a discussion.

Still, that was no excuse.

Quickly, she texted her sister, reading aloud what she tapped on the phone. "Forgot to tell you that I read Colossians 1 this morning and prayed for our family."

Colette texted back a thank-you GIF with lots of hearts.

CHAPTER TWENTY-THREE

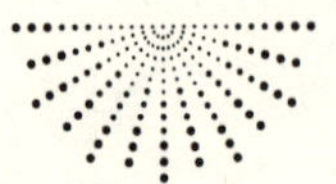

Gus arrived with his cousin Byron at Stone Mountain Park forty-five minutes before sunrise. Dawn had broken, but it was still dark, save for the parking-lot lamps.

He looked around to find Tally, but didn't see her. She had to come, since she was one of the organizers, so Gus expected to see her soon.

His heart filled with anticipation at the thought of walking up this granite outcrop with Tally. He had never been there before, and he wondered if it was like any other hike up hills and mountains.

Was the trail steep? Would there be time for him to chat with Tally? Thoughts like that filled Gus's mind as he watched a crowd gather up ahead between the parking lot and the start of the trail. Everyone wore bright-yellow T-shirts like Gus did.

"Ready?" Byron tied his shoelace with his foot on the back bumper of his SUV. "Water bottle? Phone? Hat?"

Gus nodded, tipping his baseball hat and lifting up a bottled water.

He waited for Byron to adjust his small backpack, and then they made their way through the parking lot to the Midtown Chapel group standing on the grass by the sidewalk.

And there was Tally, dressed in the yellow T-shirt and a pair of black hiking pants. She looked like a bee, but not quite a bumble bee. She carried a small backpack.

She stood next to Levi, who was wearing shorts in this cool weather. Levi carried a lantern, which he lifted above his head.

"Good morning, everyone!" Levi shouted. "If you can't hear me, come close to the front."

The people in the back moved to the front. Gus and Byron followed. In fact, Byron circled around the crowd and went to the very front, where they were several people away from Levi.

It was then that Gus saw him.

Malachi Jacobs.

Tally's crush way back when.

Do thirty-something people still have crushes?

Malachi was standing next to his sister, Maggie, who was decked out in a yellow headband, yellow jogging pants, and yellow shoes, all in an effort to go with her yellow T-shirt. She carried an iPad with her, and a cross-body bag—also in...yes, yellow.

"Welcome, one and all." Tally scanned the crowd. "Has everyone signed the liability form, especially if you're walking up the trail with children? If you haven't signed it online, Levi has it on paper."

Gus wondered how they'd confirm that everyone did sign it?

"Come to me for the form." Tally pointed toward Levi. "If you have already signed and gotten your wristband days ago, follow me up the mountain. If not, go see Levi."

Ah, so that was how they checked: the wristband.

Gus was impressed at the organization.

However, Gus didn't have a wristband, although he had signed the form. He moved toward Levi to see if he could get his name verified and receive a wristband.

"We have ten minutes—if we leave late, you're going to miss the sunrise—so let me make it quick," Tally said. "Safety first! I am assuming you've all read the safety email we sent out. There's dew on the ground from last night, and the pine needles might be slippery. If you fall on the trail, come find me. I have a first-aid kit. If you fall off the mountain, you're on your own."

Everyone laughed.

She can crack a joke. Gus had no idea.

"Everybody, keep your cell phone with you at all times, preferably with the locator turned on, just in case we lose you somewhere," Tally added.

"I'll hang around for the next half an hour for latecomers," Levi said. "After that I'll be over at the picnic grounds all morning. If you decide to give up halfway up the mountain, just go over there, and we have snacks. We don't start grilling burgers until eleven o'clock, so you have four hours to get to the top of the mountain and down again and make your way to the picnic grounds."

"Which picnic grounds?" someone asked.

"Check the Stone Mountain page on the church website," Levi told him.

Gus reached Levi and asked quietly for a wristband. Levi checked his name off his iPad roster and gave him a bright-yellow wristband.

"Five minutes left." Tally put away her phone. She pointed to Byron. "Pastor Byron, could we ask you to pray for us? Then we'll get going."

Byron nodded and remained where he was as he prayed as loudly as he could so that the crowd could hear him.

When everyone said, “Amen!” Gus looked up to see Malachi and Maggie walking toward Tally. Not to be left behind, Gus made his move to be by Tally’s side, to claim her.

“Hey, Gus.” Tally stepped closer to him, and her arm touched his.

Malachi looked at them, a tiny smile on his face.

“Glad you could join us, Mal,” Levi said. “Are you going to help me grill?”

“Sure. I’ll be there at eleven.” Malachi slapped Levi’s shoulders, as if it were an unspoken encouragement.

Levi didn’t look sad—at least it wasn’t on his face—that he had just broken up with his girlfriend, whose name had escaped Gus at this moment.

Keeping busy might be helping him.

Gus recalled that he had also kept busy in the months after splitting from Veronique.

Malachi turned to his sister. “Ready to climb?”

Maggie handed the iPad to Levi. “Our office iPad, so you know the password.”

“Let’s go!” Tally led the way with a flashlight in front of her, even though the sky was lighting up.

Some people had already gone ahead of them. They looked like they might have walked up and down Stone Mountain regularly, since they knew the way.

Gus wanted to take out a map, but the light wasn't too great under the trees. Byron walked with him and chatted a bit.

"Just follow the crowd," Tally answered someone who asked for directions. "Follow the yellow shirts."

Gus wanted to hang around Tally but didn't want to offend Byron. Fortunately, Malachi and Maggie came up to them, headlights on their foreheads. Malachi said he had something to chat with Byron about.

Gus fell back so that he was now walking beside Tally.

Their path was lined with bedrocks, the granite surface beaten smooth by thousands of hiking shoes over the course of decades.

Tally grabbed Gus's arm and shone her flashlight to a granite outcrop along the way. "People have walked up Stone Mountain since the nineteenth century, and every now and then they carved their name or year to let it be known that they were here."

"Interesting." Gus took a quick snapshot with

his phone camera. "How long does it take to get up there?"

"It's a fast walk now because the incline is not too steep, but halfway up we'll be going vertical—a little bit—and then we might slow down."

Gus nodded. "Let's get going then. Sunrise in half an hour."

They walked in silence most of the time because Tally was huffing. "I haven't exercised in a few months, so I'm in bad shape. Gained a few pounds. Last year I walked an hour a day for five days a week. This path up would've been easy for me because I walked two miles per hour."

Gus didn't tell her that he had kept fit working outdoors in landscaping, but after work hours he lifted weights before dinner. Unfortunately, he too hadn't exercised in the last two weeks he'd been here.

The climb was painless. He could reach the top in less than half an hour, but he wanted to stay with Tally.

Dawn was gone and daylight was coming. Gus could see the pine trees and other trees he didn't recognize lining their way. He was glad that he wore his hiking boots because after the small forest, it was all granite beneath his feet all the way to the top.

Tally turned off her flashlight. "Almost there."

The steel railings on both sides of the climb provided support for them going up. At first Gus wanted to hold Tally's hand to help her up, but it was impractical because they were going single file.

Gus let Tally walk in front of him.

The wind blew through his hair and through Tally's short ponytail. He had never seen her hair down, but she had cut it before he arrived in Atlanta. He wondered how she'd look in person if her hair had been longer.

Tally turned her head toward him and nearly lost her footing.

Gus held her waist. "You okay?"

"Yeah. I need to rest when we get up there."

"Sure. Is there like a gift shop?"

Tally laughed. "Yes, there is. There's also a small café and plenty of restrooms."

"Are you going to walk down?" Gus asked.

"Nooooo." Tally grinned. "I'm taking the sky lift—cable car—down. Join me?"

"Sure. Don't we have to walk back to our vehicles?"

"Yes, but it's on flat sidewalk, not vertical like this."

Gus googled to find out Stone Mountain's elevation. "What's one thousand six hundred and eighty-six feet in meters?" A random conversion app told him that it was nearly five hundred and fourteen meters.

"Not Everest," Tally said.

They cleared the steepest part of the climb and stood on top of the mountain, which was flat and had puddles of water here and there.

"You can see the city of Atlanta from here." Tally led Gus to the edge of the mountaintop and pointed this way and that.

Gus took snapshots all around and even took a few panorama photos.

"Sunrise, everybody!" Malachi walked East. They all followed.

Beyond the mountain, the vast plains stretched all the way to the horizon. A huge portion of it was covered with trees that looked like green cotton balls. Gus took more photos.

He was standing next to Tally, who was taking fewer photos than tourist Gus.

The sun rose over the horizon, a ball of fire rising into the clear blue sky.

"Psalm 113:3 says, 'From the rising of the sun to its going down, the Lord's name is to be praised.' This is my Father's world." Tally's voice faded into a swirl of wind that started whipping around the top of the mountains.

Malachi happened to be standing nearby, and he started singing the hymn, "This Is My Father's World."

Maggie and Byron joined in, and then almost everyone wearing a yellow shirt sang the chorus.

Gus sang too, but his voice was not as loud as Malachi's. He felt intimidated. Challenged, perhaps.

And he knew he shouldn't feel this way.

The sun continued to rise into the sky as everyone took photos.

Tally tapped Gus's arm. "Get a selfie of us and the sun."

"Okay." Gus turned around and tried to get the sun within the camera's view. He ducked this way and tipped his head that way.

Tally wrapped her arm around Gus, and her free hand made a peace sign. She smiled, and Gus snapped twice, for good measure.

The sun was just to the left of her head, and they leaned against each other.

Gus thought it was a cute photo.

"Let me see." She peered. "Oh, that's nice. Send it to Mom and Dad."

"Right now?"

"Uh-huh. And send one to me too."

Gus did so but wondered what Pastor Fizz

would say when he saw the two of them that close together in the photo.

Their group spread out as people milled about, chatted, took photos, and scattered.

Malachi, Maggie, and Byron decided to walk down the same way they came. It was light now, and they didn't need any flashlights.

"You coming, Gus?" Byron asked.

"I'll take the cable car with Tally," Gus replied. "I'm sure we're not the only ones."

Byron nodded. "You'll have to walk about a third around the mountain to get to the car."

"Should've parked at the cable car station," Tally said. "Oh well."

"Either way we'd have to walk, whether before or after the climb." Gus waved to the trio walking down.

"See y'all at the picnic area," Malachi said to Tally and Gus as he walked after Maggie and Byron.

"Save me a seat at the picnic table," Gus said to Byron.

"Will do. I'll get there before Tina and the kids, I'm sure." Byron waved.

A number of church members returned to the trail with them, leaving only a handful of their group members up on the mountain.

Tally looked away into the distance.

Gus stood next to her at first, then he slid his arm around her waist. After a while, he was standing behind her. His cheek brushed her temple.

"You're warm," Tally said.

"Are you cold?"

"No. Cozy."

They watched the distance together, not saying much to each other. When the sun was in the sky, they put on their sunglasses.

"What time is it?" Tally asked as she checked her own phone. "Not even eight o'clock."

She lifted her phone and took a selfie of them.

"Shall we check out the gift shop you asked about?" Tally smiled.

"I was only making small talk."

"We're heading that way though, and the gift shop is near the sky lift. We have to buy tickets and wait in line." She started walking. "Tourist season."

Gus followed Tally. They went to the restrooms and then met at the gift shop.

Tally showed him a cotton T-shirt. It had a screen printing of Stone Mountain in the back. "I'll get you one if you like."

"Me? You're buying me a T-shirt?" Gus wondered what he should do.

"Sure. It's two for one, so pick what you want."

Gus looked for something green. As expected, Tally found a shirt with red designs on it.

Tally paid and then made Gus carry the shopping bag with the two T-shirts in it.

Gus insisted on paying for their one-way ticket down the mountain.

They sat at the station, and waited for the cable car to return.

"What do you think of Stone Mountain so far?" Tally asked.

"Nice. The weather warms up quickly, so I'm glad we hiked in the morning hours." Gus's arm was stretched across Tally's shoulders.

"A bit too early for some, but we did catch the sunrise."

Tally's phone pinged. She checked the message. "Dad said he liked the photo but asked me to tell you to make sure I get home before nine at night."

She laughed.

"What does that mean?" Gus tried not to read too much into it.

"Dad's attempt at humor. Feel free to ignore."

They didn't have to wait too long. The cable car came, unloading passengers—some of whom looked like tourists with their too-much sunscreen and floppy hats and the telltale sign of following a tour guide.

Tally stepped into the cable car first, and Gus came up behind her. She went to the window and looked outside.

The cable car was crowded, and Gus felt shy about hugging Tally. He saw two other couples in the cable car, and they were cuddly with their significant others.

Gus asked if they should take another photo.

"Why not?" Tally asked.

So they took one with the window and sky as the backdrop.

Gus was happy to have those photo memories of his time with Tally. He wasn't sure where they would go from there, with the ocean between them once he went home to the Bahamas.

However, he was contented and at peace with Tally by his side.

Lord, if she is the one, then please bridge the ocean between us.

Could he give up his landscaping business and move to America to be with Tally, as Byron had done for Tina?

Could he sacrifice his peace of mind and go back to accounting or finance just to have a career here in town so that he wasn't jobless?

He wasn't sure if he wanted to do landscaping in Atlanta. To begin with, he wasn't familiar with the flora in the metropolitan Atlanta area. Besides, the more he thought about it, the less he wanted to spend the rest of his life landscaping, even though he could've gone back to college to get a landscape architecture degree.

In other words, he could not imagine leaving the Bahamas and starting over in Atlanta. As for marrying, Gus thought that it might require a very brave woman to leave her hometown and move to Nassau to be with him.

What if that excluded Tally?

Gus did not want to ask Tally to do anything that would cause her to back away from their relationship.

I know I shouldn't fear, Lord, but I fear losing Tally more than I ever did with Veronique.

That was when he knew he had gotten over Veronique.

CHAPTER TWENTY-FOUR

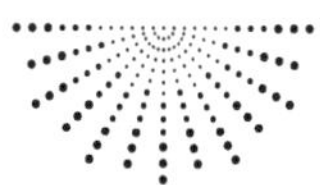

"What a fun job you have," Gus said as they hopped off the cable car at the base of Stone Mountain.

"Job?" Tally led the way out of the ticket plaza. She knew where to go without a map. She had been here many times before.

"Yes, your job as the women's ministry director."

"I see. Yes. When you said 'job,' it reminded me of what my sister said to me this morning."

"This morning? She got up early?"

Tally glanced at him. "Curious, aren't you?"

Gus shrugged. "I'm an early riser, but not all my friends are."

"My sisters and I are all early risers. More to get done in the day if we wake up at dawn."

"Exactly."

Tally navigated her way through the parking lot and onto the sidewalk by Robert E. Lee Boulevard. "We go left here and walk about a quarter way around the mountain to get back to the walk-up trail lot to pick up my car."

"Lead the way." Gus followed Tally. "So what did your sister say about jobs?"

His question made Tally hesitate. Should she talk to Gus about the discussion she'd had with Colette at dawn?

Maybe Gus had some insight she might have missed.

Here goes.

"She wants me to think about the differences between the *motion* of work and the *meaning* of ministry." Tally sighed. "Since I'm in ministry full time, either one can be perfunctory."

"I can see the dilemma. You draw a salary from the church, so your job and ministry are both in the same location."

"Right. Am I working hard because my salary demands it or because my ministry calling compels me?"

"Sounds like a good question for mental health."

"And spiritual and emotional health too."

"In other words, are you working for money or for God?"

Tally stopped in her tracks. "I hadn't thought of that connection, but you're right. Matthew 6:24, isn't it?"

Gus swiped his phone and read the verse. Tally listened.

> *No one can serve two masters; for either he will hate the one and love the other, or else he will be loyal to the one and despise the other. You cannot serve God and mammon.*

"*Mammon* being riches. Salary versus ministry," Tally said. "When your salary comes from ministry, the lines can be blurred. Some churches and ministries operate like a corporation, so that further causes confusion."

"Unless you know where you are and what you're doing." Gus moved to the other side of Tally, where he put himself between the light traffic on the road and her.

Tally smiled.

A gentleman.

She liked it because Gus reminded her of Dad. Dad was one of those old-fashioned ministers who still opened doors for women, an etiquette lost to the younger generations.

Tally wondered what it would feel like to date Gus for one week. She grinned.

"What's funny?" Gus asked.

"Inside joke."

"I think that requires two people."

"Does it?"

"I have no idea, but let's just say it does. What's funny?"

"Do you want the raw version or the sanitized?" Tally asked.

"Raw."

"You sure?"

Gus reached for Tally's hand. "Were you thinking of us? Do thoughts of us put a smile on your face?"

As they held hands, Tally felt more comfortable about sharing her thoughts. "Have you ever thought of what it would be like if you could only date someone for a week?"

"You mean like a fake relationship?"

"No, a genuine one. However, they have to separate after one week."

"Hmm. Separate forever?"

"No, just because they have to go back to work in different cities."

"If God wants them to be together, it will work out. *He* will work it out."

Tally found it fascinating that Gus corrected himself. Sometimes Christians said something ambiguous but never bothered to refine or improve their words.

Not Gus.

Gus chose precise words.

Tally liked that.

"Are we going to miss each other when I go home?" Gus asked.

At that point Tally realized they were still holding hands. "I don't know. We'll find out."

"We can call each other at least once a day?"

"Once a day?" Tally's eyes widened.

"At least. Or we can text more."

"We're both busy at work—precisely Colette's point this morning."

"If we want this relationship to work, we have to carve out time for each other," Gus said. "If we're very busy, we can talk to each other while we're eating our meals. If we can coordinate at least breakfast or dinner, we might be able to do video chats."

"All right, we'll do that, if I'm properly dressed."

"Of course."

"We'll try and see."

"Try?" Gus stopped walking.

To their left, beyond the trees and shrubs, Stone Mountain looked imposingly tall. Tourists stopped to take photos.

Tally and Gus stepped aside to let walkers pass them.

"I don't want to just try," Gus whispered in her ear. "I've fallen in love with you, Tally."

Tally glanced around her. Strangers were walking about on the sidewalk in both directions. She didn't see any yellow shirts, but she still felt shy. She dipped her head.

Gus lifted her chin with his fingers. "Look at me, Tally."

She barely did. *Why am I like this all of a sudden?*

"Do you feel the same way?" Gus asked.

She nodded.

"I know you want to marry a pastor, and I'm not one."

"Did I ever say that?" Tally asked.

"I'm not Malachi."

"What did you bring him up?"

"I had to let go of my past."

"I'm glad you brought it up then." Tally wondered how to tell Gus. She decided to just say it. "Look, Malachi is just a friend, and not even a close one at that. I used to admire him from afar, but I have let him go—just as you have let Veronique go."

"We're so adult that we can talk about our pasts so objectively."

"Aren't we, Gus?" Tally drew a deep breath. *Out with it. Clear the air. All that jazz.* "When I was in my twenties, I had a crush on him."

"You were nervous sitting next to him in Sunday school a few weeks ago."

He remembered. *Oh boy.* "It was a retroactive nervousness. When reality hit me, I woke up from that dream of marrying a pastor."

"If the Lord wills it, you could still marry a pastor." Gus's voice sounded broken, as though by saying that to her, he'd have to give up a lot.

"I understand it better now," Tally said. "Today I'm not looking for a pastor per se, Gus. Let me ask you this. Is it possible to have a pastor's heart without being a pastor?"

"I believe so," Gus replied. "Conversely, it's possible for a pastor out there somewhere to have a pastor's pulpit but not a pastor's heart."

"How can that be?"

"If you're not called to the pastor's position but you somehow obtained the chair. It might not be God's will for you. One huge indicator is whether you have a pastor's heart."

"Good points."

"Do I have a pastor's heart?" Gus asked.

"Only God knows, but you're most like my dad." Tally didn't feel like explaining that in public.

Gus's shoulders straightened up.

Tally wondered what that was about. "By the way, Maggie said that Malachi is praying about moving back to Lakeside to assist Dad."

"Why?"

"Malachi left his ex-girlfriend there."

"Oh."

"He never stopped loving her. That's why he's been single all this time. The fact that we move in each other's circles all these years caused me to think about my options with him. If we were meant to be, we would've dated a long time ago. We Fitzpatricks don't wait."

"I heard about that."

"What did you hear?" Tally's ears perked up.

"That your parents fell in love at first sight."

"Yes, they did." Tally resumed walking, and she tugged at Gus to keep up pace with her. "Not only my parents, but my great-grandparents also fell in love at first sight," Tally said.

"Interesting."

"Great-grandpa was a traveling preacher back in the day," Tally explained. "He used to tell us about doing odd jobs here and there to earn enough money to buy gas for his motorhome—that classic RV is long gone now—so that he could travel to the next town."

Gus listened as they walked through foot traffic on the sidewalk.

"One time he was in Alaska—yep, he drove all the way there—working with some fishermen at the wharf. It was raining hard. He slipped on the pier and fell into the icy water."

"I hope there's a happy ending."

"He went straight down like an anvil, and his lungs started to fill with water. He had no way to yell for help underwater." Tally's voice rose. "He thought that was it for him. He struggled in the water and was about to give up. He thought he passed out while praying in the water."

Gus waited.

"Next thing he knew, he was back on the pier. Someone had jumped into the water and saved him."

"Let me guess. It was his future wife."

"Nope." Tally chuckled. "It was his future wife's father. He was cleaning nets when he heard the commotion. He rescued Great-Grandpa, took him home, and introduced him to his daughter, Patricia. The moment they saw each other, they lost their hearts. They married three months later."

"No dating? No courtship?"

"Only engagement." Tally kept walking. "She traveled with him all over the country until they settled down in Lakeside, where they had two kids. One of them was Grandma. My great-uncle passed away last year."

"I'm sorry."

"Grandma is the only surviving McPherson. She married into the Fitzpatrick family, who owned most of the land in Lakeside. When her husband died, Grandma took over the family business to this day."

"Did your grandma also fall in love at first sight?" Gus asked.

"Funny you should ask. It skipped a generation. I think it's going to skip my generation too." Tally wove through cars in the walk-up trailhead parking lot. "However, the more important point is that Great-Grandpa did not insert his own will into God's plan for his love life. He was open to the Lord's leading. He had a blank slate of requirements and left it to God to find him a wife. And there she was, a strong Christian girl who loved the Lord and was willing to travel with Great-Grandpa."

"God is sovereign over all our lives," Gus said. "Tell me. Were you or were you not attracted to me the first time you saw me in Nassau?"

"I should've never told you that, Gus. I'll never live it down."

"I'll tell my grandchildren about it," Gus said as they reached Tally's car.

She unlocked the car doors. Before she climbed into the driver's seat, she stepped toward Gus and pecked his cheek.

Gently, he ran his hands up and down her arms. "What was that for?"

"The answer to your question."

"Which answer was it? It was an either-or question."

"Both." She climbed into the driver's seat and closed the door.

Tally waited for Gus to get in the passenger's side. She cleaned her hands with the hand sanitizer she had in the car. She handed the pump bottle to Gus, who also cleaned his hands with it.

"Thank you." Gus fastened his safety belt. "I don't want our relationship to end next week."

Tally didn't say anything as she drove the car out of the parking lot. It was almost ten o'clock in the morning, which told her that they hadn't walked very fast from the ticket plaza to the trailhead. It had been more like a stroll around a quarter of the mountain.

"What do you think?" Gus asked.

"We're both career professionals," Tally said. "We're busy at work all week, all month, all year long. To make *us* work at all, it would require cutbacks."

It echoed what Colette had told her this morning.

I suggest you make a list of the major things you do all week, and pray over them to see if you can fit in life somewhere.

"It's too bad that we have to 'fit in life somewhere.' Surely we need a balance," Tally said.

She thought about that list.

"What do you do all day when you get back to work in Nassau?" Tally asked.

"We mow the lawn once a week at the school and church. I have one crew going to each location on different days because that's how I save money on equipment," Gus said.

"Makes sense. If you have two crews going on the same day, you'd need two sets of equipment. Not just the lawnmowers, but also trimmers and edgers."

"Right." Gus had more to say. "Beyond the lawn, there are gardens to maintain daily. Vegetables, herbs, flowers. The rest of the time, we trim bushes, hedges, trees. Whatever comes up."

"What about Moss Cay?"

"Oh yeah. I forgot about that. I go there once a month, but I send a crew weekly," Gus said. "That also reminds me of Aunt Nancy's house. She has an acre of land, and she's about to end her contract and hire my company to do it."

"You know, I never did ask you what your company name is."

"Moss Green."

"Seriously?"

"Yes. We have matching T-shirts. I'll send you one."

"I will wear it." Tally promised.

"I usually call it simply my landscaping company."

"Why?"

"I don't know."

"Hmm. Perhaps you don't want it to be permanent."

"Oh? How did you figure that?" Gus looked surprised.

"Because if it's a company you're happy with and proud of, you'd call it by name. It took you this long before you mentioned the name to me."

"It's odd, isn't it?"

"Yeah. Do you see me avoiding the name Village? I say it all the time."

"You have a point there, Tally. Let me do some introspection to see whether I'm on a detour with Moss Green. Then again, I printed T-shirts and business cards."

"The business could still be part time in your mind." Tally didn't want to say more. She wasn't his career counselor. "After work, what do you do?"

"Church on Sundays and Wednesdays. If I'm filling in for a Sunday school teacher, I have to spend time preparing lessons. Sometimes the men's group has dinner out or some activities on Saturdays. The rest of the time, I tend to my own container garden on my balcony." Gus hesitated.

"And?"

"You really want to know?"

Tally nodded as she pulled into the picnic area, swarmed with yellow shirts. She found a parking spot and wondered how far they'd have to walk to Levi's grill.

Gus pointed to a spot under a tree that someone just vacated.

Tally took the space before anyone else did. After turning off the car engine, she unbuckled her seat belt, but didn't get out of the car. "Yes, I want to know."

"I must be careful here because your mom knows Aunt Nancy," Gus said. "And you've met her."

"I won't say a word. Is it really bad?"

"No."

"Then you have nothing to worry about."

Gus unbuckled his seat belt. "As I told you on Tybee Island, Aunt Nancy has been asking me repeatedly to work for her."

"Didn't you say she stopped pestering you?"

"I did. However, while I'm staying at Byron's house all week, he told me that his mom had talked to him numerous times that she's basically worn out and wants to retire, but she doesn't know if Donovan can handle Moss Enterprises."

"So?"

"She'll feel better if I can step in and help."

"She trusts you more than she trusts her own son?" Tally asked.

"Sounds like it, right? Then again, perhaps it's out of necessity. With Byron in ministry and

Donovan up to his neck dealing with Moss Resorts, Aunt Nancy is left alone at her corporate headquarters in Nassau. She thinks that if I took over Moss Cruise, then she would have some of her burden lifted."

"But you don't want it."

"I don't want to go back to the corporate world. Period."

"Wait a sec. You said the other day you don't want to go back to accounting and finance."

Gus nodded. "Still the same space. Same building. Same corporate culture."

"This invitation would put you in the VP's office?" Vice president wasn't half-bad, was it?

"Yes." A sudden realization seemed to hit him. "I should've seen it myself. Nonetheless, my aversion for my previous jobs was so strong that I wrote off all corporate jobs."

"It's not like you have to work your way up the ladder. She's offering you the top job. You're Byron's replacement."

"Am I?"

"It looks that way."

"Also, as a VP, wouldn't you hire accountants to work for you?"

"The accountants are probably already there."

"Don't even attempt to do any of the accounting work yourself."

"Don't worry. I won't." Gus looked out the window into the distance. "However..."

"Yes?"

"If I work for Aunt Nancy, I will be even busier. I won't have time to, uh, fly back here to see you."

"Isn't that expensive, though, to fly back and forth?"

"If I work for Aunt Nancy, she will let me use her personal Gulfstream at no extra charge. I do have to pay for fuel, insurance, and a pilot, but I don't have to buy my own plane."

"Wow. Like a flying Winnebago." Tally couldn't wrap her head around private jets and all. She was only familiar with economy class on commercial flights.

"Don't get me wrong. I'm just the country-mouse cousin," Gus added.

"Do you have to tell me that? I only care if you're rich in Christ." A verse popped into her head. "Colossians 3:16 says, 'Let the word of Christ dwell in you richly in all wisdom, teaching and admonishing one another in psalms and hymns and spiritual songs, singing with grace in your hearts to the Lord.' That's the kind of riches I look for."

Gus was silent.

"Let's go see if Levi needs help." Tally purposefully didn't mention Malachi, just in case Gus was jealous. Besides, Malachi was really in her past.

She only had room in her heart for Gus.

Did he know that?

CHAPTER TWENTY-FIVE

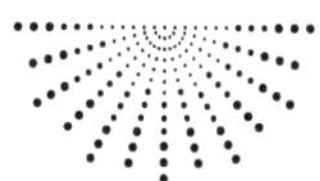

"You sure about this?" Pastor Fizz asked Gus. He leaned back in his chair in his cluttered office at Midtown Chapel.

A small window allowed in some afternoon light but kept the May sun out. The light shone on the table, highlighting the gashes and scars on the table between the two men.

Gus thought about every word he had just said to Pastor Fizz. No, he wouldn't change his mind.

"Yes." There was more to it, but it all boiled down to that for Gus.

"Why not though?"

"I don't want to influence her view of me."

"As a friend?" Pastor Fizz leaned forward in the chair, as if studying his face.

"I would like to be more than friends with your daughter, Pastor." Gus kept his face expressionless.

"I thought you two already were."

"You mean after that Friday?" Gus wondered whether Tally thought the same way as her dad.

It was true that he and Tally had shared their hearts while they had been in captivity.

"Have you asked her out?" Pastor Fizz seemed to be putting on the Dad hat.

Gus nodded. "We agreed to go to dinner."

"When?"

"No date is set." Gus waited.

Pastor Fizz waited.

Gus kept his mouth shut. If he opened it, he might confess to something prematurely.

"Tally values transparency most of all, Gus," Pastor Fizz said. "If she finds out you're secretly donating to speed up construction of the tiny homes, to buy a warehouse near the church, and to purchase the apartment complex next to the Village to house homeless teens, she'd want to know why."

"My aunt wants to remain anonymous about her share of this, and thus I have to as well. Otherwise, it wouldn't take much to guess who were in this."

"At some point in time you need to tell her."

"I will when the time is right." Gus exhaled. "If she thinks we're only friends, I don't want to embarrass myself."

"No, you won't. Midtown Chapel gets donations all the time, in bigger amounts than this." Pastor Fizz tapped the big check on the table in front of him, which came from Aunt Nancy's trust fund.

"It would be less obvious that you're doing it for her if you don't pursue her," Pastor Fizz suggested.

"Oh. Does that mean you don't approve?"

Pastor Fizz smiled. "I approve, but you've gotten your heart broken before. You might be falling in love on the rebound."

Gus only heard two words.

I approve.

"You approve?" He was on the edge of his seat.

"Don't get me wrong. Tally makes her own decisions." Pastor Fizz looked directly at Gus. "If she wants you, she will tell you. She won't hide it for years."

Years?

Like four years?

Like ten years?

"Malachi..." Gus wasn't entirely sure how Malachi came to his mind.

"You know about him too?" Pastor Fizz shook his head.

Gus nodded.

"Tally believes that she should marry a pastor just like me. It's unfortunate for you that she compares every eligible man to me." Pastor Fizz looked half humble and half proud that his daughter held him in such high regard.

"Yours is a big shoe to fill."

"You will never fill it, Gus. This is my shoe, not yours. You do exactly what God calls you to do."

"Thank you, sir." Gus relaxed in that chair. It wasn't the most comfortable office chair in the world, but there it was. It was probably there to keep counseling sessions short, although his meeting today was informal.

Gus had driven to Midtown Chapel to hand in the check, but he didn't want to meet Pastor Kim in person, and he didn't want to implicate Byron, whom he hadn't asked to participate in the donation drive. He had decided to exclude Byron because his wife, Tina, was a good friend of Tally's. Maybe they'd talk. Maybe they wouldn't. But he wasn't taking any chances.

Pastor Fizz was the best conduit to send the check to Pastor Kim.

Of course, the other alternative was to wait

until Sunday and put it in the offering plate. But then again, it was too risky, and Gus didn't trust the ushers or congregation whom he didn't know.

He trusted Pastor Fizz.

Pastor Fizz studied the check. "What has God called you to do, Gus? What has God prepared you for?"

"I don't know."

"Don't be so quick to answer. Pray about it. Think about it. Search the Scriptures. Pray some more. Seek God. Jeremiah 33:3."

Gus knew that verse. "That's one of my favorite verses. 'Call to Me, and I will answer you, and show you great and mighty things, which you do not know.' I need to save this verse in case I can use it later in a Sunday school class at home. Sometimes they call me to fill in for someone."

Pastor Fizz raised an eyebrow. "What are you doing or not doing with your college diploma? Your university degrees? Why or why not? Pray that verse back to God, and He will show you."

"Burned out." He almost whispered it.

"Sometimes we burn out not because the vocation is not our calling but because the method by which we carry out the vocation has not been prayed over and approved by God."

Gus nodded. "I get it. In other words, when

God calls me, I must do it His way, not my own way."

"Yes. Ever heard of the old idiom, 'Don't throw out the baby with the bath water?' If the water is dirty, change the water. Don't give up the precious baby."

Gus had come in to drop off a check, and now he felt like he was learning some life lessons he had missed somewhere along life's way.

"If landscaping is your calling, do your best for the Lord. If preaching is, then go forth," Pastor Fizz said.

"Byron is called to be a pastor. I don't think I am."

"You can still teach the Bible without being a pastor, but you can't be a pastor without teaching the Bible. A Christian pastor, anyway."

When Gus didn't say anything, Pastor Fizz continued. "You know my point, Gus. I'm not talking about being a preacher or a landscaper precisely. I'm saying that you need to do what God has gifted you to do, whatever it might be."

"I see. To do otherwise would be a foolish waste of my time."

"Is it? Or perhaps it would be more like missing out on opportunities to bless others and minister to the needy and fulfill the calling of God if you take detours not in God's original plan for you."

"Detours have crossed my mind."

"God will permit you to carry out your own will. You might need to learn life the hard way. Ultimately you'd get back to square one career-wise. What has God gifted you to do?"

"Right."

"If God has gifted you with a skill for numbers, if accounting comes easy for you because your brain is built that way, if you went all the way to Harvard and actually graduated with an MBA, you've got to pray about it and ask God why He had allowed all those stepping stones only to side-step them all and move you to a completely different area of work."

"You're asking why I'm a landscaper. What am I missing?"

"Don't get me wrong. Landscaping is a great job if it matches you perfectly. However, in this situation, I think you might want to consider reanalyzing the situation you have found yourself in. Your decision tells me that your analysis is flawed."

"My decision to leave the corporate world?"

"Fill in the blank, Gus. 'I burned out because...' That might give you a clue."

That's easy. "I burned out because I hated my

job. I liked my colleagues, but we all overworked. I tolerated it because I kept telling myself, 'This is my calling. This is my calling.' But..."

"Define 'this.' What are you referring to as your calling?" Pastor Fizz asked.

"Accounting. Finance."

"Not granular enough."

"No?"

"Nope. If you ask me what my calling is, I can say it's to be a pastor. But that's general, right? There are many types of pastors, as you know. Not all pastors preach at the podium on Sundays. Pastors who handle youth, outreach, administration, missions, discipleship, and counseling don't aways get to preach."

Gus waited for more.

"Just as you filled in for absent Sunday school teachers, I also fill in for pastors on vacation. So yes, you see me preach sometimes. I'll go to a church that needs a preacher. But preaching every Sunday is not my calling at all. In fact, I'm called to a very specific type of pastoral position: counseling."

"I heard you preach a lot when you travel," Gus said.

"Why, do you think?"

Gus shrugged.

"That's also a part of my counseling strategies.

I'm a counseling pastor to pastors. I show them how to connect with their congregation. Some pastors are academic, but in a church, the senior pastor has to shepherd the flock. If you're all head and no heart, what good is that? Only noisy cymbals, right?"

"You fill in for pastors on leave or churches in transition, but you're counseling all the time because that's your calling."

"Exactly." Pastor Fizz almost clapped his hands. "Churches need Timothys and Tituses. Many churches become headless when their pastors retire, get sick, or die. Then the committee looks for a new pastor out there to lead the flock that's been under the old pastor for a long time. A stranger shows up from nowhere and leads an existing congregation."

"At my home church, Pastor Dixon is training the next pastor who can take over Chapel by the Sea if he retires," Gus said.

"That's the model. Apprenticeship, so to speak."

"That's what I do with my landscaping company. I've been training enough assistants and deputies who know my routine and work such that I can take four weeks off and my business will still continue unaffected," Gus said. "I don't feel threatened by them. They won't quit and take my customers with them."

"That's leadership." Pastor Fizz pointed at Gus. "Did you learn that from somewhere?"

"I learned it as I went, I suppose, but decisions like that are natural to me. I mean, isn't it with everyone?"

"Only natural leaders have the innate ability to lead. Everyone else has to acquire that skill."

"Oh."

"When I'm at work as a counseling pastor, it's bliss for me. I can see through people's problems, show them the errors of their ways, and guide them back to Christ. I'm in my natural element. God has prepared me for this job. I'll do it until my dying day." Pastor Fizz turned to Gus. "Son, can you say that about your career right now?"

Gus cleared his throat. Gave himself a bit of time to think. "I love gardening, so I turned it into a full-time job. Ironically, it has now become a chore to me. I wish I could have a job I am truly contented with, and turn my gardening back to the hobby that I enjoyed so much."

"I think you're beginning to see what I'm getting at, Gus. Just as there are many types of pastors, there are also many types of positions for each college major or career option. Can you give me another example?"

"Writers?" Gus asked.

"Sure. Although there are many types of writers, just because they love to write, it doesn't mean they love to write anything. Some write non-fiction, some write fiction. In fiction, what genre and subgenre do they write in? Not all writers write everything. Wouldn't you say that's the same for accounting and finance?"

"Yes. You don't just take any position." Gus realized it now. Perhaps he was meant for more than what he had undergone.

"If you're doing a job in which you're constantly stressed out and you hate it all, it may not mean that you're not cut out for accounting or finance. It might just mean that you haven't found the right job that fits your particular skill set endowed by God."

"I went through trial and fire."

"You burned out. No pun intended. So you quit the entire sector of the corporate world." Pastor Fizz stood and walked around the table. "If you had been running the company you left, what would you have done to improve the working conditions of its employees?"

"Do you want a thesis?" Gus asked. "I can tell

you what they need to do to turn a profit. Top-down management restructure. Personnel and task reorganization. On and on."

"Congratulations, Gus. You just answered your own question."

"I did?"

"You sound like a financial consultant who can fix companies. If you do that, you can literally work anywhere in the world, especially with your Harvard MBA."

Anywhere in the world, including Atlanta, if Tally remained there.

Food for thought.

"Oh." Gus remembered what Tally had said to him. She had suggested that perhaps he could start a financial consulting company. "As a consultant, I can pick and choose the work I want and the duration. I don't have to stay long at any one company. I can still practice my skills, but without the pressure and burden of being an employee under duress, one who needs to flee."

"That's one way to look at it."

"Did you talk to Tally?"

Pastor Fizz looked baffled. "Tally? Why would I talk to her about something confidential between you and me?"

"Ah." That meant two independent people had

mentioned financial consulting to Gus. Perhaps this was a sign from God.

"Think about it," Pastor Fizz said. "What are you gifted in besides numbers? You might consider taking a personality test. We discussed leadership. All leaders must experience the trenches. After the trial, you have two choices—quit or move up to the next level."

"I quit."

"You answered my overarching question. What has God called you to do?"

"I quit on my own accord." Gus splayed his palms on his thighs. "What if I'm never meant to be in accounting and finance?"

"Find out what God has called you to do, and then go with God. If it's landscaping, do it to the glory of God. If it's finance, do that for the Lord. If it's both, so be it. There's no rule that says you can't be multitalented."

"What about my MBA? That's been a cloud over my head. Aunt Nancy paid for it, and it was very expensive. I feel guilty for not using it more than I am in my landscape company."

"Does anything ever go wasted in sovereign God's economy?"

"I suppose not."

Pastor Fizz sat down in his chair again. "Did

Tally tell you that she majored in English in college?"

"Yes."

"At least she graduated, right? Well, she's now the women's ministry director and uses her major very little except editing her own conference materials. However, in God's world, Tally would do well to heed Colossians 3:23–24, which says, 'And whatever you do, do it heartily, as to the Lord and not to men, knowing that from the Lord you will receive the reward of the inheritance; for you serve the Lord Christ.' God can draw from her college major to help her in her job, whatever it is."

Gus nodded. "I do use accounting and finance at my landscaping office."

"Even if your major was a dead language, God can still use it. At the very least, He can use your college experience as a whole to shape your future. Nothing is wasted."

"Perhaps your nickname should've been Pastor Fix. You just fixed the knot that I've been trying to unravel for a decade."

Pastor Fizz pointed his index finger in the air, giving credit to God. "You thought that you were coming to Atlanta for a vacation. Little did you know that God is making a course correction for you."

The course correction had led Gus to Tally.

Oh, Tally.

Gus thought of something and slumped back in his chair. "Of all the careers I would like to do, none of them includes going to seminary to be a pastor."

"So?"

"Since Tally wants to marry a pastor, does that mean I have no chance?"

"Whoa. Let's pull back the reigns a little, son. Let's not talk about marriage if you haven't gone on a first date with her."

"Ah."

"As your volunteer counselor, let me advise you not to change your career on account of Tally. Only change your career—if you need to—for the Lord and Him only." Pastor Fizz wagged a finger at Gus. "Do not dethrone God for a human being."

"Got it." He had made pleasing Veronique more important than pleasing God. As a result, he'd ended up worshipping Veronique. That had been all wrong.

Gus now believed that God had permitted her to leave him. He was the only One who could sit on the throne of Gus's heart, after all.

"God will bring to you that one bride who will

be devoted to you for the rest of her life, to love you and cherish you, till death do you both part."

Gus could almost hear the wedding processional music.

"Your bride, chosen by God, will not care if you're a pastor or not—as long as you're in God's perfect will for your life," Pastor Fizz said.

Gus smiled. Maybe grinned was more like it.

"As for Tally..." Pastor Fizz started to say.

Uh-oh. What?

Gus waited.

"As for Tally, I know she's looking for that one spiritually mature Christian man who has a pastor's heart." Pastor Fizz sighed. "Others need not apply."

"I already knew that, Pastor Fizz."

"You did?" Pastor Fizz's eyes widened. His expression looked similar to Tally's.

"Tally told me."

"She wouldn't just tell anyone."

"I'm not just anyone."

A smile appeared on Pastor Fizz's face. He nodded.

It seemed to be a thoughtful nod.

Gus wasn't sure if the pastor looked amused or impressed.

It took a good long drive through heavy downtown Atlanta traffic for Gus to finally realize that

Pastor Fizz could potentially be helping him. Earlier in the conversation, Pastor Fizz and Gus had discussed the difference between a pastor who had a pastor's heart and a pastor who did not have the ability to shepherd his flock.

Pushing aside all the banter about careers and sub-careers, Gus could see now that Pastor Fizz had sent him an implicit approval.

Would such a nod carry weight with Tally? Did that mean there was a pathway from Gus to Tally, after all?

Gus began to pray.

CHAPTER TWENTY-SIX

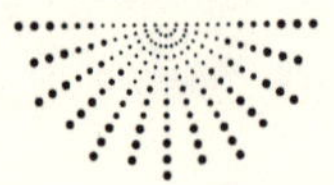

By Friday morning Gus had gone home to the Bahamas for sixteen hours. Tally cried a bit more after breakfast, and then she went to work at Midtown Chapel. After morning paperwork at her office, she drove to the Village to oversee the construction of the remaining tiny homes.

Keeping busy. Keeping busy.

A new set of funds had arrived quickly. Pastor Kim called Tally on Wednesday morning, saying that a sudden infusion of donations made it possible to speed up the Village constructions. Tally called the contractor after she hung up the phone with the pastor.

The crew had started on Thursday. Today was

only their second day, and already half the tiny houses were up.

Levi had volunteered to manage the painters and debris cleanup, leaving the yard work to individual residents. Tally walked around the property, saw the container gardens that Gus had worked on, and tried not to cry again that he wasn't there with her.

Cry?

Tally blinked.

The clock on her phone said it was 9:37 a.m. What? Not even ten o'clock?

She wondered if it was too soon to call Gus. He had texted her last night to say that he'd arrived safely in Nassau. Aunt Nancy had sent her chauffeur to pick him up at the airport, though he could have hired a car. The last thing he'd told Tally was that he would sleep in this morning.

How late was he going to sleep? Gus might be awake at this time. Tally called him on video. He answered on the first ring.

She didn't want to ask about his flight again, repeating the text conversation they'd had. Suddenly, she was tongue-tied.

A thirty-five-year-old woman tongue-tied?

Say it isn't so.

"Uh, hello." She kept her voice soft and calm, unworried and unhurried.

Her heart beat fast.

"Good morning." Gus was wearing an old faded T-shirt. He was sitting at the dining table, drinking a cup of coffee. A plate was next to the coffee cup.

"Did I interrupt your breakfast?"

"No. I just finished." Gus pointed to his empty plate. "Had eggs. What did you have for breakfast?"

"Mom made pancakes. I need to stop eating pancakes for a while." She laughed.

"Well, I like your mom's pancakes." Gus pointed at his phone screen. "What's that behind you?"

"Oh." Tally flipped her phone camera round. "I wanted to give you a tour of the newly constructed houses."

She'd be less nervous if she focused on something else other than herself. Yes, it was a good idea to show him all the new tiny homes constructed, thanks to new anonymous church donors.

"Sure. I'd like to see them," Gus said. "Sorry I'm not there with you."

"Ready for the tour?" Tally walked to the tiny house closest to her. She pointed her phone at the house and slowly panned from side to side. "This one just went up this morning, but it hasn't been painted. Levi is organizing the painting crew."

"Are you doing any painting?" Gus asked.

"Not today, but I might next week. I have two meetings this afternoon at church, and then after work we're having family dinner at my parents' house. Colette and Adalia are back in town for the weekend."

"Nice that you can see your sisters again."

"They're trying to persuade my parents to move to Lakeside."

"Oh, I see."

"But they can't make my parents do anything they don't want."

"I'm sure they'll pray about it and seek the will of God."

"Yes. First and foremost." Tally walked to the next house, the phone still in front of her. "This one is cute. Doesn't it remind you of the red cabooses at Jacobs Landing?"

"Hmm. A little."

Tally walked up the stone steps to the small porch. She opened the door with one hand and entered the house. "It's log, like the caboose. Ten feet across. You see the sitting room to the right and then the kitchen. To the left is the bed and a loft for a second bed."

"It's bigger than the caboose," Gus said.

"Looks like it." Tally pointed her phone to the ceiling. "No cupola. No skylight."

She walked out of the house and closed the door. "Levi said he might paint this house red, but we're getting input from the residents who will stay here."

"Good idea."

Tally stepped back and showed the rows of tiny homes on both sides of the stone path. "By this time next week, we'll have twenty houses up."

"That's a lot."

"Yep. That's twenty single mothers with a roof over their heads." Tally wanted to cry again.

What is wrong with me today?

"What about the teenagers?" Gus asked. "I remember that some of them are homeless."

"Pastor Kim and the ministry directors will be discussing housing for homeless teens," Tally said. "An apartment complex should be available in forty-five days. It's more for the Youth Ministry to deal with. Our church teens will help to renovate the building."

"Good for them."

"Not only the youth group though. Pastor Kim

wants this to be a church-wide project. The women's ministry will be involved, and so will some other ministries, such as outreach, benevolence, and several adult ministries. I think the maintenance department at church wants to get a piece of the pie too, and they will be handling plumbing and electrical."

"Sounds like a huge project to deal with teen homelessness."

"I'm so glad we're helping the teens," Tally said. "It breaks my heart to see teenagers trying to finish high school while not having a place to stay, let alone do their laundry or homework."

"Rooms of their own so that they can have their own private space."

"Right. Sadly, by the time we finish the project, the fall semester might be over."

"Where do the homeless teens go now?"

"Where they've been thus far. Foster homes, friends' houses, church members' spare rooms, and so forth."

Tally walked past some containers of flowers and then doubled back. "Look at these pretty flowers. You helped to plant them, remember?"

"It was fun. I do miss the Village...and you." Gus didn't sound shy when he said it.

And you.

"I miss you too," Tally said before she realized that she had said it aloud for everyone around her to hear.

She looked to see if anyone had noticed.

Well, nobody seemed to care. Everyone was busy doing something.

"That's good," Gus replied. "I thought maybe you'd forget me. Out of sight, out of mind, you know."

"How can I forget you? I walk around the Village, and I see all these containers of flowers."

"I left a mark. Is that what you're saying?"

"Definitely an indelible mark." Tally hesitated. "Wish you could come back again."

"You can always come to see me on the island."

"Maybe."

"Maybe? That's all? Don't you want to see me?" Gus sounded like he genuinely wanted to know.

Tally rounded a corner and sat on a small bench facing a square of green grass and a small fountain coming out of a clay amphora. She switched the camera back to herself.

"Of course I do," Tally said. "We barely got to know each other when you were here for four weeks."

"We have known each other for four years, love."

"As friends, Gus."

"And now more. Let's pray for time together."

"That would require us to give up some things," Tally said. "Adjusting our work schedules, maybe working less so we can have more life. Actually, that's what my sister told me I need to pray about."

A long pause. "You're doing wonderful ministry. You're much needed in Atlanta."

"Let me get to where I can talk." Tally felt that she didn't have as much privacy as she wanted, so she left the courtyard and walked to the next unpainted house. She went inside and closed the doors. There was no furniture to sit on. She leaned against the wall.

"We're considering putting Levi in charge of the Village. He's already managing our new warehouse, but the Village needs a manager—a village chief, so to speak. Levi is up for it, so he might take over from me in the fall."

"When does fall begin?"

"Not until September technically, but the school year begins in early August, so we're going by that because we want a new director in before the kids go back to school. That way the moms won't worry about transitions."

"What will you do then?" Gus asked.

"I will oversee all the women's ministry projects," Tally said. "Levi answers to me. Pastor Kim wants me to spend more time organizing the women's conferences that the church plans to turn into annual events at Midtown."

"Interesting. You love organizing events."

"I prefer to speak in the conferences than organizing them, to be honest. I love helping people, but I think there's a place for me at the podium, ministering to many women at the same time. I looked over my notes from the last ten years, and I can even compile them into several books."

"If you're speaking at conferences, that makes you location-independent, doesn't it?"

Tally understood what he was getting at. "Yes, it does."

"You can visit your grandmother in Lakeside."

"Yes."

"And you can visit me—although I don't want you to just visit."

"I'm not sure how..."

"I can quit my job and move to Atlanta," Gus said. "That way I can see you everyday. Are there job openings at your church?"

That came out of the blue.

Tally wasn't sure how to respond.

Yes, please.

No, stay where you are.

"We need to earnestly pray for God's perfect will for our lives together or apart," she finally said. "What we see now might not be what we will be, you know? Pray for God to show us what to do."

"Together or apart? Are you being objective, or are you just covering all audit trails?"

"Both. We could end up apart," Tally said.

"Not a chance."

What did he mean by that?

Tally glanced at the clock on her phone. She had two minutes to get to the community center. "Sorry, Gus. I have to run. Meeting Ming and Levi to go over some new information about Sheldon's murder."

"Let's talk later then."

"We can pray together if you want."

"Yes, I'd like that." He looked relieved on her phone screen.

Tally snapped a quick photo of him and saved the screenshot before they said goodbye to each other.

"It's not final," Tally told herself.

"No, it isn't."

"I was telling myself."

She opened the door and left the tiny house.

She had walked off the porch and onto the sidewalk before she remembered that she had left the door open. She doubled back to the house and closed the front door.

When she turned around, Levi and private investigator Ming Wei were walking toward her.

"Sorry I was about to be late," Tally said.

"No worries." Levi waved to her. "I saw you walking around talking on your phone, and I figured we'd catch you here. The homeschool activity in the community center has attracted more people than I expected, so it wasn't easy to find a place to talk in private."

"Your office?" Tally asked.

"Too close to the kids rehearsing for their drama."

Tally nodded. "I just came out of this tiny home. It's unpainted, but the AC is installed."

"Any chairs?"

"No chairs. We can sit on the floor." Tally led the way.

Immediately, Levi stretched out on the floor and closed his eyes. Ming sat cross-legged against a wall.

Tally turned on the air conditioner. "What shall we set it to? Seventy-three?"

"Works for me," Levi said without opening his eyes.

Tally sat down on the other side of Levi. Her jeans covered all of her legs down to her ankles.

"You tell her, Ming." Levi put a wrist across his forehead. His eyes were still closed.

"I've been in Atlanta all week." Ming swiped his phone. "I took Sheldon's friends to a hamburger dinner and tried to get information out of them."

"That the police didn't already have?" Tally asked.

Ming nodded. "Since I said that my wife and I are your friends, I built up a level of trust from the get-go."

"I told them they'd better talk or else Sheldon's mother will be crying forever since there is no closure," Levi said.

"That too." Ming shook his head. "Anyway, I thought I had to write off the dinner as a loss because nobody talked that night. I gave everyone my card. Nobody called me all week until this morning. Bright and early too. At five o'clock, a girl named Iliana called me. She sounded all freaked out. She hadn't slept for days."

"Iliana Wells?" Tally asked. That girl came to some of the teen Bible studies at the Village. She usually hung out with the other teenagers at the community center. Perhaps that was where she had met Sheldon.

Ming nodded.

"How did she get your number?" Tally asked.

"Friend of a friend of a friend who went to the hamburger dinner I paid for. Iliana was at the warehouse that Friday when Sheldon was murdered."

"What?" Tally stopped herself from speculating. "What on earth? I thought Sheldon was alone."

"The police thought so too. However, without security videos, there was no way to tell."

"Fingerprints?"

"Good question. However, dozens of volunteers have gone to the warehouse. Unless they tell you they were there, there's no way for us to know."

"True."

"Sheldon died protecting Iliana from being attacked," Ming explained. "He took the blows for her in the head."

"Wait. Back up a sec. Why was Iliana at the warehouse?" Tally asked.

"Because Sheldon offered her free clothes that she could modify and sew into trendy clothes she'd wear to school."

Tally wanted to cry. "Because her family is too poor for her to shop even at a thrift shop."

"The warehouse has been her thrift shop all

semester long. She's a senior, and she wants to look good," Levi said. "She wants to get a degree in fashion."

"Why didn't she just ask you or me? The donated clothes are for anyone who needs them," Tally said. "I would have said 'no problem' and driven her to the warehouse myself."

"For whatever reason she might have, it was a secret date between Sheldon and Iliana."

"There is no shame in wearing donated clothes." Tally wondered how to emphasize that to the people in the Village and yet at the same time not make a big deal out of it.

"Teenagers might not view it the way we do," Ming said. "If you recall, my parents were missionaries. Heidi and I wore donated clothes all the time. We didn't think much of it. However, I had friends who felt great shame when their parents shouted across the crowded hallway in church something to the tune of, 'Honey, your free used clothes rejected by their owners are here. Come pick them up.' Sometimes adults don't see it as a big deal, but teenagers have their pride too."

Tally nodded. "So Iliana wanted to keep it a secret. Sheldon took her to the warehouse. There was no security guard, no security camera. They walked in and out any time they wanted."

Levi sat up. "Iliana said she was sure they locked the door after Sheldon let them in. He was working the afternoon shift. Housekeeping and sorting through all the donations."

"Who else worked that day?" Tally asked.

"Glad you asked," Ming said. "There were two other people working, but both of them are volunteers. Sheldon sent them home just before Iliana showed up."

"So Sheldon was alone in the warehouse with Iliana."

"Iliana said that was what they had thought. They had no idea someone else was already inside the warehouse. She didn't know who it was because he was wearing a mask over his head. A ski mask of some sort with slits for eyes and mouth. He sounded gruff, and he had a belly. He was a big man, and he smelled bad."

"Doesn't sound like Silas, does he?" Tally asked.

"The man groped Iliana. She pulled off his mask. Saw his face," Ming said. "The man lost it. Attacked her. Sheldon stood between them. Got bludgeoned to death. Iliana ran away."

"In a nutshell," Levi said.

Ming swiped his phone again. "Anyway, I took Iliana to the police station so that she could repeat all that to them. They're looking into the mystery man who murdered Sheldon. It might not be Silas, unless he has a bigger, taller, linebacker brother."

"This doesn't sound good. Where is Iliana now?"

"Iliana has been in hiding for two weeks, so she's under the radar and can't be found. The police are handing her over to the GBI, and she's going to a safe house until they find the murderer. She's a witness, so they will protect her."

If the Georgia Bureau of Investigation was involved...

Tally thought about all the people attending Midtown Chapel and all the people who lived in the Village. "Are we all in danger?"

"I've already talked with Pastor Kim about church security. Now I'm here to talk to you about Village security." Ming put away his phone. "You two have to discuss how to keep the Village safe until the murderer is caught. You can hire security, or you can have a neighborhood watch."

"We have no money to hire security for the Village, so it has to be the latter." Tally shook her head. Feeling sad, she prayed. "God can keep us safe."

"Yes, He can," Levi replied. "I'll take the lead on organizing a neighborhood watch."

"Thank you, Levi. What about those of us who have to drive home once we leave church or the Village?" Tally thought of her parents living on their own. She decided she would stay with them until the police caught the killer.

"Most of all, we will pray for safety," Tally added. "Let's pray now."

CHAPTER TWENTY-SEVEN

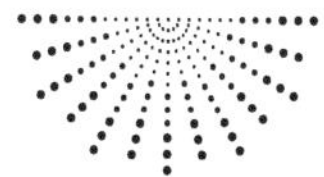

It had been seven weeks since Sheldon Everett was murdered in the warehouse in Atlanta, and two weeks since Ming Wei found a new lead for the local police detective who was investigating the case.

Gus had been following the case and getting updates from Levi on a regular basis. Gus didn't want Tally to know that he'd been curious, but she somehow found out anyway. She also found out about the donations he and his aunt had made to Midtown Chapel.

He wasn't sure who had told Tally, but he did not suspect her father at all. The counseling pastor had been trained to keep secrets, and Gus knew his secrets were safe with him.

Whether that bode well for Gus, he didn't know. He couldn't have imagined that the counseling pastor who'd helped him live with the aftermath of his warehouse ordeal could potentially end up as his own father-in-law.

This morning, Gus was at work in Aunt Nancy's new rooftop garden, which he had built for her on top of her guest house. Standing by the balcony, Gus could see a long way out to sea.

He sipped some water from his travel mug, then refilled it with cold water from a stainless-steel water dispenser, which he had brought for his crew of two.

The Caribbean sun heated up his fishing hat, and sweat streamed on his forehead, down his face, and pooled at the base of his neck, where a towel had been soaking it all up. He sat on a covered bench to take a break. The canvas canopy above him flapped in the wind.

"Nebo, take a break!" Gus called out to the only crew member he'd brought along. He couldn't afford to split up the rest of his crew, who were busy at the school and church.

Nebo nodded, made his way to the edge of the roof, and got on his phone immediately. Gus knew that Nebo had a new girlfriend and they talked a lot. Several times a day.

Gus didn't do that with Tally. Why? Perhaps they were older and didn't pine for each other. On the other hand, did that mean they didn't miss each other as much?

Gus could hop on an airplane and be by Tally's side in two hours.

Still, he wanted to give her space to think about their relationship. He wondered if it was harder for him than for her, because he was thinking of her night and day. On the other hand, Tally was pulled in many directions every day in Atlanta, and she might be too busy to think of him.

All he had to do day and night was taking care of gardens and yards, watering the flowers, pruning the bushes and trees, fertilizing the plants, and all the other maintenance that he had mostly delegated to his crew to do.

He felt that he wasn't as busy as Tally and had more time to think about her.

And yet flowers and plants reminded him of the Midtown Chapel Village in Atlanta, which in turn reminded him of Tally.

For example, this rooftop garden. When he'd stared at his aunt's container garden, he could see flowers in the Village and Tally walking by the giant containers, smiling as she gave him a tour of the new tiny homes that he had helped to build—by hiring a construction company to do the work for him.

Gus smiled a little, but he felt sad inside.

He heard a footfall. It was familiar, and he knew who was coming up to see him. He closed his eyes and prayed for God to keep him from showing his feelings.

Smile more, I suppose.

So he did, as he watched Aunt Nancy walk toward him, carrying something in her hand. A glass bowl of plantain chips. They were Byron's favorite snack, but since Byron had moved to America, Aunt Nancy had been feeding them to Gus instead.

A stand-in son?

Aunt Nancy didn't say a word as she approached him. She handed the bowl of plantain chips to him, then sat down beside him on the bench.

"You look like you're missing someone." That was Aunt Nancy. Straight to the point.

Gus couldn't reply. Wouldn't reply. To do so would be to open up his heart to thoughts he didn't want to explore at this time.

"If you want to use my jet, you can." Aunt Nancy munched on a chip.

Gus did the same so that he didn't have to talk.

The crunchy chip occupied his thoughts for a whole two seconds.

"Fly there every weekend to see her," Aunt Nancy added.

Gus turned to face his aunt. "Are you having this conversation all by yourself?"

Aunt Nancy chuckled. "I remember how Byron felt when Tina went home to Savannah."

"He had planned on going to seminary anyway, so he could have easily chosen a Bible college in America, and that's what he did." Gus tried to be logical about it. "As for us, Tally has a great job there, and I have a great job here, for now."

"Both of you have to yield."

"We're working through the process of coming together. I don't want to make her move to the Bahamas if she's not willing, and she doesn't want to force me to move to Atlanta." Gus remembered what Tally had told him recently, about how Levi had taken over the management of the Village, freeing Tally to do more speaking engagements. "We floated ideas, such as Tally doing a more location-independent career, but that's asking her to yield. I want to do my part too. How do we find a solution that is amicable and fair to both of us? That's our prayer."

"And it will be a test of your love," Aunt Nancy said.

"What do you mean?"

"It's not like you're starting out. You've been working for years building up your career, and so has Tally. The test will be to see how much you're willing to sacrifice in order to make your relationship work."

Gus sighed. "Yes. What are we willing to give up in the name of love?"

"Being flexible will get you to where you want to be."

"Hmm. Do you know something I don't?" Gus asked.

"I'm older than you, so I know many things you don't." Aunt Nancy laughed. "However, there's something you do know that I don't."

"How could there possibly be anything?" Gus wiped sweat off his neck.

"You're still the finance person I trust the most."

"Ah. There are many of us."

"No, Gus. I'm serious. You know me well enough to know that it's hard for me to trust anyone outside the family. I do have one or two VPs whom I trust, and we're not related, but other than them, I have a hard time trusting."

"I know. God will show you who you can trust."

Aunt Nancy's eyes bored into his. "Like I said, I trust you."

Gus didn't answer. If he did, she would make that job offer again.

"Moss Enterprises needs you. Donovan is handling Moss Resorts. I'm taking care of the rest of it right now, and I'm overwhelmed, to tell you the truth. I want to retire, Gus. If you can manage Moss Cruises for me, that's one less thing to worry about. Then I'll feel better about retirement. I don't want to hand over my family's hard work to a stranger or a board of directors."

Gus wasn't sure how to tell Aunt Nancy for the millionth time. *No, he wouldn't do it.*

"You've told me that you like landscaping and gardening," Aunt Nancy said.

Yes, repeatedly.

"You said all that while you were still single."

"What are you getting at?" Gus laughed, picked up another plantain chip, and chewed it slowly so that he didn't accidentally open his mouth and say something he'd regret.

"You're not single anymore. You and Tally are in love with each other. From what you've been telling me, you're serious about her."

"I'm forty-one, so yes, I need to be serious." Gus wondered how much to tell his aunt. "I want to marry her and love only her for the rest of my life."

"If God wants both of you to be together, what are you willing to sacrifice?"

"I'll give up my career in the Bahamas to be with Tally wherever she goes." Gus surprised himself. Give up his landscaping business? Give up living on his favorite island in all the world? Give them all up for Tally?

His heart told him he would be willing to do it.

"When you marry..." Aunt Nancy wiped her eyes. "If you want to have at least two or three kids, you'd better start sooner than later."

"Kids?" First, Gus had to find a way to spend more time with Tally.

"Two will be nice because they can play with each other." Aunt Nancy ignored Gus, who couldn't get a word in at this point. "If you're serious about starting a family, then you need to consider your finances. I'm sure you can raise a family on your landscaping income, but if you have a business opportunity to raise your income, wouldn't you do it? It's for the family, after all."

Aunt Nancy wasn't done. "You can buy a nice house and furnish it well for your wife and kids to enjoy. If you can do it, why not? Why hold yourself back?"

"I'm not . . ." Gus had to think about this. Was Aunt Nancy right, that he was holding himself back?

"How does ten percent of Moss Enterprises sound to you?" Aunt Nancy said.

Sounds desperate.

Caught by surprise, Gus didn't know how to respond.

Ten percent of Moss Enterprises would be about a hundred million dollars. Could he buy a nice oceanfront house for Tally with such a salary?

Yes, I can.

A ten-bedroom oceanfront manor like Moss Mansion, connected to this guest house via a covered walkway.

Then again, Gus didn't need to mull over the multimillion-dollar offer. He had made up his mind a long time ago not to return to the corporate world.

He sighed.

"But your Harvard MBA is still in your pocket. Unused." Aunt Nancy's voice was kind, but there was a strain there. Gus sensed it, but he couldn't pinpoint why.

Unused, yes, but she probably meant *wasted.*

"Pray about it?" Aunt Nancy had always been the pushy kind.

Then again, if she hadn't been so assertive, nothing would have happened to Moss Enterprises. It would have still been in the red since her husband passed away.

Single-handedly, this wonder woman had travailed through the trials and against all odds, pulling a near-bankrupt company into the billion-dollar tourism power that was Moss Enterprises today.

The only way to deal with such a powerful woman was to change the subject.

"How is it going with the women's conference preparation at church?" Gus asked casually, as a matter of conversation.

Aunt Nancy took a deep breath. "I bit off more than I can chew, Gus. I volunteered to replace someone who could not make it, but I've been so busy that I didn't have time to prepare for the workshop they want me to lead."

"What kind of workshop?"

"About career Christian women." Aunt Nancy picked up several plantain chips from the bowl that was still sitting on Gus's lap. "They want me to talk about independence—not from God, mind you—in which Christian women can do jobs that make them feel more confident about being able to support themselves."

"Do you need any help with that?" Gus knew just the person who might be able to give Aunt Nancy pointers about such a topic.

"Help?" Aunt Nancy chuckled. "I need someone to replace me altogether."

Sounded like she had overbooked her schedule. She had an administrative assistant, but only at the Moss Enterprises office. Aunt Nancy still handled her own personal schedule herself.

"Why did you agree to handle the workshop?" Gus asked. "Your plate runneth over, dear aunt."

"Because there was no one else."

That perfectly described the Moss attitude. They'd take care of things because someone had to.

"Problem is, after I told Pastor Dixon I'd take over the workshop from the speaker who had to drop everything and take care of her dying mother... Ah. My fault." She threw up her hands. "I try not to schedule personal events past the current quarter, but it happens. I had no idea that two months after I signed up to speak at the conference, my life would be thrown into a tailspin."

A tailspin? "What happened, Aunt Nancy?"

"Moss Cruises." She looked at him. "Moss Cruises should have been yours. However, since you didn't want it, I had to hire some total stranger—whom I shouldn't have trusted in the first place—to take care of the family business."

"Is it my fault now? I didn't put you in a tailspin."

"No, no. I'm just venting. Can a seventy-something woman vent?"

"Anyone can vent. Please forgive me."

Aunt Nancy continued. "With the chaos in Moss Cruises, I don't have time to prepare for the women's conference. In fact, I might not even attend it this year."

Gus was processing what his aunt had just told him, when one word rose above the rest.

Chaos.

"Wait." Gus wondered if he should even go there. "What chaos are you talking about?"

"Chaos?" It was like she had forgotten her own words spoken merely seconds ago.

"You said that there's chaos at Moss Cruises."

Aunt Nancy didn't reply. The chips fell from her fingers, and she slumped to one side.

"Aunt Nancy?" Gus was on his feet, facing his aunt.

She was trying to say something. Gus couldn't understand what she said. It was something like "itchy," but after she touched her head, Gus guessed that she meant to say, "Dizzy."

Her left hand tried to lift her right arm, but her right arm wasn't moving.

Now her face drooped on one side.

Gus tapped the Nassau emergency number on his phone to call for an ambulance. His hands shook, and he prayed to God to save Aunt Nancy.

CHAPTER TWENTY-EIGHT

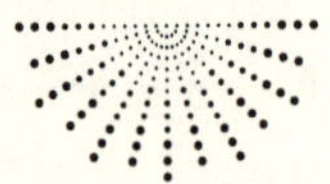

As soon as Gus texted Tally about Nancy Moss's ministroke, Tally informed everyone at church about it in an email blast to the staff. That covered the prayer and women's ministries as well as Levi at the Village.

Tally wasn't surprised that most people who were praying for Nancy's healing from the transient ischemic attack knew who she was. Midtown Chapel was a sister church to Chapel by the Sea, after all, as was Riverside Chapel in Savannah.

Thankfully, Gus's quick reaction in calling for emergency help saved her life. Only one day after being hospitalized under a doctor's care, Nancy went home.

However, the difficulties in Gus's life began.

Tally left him alone for the next two weeks, not disturbing him as he took an unpaid leave from his landscaping business to work at Moss Enterprises, filling in for President and Founder Nancy Moss as she recuperated at home.

Gus's texts grew increasingly infrequent. Sometimes he'd go for days without texting or calling her. Then one day in late June, he'd called her on video while she was sitting in her office at Midtown Chapel, going over her schedule for the rest of the year.

Maggie was also in Tally's office, but left to give Tally some privacy as soon as Gus called at five o'clock.

On the video screen, Gus was sitting in an office chair.

Tally tried to see what was behind Gus, but all she saw was a giant painting. "Where are you?"

"In Aunt Nancy's office." Gus spun his chair around, still holding his phone in his hand. "Not in my home office, which is austere compared to this one on the tenth floor."

"Moss Enterprises or Moss Cruises?" Tally recalled what Gus had told her briefly when they had spoken two weeks ago.

"Enterprises. The head offices of Moss Cruises

and Moss Resorts are both downstairs. Same building."

"How long are you going to be there?" Tally looked up. Maggie peeked in the door. Her purse was over her shoulder. She waved.

Tally waved back. "Thanks, Maggie. Drive safely home."

Maggie nodded and disappeared, closing the door behind her.

"I thought I'd just be here for a week, but it's been two weeks," Gus said. "I'll leave when Aunt Nancy returns to her office."

"Which is..."

"She didn't give me a firm day, but I made her sign a contract with me for only one month."

"Clever man."

"When it comes to business, contracts provide clarity so that we don't get into he-said-she-said arguments, you know?"

"I agree."

Gus leaned back. "How was your day?"

Tally could read that question in many ways. Perhaps Gus missed Atlanta...and her. Or Tally's day was more interesting than his.

"Before I answer that question, may I ask why you ask?" Tally wondered if she was reading too much into it.

"Making small talk," Gus said. "I didn't want us to stare at each other on this video call without having anything to say."

Yeah, I read too much into it.

"Truth be told, I'm sure many people ask you how you're doing without really wanting to know," Gus said. "I asked because of the opposite reason. I care and I want to know. So. How was your day, love?"

Tally drew a deep breath. "I was up at three o'clock in the morning. Mom called me and woke me up and asked me to meet them at the hospital."

"So you went back to your own house." Gus looked concerned. "Is it safe?"

"Yeah. It's fine. Remember the battered woman who went to my parents' house early morning when you were in town?"

Gus nodded.

Tally didn't have to tell him her name. She'd rather keep Karissa's name confidential, if Gus hadn't heard it or didn't remember. "Well, she went back to her abusive husband, and he beat her up again. This time she went to my parents' house with a broken wrist."

"Oh no. Did you make a police report?"

"Dad did. He was talking to the police when I arrived at the hospital." Tally shook her head. "I don't understand why the woman went back to her husband. We tried to get her a job so that she could be self-supporting. Lots of work around town she could've done."

"Maybe she should leave town and start over in another city far away."

"That was among the suggestions we all gave her too, but she has to make her own decisions. All we can do now is pray that she will have God's wisdom."

"Is she a Christian?"

"I don't know." Tally sighed. "What did you do all day?"

"No, let's finish with your day first."

"All right. After we were done at the hospital, Mom and Dad took Kar—her—to a women's shelter. I'll keep in touch with them, but they know best regarding what to do about her. It's not the first time they've seen such a case."

"Understandably. Then you went back to sleep?"

Tally laughed. "No such opportunity. I went to the Village because Jacinda is having another bout of emotional roller coaster."

"Jacinda, the mother of the teenager who died at the warehouse?"

"Murdered. Ming Wei managed to get Sheldon's friends to talk. Did I tell you?"

"You might have mentioned it in one of your short texts."

"Sorry. I was busy." Tally felt guilty for only sending short texts.

"No worries. So Sheldon's friends talked to Ming?"

"And to the police and the GBI. Thank God they finally had some leads."

"Are they closer to finding the murderer?" Gus asked.

"Very close."

"Then you need to stay safe until they find him. How's the security at church?" Gus's voice sounded grave. Tally had no idea he could sound more serious than he had been.

"It's fine. Really. Don't worry about it. Pastor Kim and the deacons hired three more off-duty police officers to protect the staff."

"Good. I was worried."

"I know you are. Ask me about something else."

"Are you finished with work for the day?" Gus asked.

His voice was calm, but Tally knew that behind that cool voice was a heavy burden of responsibilities he hadn't expected before Nancy's ministroke.

On top of that, he probably worried about Tally more than he needed to.

This was why she didn't like long-distance relationships.

Tally nodded into the video camera. "Maggie and I were going over my schedule to make sure I'm not stretched too thin between now and Christmas. She just left, so we'll work on this tomorrow morning."

"Good idea not to overbook," Gus said.

"Can you believe it's Friday again tomorrow?"

"It's been a very long week." Gus expelled a breath. "When this is over, maybe you could make time to come to the Bahamas to see me."

"*This* being what?" Tally laughed. "If you mean our jobs, they are never ending, right? I don't know when I'll have free time to travel the rest of this year with all the church events coming up."

"Maybe I could come to Atlanta then. My hours are more flexible than yours because I run my own company."

"But it isn't enough, is it?" Tally wanted to cry.

"It's okay. If God wants our relationship to work, it will work out."

"Is there something He wants us to do though? Perhaps we can make changes so that we can see each other more often," Tally said. "I told you that

I'm booked the rest of the year, but that's where it stands right now. When Maggie and I resume going over my schedule tomorrow, I plan to cut back on more things I don't need to be doing."

"Like what?"

"I don't want to cite specific examples right now because I don't know what I will be deleting from my schedule or delegating to someone else to handle. I can always play a support role. That also helps me train future leaders."

"Wise."

"It's a matter of practicality. You know what the statistics says about church ministries, right? That twenty percent of the people do eighty percent of the work, or something like that. At Midtown Chapel, I submit that ten percent of the people do one hundred percent of the work. Pastor Kim has been reminding all the ministry directors to train up our Timothys and Tituses. So far I only have one person trained—Maggie."

"What about Levi?"

"He comes trained to minister. He draws a salary as our warehouse manager, and now as the Village chief—still another manager position."

"By delegating and cutting back on your schedule, you free up time for us," Gus said. "I will do the same here too. I'll be busy for one more week, and then I'll hand all this back to Aunt Nancy. She's recovering well from her ministroke. In fact, she was well within two days, but she decided to take time off to rest some more. She hadn't had a proper rest since her husband passed away decades ago."

"That's the thing, isn't it? We don't know how much time God has given us to spend with our loved ones."

Gus smiled. "Yes, we want to see each other while we still have time."

"But there's no way right now."

"Unless we make time."

"Gus, that's one of my pet peeves."

"Oh?"

"People say we ought to 'make time,' but no one can truly *make* time except for almighty God Himself. Do you agree?"

"Ah, yes. I know what you mean. It's a figure of speech to me. It only means that we are looking for available time slots or opportunities in our busy schedule."

"Practically, we can strive to be wiser about managing the twenty-four hours we all have, and perhaps arrange our day and night in such a way that we have time for all the things we want to do, in addition to all the things God calls us to do."

"My thoughts exactly." Gus leaned back in his office chair.

"You know what it says in Ecclesiastes 3:1–8. There's a time for everything."

"Let me look up the passage on my laptop," Gus said. When he found it, he read it aloud.

Tally listened. She loved Gus's voice, including the slight British accent and his Caribbean lilt. Maybe he could read the Bible to her more often—while she lay down, eyes closed, on a hammock...on Moss Cay.

To everything there is a season,
A time for every purpose under heaven:
A time to be born,
And a time to die;
A time to plant,
And a time to pluck what is planted;
A time to kill,
And a time to heal;
A time to break down,
And a time to build up;
A time to weep,
And a time to laugh;
A time to mourn,
And a time to dance;
A time to cast away stones,

And a time to gather stones;
A time to embrace,
And a time to refrain from embracing;
A time to gain,
And a time to lose;
A time to keep,
And a time to throw away;
A time to tear,
And a time to sew;
A time to keep silence,
And a time to speak;
A time to love,
And a time to hate;
A time of war,
And a time of peace.

"There's 'a time to embrace' and 'a time to love.' Yet we're constantly running out of time." Tally got up from her chair and stretched. She had sat in that chair for hours.

"You're tired. I'll let you go," Gus said. "You have to fight Atlanta rush-hour traffic to get home."

"It's all right. When you called me, you made my day. I've wanted to call you for two weeks, but I didn't want to bother you."

Gus looked touched. "You can call me at any time."

"Even when you're in a meeting?"

"I know you won't bug me in a meeting, just as I won't bug you in your meetings."

"You know me well."

"I want to know you more. I want to spend the rest of my life knowing you more, Tally."

What he said warmed Tally's heart. She was bursting with words she wanted to say to him, such as, "I love you. I love you. I love you."

But she restrained herself. Firstly, she was still in her church office, where a certain decorum was required—even though if Gus were here right now and wanted to kiss her, she'd let him.

Secondly, she didn't want Gus to think that she was a giddy schoolgirl. She felt that she was too old for childish behavior in front of a man she had fallen in love with, who also loved her back.

So she said, "Well, if you want to talk to me for an hour, then traffic might be lighter by the time I leave."

Kind of official like.

"I'm concerned that you're downtown alone," Gus said. "With Sheldon's murderer on the loose..."

"You mean walking from the church staff door to my car bothers you?"

Gus nodded.

"You worry too much. It's a short walk, and I've done it for years since college."

"You're in downtown Atlanta though."

"Midtown technically," Tally corrected him.

"Regardless. Have they caught the killer?"

"Not yet."

"See? I rest my case."

"Don't worry, Gus. It's okay. If you live here, you know what to do to take care of yourself and stay safe. The sun is still up in the sky at six or seven o'clock this time of year, so I'll be fine. Besides, there's security."

"Ask them to escort you to your car."

"On a half-a-minute walk?" Tally leaned into her phone camera. "Gus, are you overly concerned?"

"Not overly. I think it's enough concern."

"All of a sudden? Did anything happen to you at work today to make you think about my safety all of a sudden? Did someone threaten you?"

"Well..."

"Any juicy story?" Tally tried to joke about it. Yes, she knew safety was a serious matter, but Gus seemed visibly worried. She didn't know why he would be, but she didn't want him to worry about her on top of the stress he had at work.

"How did you turn this around? Why do I have to tell you a 'juicy story'?" Gus asked.

"It was fine until you complained about safety."

Gus drew a deep breath. "I'm sorry. I've had a long day. I'm snappy."

"Why? Was it only the long day at work, or is it something else?" Tally asked.

"Both maybe. Aunt Nancy is offering me a new job."

And just like that, Gus hadn't told her about the problem he seemed to have had that day.

"Gus," she said.

"Yes?"

"You avoided my question."

"Which one?"

"Let me just summarize. You were suddenly concerned about my safety in Midtown, which is not quite downtown Atlanta. When I asked if something happened to you today, you didn't answer, but you didn't deny it either."

"No, I wasn't threatened. The police were here at Moss Enterprises this afternoon, arresting employees—former employees now—who stole money from my aunt. They're white-collar crimes, but they made me think of other types of crimes, including those involving the taking of lives. That led me to thinking about you living and working in

Atlanta, which statistically has a lot of violence in the city."

"Crime is everywhere, Gus. All over the world. Besides, I grew up here, dear. Don't worry about me."

"Can't be too careful."

"Right. But I can't live in a state of paranoia either."

"True. I wish I was there with you so I wouldn't worry too much." Gus rubbed his temple.

"You're tired. Probably need more sleep. Worries crowd your mind."

"Oh, Dr. Fizz, you're brilliant." Gus laughed.

"Now that you're feeling better, let's get back to what you said earlier. Nancy Moss offered you a job."

"To be fair, she has offered me one job or another many times in the last several years. I've turned them all down."

"This time you're considering it." Tally was sure she'd hit the nail on the head.

"It upsets me that my mind even wants to think about this potential. I've left the corporate world, and I did not plan to go back," Gus said. "However, she offered me ten percent of the parent company if I take the job."

"What job?"

"VP of Moss Cruises, which is one of the two subsidiaries of Moss Enterprises. The other one is Moss Resorts, and Donovan is in charge of that. Above these two entities, Aunt Nancy is the president."

A vice president position plus ten percent of the parent company.

Hmm...

"When the time comes for me to settle down, this VP post would be stable enough to support my family." Gus explained his rationale.

"Isn't your landscaping job stable too?" Tally had to know. What was on Gus's mind right now?

"Yes, but this pays more."

"Well, if your future wife is someone who thinks that landscaping is beneath her, then no amount of income will satisfy her," Tally said. "The love of money will be her driver, you know?"

Gus nodded on the little phone screen. "First Timothy 6:10. 'For the love of money is a root of all kinds of evil, for which some have strayed from the faith in their greediness, and pierced themselves through with many sorrows.' That verse?"

"Yes."

"Let me ask you this, Tally. Would you marry a self-employed landscaper or a VP of a multimillion-dollar company?"

"Are you kidding me, Gus?" Tally laughed. "I'm an independent woman. I don't need to marry anyone. If I do, it won't be because of his job. It would be a hundred percent for love."

"Hypothetically?"

"Hmm." Tally wasn't sure what he was getting at, but she figured that he really wanted to know. "Then I choose a godly man who focuses on God every day. Whose heart is bent toward God and things of God. Who does not love the world and the temptations therein. Who will be a trustworthy husband to me—stable, kind, thoughtful, wise, et cetera. Oh yes, and who will be a wonderful father to my children. He'll spend time with them and watch over them."

"A man with a pastor's heart," Gus said quietly.

"Someone like my dad. He's my role model—my template for the ideal husband."

"Have you found him?"

Tally kept her eyes on the phone, trying to read Gus's face on the small screen, wondering how he would respond if she told him.

"Ten years ago I thought I had." She sighed.

"You found a man who fit the bill."

"I almost did, but he got away. Then I almost married someone in his profession. That was a mistake that God saved me from. Years later—like last month—I realized that my old crush was not the one."

"Oh?"

"He was a placeholder for someone whom God has brought into my life."

"Placeholder?" Gus chuckled. "How would he feel if you'd told him he was only a placeholder?"

Tally shrugged. "I won't ever tell him."

"You told me."

"Because you're not the placeholder."

Gus sat back in his seat. "When you know someone is not the one, do you feel relieved?"

"As a matter of fact, yes."

"Same here. I thought I was still in love with my ex, but last month I realized that I felt nothing toward her. I spent a year trying to let her go, when actually, I already had. The memories are still there though."

"Memories." Tally sighed again. "What are we going to do with those?"

"They're slowly being replaced by new memories, new experiences, new love."

"Makes sense."

"Since this conversation is top secret between the two of us only, tell me something new that nobody else knows," Gus said.

"What exactly do you want to know?"

"I told you back at Stone Mountain that I'd fallen in love with you." Gus's voice was calm. He didn't sound emotional at all. It was as though he was merely stating a fact.

Tally nodded.

I've fallen in love with you too.

Suddenly shy, she wasn't sure why she couldn't say it aloud yet. "Are you looking for a response?"

"Yes. Something like that or some sort of statement."

A statement?

What could she say?

Gus, if you ask me to marry you right now, I'll say yes.

Funny how the human heart was.

Once you know, you know.

CHAPTER TWENTY-NINE

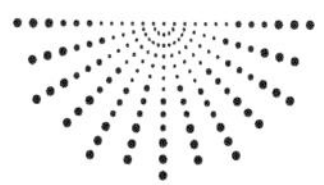

"Thank you for your help the last three weeks." Aunt Nancy cut into the filet mignon on her dinner plate. She liked her steak rare—almost raw.

On the other hand, Gus liked his steak almost too well done. Sitting across the table from Aunt Nancy and her youngest son, Donovan, Gus also started eating his dinner.

"For the first time in three weeks, I feel like I can relax," Gus said. It was Friday night, three and a half weeks since Aunt Nancy had a ministroke.

"I know what you mean." Donovan pointed a fork at him. "I thought Mom was going to die and I'd have to run Moss Enterprises. Freaked me out a little."

Aunt Nancy made a face. "You can't get rid of me that easily."

Donovan put down his knife and fork, leaned toward his mother, and planted a kiss on her cheek.

Aunt Nancy smiled broadly. "I wish your sisters and brother were here, but this is our business dinner."

"And they're not invited." Donovan laughed.

Gus continued eating, not thinking much about things at this time. His brain was tired—tied up in financial spreadsheets and accounting fiascos—from the last three weeks, which felt like an eternity.

"I could use a vacation," Gus said.

"You just came home from one." Donovan went on to say that Byron missed them. "I try to go to Atlanta twice a year, but I don't think I'll be doing that much. I'd be doing good if I can make it once a year from now on."

Gus nodded. "God will work it all out."

"Indeed He will." Aunt Nancy smiled. It was a genuine smile, perhaps close to pure happiness, that Gus hadn't seen in years.

God had lifted her burden of shouldering Moss Enterprises and Moss Cruises because she didn't trust anyone outside the family.

Unfortunately for the family business, her fears had been realized.

"I still cannot believe Morton embezzled money from Moss Cruises," Donovan said.

Gus almost hushed him, in case Aunt Nancy had another episode of TIA, but she appeared normal. The ministroke had run its course, and she was back to her normal, fully functional self.

The chaos that Aunt Nancy had tried to tell Gus about on her rooftop garden—that morning when she'd suffered a ministroke—was all about Morton and the missing money. He'd gone unnoticed for years because his brother-in-law was the vice president of operations at Moss Cruises. Morton had sailed through scrutiny.

That whole situation had aged Aunt Nancy.

"A brilliant strategy, ma'am, to let Donovan handle both Moss Resorts and Moss Cruises," Gus said to Aunt Nancy. "Donovan started out handling cruise ships anyway, so this is a full circle for him."

"Not that I've left it altogether. I still sail a yacht," Donovan added. "Now I get to expand it into a fleet."

"Don't overspend," Aunt Nancy said.

"No worries, Mom. Moss Cruises is in good hands." Donovan smiled.

If he does say so himself.

Donovan turned toward Gus. "Thank for cleaning up Moss Cruises for me. You sure you don't want to come work for us and be my VP?"

"I'm sure that's not my calling," Gus said.

Gus worried a bit for his cousin. Then again, Gus had fixed the financial woes at Moss Cruises, overhauled their accounting system, and set them on the right path. Donovan did not have to be concerned about the past.

Aunt Nancy's butler came into the dining room and spoke to her. "They've arrived, ma'am. Should I show them to their rooms?"

"Please." Aunt Nancy nodded. "You have my instructions."

"Yes, ma'am."

After the butler left, Donovan asked the question before Gus did. "Who arrived?"

"Our guest speakers for the women's conference next week," Aunt Nancy said. "Since I'm hosting all three of them, I asked them to come for the weekend so they can have a bit of rest and relaxation. I invited them to church on Sunday as well."

"Oh." Donovan's eyebrows rose.

"No. This is not a dating game, son." Aunt Nancy shut him down. "They're Christian speakers who will be conducting workshops next week at church, so leave them alone, please."

"I didn't say anything," Donovan protested.

"You said *oh*. That says everything."

Gus recalled the conversation he'd had with Aunt Nancy, about how she had been overwhelmed with the workshop she was supposed to handle. "Does that mean you're not going to run a workshop next week?"

"Precisely. I told Pastor Dixon that I can't do it on account of my health, but I called a friend, who knew a speaker who could fill in for me. I knew it was from the Lord when she happened to be available next week."

"If she wasn't available?" Gus thought that Aunt Nancy could have called Tally. He'd be more than willing to pay for her airfare and hotel. Then again, he wasn't sure if Tally would be available. It was last minute.

"If she couldn't make it, we'd have canceled the career workshop altogether," Aunt Nancy said. "People would have complained, but they could come back next year if they want."

"They don't have to stay here, Mom," Donovan said. "I can put them up at Nassau Island Breeze Resort. That's only ten minutes from your church."

Your church.

Gus prayed that someday Donovan would meet Jesus, call Him Savior, and be able to call it "my church" or "our church" instead of "your church."

Aunt Nancy shook her head. "I was unable to keep a promise to speak at the women's conference, so this is how I'm making up for it. They'll have their own rooms, and Chef Ana will take good care of all their meals."

"If you get tired of them, Moss Resorts is ready to serve," Donovan said.

"No need. All three speakers are my friends. This is their sleepover." She chuckled. "We'll talk about grandkids."

Grandkids.

Gus wondered how old the speakers were. Then again, Aunt Nancy had many friends of all age groups.

As Gus listen to Aunt Nancy and Donovan going back and forth, he didn't say anything because the women's conference didn't concern him. However, the mention of such a conference made Gus recall his time in Atlanta with Tally.

And it made him sad.

As if sensing a change in mood, Aunt Nancy turned her attention to Gus.

"Gus, thank you again," Aunt Nancy said.

"Don't mention it. This is what family is for," Gus said.

"I want you to know that I am touched. You've selflessly covered for me for three weeks. No complaints from you. You worked quietly and efficiently, and you got the job done. The embezzlers are behind bars, Moss Cruises is on the way to a better fiscal year, and you gave me three weeks to rest at home."

"Thank God for everything," Gus said.

"Donovan, Byron, and I have agreed to give you ten percent of Moss Enterprises as a fitting payment for all that you've done," Aunt Nancy added.

"What?" Stunned, Gus couldn't say another word.

"We're very happy to do it," Donovan said. "You're family too. If you weren't already my cousin, I would've asked Mom to adopt you. After all, Byron's left the country, so I need an older brother to complain to."

Gus laughed. Still amazed at the windfall, he could only thank God.

"Take the ten percent. You don't have to work at Moss Enterprises," Aunt Nancy said. "Go back to what you love to do. Spend time outdoors. Take in God's sunshine. Plant lovely flowers. Enjoy your life."

"Thank you, Aunt Nancy." Gus wasn't sure how long he'd keep calling her Aunt Nancy. Probably for the rest of his life.

To Aunt Nancy, Gus was still the little orphaned relative she'd taken in and raised as her own. God had indeed brought a motherly figure into his life when he needed guidance the most.

"That's not all," Aunt Nancy said. "I have another thank-you gift for you, and it's in the library."

"Oh? What is it?" Gus asked.

"A surprise. Go to the library and you'll see." Aunt Nancy smiled. "But first, let's have dessert."

When she said that, she gave Gus the impression that there was no hurry. The gift box would still be there in the library, waiting for him after dinner. It would not be a perishable product, unless it was in a cooler. It was probably not lawn equipment because she wouldn't have put that in the library.

What on earth is it?

What more could she give him that was better than the ten percent stake in Moss Enterprises? Knowing Aunt Nancy, it had to be something more precious or priceless.

What was more priceless than a hundred million dollars?

Meanwhile, Aunt Nancy's personal chef had outdone herself again. The strawberry shortcake was to die for. The strawberries on top had just the right amount of sweetness in them.

"Chef Ana grows these organic strawberries herself in her greenhouse," Aunt Nancy said.

"Did she? It's delicious." Gus meant it. Then he wondered if Tally might like to try this dessert.

When Gus finished his cake, Aunt Nancy told him to leave. "Go now. Your gift is in the library."

Gus drank some water to wash down all that sugar in the shortcake. Then he excused himself and left the dining room.

He walked down the hallway toward the grand staircase. On the other side of the staircase was another hallway leading to Aunt Nancy's home office and the small library she loved to read books in.

He swiped his phone to see if Tally had sent him any message.

None.

At the foot of the stairs, he looked up and...

Tears puddled in his eyes.

The love of his life was walking down the steps.

"Hello, Gus," Tally said.

"Tally?" He blinked. Was he hallucinating? What had Chef Ana put in the strawberry shortcake?

He broke into a big smile and walked toward Tally just as she stepped onto the marble foyer. "Are you really here, or am I imagining things?"

"I'm here." Tally wrapped her arms around Gus's waist. She rested her head on his shoulder.

Gus gave her a tight hug, as if letting go would make her disappear from sight. He could feel his heart beat rapidly.

"I missed you so much," he whispered into her hair.

"Same" came the muffled reply.

They held each other for a while. And then some.

"I was supposed to wait for you in the library," Tally said.

"You're the gift from Aunt Nancy?"

"She wanted to surprise you, so she told me not to say a word. It was all very last minute anyway. I was invited two days ago, and had one day to prepare my workshop materials—which I happen to have since I've spoken at many women's conferences."

Gus kissed her forehead. "I suggested you when Aunt Nancy couldn't get her workshop materials together. I thought of you as a fitting replacement for her when she had the ministroke. I'm glad that she had the same idea too."

"She called my mother," Tally said. "If you recall, they've been friends for years."

"Aunt Nancy called your mom?" So Riona Fitzpatrick had been the person Aunt Nancy called to ask for speaker recommendations. "Your mother recommended you."

"It happens. I'm available this weekend. Next week I'm driving my parents to Lakeside."

"You told me they were going to do a trial run there. In any case, I'm glad you're finally back in the Bahamas." Gus ran his fingers through her hair. "Now we've come full circle."

Suddenly looking self-conscious, Tally pulled away. "We're in the foyer of someone else's house."

"So?"

"Shall we go talk in the library?" Tally asked.

"How about a walk outdoors? You haven't seen the rooftop container garden I made for Aunt Nancy before she had the ministroke."

"Is it okay for you to show it to me?"

"Of course it is, sweetheart, my love." Gus kissed her forehead again.

He wondered when she'd let him kiss her on the lips. He didn't want to take advantage of the situation, but here they were. Their relationship was certain at this point, and they both knew it.

"Lead the way." Tally entwined her fingers in his.

They walked side by side, hand in hand, out of a side door leading to a courtyard that had strings of lights all around it. The roar of the ocean on the other side of the garden permeated their space, as did the wind that blew their way.

"Ooh, I can hear the ocean." Tally retied her ponytail into a bun on top of her head.

She grinned.

Gus could guess what that was about. "Our rain-check beach walk."

"You remembered." Tally squeezed his hand.

With his free hand, he checked the weather app on his phone. "No rain tomorrow morning. Would you like to walk with me on the beach at sunrise?"

"What time do I have to get up?"

"Sunrise is at six thirty."

"Oh. So you're driving here from your house?"

Gus nodded. "It takes me only thirteen minutes to get here."

"What time should I be ready for you?" Tally swiped her phone to schedule it.

"How about six fifteen? We can walk out to the

beach through this garden."

"Okay." Tally set her alarm and pocketed her phone.

Gus put an arm across her shoulders and led her to the guest house on the other side of the infinity pool.

"Sparkly." Tally pointed to the pool just as clouds cleared and the moon shone down.

"Watch your step," Gus said as they climbed the side stairs to the guest house roof. "Aunt Nancy wants to install an outdoor elevator here soon so that she doesn't have to climb all those stairs."

"Safer too, I think. These steps look like they might be slippery when wet."

"They are. It rains quite a bit here, so better safe than sorry."

On the rooftop, Gus turned on the lights. The lanterns went all around the walls. There was enough light for Gus to show off the container gardens he had planted for Aunt Nancy.

"My crew waters them now instead of me, but one of my gardeners and I planted all these flowers."

"I bet they are bright and beautiful in the daytime." Tally followed Gus on their mini tour.

After introducing her to some of the tropical flowers that she might not have heard of beyond the hibiscus, Gus led her to a teak bench up against a wall.

Sitting on the bench, they could look out to the silvery sea under the moonlit night. Tally tried to take a photograph of the ocean, but it turned out all dark with a fuzzy blob for the moon in the sky. She didn't delete the photo.

She pointed her phone camera at Gus. Gus smiled as she snapped away.

Then Gus gently pulled Tally toward him, his arm over her shoulders. Tally handed him her phone, and he took a photo of them grinning under the moonlight.

"What time is it?" Tally asked, checking the phone herself. "It's almost nine o'clock. I can't stay up too much longer."

"What time did you arrive in Nassau?" Gus asked.

"Late afternoon. We went to dinner with some of the women from your church. Then someone drove us to Nancy's house."

"I was having dinner at the house with Aunt Nancy and Donovan. Aunt Nancy told me that she had a special gift for me in the library. I was trying to figure out what it was." He squeezed her shoulder. "I was so happy that it turned out to be you. God is so good to us."

"Yes, He is. So let's pray and thank God for keeping us safe all this time we were apart." Tally leaned toward Gus and placed a palm on his chest. She closed her eyes and waited.

It meant she wanted him to pray now.

"Father God, thank You for bringing Tally here safely this afternoon. I am happy that we can see each other in person again. Thank You for directing Aunt Nancy to make it all happen. What a pleasant surprise!" His chest felt warm as Tally's palm remained there, where his heart was beating wildly. "Thank You for keeping Tally and me safe these five weeks we've lived apart. I missed her so much and I can't live without her—but neither of us can live without You, Lord."

"Thank You, Jesus," Tally said quietly.

"Father God, please protect us this weekend and give Tally and me a lot of time together to make pleasant memories. Next week Tally will be busy with the women's conference, and I don't know if I can see her much. I pray that You will help me not to be selfish. I understand that Tally is ministering to the Christian women who have come from all over the place to attend the conference. Give her Your words to speak and show her what to do. In the strong name of Jesus, I pray. Amen."

"Amen." Tally looked up lovingly at Gus. "I miss you too."

When she didn't turn away, Gus wondered if he had her permission to kiss her. After all, their lips were centimeters apart.

"We were seven hundred miles away from each other for more than a month, and now we're inches away from each other." Tally reached up and touched Gus's chin. She ran a finger along his jawline.

I think I've been invited.

With his thumb and index finger, oh so gently Gus lifted Tally's chin toward his. The moon shone down on her face, revealing glistening eyes.

"Are you crying?" Gus whispered.

"Happy tears." Tally smiled.

"I don't ever want to be apart from you again."

"I go home to Atlanta next Friday afternoon, and I don't know when I'll be back."

Stating the facts, she is.

Why did that hurt his heart so?

Gus lowered his lips. Tally closed her eyes.

Her lips tasted like honey. Must be her lip balm.

"Mmm. Strawberry shortcake." It was all Tally said before she deepened their moonlight kiss.

CHAPTER THIRTY

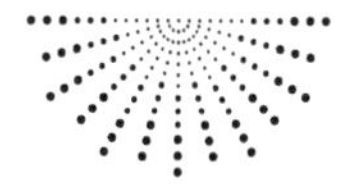

Tally could barely sleep all night. Too excited. She got up at four o'clock and could not go back to bed.

She read her Bible and prayed. Her list of prayers was so long that it took a whole hour to pray through everything. By the end of her prayer time, she had covered Gus and her family, Midtown Chapel, the Village, Lakeside Chapel, Riverside Chapel, Chapel by the Sea, and next week's women's conference.

She also said a prayer for God to heal Nancy Moss completely. It was because of her that Tally had been able to go to the Bahamas and see Gus again.

Even though the windows of her bedroom were

closed, she could still hear the ocean in her ears. She recalled her rooftop rendezvous with Gus, the breeze all around them as they kissed and hugged each other.

The kiss was a long time coming.

She was sure now more than ever that Gus was the one for her. Mentally and emotionally, she had forsaken Malachi—representing all others.

At a little after five o'clock, Tally took a shower and then paced up and down the walk-in closet looking for something to wear among the seven sets of outfits she had brought for the conference—one for each day, one for Sunday church, and one spare.

She checked her suitcase for the T-shirts and shorts she'd brought. They were her favorite clothes —comfortable and all cotton. However, she wasn't sure if they would be suitable for her to wear while she walked on the beach with Gus.

Gus knows me already. Stop fussing.

Tally settled on a faded red T-shirt, exercise shorts, and a pair of flip-flops.

She was downstairs in the kitchen looking for coffee before she realized she hadn't put on any makeup. She didn't know where the coffee was, and the coffee maker looked too fancy for her to use.

She settled for a bag of tea in a microwaved cup

of hot water and told herself that by the time she returned from her sunrise walk, someone would be up making coffee.

Hopefully.

Gus texted her at six o'clock.

She called him back. "I'm ready to go. Do you want me to go outside and wait for you in the courtyard?"

"Yes. I've already notified security that I'm coming. I won't go inside the house, so let's meet by the infinity pool. I'm parking my car now."

"See you there." Tally walked to the back door and then stopped. She wasn't sure if opening the door would set off the alarm. She called Gus again.

"I'll call security for you," Gus said.

Within seconds the back door clicked. Security must have unlocked it.

Dawn had just broken, and the sky was getting lighter by the minute. She was looking at the sky when someone called her name.

"Good morning, sweetheart." Gus came up to her, wearing a faded green T-shirt.

Tally had to laugh. "We're wearing Christmas colors."

"Only our favorite colors." Gus hugged her from the back, locking his hands in front of her tummy.

Suddenly feeling overweight, Tally held his wrists and tried to pry his hands away.

"Why?" Gus asked. "You don't like me anymore?"

"I don't want you to feel the flab on my waist."

He held her even tighter. "I'd rather not be hugging bones."

"Let's get going because sunrise is at six thirty, you said." Tally started walking.

Gus let go of her waist. "Six thirty-six, according to my weather app."

He held her hand as they walked across the lawn, past the pool, onto more grass, and then to the stretch of fine quartz sand.

"East is that way." Gus pointed to the right.

They left the Moss Mansion property line and walked toward the sunrise. Above them the sky was filled with clouds that looked like a tray of marshmallows suspended in air.

Tally took off her flip-flops and carried them in her left hand. Her right hand was in Gus's left hand as they walked along the shoreline, kicking up saltwater.

The sun rose over the horizon, and Tally stopped. "I want to get some photos."

Gus waited as she took some photos. "Let's get a photo of us and the sunrise."

They turned to face away from the sunrise. Gus held Tally tightly and snapped a photo of them with the sunrise in the background.

"Let's take one with your phone too," Tally suggested.

By the time they were done, the sun was rising quickly into the sky. They continued their beach walk eastward, hand in hand.

Tally wanted to walk in the water, and so she did. The sand shifted beneath her feet, and she lost her balance.

Gus caught her.

But not before the sea took a swipe at the bottom of her shorts, soaking them.

Gus helped her out of the water. "Do you want me to hold on to you so that you can wade in the water without falling in?"

"No need." Tally walked on soft sand along the ocean's edge. "There's a spiritual lesson here."

"I know." Gus swiped his phone. "Are you thinking of Matthew 7:24–26 about rock and sand?"

"Yes." Tally stopped where they were and checked her phone. "How about you read the two verses about the house built on the rock, and I'll read the next two verses about the house on the sand?"

"Sure. 'Therefore whoever hears these sayings of Mine, and does them, I will liken him to a wise man who built his house on the rock: and the rain descended, the floods came, and the winds blew and beat on that house; and it did not fall, for it was founded on the rock.' Good reminder to be anchored in Christ."

Tally nodded. "The next two verses say, 'But everyone who hears these sayings of Mine, and does not do them, will be like a foolish man who built his house on the sand: and the rain descended, the floods came, and the winds blew and beat on that house; and it fell. And great was its fall.' A warning for us."

"Let's pray that we will build our spiritual house on the solid rock of Christ and not on shifting sand," Gus said.

"That we will listen to God carefully, keep His Word in our hearts, and obey Him thoroughly so that we will not sin against him," Tally added.

"Good." Gus extended his hand.

Tally put hers in his.

And Gus prayed.

They walked again after they said "amen" in unison.

"Nice that we can read the Bible together," Tally said.

"Back in the medieval days, Christians required priests to interpret the Scripture for them because most commoners didn't read Latin, Hebrew, or Greek."

"Today we can read the Bible on our own. The Holy Spirit gives us understanding of God's Word."

"What's the verse that talks about the Holy Spirit as our teacher?" Gus asked.

"John 14:26? 'But the Helper, the Holy Spirit, whom the Father will send in My name, He will teach you all things, and bring to your remembrance all things that I said to you.' That one?"

"Yes. You're good at this."

"That's what happens when your dad is a pastor."

"Not all pastor's kids turn out fine," Gus said. "Or missionary kids, for that matter."

"True. By the mercy of God my parents worked on my sisters and me so that we don't stray away from God's Word," Tally explained. "Don't get me wrong. We sin too, but the Holy Spirit convicts us of the errors of our ways, and we repent and get back on track. Our perfect Savior forgives us and helps us."

"Your parents will have wonderful rewards in heaven for teaching their kids well."

The temperature was warm, and Tally started to sweat.

"Go indoors?" Gus asked.

"No. Since we're here, we might as well get some exercising done, right? I usually walk two miles per hour on the treadmill, but I don't have my walking shoes today."

"Let's stroll. How far do you want to walk?"

"As long as we want. I have the day off," Tally said. "However, the sun is getting hot. If we walk half an hour there, we have to walk half an hour back."

"Up to you. We can do whatever you want. I'm just happy to see you again."

"Then let's walk."

Every now and then, Tally and Gus stopped to look at the ocean and the occasional seabirds flying around. Tally sent some ocean videos to her parents and sisters back home.

Mom texted back that she wanted to return to the Bahamas someday.

Tally decided not to call Mom at this time. She wanted to save the time for Gus.

"You're off today, you say."

Tally nodded. "Today is our free day."

"What are your plans for the rest of the day?"

"I'm all yours," Tally said.

"Then we might as well have our rain-check dinner tonight, if you like."

"You still remember." Tally locked arms with Gus. "It seems such a long time ago that we agreed to go out to dinner as survivors of the warehouse captivity."

"God set us free. We celebrate that."

They stopped to look at seabirds. Tally pointed here and there. "Beautiful sunrise. Ocean waves."

"What do you think of Paradise Island and the Bahamas in general?" Gus asked.

"I love it." Tally gazed out to the ocean. "If I have a good reason, I could move here."

"What reason might that be?" Gus's voice was gentle, as if reminding her that they had kissed the night before. Under the moonlight, no less.

"I'm thinking about it," Tally said.

Gus kissed the edge of her lips gently. "Is that a good reason for you?"

The sun rose all around them.

Tally smiled. "Not sure if that's compelling enough."

"Compelling enough?" Gus kissed her again. "Like this, maybe?"

"Well... If you want to persuade me—"

Gus cupped her face in his palm and planted a

third kiss on her puckered lips. She smiled as he tried to prove his point.

They had to stop kissing because they laughed too much.

"See, you want to live here because of me," Gus said.

"No, Gus. I will only go where God leads me. So if God leads us to stay here in the Bahamas, then we will stay here."

"We. Thank you for including me."

"What if God leads us back to the States?" Tally asked. "Will you go with me?"

"In a heartbeat."

"Why?"

"Because God leads us, as you said. Wherever God leads us, we go."

They kept walking, assured of their decision.

It didn't seem like they had walked too far away from Nancy's house, but when Tally turned to look, she couldn't spot Moss Mansion.

"Looking for Moss Mansion?" Gus asked.

Tally nodded.

"Does that mean it's time to turn around?"

"We can go back if you want." Gus glanced at his phone. "It's seven thirty-six."

"Early."

"Do you want to hang out with me? We can

drive around town and spend the day together, ending it with a dinner date somewhere. What would you like to eat?"

"Breakfast right now. Thank you very much."

"Breakfast it is." Gus led the way back to Moss Mansion.

Before they reached it, Tally could hear people laughing and talking. Women mostly. At the edge where grass met sand, she saw the other two speakers and Nancy gathering around a chef.

The chef was cooking something on the outdoor stove, and it smelled like eggs and cheese.

Tally's tummy rumbled.

"Looks like Chef Ana is going to cook your breakfast for you." Gus followed Tally across the lawn.

When the ladies saw them coming, they waved, gasped, and then started clapping.

Tally wasn't sure what that was about. She turned to ask Gus—

Gus was kneeling on the grass. His arms extended in front of him, a red heart-shaped box in his hands. The velvet box was closed, but Tally could guess what was inside.

He had tears in his eyes. "I thought we'd be alone on the lawn. I planned to do this after we returned from our beach walk. I didn't want to wait, whether there were people here or not."

"It's all right. They can be our witnesses."

Now Tally was crying. She felt sticky and sweaty under the Caribbean sun. She wanted to run indoors and go take a shower. But her feet didn't know what running was today.

She stood rooted to the spot of grass in front of Gus.

"Tallulah Fitzpatrick," Gus said.

"Yes?"

"Four years ago when you first came to the Bahamas, you saw me and felt something for me. Am I right?"

"But there was no love between us then." Tally was glad there hadn't been because she would never want to break up a relationship.

She had no idea four years ago that Gus and his then girlfriend weren't meant for each other. Gus himself hadn't known either until a year ago.

"I agree. I started to notice you when we were the only two people in some meeting who liked Christmas colors. You liked Christmas red and I liked Christmas green. Remember?"

"I still do."

"Same here."

"Why are you rehashing all these things—our favorite colors, the time we first met?"

"Well..." Gus cleared his throat. "Fast-forward four years, and we're both single now, free to love each other the way God intended. Do you believe that God brought us together?"

"Yes. No doubt in my mind. The evidence is clear." Tally didn't go into details. She could, and Gus might enjoy her analysis, but the dude was kneeling on the grass holding a ring that was meant for her finger, so she didn't want to delay it any longer.

Besides, the sun is hot this morning.

"Since we're practical people, let's get to the point so that we can eat breakfast," Gus said.

That's my man.

"In the time I spent with you in the merry month of May, I have fallen in love with you, and I know in my heart that I cannot love another. You're the only one for me for the rest of my life on earth."

"You're the only one for me too."

Gus's lips quivered. "I was worried about how quickly we fell in love, since I don't quite believe in love at first sight—though I respect that point of view, since your parents fell in love at first sight. However, there is such a thing as *koi no yokan*, that Japanese phrase that doesn't quite mean love at second sight. I take it to mean that, having met each other, we would eventually fall in love."

"Hey, Gus!" A male voice sounded out of nowhere. "You're not writing a master's thesis!"

Tally turned to find Donovan walking toward them. His mother stopped him as he walked by her.

Nancy tried to hush him, but he kept talking, raising his voice, in case Tally and Gus couldn't hear him.

"I came over to see if all our effort last night was in vain," Donovan said. "And here I am listening to a discussion of dictionary words. What happened to the romance?"

"Effort? What did you two do last night?" Tally asked. She didn't want to think what that could possibly be.

"I'll tell you after you answer his question." Donovan pointed to Gus.

Nancy laughed. "He has to ask the question first."

Tally turned back to Gus, small beads of sweat trickling down her temple and checks.

"Tallulah Fitzpatrick," Gus said, as if starting over. "I've heard this phrase multiple times, but now I've experienced it myself: when you know, you know. We don't need a long courtship. We don't need to date for five years. We've prayed about this. I know you're mine. You know I'm yours. Do you agree?"

"Yes I do. Very much so."

"Tally, I want to marry you, love you, cherish you, care for you, protect you, honor you, and please you the way the Bible says I'm supposed to as your husband. I can't wait to start a family with you and raise our children in the ways of the Lord, just like your parents have raised you and your sisters." Gus lifted the box a little higher in the air and opened it.

The tiffany-cut diamond engagement ring sparkled in the sun.

"Tallulah Fitzpatrick."

It was the third time Gus had called her Tallulah.

"What's my middle name?" Tally suddenly asked.

Does he even know?

"Riona. Your mother's name. I asked your dad," Gus said proudly. "Tallulah Riona Fitzpatrick, will you marry me and be my one-and-only wife and lover for the rest of my life?"

Hot tears streamed down Tally's face. "Yes, Augustus Isaac Moss III. I will marry you."

As everyone applauded, Gus took out the

engagement ring from the box and slid it onto Tally's ring finger.

It fit perfectly. "Wow."

"Your ring finger is the size of my little finger," Gus explained.

Donovan stepped forward. "Now I will tell you a story about how we had to open the jewelry store on board one of our docked cruise ships so that Gus here could shop for a ring for the love of his life. But before I do that, aren't you supposed to kiss each other?"

Gus rose to his feet and kissed Tally on the forehead. Instead of complaining or letting it go, Tally reached for Gus's T-shirt neckline, and pulled him toward her until their lips almost touched.

Then she waited, knowing he wanted this. He hadn't been shy on the beach when he knew they were surrounded by strangers. Here on the lawn, Aunt Nancy was watching him, and his cousin's nose was practically upon them.

As Tally waited, she sensed that Gus mustered up his courage.

Sure enough, Gus completed what Tally had started by sealing their engagement with a long kiss under the hot morning sun.

Breakfast had to wait.

CHAPTER THIRTY-ONE

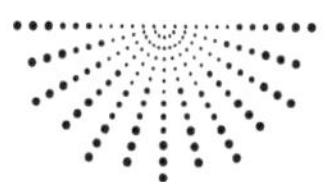

Nine months after Gus proposed to Tally in the Bahamas—during which time, Dad managed to squeeze in six months of premarital counseling—winter started to thaw out in Atlanta on that blustery February morning. It looked like it was going to rain outside, even though multiple weather forecasts said Saturday would be sunny all morning.

So much for that.

Unprepared for rain, Tally hadn't thought about providing umbrellas as party favors.

Oh well.

The old church with its stone walls and stained-glass windows looked dark now save for the ceiling lights. If it was sunny outside, then the stained glass would provide a multicolored light show on the walls and floors of the hundred-year-old sanctuary in midtown Atlanta.

As it was, this morning, all focus was on God alone.

The heavy wooden doors opened when the Midtown Chapel sanctuary orchestra played Bach's "Jesu, Joy of Man's Desiring."

In a simple white bridal gown with a veil and train, Tally walked slowly down the aisle, arm in arm with Dad. She dared not look at him for fear of bursting into tears.

Dad hadn't said much beyond the prayer he'd prayed with his wife and daughters in the bridal room. Maybe he was sad or happy or both. Tally couldn't read his mind.

Tally was his first daughter to get married.

And his first daughter to undergo the extra-rigorous premarital counseling he had meted out.

Mom had told Dad that it would be easier with Colette and Adalia. Speaking of whom, Tally's two sisters were behind her, carrying her train.

She hadn't wanted a long train, but Colette and Adalia had told her that they must each hold it. Anyway, it hadn't cost much more to have a train that was a few feet longer than she had anticipated.

No train at all would be ideal, but here we are.

From a distance, Tally saw Gus, standing next to his best men and cousins, Byron and Donovan. Gus's jaw dropped for a quick moment, and then he smiled broadly at her.

Colette, the newly minted wedding planner, had done Tally's makeup. So Gus could be shocked at it being too much or too little or just right. Tally had no idea what might be on his mind.

Tally drew a deep breath as she tried to remain calm while walking down the red carpet strewn with rose petals. She hadn't wanted the petals because she didn't want to destroy hundreds of roses just to have a forty-five-minute wedding ceremony. Fortunately, she was able to pressure Colette to go for silk petals that could be reused in another event.

The wedding meant the world to her parents and sisters. If it were up to Tally, she'd have a very small and simple-budget wedding and give away the rest of the money to the church to be allocated for ministry at the Village and to battered women shelters around the city. Then many women would benefit from it, not just her.

Yes, this was Tally's wedding, and she could do whatever she wanted with it, as Colette had reminded her over and over.

Ah, Colette.

What a godsend her sister had been to Tally. Then again, it was a win-win for them. Colette wanted to continue being the event planner at Lakeside Resort, but she needed more experience in the wedding department. She had recruited her friend and photographer, Henry Grayson Ford, to help her, and they had both decided to handle Tally's wedding for free, donating their income to the Village as their wedding present to Tally.

It was one of the best wedding presents ever.

A sea of smiles greeted Tally as she walked past rows of old bench pews, seats reclaimed from an abandoned church in England and shipped to Atlanta sometime in the nineteen fifties. There were no cushions on the seats, but the eighteenth-century carved pews made the whole church look like a setting out of time.

Tally nodded to Pastor Kim, his wife Lydia, and their daughter, Iseul. They sat in the same pew as Jacinda Everett, surrounded by Iliana and other teenagers she had started to mentor as her way of dealing with the grief of losing her own son. Some of them were Sheldon's friends from school, but some of them were orphans.

Iliana Wells's arm wrapped around Jacinda's. Almost eighteen now, Iliana had been the last person to see Sheldon before he was murdered at the warehouse back in May. Iliana had cooperated with the Decatur Police and the GBI, and her vivid memory resulted in a detailed police sketch of the assailant who'd attacked her and Sheldon.

Sitting on the pews in front of Iliana, Tally's fellow church members from Midtown Chapel clapped as she walked by. She silently thanked God again for them, pooling together the reward fund for the arrest and conviction of Sheldon's murderer, seeded by more affluent members, such as Logan and Marie Urquhart, Byron and Tina, and Gus—bless his heart—who always stepped in for Tally's sake.

Volunteers had distributed the suspect's sketch far and wide—on social media, in grocery stores, in soup kitchens, halfway houses, schools, apartment complexes, wherever they were allowed to pin the flier on bulletin boards. They continued their effort for weeks, encouraged by the church leadership.

Shortly thereafter, someone living under a bridge came forward to collect the reward money. When the GBI and local police questioned the homeless man, he outed a friend who had boasted about sleeping in a warehouse for several days. The friend matched the police sketch, and they put him in a lineup for Iliana to identify.

After Iliana was sure that he'd been the one

who had bludgeoned Sheldon to death, the suspect confessed that someone he didn't know had approached him with a stash of cash, a key, and instructions to go to a specific warehouse to set it on fire.

It was the same warehouse.

Instead of burning down the building, the homeless man thought it was a waste of indoor space to ruin like that. He used the warehouse as his new home, sleeping there day and night, high on drugs, unable to carry out the deed he'd been paid to do. That Friday he'd run into Sheldon and Iliana by accident, and the rest was as tragic as it was unnecessary.

The would-be arsonist had failed that Friday, but one week later, Silas made up for the slack. Tally wondered if Silas had gotten the fire idea from the local news. However, with Silas dead and gone, the story died with him.

After seven months of investigation, the authorities discovered a web of money laundering activities masterminded by a group of criminals, including the warehouse owner, who'd sent his people to hire the homeless man to burn down the warehouse to hide nefarious activities he'd been allowing in his facility. Apparently, Sheldon hadn't been the first person to die in the warehouse.

And he certainly hadn't been the last. Joey the security guard had also perished in the same place, killed by Silas one week after Sheldon had died—although Joey's case seemed to be unrelated to the money laundering. Another needless death.

Beyond that, Tally had no news about the conclusion of the money laundering scheme because such investigations were done at the federal level by the United States Department of the Treasury.

Back at the local level, Iliana's first-person eyewitness account and her memory of the homeless man's face had led to the capture of Sheldon's killer. After spending time with local law enforcement officers, helping them to solve the case, and then with prosecutors in the court system, seeing them convict the suspect of involuntary manslaughter, Iliana decided to go to law school.

Her desire to study law spurred Jacinda to earn her GED and enroll in a local community college to major in cosmetology so that she could build her career as a makeup artist.

Tally thanked God that Jacinda and Iliana were able to carry on with their lives after Sheldon's death.

While it would have been much better had Sheldon been alive to see his mother get back on her feet, no one on earth could rewind the clock. Sometimes God allowed things to happen without any explanation to anyone.

Tally accepted that God was sovereign. He had the right to keep certain things secret, as it was written in Deuteronomy 29:29.

> *The secret things belong to the Lord our God, but those things which are revealed belong to us and to our children forever, that we may do all the words of this law.*

Tally smiled at Ming and Sabine Wei, Heidi and her husband, Pastor Flores, and several other friends from Riverside Chapel in Savannah, where she had spoken at women's conferences and conducted workshops. Sitting next to them, Roger and a pregnant Cheyenne Patel smiled broadly, as did Priyanka and Hunter Jacobs, one pew in front.

Priyanka and Hunter had gifted them two nights of honeymoon in the red caboose at Jacobs Landing on Tybee Island. At first only the yurts were available, but Hunter worked his campsite-manager charm and persuaded their other renters to let the honeymooners have two nights in the caboose.

Really, they didn't need to be in that particular

caboose, but Tally and Gus accepted the gift anyway. Finally, they just might be able to make it to their planned sunrise walks on the beaches of Tybee Island. Tally prayed it wouldn't rain.

Tally nodded and smiled at friends from the Bahamas. Pastor Dixon and his wife had flown all the way from Nassau to attend the wedding. They sat next to Nancy Moss, who was dabbing her eyes with a monogrammed silk handkerchief.

Absent from the sanctuary were people from Tally and Gus's past. Veronique was a happy new mother in the Bahamas and had told people that she wouldn't have attended even if invited. Malachi Jacobs was busy handling pastoral duties at Lakeside Chapel so that Dad could come to Atlanta to officiate the wedding and walk Tally down the aisle.

Just as well, because Gus and Tally wanted a new beginning for themselves. This was a new start that God had given them. Saying goodbye to people in their past would be one of the indications that they had moved forward with God.

The sweet music ended just as Tally and Dad reached the podium.

Without a word, Dad put Tally's gloved hand in Gus's, and then Dad took the stand as the officiating pastor.

Tally felt nervous looking at Dad, even though she knew that he had approved her marriage to Gus. In fact, Gus had talked to Dad and received his and Mom's blessings before he proposed to Tally nine months ago on Paradise Island in the Bahamas.

Tally smiled as she recalled that proposal morning.

Both sides of the family were supportive of their relationship. Tally and Gus decided to look at their support as a confirmation of God's approval of their marriage.

"Mark 10:9 says, 'Therefore what God has joined together, let not man separate.' Dearly beloved, we are gathered here to witness what God has put together." Dad's voice boomed though his microphone.

Tally thought a sermon was going to break out.

However, it did not.

Mom must have told Dad to keep it short.

The more Tally looked at Dad, the sadder she became. She did not want to leave Atlanta and move to the Bahamas. No, truly. She wanted to be closer to her parents, who were up there in age. She wanted to care for them and be there when they needed her.

Could Gus understand that?

Yes, she had told him that she could live in the Bahamas. However, now that she was standing there in the wedding chapel, looking at Dad getting old before her eyes, she couldn't leave them.

How could she?

Then again...

"Genesis 2:24 says, 'Therefore a man shall leave his father and mother and be joined to his wife, and they shall become one flesh.' When you are married, you and your spouse stay together, wherever God leads you." Dad's voice was sure.

How did Dad know what she was thinking?

Tally almost laughed at the thought of the jokes about tinfoil hats.

Gus squeezed her hand, as if to say, "Calm down."

She took a deep breath and listened as Dad preached his wedding sermonette. That was Dad all the way, and she had to accept it.

She had already agreed to move to the Bahamas with Gus. Perhaps they could try it out for a year and see if they liked living in Nassau. She'd be speaking at women's conferences in the States and would be flying back and forth. She would still see her parents whenever she traveled.

She knew that Gus was open to living in Atlanta as well, though Mom and Dad were moving to Lakeside, Florida, to take care of Grandma. No one in the Fitzpatrick family would remain in Atlanta.

In fact, this was the last wedding Dad would conduct at Midtown Chapel.

Tally sniffled. She missed this church already. The church of her youth.

She'd also miss her friends at the Village, many of whom were here today, filling both sides of the aisles, sitting among Gus's family and their friends from many churches. They could all barely fit into the sanctuary, and there was even an overflow livestream downstairs in the fellowship hall, where the reception would be held.

Tally had to leave Atlanta to live with her husband in the Bahamas. She was willing to do it as long as she and Gus were in God's perfect will for their lives. That was the only reason.

Lord, I know You will work it all out.

For sure, their first year of marriage would be spent in Nassau, but beyond that, who knew.

After all, Gus had taken her advice to start a financial consulting company, which he called Moss Tally, with "tally" being an accounting term denoting a score or count. Who'd think her name could have that many meanings?

Tally chuckled at the irony of it.

Gus glanced at her. So did Dad.

What's so funny?

Tally tried to return to a poker face, but she couldn't hide the grin.

Her new husband had named his company after her. Tally was pleased.

Gus had kept Moss Green, his landscaping company, as something he'd do during the day. However, whenever Moss Enterprises, Moss Cruises, and Moss Resorts needed his assistance, Gus would go under the banner of Moss Tally.

In the future, he'd hire a couple of accountants to assist him. If needed, he'd send them over to the job corporate job sites while he pruned some fruit trees or flowers.

Nancy Moss was as happy as a lark. With Gus to rely on for freelance consulting, she semiretired and spent more time at the spa than at the Moss Enterprises headquarters. Her son Donovan learned a lot of things from Gus and was on his way to becoming one of the best CEOs that the Moss family could produce.

All was well that ended well.

After she and Gus exchanged traditional vows and rings, Tally realized that she didn't recall what she had said. She was so nervous that she had blindly repeated after Dad. However, she and Gus had gone over the vows themselves weeks before, and had approved them.

Tally reminded herself that all these things were recorded on video, and she could watch it later.

"Ephesians 5:25–33 is a long passage meant for Christian husbands and wives," Dad said. "I'm going to read just a couple of verses from this passage. The entire passage is in your wedding program."

Dad waited for people to find it in their wedding programs.

"Ephesians 5:28–29 says, 'So husbands ought to love their own wives as their own bodies; he who loves his wife loves himself. For no one ever hated his own flesh, but nourishes and cherishes it, just as the Lord does the church.' Husbands, that is your task."

Dad looked around the room.

Tally was happy for the delay because after this, Gus had to kiss her in front of all these people they knew.

"Ephesians 5:33 says, 'Nevertheless let each one of you in particular so love his own wife as himself, and let the wife see that she respects her husband.' That last part is your task, wives." Dad closed the

Bible. "There are other Bible passages for husbands and wives, but we will save them for the marriage itself. That means a lifetime of learning, y'all."

Tally and Gus smiled at each other.

A lifetime with you.

"By the power vested in me, I now pronounce you husband and wife." Dad turned to Gus. "You may kiss the bride."

Nervous, nervous.

Tally waited. Gus took his time. He lifted Tally's veil, a slight smile on his lips. Tally waited in anticipation. Somehow that put Gus at ease.

He cupped her face in both palms, and their lips met to the jubilation of the crowd, who clapped rambunctiously.

"Please welcome our newlyweds, Mr. and Mrs. Augustus Moss," Dad announced.

The wedding guests clapped again. They all stood as Tally and Gus made their way down the aisle and out the door. The hallway took them to the elevator to the fellowship hall downstairs, where the bride and groom greeted their friends.

Levi came over to congratulate Tally and Gus, when sudden applause in the hall made everyone turned their heads. Tally peeked through the crowd but couldn't see a thing. A live feed appeared on the big screen. One of the videographers had fed the scene into the projector.

Tally saw Soline Ang-Ferrera standing with her palms covering her face, and her boyfriend—her first love from college—on his knees.

"Yes, yes," Soline said as he put a ring on her finger.

"How sweet," Tally said.

Standing next to her, Levi took a deep breath. "Excuse me."

He walked away.

"Levi!" Tally called out. He didn't respond. He kept walking until he disappeared down the hallway.

Gus moved. "I'll find him."

Tally grabbed his arm and shook her head. "He might want to be alone."

"I'll call him tomorrow then."

"Good idea." They'd be at Jacobs Landing on Tybee Island, enjoying their honeymoon in the red caboose. Maybe they'd roast marshmallows and make s'mores again.

And certainly go walk on the beach.

Tally prayed silently for her colleague and friend. Levi must be heartbroken.

Around her, Tally heard some people mumbling about how rude it was for someone to propose at another person's wedding reception. She wanted to say that she didn't mind sharing other people's happiness, but she decided to keep silent, smile, and greet another guest.

Gus squeezed her hand gently.

The music started to play a slow romantic waltz. Gus swept up Tally in his arms. In the weeks prior to the wedding, Gus had taught Tally to waltz. She knew that she could last for maybe twenty seconds on the dance floor without embarrassing herself.

This morning they danced for the video so that they could show their future children that Mommy had learned to waltz for twenty seconds.

Gus leaned toward Tally's ear. "I love you and only you for the rest of my life. There's no one else."

Tally couldn't help smiling. Somehow, she knew he'd told the truth. Whatever his past relationships were, they could move forward.

"And I, you. Ditto. Ditto." She grinned. An English major at a loss for words.

"What?" Gus asked.

"Inside joke."

"Are we exclusive?" Gus asked, almost too casually.

"One man, one wife. Our vow before God. So

yes, let our marriage bed be undefiled." Tally wondered why he'd asked.

He looked in a certain direction, and so did Tally.

Oh, I see.

Malachi and his sister, Maggie, were at the buffet table nearby.

"I thought he was at Lakeside," Tally whispered to Gus.

"He's here now."

This is a test, yes? "Did he fly here?"

"Who knows. Seven hours to drive. If I can do it, he could."

Tally glanced one last time at Malachi. She felt nothing. Truly, she no longer had feelings for him. Whatever she'd had six years ago might have been puppy love.

"I love you," Gus said again as he led her away from Malachi and Maggie to the other end of the dance floor. "And no one else."

No one else.

He'd said that twice in five minutes, as though she needed assuring. Perhaps he wanted to hear the same from her.

"I love you too, Gus, and no one else."

And she meant it.

DEAR READER:

Thank you for reading *Pray for Me*, book 5 in my Vacation Sweethearts collection of Christian travel romances. While *Pray for Me* is set primarily in a bustling metropolis, the next novel, *Care for Me*, takes us from the big city of Atlanta all the way to the top of the Great Smoky Mountains to the small town of Misty Mountain. It's Seth Moreno's hometown, the place where he left his first love behind. Seventeen years later, has April Madison married? Seth is about to find out when he is tasked to deliver a Bible to his mother's old friend, April's great-aunt. Sign up for my newsletter to be notified when this novel is published.

Care for Me (Vacation Sweethearts Book 6)
JanThompson.com/care

Jan Thompson's Book News Mailing List:
JanThompson.com/newsletter

COLETTE, ADALIA, AND MALACHI ARE IN LAKESIDE CHAPEL

In *Pray for Me*, Tally's two sisters are mentioned but are mostly absent from the story. That's because while Gus is in Atlanta, Colette and Adalia are in Lakeside, Florida, helping out in their grandmother's resort by the lake. They headline a new upcoming series, Lakeside Chapel, which is a sister series to Seaside Chapel. Sign up for my newsletter to be notified when the series launches.

If you haven't read Seaside Chapel, you can find the link below.

Jan Thompson's Book News Mailing List:
JanThompson.com/newsletter

Seaside Chapel (sister series to Lakeside Chapel)
JanThompson.com/seaside

TINA AND BYRON ARE IN SMILE FOR ME

In *Pray for Me*, we meet several characters who have appeared in past books. For example, Gus's cousin Byron is married to Tina. These two are the main characters in *Smile for Me*, the first novel in the Vacation Sweethearts series. When Tina goes back to the Bahamas to teach in a summer art camp, she has to confront her nemesis, Byron Moss. Has their relationship changed two years later in this opposites-attract international romance?

Smile for Me (Vacation Sweethearts Book 4):
JanThompson.com/smile

MING AND SABINE ARE IN TELL YOU SOON

Private investigator Ming Wei and real estate agent Sabine have their own drama in *Tell You Soon*, book 2 in the Savannah Sweethearts coastal city and beach romance series. When Ming asks Sabine to sell his beach house, he has no idea it would lead to trouble in this coastal romance with a side of suspense.

Tell You Soon (Savannah Sweethearts Book 4):
JanThompson.com/tell

HUNTER AND PRIYANKA ARE IN KISS YOU NOW

In *Pray for Me*, we meet Hunter Jacobs at Jacobs Landing, a glamping campsite on Tybee Island, where the Fitzpatricks and Gus stay for a weekend. Hunter meets his wife, Priyanka Patel, when she first arrives on Tybee Island and gets a job as a people walker at the Savannah Senior Living Resort. What is a people walker? Find out in *Kiss You Now*. Priyanka's centenarian friend, Pastor Hiram Jacobs, has a large family, including his great-grandson Hunter, a down-and-out novelist. When Hiram asks Hunter and Priyanka to work together in a writing project, they have no choice.

Kiss You Now (Savannah Sweethearts Book 7)
JanThompson.com/kiss

ROGER AND CHEYENNE ARE IN FIND YOU AGAIN

In *Pray for Me*, before Gus gives his testimony at the Savannah Senior Living Resort, the person who introduces him is none other than Dr. Roger Patel, who runs the resort. A bachelor, Roger is not looking for love. However, when his firefighter friend, Cheyenne Endecott, brings her widowed aunt to SSLR, they find each other again.

Find You Again (Savannah Sweethearts Book 8)
JanThompson.com/find

HELEN HU IS IN ONCE A THIEF

In *Pray for Me*, Midtown Chapel asks Helen Hu to help find closure for Sheldon's family. Helen is super busy, so she dispatches her brother-in-law, Ming, to Atlanta. Helen has her own story in *Once a Thief* (Protector Sweethearts Book 1), where she goes to Greece and Italy to find her missing mother, an erstwhile thief with a belated conscience. Fifteen years ago Mama Hu stole some bejeweled eggs, and now she tries to return them to the wrong owners. In the process, she gets abducted. How does Helen find her mother? She sets a thief to catch a thief, but does reformed criminal Reuben Costa have other plans?

Once a Thief (Protector Sweethearts Book 1)
JanThompson.com/thief

READ TIME FOR ME FOR FREE

Time for Me is the only prequel to this Vacation Sweethearts series. When art gallery archivist Sheryl Breckenridge tries to get world-famous sculptor Winton Pace to display his artwork at Simon's Gallery, she doesn't expect him to fall in love with her. Will she reciprocate in this friends-to-more romance? You can buy the book at popular online retailers, but this novella is also available for free.

Download *Time for Me* for free:
JanThompson.com/time-free

READ ASK YOU LATER FOR FREE

A Christian beach romance novel, *Ask You Later* is the story of artist Leon Watts, who returns to Tybee Island and Savannah to jump-start his fledgling career, and meets a non-artistic art gallery director getting in his way. This prequel novel is a part of the Savannah Sweethearts collection, the series that comes before Vacation Sweethearts.

Download *Ask You Later* for free:
JanThompson.com/ask-vacation

Have you read *Smile for Me* (Vacation Sweethearts Book 1)? Read on for a sneak preview of Chapter 1.

HAVE YOU READ SMILE FOR ME?

VACATION SWEETHEARTS BOOK 1

She is laid back.

He is uptight.

Never the twain shall...kiss?

A deadline-driven workaholic assistant school principal who meticulously plans his schedule months in advance meets an easygoing art teacher and studio potter with no sense of time, living her life as the seasons come and go. When they cross paths again at the Summer by the Sea Day Camp sponsored by his church in Nassau, Bahamas, how can they get along if they cannot see eye to eye?

TINA MACFARLAND IS LAID BACK...

Come to the Bahamas, they said. It will be fun, they said.

Well, arriving in Nassau, I feel I could be okay if Byron's not around. I made it! I'm here! That's good enough for me, but apparently it's not good enough for Mr. Uptight.

Why does he bother me so? I don't need his approval—

Oh yes, I do.

As a volunteer art teacher at the day camp, I have to answer to Byron for four weeks.

Well, thank God it's only for four weeks. And then I'm outta here, and he'll be out of my hair.

Surely I can last through day camp. What could possibly go wrong in a month? Nothing I can think of...

—TINA MACFARLAND, CERAMIC ARTIST, POTTER, ART TEACHER, VOLUNTEER AT THE SUMMER BY THE SEA DAY CAMP IN THE BAHAMAS

When invited back to the Bahamas for a second time two years after a disastrous mission trip there, potter and art teacher Tina MacFarland isn't sure she wants to face the obnoxious assistant principal of the Chapel by the Sea Christian School again. The last time she encountered Byron Moss, he found fault in everything she did. It seems that nothing she ever does is good enough for Mr. Uptight, as attractive as he may be to her.

Regardless of her personal concerns, they need art teachers at the Summer by the Sea Day Camp, and Tina answers the call to go. Surely God will help her last for four short weeks. What can possibly happen in a month? Nothing she can think of.

BYRON MOSS IS UPTIGHT...

> This is what I've always wanted, right? Then why does this assistant headmaster position hem me in?
>
> I feel constricted, restricted, afflicted. I fear I have taken a wrong turn in my career.
>
> What is God's will for my life?
>
> And what does Tina think about—
>
> Tina? What does she have anything to do with my career decisions?
>
> — BYRON MOSS, ASSISTANT HEADMASTER, CHAPEL BY THE SEA CHRISTIAN SCHOOL IN THE BAHAMAS

Assistant Headmaster Byron Moss is at a crossroad in his career. On the one hand, he has worked very hard to get to this position at the Chapel by the Sea Christian School. One more step up from this assistant principal position, and he'd be in charge of the entire school.

On the other hand, when Tina returns to Nassau, Byron suddenly feels hemmed in by his career choice. He is restricted from showing his transforming feelings for Tina. He fears he has taken a wrong turn in his career, and that if he keeps going on that route, he may lose his chances with Tina. More importantly, what is God's will for his life? Somehow, he knows that Tina is part of all that. But she's so...chaotic! And it drives him nuts. For the first time in his life, Byron is confused about what he needs to do.

NEVER THE TWAIN SHALL...KISS?

Ah, Byron and Tina... How would they navigate the super-conservative work environment where office romance is frowned upon? Can they change the old rules? Or will the old rules change them?

Let's find out in the Caribbean, where the waters are blue, skies are pretty, and hearts are warm...

An interracial summer vacation Christian romance set in the Bahamas, *Smile for Me* is Book 1 in *USA Today* bestselling author Jan Thompson's Vacation Sweethearts series of traveling romances, a spin-off of her Savannah Sweethearts series.

While the novels of Vacation Sweethearts are loosely connected, they do not have to be read in order, though it would be more fun to start from the beginning.

Smile for Me (Vacation Sweethearts Book 1)
JanThompson.com/smile

Sign up for Jan Thompson's book news mailing list:
JanThompson.com/newsletter

Continue reading for a chapter 1 preview of *Smile for Me.*

SMILE FOR ME CHAPTER 1 SNEAK PEEK

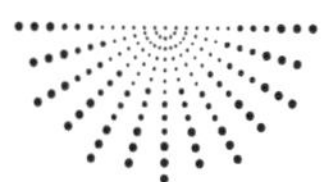

VACATION SWEETHEARTS BOOK 1

Byron Moss had called that woman *Veronique* in a singsong fashion, and that had rubbed Tina MacFarland the wrong way.

She would have to admit that Veronique was a pretty French name—too French for this ex-British colony, but then again, nobody had asked her.

She watched both of them whisper to each other at the front of the long school bus, identical iPads hanging off their necks like some sort of Horn books from the nineteenth century.

At first Tina had thought that Veronique was taller than Byron, but that idea went away when Tina saw the day camp assistant director's five-inch stiletto.

Try walking on Bahamian sands with those—

Lord, forgive me.

Thank You, Jesus.

Tina didn't know what had overcome her, but every time she had been with Byron, she only thought of the worst of him.

Meticulously overbearing was the last double adjective she had used for him.

Uptight.

A pain in the neck.

The moment the volunteers from Riverside Chapel, Savannah, and a couple of other churches had disembarked from the airplane, Byron was at baggage claim waiting for them.

The way he had checked off their names as if they were school children had bothered Tina.

Then he had herded them into this non-air-conditioned school bus. Everyone just cracked jokes and laughed with him as he checked off their names one more time.

However, when Tina passed by him, he didn't say anything except to call her name.

The way Byron had said her name was very unlike how he had called Veronique's name. Veronique's name rolled off Byron's tongue in a smoother way than when he had snapped out Tina's name.

"Ti-nah!"

It was curtly British, clipped at the end of the second syllable, as if his disgust of her had taken its toll and he couldn't bear to say her name at all this time around.

Two years ago they had butted heads like two rams or goats. Horns locked as Byron had hissed out her name and stretched it in the air as though he was mentally wringing her neck every single time.

"Tee-yee-yee-nah! Teeenaaah!" Byron would yell at her in disgust because she hadn't done things the way he had wanted.

Well, sure, there was the bell before and after class, but she hadn't finished teaching, and besides, the kindergarteners were having fun, weren't they?

After all, it was Vacation Bible School, not a bar exam.

Come on!

In any case, her name sounded awful when Byron had said it aloud.

Well, it wasn't her fault she was named after a citrus fruit. A tangerine, to be exact.

Clementine Gracielle MacFarland.

No one ever called her Clementine, not since birth, according to everyone. It had always been Tina, as if Clementine was a shame of a first name.

Her brother had the better name, Martinelli, though everyone called him Martin.

But Tina.

"Tee-yee-yee-nah! Nah! Nah! Nah!"

"Stop," Tina muttered. "Stop it..."

A nudge and a couple of hard jabs on her shoulder made her jerk straight up and open her eyes.

"Oww... Who did that?"

Two brown eyes, eyebrows raised, edged by a smile, were in her face.

Tina recoiled, but there was nowhere to go. The seat back was stiff. She bumped her head on the metal bar that went all the way across the top of the seat.

"Ouch." She rubbed the back of her head.

Byron Moss straightened up, looming over her. Byron with the lovely brown eyes that kept her out of focus whenever she remembered them—

She cleared her throat.

"You fell asleep. Had a tiring flight?"

His voice was somewhat gentle and quiet, and Tina was beginning to think she had been dreaming that his tone had a sharp edge to it.

Yeah, must be having a nightmare.

She yawned and rubbed her eyes.

"We got off the plane?" As soon as she had said it, Tina felt dumb, like she had just given Byron one more "scatterbrained" remark for him to pick on later.

"You got off the plane. We loaded your luggage—all five pieces—onto this bus. We drove all the way from the Lynden Pindling International Airport to Montagu Bay, taking thirty-one minutes due to traffic. And we are now parked outside the Nassau Island Breeze Resort."

Byron waved toward the window. "We unloaded your luggage—three heavy, hard case luggage, two soft sides, but equally heavy—what in the world did you bring?"

Tina didn't feel obligated to answer him.

"Everyone is checking in at the front desk."

"Now?" Tina tried to get up, but her head spun.

"Yes, dear. Did you take Dramamine or some air-sickness meds, perchance?"

Dear?

Perchance?

Yep. That was Byron for her. He'd say strange literary things like that.

Byron stretched out his hand to help Tina to her feet.

She felt groggy. "Sorry. I stayed up all night to pack my art supplies. Then I couldn't sleep on the flight. Turbulence or something."

"We can get art supplies in Nassau, you know." Byron smiled with his eyes.

He was the only man Tina knew who could smile with his eyes.

"Well, I thought that—I mean, the last time I was here..." Tina wasn't sure how much she should remind Byron of what had happened two years ago when she had come to the Bahamas on her first mission trip outside the United States.

"Yes. Two years ago." Byron stepped back between two seats to let Tina go first toward the exit at the front of the bus. "You forgot all your brushes and canvases."

"You don't miss a thing, do you?"

"I missed you last summer," Byron said. "Why didn't you come?"

Missed?

Did he just say he missed me?

Tina tried not to read too much into it.

Byron was the last person on earth who would miss Tina.

"The kids at day camp asked for you by name. Where's Miss Tina? Why isn't she here? Doesn't she love us anymore?"

Love?

Tina stumbled out of the bus into eighty-something-degree heat. The June sunshine was bright, bright, bright. The sky was clear and blue, and Tina wanted to go for a swim.

Behind her, Byron was on his iPhone.

Tina shed her cardigan she had worn since she sat down in the cold cabin on the tarmac at the Savannah / Hilton Head International Airport. She was always cold in an airplane cabin, even when the flight was full and the passengers were packed in like paint tubes.

But now she was hot.

"What time is it?" Tina rolled up her cardigan and stuffed it into her worn, oversized zippered tote bag she had been using as her purse for over a year now.

"Two o'clock. Actually, six minutes after two."

"Are you sure it's not six minutes and fourteen seconds after two?"

Byron frowned at his watch. "Well, I don't know..."

Tina gently punched his arm. "Lighten up."

"Did they give you lunch on board?" Byron stood there a minute.

"I guess. I slept through."

"Why didn't they wake you up? You paid for the meal."

"Why are you asking me all these questions, Byron?"

"Because I don't want you to be hungry. Everyone else said they've eaten." Byron stepped toward her. "If you haven't, I'll take you to lunch."

"You'll take me out to lunch?"

Byron nodded. "Yes. Is that a problem?"

"No." Tina wondered why they were standing on the sidewalk. Shouldn't she be checking in?

Then she saw her.

Veronique and her five-inch stilettos, walking briskly toward them as if she were strutting on a catwalk.

She was amazingly graceful.

Clumsy me, I can't compare.

Tina watched as Byron dangled the bus keys in

front of Veronique. "Thank you for taking the bus back to the school."

Tina wondered how Veronique was going to drive this mammoth of a bus in those heels. Then again, it wasn't her problem, was it?

"How are you going to get home?" Tina asked Byron.

"I left my car in the hotel car park."

Car park? His way of saying parking lot.

"You thought of everything." Tina started walking.

"Not everything. You still haven't eaten lunch."

"Don't worry about me. I'll just eat in the hotel restaurant. Surely they have a café of some sort."

Byron stopped at the lobby, and so did Tina. She turned to see what the matter was.

"We need to learn to get along, Tina. Otherwise the Lord's work is not going to happen the next few weeks you're here, or two months, if you decide to stay for the entire camp."

"What does that have to do with where I eat lunch?"

"I get along with everyone else."

"So do I."

"But you and I don't get along with each other."

"Maybe it's best if we stay out of each other's hair," Tina said.

"Or we can have lunch and do things together to break down this wall of ice between us."

"Do things?" Tina widened her eyes. "Like what kind of things?"

"Like maybe we could work in the same classroom and be on the same field trips this summer."

"No. We'd drive each other insane."

Tina went to the end of the shortest line. There were gobs of people in the lobby, checking in. Summer vacationers, possibly. She waved to her teammates and the other fellow volunteers, some of whom were in the front of their lines while others were done and wheeling their bags to the elevator.

"Not if you try to be on time—for once," Byron said.

"Whoa. You just insulted me, and I haven't even checked in."

Byron stared at her.

"Go away, Byron."

"Can't. I'm in charge of the Summer by the Sea Day Camp, remember?"

"Well, bummer. I'm not going to congratulate you for being promoted to assistant headmaster." Even though he probably deserved it. Byron Moss, in spite of his many flaws, was one of the most hardworking men Tina had ever known.

"Can we still do lunch?" Byron's voice was

almost pleading. "We have to make the day camp succeed."

Tina's tummy growled.

"Your stomach is begging you on my behalf," Byron said.

Tina burst out laughing. "All right. I'll have to give it to you. You're not only stubborn, but you're also persistent."

"I think those two words mean about the same thing."

"Just say thank you, Byron."

"Thank you, ma'am." Byron glanced at his watch. "I'll help you take your bags to your room after you check in, and we should be on our way by three o'clock."

"You'll help me with my luggage because you don't want me to be late coming back down here to meet you for our already late lunch?"

"No, because your bags are heavy."

"Oh." *How considerate.*

"While you check in, I'll get you a Fanta Grape."

Tina froze. It had been two years since she last had that soda. "You remember."

"I remember everything about you, Clementine Gracielle MacFarland." And off he went.

Smile for Me (Vacation Sweethearts Book 1)
JanThompson.com/smile

Sign up for Jan Thompson's book news mailing list:
JanThompson.com/newsletter

ACKNOWLEDGMENTS

Many thanks to my Georgia Press publishing team for keeping up with my writing schedule.

A huge thank you to editors Lesley Ann McDaniel for copyediting and Dori Harrell for proofreading this novel.

I appreciate my early readers! There are many, but I want to make a special mention of these avid readers who read this long novel in record time before the rest of the world: Bernadette Cinkoske, Debbie Jamieson, Kim Brougher, Paula Santos, and Pat Carpenter. Thank you, ladies!

Thank you to firefighters William R. Metcalf, Bob Bonanno, Ken Shoemaker, and Martyn Doolin of the Author Fire/Rescue group for answering my questions about search-and-rescue in the midst of a building fire.

I am grateful to God for my husband, my son, and my brothers for their encouragement as I write the books that I want to read.

I'll always appreciate my beloved mother and my late father for having instilled in me the love of reading and writing from a very early age, all the way to my childhood days of nursery rhymes in books and on vinyl records.

Most of all, I am eternally thankful to my Lord and Savior, Jesus Christ, who died on the cross to save me from my sins and rose again from the grave to give me eternal life. Without Him, I can write nothing (John 15:5).

Jan Thompson
John 3:16

BOOKS BY JAN THOMPSON

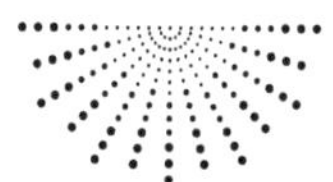

CHRISTIAN ROMANTIC SUSPENSE & BEACH ROMANCE

BINARY HACKERS (NEAR-FUTURE INSPIRATIONAL ROMANTIC THRILLERS)

- Book 1: Zero Sum
- Book 2: Zero Day
- Book 3: Zero Base
- Book 4: Zero Trust

PROTECTOR SWEETHEARTS (CHRISTIAN ROMANTIC SUSPENSE)

- Book 1: Once a Thief
- Book 2: Once a Hero

- Book 3: Once a Spy
- Book 4: Twice a Fighter
- Book 5: Twice a Convict
- Book 6: Twice a Soldier

DEFENDER SWEETHEARTS (CHRISTIAN ROMANTIC SUSPENSE)

- Book 1: Never a Traitor
- Book 2: Never a Hostage
- Book 3: Never a Fugitive
- Book 4: Always a Maverick
- Book 5: Always a Champion
- Book 6: Always a Guardian

SAVANNAH SWEETHEARTS (CHRISTIAN COASTAL CITY & BEACH TOWN ROMANCE)

- Prequel: Ask You Later
- Book 1: Know You More
- Book 2: Tell You Soon (Romance with Suspense)
- Book 3: Draw You Near
- Book 4: Cherish You So
- Book 5: Walk You There

- Book 6: Love You Always (Romance with Suspense)
- Book 7: Kiss You Now
- Book 8: Find You Again
- Book 9: Wish You Joy (Christmas Year Round)
- Book 10: Call You Home

VACATION SWEETHEARTS (CHRISTIAN TRAVEL ROMANCE)

- Book 1: Smile for Me
- Book 2: Reach for Me (Romance with Suspense)
- Book 3: Wait for Me (Romance with Suspense)
- Book 4: Look for Me (Romance with Suspense)
- Book 5: Pray for Me
- Book 6: Care for Me
- Book 7: Cheer for Me

SEASIDE CHAPEL (CHRISTIAN SMALL TOWN BEACH ROMANCE)

- Book 1: His Longing Heart (second edition of Share with Me)
- Book 2: His Wake-Up Call (second edition of Step with Me)
- Book 3: His Morning Kiss (previously published as Sing with Me)
- Book 4: His Quiet Serenade
- Book 5: His Waiting Love
- Book 6: His Beach Retreat

Subscribe to Jan Thompson's mailing list:
JanThompson.com/newsletter

SEASIDE CHAPEL

Welcome to *USA Today* bestselling author Jan Thompson's Seaside Chapel Christian beach romance series. These novels are set on real-life St. Simon's Island, Georgia—a beach town where history is all around and the future is a moment away—and the neighboring fictitious Seaside Island, where the rich and famous live.

Savor the small-town atmosphere and the warm southern beaches of St. Simon's Island and the idyllic Golden Isles along the Atlantic Ocean. Enjoy the music of the orchestra and hymns of the church, and hang out with our Christian friends who attend Seaside Chapel, a little church by the sea known for its beach weddings and fair share of love and life.

As these Christians grow in their knowledge and understanding of God, they are tested in their spiritual maturity, their love lives, and their relationships with others. Share their heartaches and healing, and cheer them on as they celebrate faith, family, and friends.

~

JanThompson.com/seaside

- Book 1: His Longing Heart (second edition of Share with Me)
- Book 2: His Wake-Up Call (second edition of Step with Me)
- Book 3: His Morning Kiss (previously published as Sing with Me)
- Book 4: His Quiet Serenade
- Book 5: His Waiting Love
- Book 6: His Beach Retreat

SAVANNAH SWEETHEARTS

Welcome to the new south! From *USA Today* bestselling author Jan Thompson come these clean and wholesome, sweet and inspirational Christian romances set on the romantic beaches of Tybee Island and in the coastal town of Savannah, Georgia.

Meet a group of multiracial and multiethnic churchgoing Christians who love the Lord, work hard in their careers, and seek God's will for their love lives. Against a backdrop of ocean, sand, and sun, these inspirational romances showcase aspects of the human need for God and for one another. Have some tea, settle in a comfortable reading chair, and enjoy these sweet celebrations of faith, hope, and love in Jesus Christ.

JanThompson.com/savannah

- Prequel: Ask You Later
- Book 1: Know You More
- Book 2: Tell You Soon (Romance with Suspense)
- Book 3: Draw You Near
- Book 4: Cherish You So
- Book 5: Walk You There
- Book 6: Love You Always (Romance with Suspense)
- Book 7: Kiss You Now
- Book 8: Find You Again
- Book 9: Wish You Joy (Christmas Year Round)
- Book 10: Call You Home

VACATION SWEETHEARTS

Travel with our friends from Savannah, Georgia, to the coast and to the mountains. Cheer them on as they celebrate the immeasurable grace and undeserved mercy of God through Jesus Christ.

The Vacation Sweethearts novels are a spin-off of Jan's Savannah Sweethearts series, and fans will recognize familiar faces from Riverside Chapel, a church in the coastal city of Savannah, Georgia. In fact, we might even visit the beach town of Tybee Island from time to time to visit old friends and beloved families...

JanThompson.com/vacation

- Book 0 (Prequel): Time for Me
- Book 1: Smile for Me (International Romance)
- Book 2: Reach for Me (Romance with Suspense)
- Book 3: Wait for Me (Romance with Suspense)
- Book 4: Look for Me (Romance with Suspense)
- Book 5: Pray for Me (International Romance)
- Book 6: Care for Me
- Book 7: Cheer for Me (International Romance)

PROTECTOR SWEETHEARTS

Private investigator Helen Hu and her associates specialize in searching for missing persons and hunting for lost treasures. Join them in their adventure suspense around the world in *USA Today* best-selling author Jan Thompson's Protector Sweethearts, a series of Christian Romantic Suspense with a side of mystery. Protector Sweethearts is a spin-off of Savannah Sweethearts and Vacation Sweethearts.

JanThompson.com/protector

- Book 1: Once a Thief

- Book 2: Once a Hero
- Book 3: Once a Spy
- Book 4: Twice a Fighter
- Book 5: Twice a Convict
- Book 6: Twice a Soldier

DEFENDER SWEETHEARTS

Defender Sweethearts is a sister series to the Protector Sweethearts Christian romantic suspense collection. While the heroes in Protector Sweethearts search for lost treasures and lost people, the Defender Sweethearts novels focus on protecting the helpless and hopeless. The main characters in Defender Sweethearts come from the supporting cast in Protector Sweethearts.

JanThompson.com/defender

- Book 1: Never a Traitor

- Book 2: Never a Hostage
- Book 3: Never a Fugitive
- Book 4: Always a Maverick
- Book 5: Always a Champion
- Book 6: Always a Guardian

BINARY HACKERS

Like more suspense with your Christian romance? Like to read suspense thrillers? If you're looking for clean near-future romantic suspense without compromising the Christian faith, these books are for you.

From *USA Today* bestselling author Jan Thompson come these inspirational near-future cyberthrillers combining technothriller and romance, starting with Binary Hackers that feature computer specialists living at the edge of cyberspace, where they have to juggle being law-abiding truth-telling Christians while carrying out their assignments by any and all means possible.

The Binary Hackers series is set in the same story world as Jan's other books, and characters from the other series may make cameo appearances in this series and vice versa.

JanThompson.com/binary

- Book 1: Zero Sum
- Book 2: Zero Day
- Book 3: Zero Base

ABOUT JAN THOMPSON

USA Today bestselling author Jan Thompson writes clean and wholesome contemporary Christian romance with elements of women's fiction, Christian romantic suspense with an air of mystery, and inspirational international thrillers with threads of sweet Christian romance. Jan's books are for readers who love inspiring stories of faith, family, and friends.

Raised on a tropical island in the eastern hemisphere, Jan now lives and writes in the western hemisphere. Her international background gives her a unique multicultural and multiracial perspective to her novels and books. The island has never left her, and she reminisces about beach life in her beach romance novels.

When Jan is not busy writing small-town stories, she writes big-city romantic suspense and international technothrillers, a nod to her previous career in computer science. She weaves technology with human interests, reflecting the current and future digital world. And romance. There's always romance.

Beyond the printed page, Jan is a wife, mother, family scribe, avid reader, occasional artist, erstwhile pianist, and chief of staff to the family cat.

For God so loved the world
that He gave His only begotten Son,
that whoever believes in Him
should not perish but have everlasting life.
—John 3:16

Made in the USA
Columbia, SC
16 June 2025

59497015R00381